Lupine

Renton Wolfe

ISBN: 979-8-9918362-1-0

DEDICATION

To my family, filled with the strongest people I know—your support, love, and resilience have been my constant source of strength. This book is as much yours as it is mine. Thank you for always believing in me.

CONTENTS

THORNWALLOW

VELORA

SYLPHREACH

LOSTSUMMIT

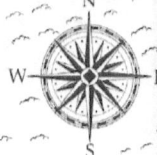

Nyxaris

Eclipsia

SELUNARIS

Noctiluna

Crescentia

Lunaria

MOONVEIL

CHAPTER 1

It was cold—no, it was freezing. The world around me had transformed into a landscape blanketed in a thick white sheet of snow that stretched endlessly across the terrain. Each breath I took formed small clouds in the air, and chill seeped into my bones. Undoubtedly, a harsh winter took hold across the land.

The sound of snow crunching beneath my boots gave a rhythm to listen to in the otherwise silent wilderness. With each step, the cold pressed on me, only the furry cloak I received from that treacherous town in the Madlands barely offering any respite.

The expanse in front of me was quiet and devoid of any paths. Being disoriented in these unfamiliar woods was becoming routine.

Celine and I ran for what felt like an eternity, trying to avoid our pursuers. Though the town was behind us now, their shadows lingered in the corners of my vision. We made sure to double back on our tracks extensively, though I knew they were still on our trail, still hunting us to end what they started. The wolf tracks that came dangerously close to our camp were proof enough of that.

I adjusted my grip on the bone hunting knife that Celine crafted for me. Its cold hilt stuck to my skin slightly because of the biting wind. I knew I needed to find food, but hunting in this weather was a gamble. The game was scarce, hiding from the frost to shelter themselves from the cold, something I wish I could've been doing.

A reminder pressed into my brain. *Come on Isaac, keep moving.* Every sound, every single snap of a twig, could mean the difference between life and death.

I leaned against a nearby tree, breathed into my frozen hands, and tucked them under my armpits, desperately trying to get the blood circulating through them. Then, for a moment, I listened to the world around me. There were no birds singing, no bugs buzzing, and no animals scurrying. Everything was still.

Finally, a faint trail caught my eye—a sign of life. I lowered my profile to be quieter and moved along it. There were pronounced tracks in the snow—some type of hare. The hunt started, and I could only hope that this day would be different; that I could return with something more than just a disappointed look on my face.

White and gray swallowed the world around me, draining it of all detail besides the tracks at my feet. If they slipped from view, so too would any hope of finding them again.

Out of the corner of my eye, I caught a flicker of movement. It was subtle, and I could barely make it out. A snow hare with its white fur perfectly camouflaged against the snowy backdrop. It paused momentarily, its large ears twitching as it sensed something amiss. I did the same, pausing in my tracks, scared that any movement would send it running into the blank forest.

My fingers inched towards my belt, where the slingshot I made a while back rested. A stone from my back pocket came next, one large enough to get the job done.

I loaded the stone and pulled the sling back, training my eyes on the unsuspecting hare. The slingshot drew taut as I prepared to take my shot. But right as I was about to release, a sudden whisper brushed against my ear—soft yet unmistakable.

"Truth..."

My head whipped around, eyes wide as panic gripped me. The unexpected sound sent my heart racing and in that split second of distraction. The slingshot slipped from my hands, and the stone flew wide, missing the hare by several feet.

"Damnit," I cursed under my breath as the hare bolted away, disappearing behind trees.

Confused, I looked around the area once more; though nothing was out of the ordinary. *Strange.*

These odd whispers started happening a week ago. Seemingly at random times, they'd come from the forest, other times from within my own skull. I figured it was the paranoia of Celine and my situation getting to me.

But deep down, I couldn't shake the feeling that it was more than just paranoia. The whispers were too real, too intimate. It almost felt as if someone—or something—was living in my brain, trying to relay information to me.

Each time it happened, it left a lingering sense of panic. I kept telling myself it was nothing but nerves, but the whispers refused to fade, growing harder to ignore with each passing day.

With a sigh, I turned my focus back to the task at hand. Regrouping and gathering my wits were all I could do if we were going to eat today. I took a moment to control my breathing, feeling the cold air fill my lungs. One missed shot didn't have to mean another chance wouldn't come.

My attention returned to the ground again, looking for the tracks the hare would have left behind in its haste.

Then, right as hope began to fade, a faint set of paw prints leading away from the thicket caught my eye. They were small but distinct, a sign that the hare hadn't fled too far away. My heart lifted slightly; perhaps this day wouldn't end in failure after all.

With renewed determination, I followed the tracks, tiptoeing in case the hare was nearby. There is no way that I'd let the whispers get to me again.

The chill in the air wrapped around me like a thick blanket, slowing my movements, but the promise of a meal lit a fire in my stomach. Slowly, the light of the day began to fade, making the naked trees create long shadows on the forest floor.

Not good. I needed to make my move soon.

After navigating for a few moments, I spotted movement again—another flash of white. There it was—the snow hare, nibbling on a few exposed blades of grass. I sank low, taking a quiet but deep breath.

I lined up my shot yet again. Oblivious, the hare nibbled in peace, ears twitching at nothing. I pulled the slingshot back, taking my time to make sure this shot would land. I couldn't let another opportunity slip away.

Release. The stone flew through the air with a whoosh, striking the hare squarely on the side of its skull. The creature let out a startled yelp and collapsed into the snow.

"Yes!" I let out in a hushed whisper as I quickly approached my catch.

"Got ya," I murmured, a grin breaking across my face. It was smaller than I hoped, but I felt a wave of relief. Food was food, and this would be a welcome meal after the days we'd spent wandering without sufficient sustenance.

I knelt down and picked up the hare, glancing around to make sure no one was following. It would be smarter to skin the animal elsewhere and bury the guts a good distance from our camp, just in case the smell would lead anyone back to us.

After some walking, I found a suitable spot. My eyes glanced around yet again. The last thing I needed was for our location to be compromised. The last rays of light softly illuminated the hare's soft fur as I set it down in a small clearing.

Slowly, I drew the bone knife from my belt and began skinning my catch. The cold air stung my fingertips, but my focus remained on the precise cuts that needed to be made. The more meat I could get off of this thing, the better. Once the skin was removed, I set it aside, then cut away the innards.

After a moment of digging into the snow with my hands, a hole was dug deep enough to bury the waste. I packed the snow down firmly against the remains. Hopefully, they were pressed down enough to erase any evidence of my presence.

I retrieved the hide-knapsack that Celine fashioned for me. Carefully, I packed it with snow, using the icy flakes to keep the hare's body fresh for the journey back to our camp. The carcass settled snug within, secured for the return long trip back.

The thought of a warm meal made me drool. But as I walked, a rustle echoed through the stillness of the forest. I froze mid-step to listen, a jolt of fear coursing through me. The noise came again, footsteps, and a good amount of them.

I quickly ducked behind a nearby tree, my heart already pounding. Peering around the rough bark showed the same people who followed us from the Madlands, the queen's guards. Their presence sent a chill down my spine. Some of them were in their wolf forms, sleek and powerful, their fur contrasting deeply with the white of the forest. Others stood in their humanoid forms, eyes scanning the area with keen intensity.

Why can't they just leave us alone! My mind screamed.

Though I knew they never would. To them, Celine and I committed the ultimate sin—the slaying of their beloved queen.

They moved cautiously, stopping now and then to look around and sniff the air. It was clear that they were searching for any sign of us. A lump formed in my throat as my body froze in place. I could only pray that the tree would provide enough cover.

One of the wolves lifted its head, nostrils flaring as it caught the scent of the air. Quickly, I placed the knapsack under my cloak, remembering the words that the female guard told me before she helped me escape the cave.

The cloak will help conceal your scent.

I still wasn't sure of it, but the cloak seemed to be the only reason the guards couldn't find us all this time.

The wolf dropped its nose and returned to sniffing the ground, seemingly convinced that nothing was amiss.

I carefully peered out further to get a better view.

The group was moving in a loose formation, communicating silently. Though their body language told me they hadn't seen or heard anything of interest yet.

Relieved, I let out a slow breath as the group continued down their path.

Glancing in the direction of our camp, I calculated my next move. We couldn't afford to stay here much longer with the guards so close.

I slunk away from my hiding spot, moving slowly as I mapped a route back in my mind.

Right as I took a step, a twig snapped beneath my feet, sending a harsh crack echoing through the forest like a gunshot.

I froze, shock crackling in my limbs. The world held its breath as I stood perfectly still, praying that the sound went unnoticed.

But the tension in the air thickened as I heard the group pause, their voices barely close enough to make out.

"Did you hear that?" one of them asked.

"It came from over there!" another replied, followed by

the rustle of movement as they began to turn in my direction.

I crouched down even more behind the tree, trying to make myself as small as possible. My mind raced—did they spot me? Should I run or stay hidden here?

I wrapped my hand around the hilt of the sword on my belt. Every instinct begged to look, to know how close they were, but it would've blown my cover. I was outnumbered, but they wouldn't take me down without a fight.

"Split up," someone commanded, and my stomach sank. "Search the area. We cannot afford to lose them again."

Footsteps drew closer, each crunch of snow echoing in my ears, urging my body to move. Despite the cold, my body was extremely warm in anticipation of what was to come next. Each second that passed felt suffocating as the realization of being caught hung over my head.

Just then, something white ran right in front of me. Another hare darted from behind a nearby tree, right past my hiding spot.

Shit, not good. This could lead them right to me.

The crunch of the guards' footsteps paused.

"It is merely a foolish hare," I heard one of them remark, his voice heavy with irritation.

"We are wasting our time chasing rabbits. Let us focus on finding the boy and girl," one of them snapped.

I held my breath. I wasn't out of danger's path yet.

"Indeed," another replied. "The scent is faint, but I am certain we will find them eventually. We must remain diligent. They have evaded us for far too long."

The crunch of boots on snow slowly receded away from my position. As their voices faded into the distance, a shaky breath escaped my lips. The hare, blissfully unaware of the danger it almost brought to me, continued its frantic dash through the trees, eventually disappearing behind an outcrop.

With the guards a good distance away and my heart still pounding, I scooped up a handful of snow and put it in my mouth, trying to cool down. The tension in the air was still thick, but I knew this was my chance to slip away. Celine would worry if it got too dark before I made it back.

One last look around the tree confirmed the coast was clear. Step by step, I eased from my cover, praying that—for now—we were beyond the reach of those who hunted us.

With another deep breath of relief, I started the trek back through the woods. The air was frigid, making my movements sluggish, but caution kept me keenly aware of the need to remain quiet.

The sky above already darkened immensely. I needed to take great care to walk back through the tracks I already made. Doing so would confuse anyone pursuing us, making it appear as though my tracks led nowhere. I mentally calculated the time it would take, knowing this would only add to my journey. It was annoying, but the risk of being careless was far worse.

After about an hour passed, I needed to complete the harder task of laying down false trails.

I kicked snow over the first set of footprints, then walked in another direction for the next 10 minutes before doubling back again. To any who followed it would look like I split off from the path once more. I repeated this periodically during my hike back if I wanted it to be effective.

After what felt like forever, I caught sight of the familiar outcrop of rocks nestled among trees. Finally, the cave Celine and I hunkered in was in view and my pace quickened.

It was dark; I knew she wouldn't be happy about how long I was out.

As I got closer, I noticed that more snow gathered around the jagged edges of the rocks around the cave's entrance.

Perfect. Maybe the extra snowfall obscured any of the tracks I left behind.

The mouth of the cave was dark, a small glow barely pulsing from the inside. This cave became our refuge, a place where we could regroup and plan our next steps away from not only the elements, but the dangers lurking in the woods.

"Finally." The word slipped out with a sigh. I spent the entire morning hunting, and though the results were meager, Celine would understand. She always did—patience was one of her many strengths.

Entering the cave, the darkness swallowed me momentarily before my eyes adjusted to the dim light within. The air was noticeably warmer, instantly melting the ice that clung to my cold bones.

The space felt intimate and cozy despite its simplicity. Celine made the best of our limited resources; a small fire sat in one corner, the cold ashes of a previous fire reminding me of the warm night we shared days prior.

Next to it were the makeshift beds we fashioned from dry leaves and moss that we hastily gathered from drier parts of the forest. Of course, they weren't comfortable, but they gave us enough rest to keep us going throughout our days.

In one corner of the small cave sat Celine, cross-legged. The dark navy cloak I gave her was wrapped snuggly around her body. The fabric contrasted nicely with her warm orange-brown hair, which she let fall in loose waves around her shoulders. She was focused intently, weaving something between her hands.

As I approached, her furry ears perked up and twitched, picking up the sound of my arrival. She looked up, her violet eyes lighting up with a slight display of relief.

"I thought you might not return," she said softly, a hint of tease in her voice. "Were you off chasing shadows again?"

A smile plastered my face. "You know me too well," I replied, dropping the knapsack to the ground. "But I did manage to catch something this time." I pulled out the skinned hare and held it up as if it were a small trophy.

Her expression shifted with a flicker of approval in her eyes. "Well done, Drifted. It is not much, but we will cherish it all the same."

The quiet pride in her words meant more than any loud cheer could.

"Yeah, it's small," I admitted, setting it down in front of her. "But I figured it was better than coming back empty-handed."

"Aye, every source of sustenance counts." Her gaze lingered on the hare as she turned it over in her hands.

There was no need for extravagant praise. Celine's acknowledgment alone spoke volumes. I was used to the way she showed her feelings—or lack thereof.

"What were you working on before I came in?" I asked, nodding to the bundle of fabric and materials sitting in her lap.

She paused, and a pleased smile curved her lips. She held up one hand to reveal a completed handmade fur shoe. The craftsmanship spoke for itself; it was carefully stitched with rabbit fur.

"Something to aid me in keeping warm," she replied, trying to keep her voice calm, but I could hear the hint of pride seeping through.

I nodded, taking in the sight of the shoe. Since our escape from the Madlands, Celine was barefoot after her transformation ended. More than once, I offered her my shoes, insisting she wear them. Each time, she'd brush off my concern, claiming that being barefoot didn't bother her.

Of course, that was before the snow came.

"Finally admitting defeat?" A wry smile crept onto my face. The memory of her stubbornness made me chuckle softly.

She shrugged. "I believed I could manage. Though it seems winter has a way of changing one's perspective, does it not?"

"Yeah—especially when the ground is as cold as it is now," I replied, keeping my tone light. "Regardless, they look well made. It's like you have a gift for finding potential in everything around us."

Celine sewed and created various items for us during our travels. Her resourcefulness never ceased to amaze me. The bone knife, carved from a carcass and sharpened against stone, became vital to our survival. The leather knapsack, stitched from animal hide, carried all we needed. And now— these shoes.

She looked up from the hare. "It is not a gift, Drifted. It is necessity. When you have little, you learn to use what you find. The world provides if you are attentive."

"You make it sound so simple," I replied, shaking my head. "I could never come up with half of the things you've made."

Celine smiled. "Perhaps you need more practice. It is not merely about grand ideas; it is about recognizing the value in minor details."

There was always some lecture tucked inside Celine's words. Many of them flew right over my head, but this one stuck. There was usefulness even in the smallest things. The items she made weren't only practical; they also represented our resilience and ability to adapt.

"Whatever the reason, I'm grateful to have you by my side," I said, full of sincerity. "You keep us one step ahead."

Her expression softened. "And you provide balance, Drifted. That is why we will be able to navigate the challenges that lie ahead—together."

I gave her a smile and a slight nod, relieved she would be on my side for whatever obstacles lay ahead of us.

The next few hours passed in a comfortable rhythm as Celine and I set about cooking the hare. The small fire crackled softly, warming the cramped cave that protected us. And the smell of roasting meat was strong in the air as we set about eating with occasional small talk.

"Do you remember the first time we had a meal like this?" I asked, glancing over at her while tending to the fire.

Celine nodded back. "You nearly burned the meat that day. I was convinced I would have to teach you how to cook."

Her words drew a small laugh from me, the sound echoing softly in the cave. The rest of the meal carried on in quiet— warmth from the fire, the taste of food, and the rare comfort of feeling almost at peace.

Eventually, as the last of the hare was consumed, and the fire dwindled, I felt the weight of exhaustion settling in. Celine had returned to her corner, her cloak wrapped tightly around her as she set to working on the second shoe.

I stretched out on my makeshift bed, feeling the rough leaves on my back.

"Celine," I began, hesitant to ruin our peaceful night. "There's something I need to tell you."

Her eyes lifted from her work, curiosity strong in her violet eyes. "Yes, Drifted?"

A deep breath escaped my lips as I recalled the close call in the woods. "While I was hunting, I heard the guards. They were combing the area, and I nearly got spotted."

Celine sat up quickly, her demeanor quickly growing intense. Her piercing eyes bore into mine, and the calmness of the cave felt suddenly charged with tension. "Why is it only now I am hearing of this?"

Her sudden shift in her demeanor startled me. "I didn't want to worry you," I admitted, feeling a rush of guilt. "I escaped without any issues."

"Worry me?" she echoed. "Drifted, you must understand—your safety is paramount. Never hesitate to share these things with me."

I met her gaze, feeling the guilt from my silence. "You're right. I should have told you sooner. I didn't mean to keep you in the dark."

Celine nodded and exhaled. "Regardless—how far were you when this transpired?"

I thought for a moment before responding. "I would say about six miles away from the cave."

Her lips pursed slightly. "That is too close. We cannot afford to remain here any longer. We shall depart first thing in the morning."

I nodded, agreeing with her assessment. This was the longest we've ever lingered in one spot since we've been on the run. Admittedly, we were growing complacent, and that could cost us dearly.

"Rest, Drifted. I will keep watch and continue working on my remaining shoe."

I opened my mouth to protest, but she raised a hand. "It is important that you conserve your strength. I will remain alert."

With a resigned sigh, I nodded, too tired to argue any further. "Alright, but if you need me—wake me."

"Of course," she replied softly. "But for now, you must rest. I will be here."

The makeshift bed cradled me as the fire's warmth lulled me into a sense of security. From across the cave came the quiet rhythm of Celine stitching the fur shoe.

With thoughts of tomorrow fading into the background, I

drifted off to sleep.

CHAPTER 2

A harsh mix of frantic voices bounced around my mind, both disjointed and chaotic, as I fell deeper into a swirling darkness. Words collided in my head—snippets, shouts, screams, and laughter all blended together into a symphony that set my heart racing. I tried to make sense of it, to find any sort of meaning among them, but the more I struggled, the more entangled everything became.

"... You must see..." a voice urged.

"... You must hear..." another whispered, seemingly from every direction.

"Blind..." came a third, low and daunting.

"You... you are blind..." the voices continued, mocking me with laughter.

"Truth!" the final yelled.

I stumbled forward, searching for a way out, but every step disoriented me further. The voices grew louder, swirling around me, as I kneeled in a desperate attempt to make myself small. My hands covered my ears, frantically trying to keep the words from boring any deeper into my mind. All around me, the words desperately pleaded to heed their callings, but there was nothing I could do.

New eyes glimmered at the edge of my vision, watching me from the shadows. I turned, and there they were— thousands of glowing orbs, deep crimson red, watching over me. Each of them bore into my soul with such intensity that rooted my legs in place. They pulsed with anger, hunger, and malice, causing my blood to run cold.

"Drifted..." a voice whispered out to me.

It gripped tighter as I strained to break free. Shadows pressed in, ensnaring me like a web. I felt paralyzed, trapped in a web of fear and uncertainty.

The next thing I knew, I was floating in a vast sea—except there was no water. Just pitch-black crashing into me like waves as the red eyes watched from above. I struggled to stay afloat as the waves hit me. Each time my head went under, it took longer for me to break the surface and gasp for air.

As I went under again, the exhaustion in my legs pulled me deeper into the sea. My limbs were sapped of energy, and the fight to stay afloat faded. The darkness surrounded me, and the echoing whispers of the frenzied voices came once more.

"Drifted..."

"Drifted."

"Drifted!"

Their calls grew more urgent, each repetition desperately trying to bring me to the surface. I tried to respond, to fight against the waves dragging me down, but there was nothing left for me to give.

As despair threatened to consume me, hands plunged into the darkness and grabbed me by the shoulders. Then, in an instant, they began dragging me from the murkiness, pulling me back toward the light.

I shot upright, gasping for air, my heart racing as I came to. Celine was there, her hands still on my shoulders, concern etched across her face.

"What ails you, Drifted?" she asked, her voice filled with urgency.

I wiped the cold sweat from my forehead, still trying to convince myself that it was only a night terror. "Nothing," I replied, my throat bone dry. "It was just a nightmare."

Celine studied me for a moment, looking for any signs of lingering fear. Her expression lightened, and before I could dwell on the remnants of the nightmare, she spoke.

"Nightmares often reveal our deepest fears, Drifted," she said, her voice steady. "They are reminders that we must confront the darkness if we wish to understand our true selves."

She paused, a thoughtful glint in her eyes. "I would love to explore this further with you, but we must depart before the sun rises any higher."

The brightness of the morning flooded the cave, illuminating the area in a warm glow. The sun was already well up in the sky, and the fire crackled softly in the corner. Celine must have stoked the flames during the early hours to keep us warm against the chill of the morning air.

I rubbed the sleep from my eyes and pushed myself up, the dry leaves and moss crunching beneath my weight. At the cave's mouth, the view stretched wide: snow blanketed the ground in shimmering white, glistening beneath the hanging sun.

"Did you manage any rest?" Celine asked as she began gathering our belongings.

I nodded, stretching my limbs as I stood. "I did, except for the nightmare, of course. It felt good to go to sleep with a relatively full stomach for once."

Celine sat on the floor, slipping on her newly crafted shoes. "We should take our leave soon. I am positive the guards remain in pursuit."

"You're right," I replied, quickly gathering my things.

Together, we packed our belongings, breaking down the camp to leave as little sign of our presence as possible. I gave the cave one more look over to ensure we'd left nothing of importance.

Then, side by side, we stepped out together.

As we walked, I glanced over at Celine. "So, we're still heading north?" I asked, trying to forget about my nightmare.

She gave a small nod. "Yes—though our journey bends to the northwest now."

"Do you have any idea of how far we are at this point, after being thrown off track by the Madlands and all?"

Celine shook her head, a faint crease growing on the corner of her lips. "No. Yet I can sense the journey is far."

We were back to square one—no clear sense of what our journey was about. There was no map to guide us, just Celine's innate sense of direction. It was unsettling knowing that our fate rested on a hunch.

Even so, I didn't mind. I trusted Celine's judgment more than I trusted the unpredictable paths of the wilderness.

But I wasn't completely in the dark anymore. Celine mentioned something about our journey a few weeks ago. We were on the way to meet her father, a figure we hadn't discussed since she first mentioned him. I hadn't brought it up since because I never found an appropriate time to. But now, while things were quiet, perhaps I could get some answers to at least some of my questions.

"Celine," I began, hesitating for a moment. "You said we were going to see your father. Is that still the case?"

Her ears perked up slightly, and she nodded. "Aye, that is correct, Drifted."

"Well... What do you know about him—your father?"

She paused in her tracks, her brow furrowing as she considered her response. "I do not know him at all, Drifted. I have never met him." Her voice was calm, though I could see the complexity of emotions on her face.

I stopped next to her. She never met him? Perhaps he

walked out on her family when she was too young to have any memory of him? Embarrassed, I quickly backtracked on my question. "Sorry, Celine. I didn't mean to pry. I didn't know he abandoned you at such a young age."

A puzzled look grew on her face. "No, you are mistaken, Drifted. I have no memory of my father because there is no memory of him to have. There is only a sense of him, an instinctual feeling of him. Somehow, this man is connected to my past—to who I am meant to be."

I frowned, trying to process her words. "That's... confusing. How can you trust a feeling about someone you've never met?"

Her deep violet eyes held mine. "It is difficult to explain, Drifted. At times, it is not about knowing someone through experience, but understanding what they represent. He is in some way connected to my heritage, and he will have the answers to many of our questions."

In usual fashion, Celine's answers left me with more questions. "What about your mother? What memories—if any—do you have of her?"

She put a finger to her chin, presumably searching for the right words. "I recall someone who I believe would have fit the role of a mother," she said slowly. "Her presence was warm and kind. She taught me what I know about survival, how to navigate the world around me. But I am not certain of much else."

"That sounds... comforting?" I questioned. I didn't quite know how to feel about what Celine was telling me. She had two parents—if I could call them that—that she barely knew.

"Yes," she continued. "But I have no recollection of what she looked like, her name, or even her voice. It is as if those details have been lost to time, leaving behind only the feelings she instilled in me."

Her words hung in the air for a moment. Celine never shared much about her family with me because she knew nothing about them herself. It was clear that she wasn't from Moonveil—her roots were somehow tied to the town we had escaped from in the Madlands. How she was connected remained a mystery to me—but the furry ears perched atop her head and her ability to transform into the same wolfish beast they did were unmistakable.

"Do you think you will remember more about her if we meet your father?" I asked.

Celine gave a slight nod. "Perhaps. There is a part of me that believes understanding one may lead to insights about the other. Though there is no way to tell until the journey is taken."

Though I didn't know much about the journey ahead, I understood it was important for both of us. What started as a desperate attempt to rectify the growing fiend presence threatening to encroach on Moonveil, had transformed into something more significant: a chance for Celine to learn about her past, to uncover who she was and where she belonged.

"I'll be there every step of the way then," I promised, realizing how shared our paths really were.

Celine returned my nod with one of her own and gave me a long, silent stare. Seemingly grateful for my commitment to our goals.

As we pressed on through the woods, I couldn't help but note how remarkably quiet it was. While I was thankful that there were no howls or distant calls of the creatures we had come to dread, It still struck me as odd.

Throughout our travels, we hadn't encountered a single fiend in this region. No Dreadbeaks swooping overhead, no Fungoids stomping around—nothing.

The absence of fiends felt surreal to me. I lived with their threat hanging over me my entire life. To no longer hear the far screeching of the foul creatures was extremely out of place.

"So strange," I muttered, more to myself than to Celine.

Her head tilted. "What is strange, Drifted?"

"That we haven't seen any fiends since we began traveling," I said. "In Moonveil they were everywhere—you could hardly walk more than a few miles without crossing paths with one."

"That is correct," Celine started, looking up at the sky. "Though, perhaps we should take it as a reprieve from the constant stresses we were once under."

"It's not like I don't appreciate the peace, it's just that it feels... misplaced. Especially knowing what Aldhard told Brute—"

I stopped in my tracks as uttering the name brought an icy wave of grief over me. A knot formed in my stomach as I recalled the betrayal that happened a few weeks ago.

Celine, noticing my hesitation, stopped slightly in front of me. "You are referring to the tale you shared—the one of you and the man we now know as Remus, correct?"

I nodded slowly. The pain still fresh in my mind, and the scar on my forearm still visible from that day. 'Yeah... I can't shake the feeling that something is off."

"Remember, Drifted," Celine said gently. "The betrayal was not your fault. You only followed who you thought was trustworthy."

A sigh escaped my lips as I looked down. "Sure, but if only I had listened to you back then... maybe we wouldn't be in this position now."

Celine shook her head and rested a hand on my shoulder. "Dwelling on the past will not change what has already taken place. We must learn from it and continue forward. Regret is a heavy burden, but it does not define us."

Her words were soothing, something Celine excelled at, minimizing my mistakes by disguising them as a learning opportunity. "You're right, Celine, thanks—."

But when I looked up to meet her gaze, she wasn't looking at me. She was staring off into the distance, lost in thought, as if something had captured her attention beyond the trees.

"Celine?" I called out, but she gave no response.

Confused, I looked at her from head to toe. Her ears twitched and turned as though they had caught something I could not hear.

"Celine?" I tried again, a little louder this time.

Finally, her eyes met mine, but they were filled with fear. Suddenly, she shoved me hard, and I stumbled backwards, hitting the snowy ground.

A blur of color flashed in front of my eyes. My head snapped toward Celine just in time to see a wolf hit the ground to our left, its pelt a mottled mix of brown and gray. It bared its teeth, a guttural growl rumbling out, so raw and graveled it froze me where I sat.

"Drifted, on your feet!" Celine shouted.

I scrambled to my feet, frantically kicking the snow. But before I could fully stand, the wolf jumped, its legs propelling it forward with an intensity that took my breath away.

It slammed into my chest, knocking me back to the ground. I gasped as the air was ripped from my lungs, the weight of the beast pressing down on me. Its jaws snapped inches from my face as it tried to end my life. I pressed my arm into its thick fur as I fought to keep its mouth away from my throat.

"Drifted!" Celine shouted in the background as I struggled.

Out of the corner of my eye, I caught more movement. Another wolf leaped into the fray, intercepting Celine and blocking her path to me.

Damnit, not good. I thought to myself. These were probably scouts that they sent out on our trail. They must've found a way to follow me back near the cave, despite all my precautions.

"Drifted, keep fighting!" Celine's voice rang out again.

I shot a look in her direction. She was hopelessly trying to get past the wolf to assist me, but it wasn't letting up, staying one step ahead of her.

The wolf on my chest snapped its jaws closer, and I pushed hard with all my strength against its fur, feeling the heat of its breath hot against my face. I knew I had to act fast. With Celine held at bay, I wouldn't last much longer.

With my free hand, I fumbled for the bone knife secured at my belt. As my fingers got around the hilt, I drew it free and thrusted the blade toward the side of the wolf's neck, aiming for any sort of vital spot.

The knife sank deep, and the wolf yelped out in pain. Blood sprayed as I twisted the blade, forcing it deeper.

The beast reared back, shaking its head violently as it tried to dislodge the knife. I watched in shock as the beast gradually transformed back into its humanoid form. The once wild animal was again a man, clawing at his neck in desperation.

I stood frozen in shock as the man went limp on the ground. I couldn't comprehend the reality of what I had done. Another life had been lost at my hands.

The second wolf ceased growling and darted toward the fallen guard. It nuzzled against the man's limp body, whimpering softly. A sound that only added to my numbness as I stared in silence.

A hand gripped mine tightly, and before I knew it, my feet were running. I looked up to see Celine dragging me away from the scene, trying to put as much distance between us and the battle as possible.

I hesitated, glancing back at the fallen guard and the grieving wolf, but Celine pulled my hand harder. I shook my head, following her lead through the trees as the adrenaline surged within me.

Behind us, I heard the distant sound of a wolf howling, a call that pierced through the quiet of the woods.

More noise followed shortly after. The unmistakable sounds of multiple footsteps behind us. I glanced over my shoulder, my heart racing and my breath shallow as I grew more tired.

Following behind us were several wolves—at least seven or eight—chasing us down with so much bloodlust in their eyes that I nearly tripped. The only thing that kept me moving was my instincts taking over, controlling my movements.

"Celine!" I shouted. "We need to move faster!"

She nodded, her eyes focused ahead of us. "Aye, Drifted. Do not let up!"

We pushed harder, darting through the bare trees, but the wolves were relentless. Their footfalls pounded closer behind us as the sound of panting and snapping twigs filling my ears. My brain went into overdrive, thinking of everything it could to keep me alive. One false move, one bad step, would be the end of it for us.

Suddenly, a thought struck me. If Celine could take on her wolf form like she did back at the Madlands, we'd be able to escape easily—just like we did back then.

"Celine!" I cried out, desperation climbing through my voice. "Can't you transform like you did back at the town?"

She shook her head. "No, I have no recollection of how that occurred. I cannot replicate that now."

"Damnit", I cursed. We wouldn't be able to run much longer, but fighting was out of the question with so many wolves behind us. The odds were stacked against us, and we were quickly running out of time.

Then, as if things couldn't get any worse, Celine skidded to a halt in front of me. I barely managed to stop in time as my feet slipped in the snow. When I caught myself and looked past her, my heart fell into my stomach. We ran all the way to a cliff.

I looked to the left—nowhere to go.

I did the same to our right—nope, equally as hopeless.

We were trapped, and there was no other direction to run. The wolves were closing in fast and soon would be upon us. I could see the deep red of their eyes set intently on us. I could hear their heavy breaths, feel their anticipation as they got closer.

I looked over the precipice, and my stomach dropped. Beneath us was a far drop into a dense forest of evergreens. It was a long way down, and I didn't want to weigh our odds of surviving a fall that great.

"What now, Celine?!" the words tore from me, though I already knew our options were exhausted.

The wolves closed in, growling loudly as they stalked toward us. I reached for my sword, but as I went to draw it, Celine took my hand and pulled me in close.

"Now, we do the only option left to us, Drifted."

Before I could process what she meant, she stepped forward, dragging me with her as she pulled us both off the cliff.

The air rushed past me, and my spit caught in my throat as we plummeted toward the canopy below. My vision blurred until the only thing that filled it was a singular tree branch, rapidly closing in on my face.

CHAPTER 3

My eyes slowly fluttered open, and the first thing that greeted me was a pounding headache. The world came into view at a sluggish pace as my brain came to, the corners of my vision still dark.

The sound of barking broke above me and I shot up—my body protesting in pain as I got into a sitting position.

Far above, I could make out the wolves barking down at me.

My mind filled with worry as I remembered Celine. Looking to my left, I saw her a few feet away, unmoving.

Panicked, I crawled over to her, hoping that she was okay.

"Celine..." I shook her shoulder, but she didn't stir.

"Hey, Celine!" I shook her again, harder this time.

Her eyes flew open with a wild stare, and she sat upright.

"Are you alright?" I asked her, worried.

Her eyes locked with mine, and she relaxed a little. "Aye, Drifted, I am okay."

She looked up towards the wolves barking and then turned her attention back to me. "We must move. They are too far to pursue us now."

"Right, let's go," I croaked.

Staggering to my feet, I swayed slightly as the pounding in my head grew worse—clearly, the fall was rougher than I thought.

Reaching out, I offered Celine a hand. She grasped it, but the moment she tried to stand, a sharp breath escaped her and she collapsed back down with a wince.

"Hey, what's the matter?" I asked, trying to keep the worry out of my voice.

"There is nothing the matter, probably a mild sprain," Celine replied, holding her hand out to ask for mine once more.

I tried to pull her to her feet again, but her leg buckled, and she went crashing to the snowy floor once more.

"Celine!" I exclaimed as I knelt beside her. "Let me see."

I carefully pulled up the hem of her cloak to reveal her leg.

I recoiled at the sight. A mess of bruises covered her skin, shades of purple and blue, blooming across her calf. The injury looked far worse than any mild sprain.

"Sure, looks like more than nothing," I said. "Celine, this doesn't look too good."

She grimaced, shaking her head slowly. "I shall manage Drifted, help me up so we can depart!"

"You're not going anywhere on that leg," I replied.

That's when I noticed the barking of the wolves stopped. I looked up toward the top of the cliff.

To my horror, they were gone, probably trying to find a route down to catch us.

"We have to move," I urged. "Let's go—you have to ride on my back."

Celine frowned, her pride evident in her posture. "I will not ask you to carry me like some burden."

"Burden?" I replied. "Come on, Celine, we don't exactly have the luxury of time on our side. We need to go—now."

She hesitated; I could tell she was torn between pride and necessity. "I won't be a hinderance to you."

"Celine," I said, softening my tone a bit more. "Remember what you told me? 'Our fates are intertwined.' I'm as good as dead if I leave you out here alone. Let me help you."

Her eyes narrowed as she wrestled with my words. Finally, she relented. "Fine," she said, defeat thick in her voice. "But if I sense I am holding you back, I will sacrifice myself immediately."

"There won't be a need for that," I replied, kneeling down and motioning for her to get on my back.

"Hold on tight," I said, bracing myself for the added weight.

As I stood up, I took in how light Celine was. Though it made sense, given her slender build.

I assumed she'd be heavier. Probably because she was the first person my age I've ever carried.

I was thankful, though, as the last thing we needed was for me to struggle to carry her as we were trying to avoid these wolves.

We moved through the thick snow slowly as I got used to the added weight. The cold air hurt my lungs, each breath growing more labored with every step.

But to my surprise, I felt a large amount of warmth radiating off Celine. It enveloped me like a protective layer, comforting my body and pushing me to keep moving despite the exhaustion.

"What do we do now?" I asked Celine, unsure of where to go next.

"It would be wise for us to look for a location to hide and regroup. Possibly a ridge or an outcrop or another cave. The wolves are surely still tracking us, and we are in no position to stay out here until dark with my broken leg."

She was right. The quicker we found somewhere to camp, the more rest we could get.

Falling off that cliff put a good amount of distance between us and our pursuers, so we wouldn't have to worry about them for a small while.

If we could find somewhere inconspicuous to hide, we might be able to catch our breath and devise a plan.

I glanced toward the sky, searching for the sun, but it was lost behind a blanket of thick gray clouds. Only the faintest glow remained, low and dim, hinting that the day was beginning to slip away.

I held still, listening. But there was nothing. The world was quiet. Towering trees stood in stillness, their branches swaying gently, filling the silence with a soft chorus of creaks and groans.

"Do you hear anything?" I asked Celine, knowing that her ears could catch anything far before mine would.

"No, it seems we have lost them for the time being. Though we must remain cautious. I will keep my ears at the ready."

I nodded. "What about somewhere to rest?"

She straightened herself on my back to get a better view. "There, to our right," she pointed toward a tall vertical rock-face partially obscured by snow-laden trees in the distance. "This will provide us with the cover we need."

"Good eye," I agreed, picking up my pace, treading carefully on the uneven ground.

As we approached the wall, I felt a sense of hope. If we could make this a suitable hiding spot, we might get enough rest for Celine's leg to heal; even if only slightly.

When we reached the base of the wall, I looked around, taking in the surroundings. The rocky surface jutted out at odd angles, giving us plenty of nooks and crannies where we could hide ourselves.

The area was dense with pine trees, forming a sort of hideaway from the rest of the woods. Even better, with the wall behind us, we'd only have to watch our sides, and directly in front of us. There would be no way for the guards to sneak up on us from behind.

"This is it," I said, feeling secure enough to let out a deep breath. "It seems like the perfect place to rest."

"Aye," Celine replied. "Let me down, Drifted. You need to rest."

I hesitated for a moment, and then slowly lowered her to the ground. She winced slightly as her weight shifted, but then steadied herself against the rock wall.

"Careful," I cautioned, watching her closely. "We need to keep you off of that leg as much as possible."

"I shall manage," she insisted, though I could see the strain in her movements. "I just need but a moment."

I crouched beside her, glancing around to make sure we were concealed enough. "You stay here and catch your breath; I'm going to go gather some firewood."

Celine nodded, her eyes flickering to the surrounding trees. "Do not stray too far. If we get caught while separated, it will mean certain death for the both of us."

I returned her caution with a slight smile, trying to lighten the tense mood. "We'll be alright, we've faced worse."

She managed to give me a small smile back. "You are correct. Though, don't take my words lightly."

I got to my feet and moved away from our makeshift camp. Every now and then, I stopped, straining my ears for anything out of the ordinary. Everything was quiet, but I couldn't shake the feeling that there was still danger nearby.

As I walked, I spotted a large, sturdy pine tree. I approached it carefully, assessing its size. It would provide good, dry wood for a fire, but I needed to be cautious about the noise I made.

I unsheathed my sword and began to hack at the tree trunks, taking short, controlled strikes.

Thankfully, the sound of the metal against the wood was

muffled by the snow, but I still worked quickly as I kept one ear tuned to the surrounding forest

After a few minutes, I managed to break off a decent-sized branch. I dropped it onto the ground and began working on the tree some more.

Taking my sword, I stripped the tree of its bark, gathering strips of various lengths and thicknesses.

Several minutes later, I gathered up a decent amount of firewood and materials. Looking around, I saw a large number of pinecones on the ground.

Knowing that I wouldn't have enough time to hunt for food before dark, I added the cones to the top of my woodpile, as they would be able to provide some nourishment, albeit minimal.

As I bent down to pick up everything from the ground, an intense pain shot through my head.

It felt like a rope suddenly been wound around my skull.

I staggered slightly, clutching my forehead with one hand and using the other to balance myself on a tree.

Then I heard it, the strange whispering that kept haunting me, echoing in my mind with a painful intensity.

"Blind..."

"Truth..."

"Pain..."

The words jumbled together, swirling in my head chaotically.

Before long, they became too loud, and I couldn't decipher the words floating around. Each syllable was twisted and smashed together, digging deeper into my mind as I grasped for clarity.

I put my back against the tree and slid to the ground, feeling the cold seep through my clothes. My head felt uncomfortably hot, as if I were coming down with a fever.

The pain became unbearable, and I grabbed a handful of snow and pressed it tightly against my forehead.

I buried my face in my hands, hoping the cold would numb the heat and quiet the noise inside my skull. I took ragged and deep breaths, hopelessly trying to grasp any sense of control.

Then, suddenly, as quickly as they came, the voices disappeared.

The silence was quick and profound, almost deafening with my head was so quiet.

I blinked slowly in disbelief, lowering my hands from my face.

What the hell was that? My mind questioned.

I stayed still for a moment, my heart beating roughly against my chest. I was no stranger to the weird voices that were plaguing me, but this pain was new.

I shook my head, trying to clear my mind. It wasn't surprising that I was seeing and hearing things. My mental health must be suffering because of the fatigue, I convinced myself.

I hadn't been getting much sleep, and the constant paranoia from being pursued by the guards must be affecting my mind.

Taking a deep breath, I pushed myself to my feet and brushed the snow off of my clothes. The chill in the air coupled with my soaked clothes snapping me back into reality.

I needed to focus on the present, on keeping Celine safe until we reached our destination. The last thing we needed was for me to spiral into some panic.

"Okay," I murmured, shaking off any lingering doubt. "Breathe. We have to keep moving."

With that, I picked up all the materials and stepped away from the tree.

As I made my way back toward Celine, I noticed her staring

at me with her face covered in a mixture of curiosity and worry.

"You took longer than I anticipated, Drifted," she started. "Did you face any trouble?"

I shook my head as I knelt beside her, dropping the items to the floor. "No, none at all. I guess I wanted to make sure we had enough wood."

But the moment I said it, I could see the skepticism flicker in her eyes.

"Are you certain?" she pressed, studying me closely with her eyes. "You can tell me if something is ailing you. I am not blind to your struggles."

I hesitated, her concern weighing heavily on my conscious. "Really, Celine, I'm fine. Just tired, I guess. It's been so cold at night it's hard to sleep sometimes!"

She frowned slightly, raising an eyebrow. "Tired or not, we're in a precarious situation. If there's something more— anything at all—it's better to share it."

I took a deep breath, returning her frown with a smile to lighten the mood. "I'm alright, Celine. I promise."

I didn't want her worrying about me. She knew I hadn't been getting much sleep because of the routine nightmares, though she didn't know the full extent.

It would do us no good to have her worrying about me when there was already so much more to worry about.

"Let's get a fire started," I said, trying to shift the focus away from myself. "After that, we can take a look at your leg."

Celine nodded, and I turned my attention to the materials I brought back. I arranged the wood in a small open area sheltered by rocks.

I started with the smaller sticks and strips of bark, arranging them in a teepee formation to allow for good airflow. Breaking a few of the pinecones, I nestled them in the center of the structure, knowing they would catch quickly.

Next, I searched the area for decently sized rocks to place around the base of the structure—enough to keep the wind from snuffing out the flame if it picked up.

With everything in place, I looked around for something to spark a flame. Thankfully, I remembered Celine always kept a few pieces of flint in my knapsack to start fires with.

I rummaged through the bag until I found one, and then found a slightly larger rock nearby.

I struck the flint against the rock and watched as it sent tiny sparks flying into the wood and broken pieces of pinecone.

It took a few tries, but finally, a small flame flickered to life as it caught hold of the dry materials.

"Come on," I whispered, leaning in closer to blow lightly on the flames.

Slowly, I coaxed it until it grew into a steady fire. Immediately, the surrounding area filled with warmth as it radiated outward.

"Nicely done, Drifted," Celine said, her voice filled with approval as she watched the flames grow.

"Not too shabby, eh?" I replied as I turned to her. "Now, let's take a look at that leg."

I stood up and looked towards the remaining materials. There was a longer, thicker branch that I brought to create a makeshift splint. I picked it up and knelt beside Celine, taking a moment to gather my thoughts.

"Alright, let's see if I can help any," I said as I gently pulled up the hem of her cloak.

The sight of her calf formed a knot in my stomach. The bruising had spread; dark purple and blue splotches made their way further up her calf.

"Celine, this looks serious," I said, trying to keep as much concern out of my voice as possible. "The splint may help, but only slightly."

"I will be okay, Drifted," she insisted, but I could see the pain in her eyes.

Unconvinced, I positioned the thick branch alongside her leg, making sure it extended a few inches beyond the knee and ankle.

I then took my sword and cut strips of fabric from the fur cloak I wore.

"Alright, let's get this secured," I said, tearing the strips to an appropriate length.

I began to bind the splint to her leg, making sure it was snug, but not too tight.

Celine winced as I tied the first knot, but quickly turned her face in an attempt to hide the pain.

"You know, showing a little weakness now and then won't kill you," I teased, letting out a small chuckle.

She turned her eyes back to me, a small smile tugging at the corners of her lips. "I have no reservations about showing weakness. This is simply uncomfortable, that is all."

"Ah, I see. Well, forgive me for assuming otherwise. How foolish it was of me to think that a broken leg could ever be painful to you, Celine."

As I finished securing the splint, I jokingly brushed my hand against her leg a bit too hard, and she winced again.

I raised an eyebrow, unable to resist the opportunity. "That wouldn't happen to be a show of weakness, would it?"

Celine's ears started to twitch, and her face took on a reddish hue. "I swear, Drifted, if you keep this up, I'll let the wolves have you!"

I laughed, holding up my hands in surrender. "Alright, alright! It won't happen again."

She huffed and crossed her arms, turning her head away.

"If you are looking to lighten the mood, lighten it by easing the pain in my leg."

"Okay, okay," I said, trying to cover my grin. "Though, you have to admit. It was a little funny, wasn't it?"

Celine rolled her eyes. "Focus on preserving your strength instead of playing childish games," she shot back. "There is no amusement in pain."

"Your wish is my command," I replied to her, tying off the last knot to secure the splint. "There, it should be able to heal up nicely now."

She looked at her leg intently, then tried moving it in the splint. "It really hinders mobility, does it not?" She asked.

"Yeah, that's kind of the point." I replied.

"Aye, I do suppose so," she said, lowering the hem of her cloak down. "Thank you, Drifted."

"Anytime," I said, giving her a reassuring smile. "Now, let's sit back by the fire and rest for a bit. We've earned it."

As we settled back near the warmth of the flames, I felt the tension in the air ease slightly. Despite our dire situation, the soft crackling of the fire was a comforting reassurance.

As I got mesmerized by the flames, a sudden grumble broke me out of my trance.

It took me a second to realize that it was my stomach.

"Let's see what we can scrounge up to eat," I said, rummaging through the pile of wood to pick out the pinecones I collected earlier.

I picked a few of them up, brushing the snow off of them.

I cracked a couple of them open against the edge of a nearby rock. Then, I removed the small and nutty seeds from inside, collecting a handful.

"It isn't much," I said, looking over at Celine as I held my hand out to her. "But it's at least something to help keep our energy up."

Celine took the nuts from my hand and placed one into her mouth. "Thank you Drifted, while it isn't much, it will have to do."

"Yeah," I replied, popping a few into my mouth. "They're a little bland, but not too bad, right?"

Celine popped a few more into her mouth and nibbled softly. "I did not realize that pine nuts were edible. They are actually quite a treat."

I ate another nut. "You've never had them? I used to eat them all the time as a kid."

Celine shook her head. "No, never."

I leaned back against the rock face and began cracking open a couple of more pinecones. "When I was younger, I'd sometimes gather pinecones and climb a tree near town and spend the day watching the world from above."

Celine turned her gaze to me and listened intently. She always got intrigued by stories from my past. "What did you observe from up there, perched in the tree?"

"Oftentimes I'd see wolves," I continued. "Two groups would come together and fight. Maybe over territory or food, I don't know. But they'd fight so often I eventually could distinguish which wolf was who."

"You mean to say that the same wolves were fighting that often?" she asked, leaning in, deeply invested.

"Mhm, for the most part. There was one in particular, with dark brown fur, that I always rooted for. He was always my favorite. Strong, quick—insanely cool."

Celine's eyes were burning with curiosity now. "Were you ever scared of the wolves?"

"Not really," I said with a shrug. "Being so high up in the tree made me feel invincible. I was only a kid, full of stupid bravery. That was until that one day…"

"Yes, continue, Drifted," Celine urged, leaning in until her face was just inches away from mine.

I swallowed, feeling embarrassed at having her face so close to my own. "Well, one day I was so focused up there, watching my favorite wolf, that I didn't pay enough attention to my surroundings. He was battling another wolf, and I was completely immersed. Then I heard some rustling in the tree beneath me, so I leaned over the edge of the branch to get a better look."

Celine's violet eyes widened. "Aye, and then?"

"Honestly, I don't remember much after that. I fell from the tree, and then everything went dark. When I woke up, I found myself on the front steps of my house. Aunt Silvia and my parents were there screaming at me to tell them what happened. They thought I'd gotten lost or worse."

Celine's brow furrowed. "Though how did you get home after you fell from the tree?"

I chuckled, sharing her confusion. "Your guess is as good as mine! To this day, it's been a mystery to me. One that will probably never be solved. After that day, my parents kept a closer watch on me and made me promise to not climb trees anymore."

Celine leaned back against the wall, rubbing her splinted leg. "It seems like you learned your lesson, even if it took a fall to do so."

I nodded with a grin. "Definitely. But I still miss watching those wolves fight. It was exciting being able to watch nature unfold before me."

"I would venture to say we've been as close to nature as we've ever been. Being hunted is certainly an intimate experience," Celine said, letting out a sigh. "Perhaps not the kind of intimacy one wishes for, but intimacy nonetheless."

I laughed. At least she could find some form of humor in our circumstances. "True enough. Though I'd prefer to be the observer rather than the prey for a change."

Celine ate the last of her pine nuts. "We will find a way to navigate this wilderness without becoming its victims. We just need to stay alert and keep our wits about us."

"Agreed," I said, grateful that Celine could continue to be so optimistic. "As long as we stick together, we'll make it through whatever this place throws at us."

As the sun dipped further and the darkness continued to envelop us, there was a certain calmness in the air.

And though I was sure it wouldn't last, I allowed myself to be at peace with it.

CHAPTER 4

It was night, and the only noises was the occasional hoot of an owl somewhere in the distance and the crackling of the fire.

Celine stirred beside me, glancing at the fire illuminating our makeshift camp. "Drifted, we should put out the flame. The light will give us away in the darkness," she said.

I nodded. She was completely right, though without the fire I wasn't sure we'd make it through the harsh cold. Regardless, I agreed, as I'd rather deal with the cold than get mauled to death by those guards. "You're right. I'll take care of it."

I got up and knelt beside the fire, placing my hands near it one last time to soak up the warmth. With a deep breath, I kicked some snow over it, smothering it until the last flicker of light disappeared.

We were in darkness, with the only light being the white full moon above. The sudden quiet felt awkward, and I found myself shifting in the snow as the cold seeped into my bones. The absence of the flame left me feeling vulnerable to whatever dangers lurked in the shadows.

"Celine," I said, glancing at her. "You should try to get some rest. You've been through a lot today."

She looked at me, trying to keep her usual relaxed demeanor, but I could see the fatigue written on her face. "I appreciate your concern, Drifted. But I shall manage."

"You're not okay," I insisted gently. "You hurt your leg and need all the rest you can get if you're going to heal."

She hesitated, clearly torn between her pride and her need to recover. "I can go on much longer than you can, Drifted. You rest; I will take first shift."

"Celine," I said, softening my tone. "You've done so much already. You need to take care of yourself. I promise I'll wake you if anything happens."

Reluctantly, she sighed, and I could see the tension ease in her shoulders. "Alright. I shall rest, but only for a short while. If you sense any disturbance—any at all. You had best wake me."

I couldn't help but smile at her stubbornness. "Yes, ma'am, don't worry, nothing will get past me."

Celine leaned against the rock wall, pulling her cloak tighter around her as she got into a more comfortable position. I watched as her eyelids fluttered closed, and soon enough, she was asleep.

As the night dragged on, I kept my wits about me, occasionally cracking more pinecones to munch on. The moon was high, illuminating the ground with shadows of swaying branches and flying owls.

But as the hours passed, I felt the cold of the forest becoming unbearable. Eventually, I found myself shifting on the floor again. This time not because of the quietness, but as a way to keep myself warm.

I wrapped my arms around my knees and pulled my fur cloak closer to preserve whatever heat I had left, but it was a losing battle.

I glanced over at Celine; she was calm in sleep, and her breathing was steady. A large contrast to the growing discomfort I was feeling. I tried to distract myself from the cold, reminding myself that I was on guard duty and needed to be alert and ready at any moment.

Yet, the chill continued to seep deeper into my bones, and

I wished for even a spark of warmth as I kept watch.

Movement stirred beside me. Celine had awoken from her sleep, and before I could fully grasp what was happening, she scooted over and pressed herself against me.

I could feel my face growing warm in surprise as she nestled her head onto my shoulder, her eyes still closed throughout the movement.

"Ce... Celine?" I whispered, half in shock and half in confusion.

She looked up slightly, her voice soft and soothing. "I can sense you are cold, Drifted. I am warm. We shall keep better warmth between us if we remain close."

My heart began beating quickly in my chest, and I swallowed hard, trying to gather my thoughts. "You really don't have to do this," I replied, growing warmer despite the cold in the air. "I'll be okay. You shouldn't worry about me."

Celine opened her eyes more, and now her gaze felt as if it were boring into my soul. "If you remain cold, you'll be distracted from keeping watch. This way, you will be able to stay focused on the task at hand."

I hesitated. The practicality of Celine's words made sense, though the closeness felt immensely intimate. "But Celine—"

Before I could argue more, she cut me off. "This will ensure we remain safe. You do not have a problem with ensuring our safety, do you, Drifted?"

Of course I cared about our safety, but having Celine, hell—anyone this close to me wasn't something I was used to.

With a sigh, I conceded. This wasn't an argument I was going to win. And besides, Celine was warm. I would be lying if I said it didn't feel good. "Alright, but if you feel uncomfortable at any point, let me know."

Celine nodded and settled back against me. Her warmth enveloped me in a way that made the cold feel almost insignificant. It felt as if I were sitting next to the fire again.

How could she be so warm?

"I hope I was not too heavy for you earlier, Drifted," Celine asked. Her voice still sleepy from waking up.

"Of course not," I replied, clearing my throat. "You were as light as a feather. Though, it's going to be a bit awkward carrying you now with your leg splinted like that."

She chuckled softly, the sound as pleasant as the warmth radiating from her body. "Aye, well. That will be your problem to sort out in the morning."

I felt a lightness in my chest at her words. The combination of the warmth and closeness of Celine made the situation all too overwhelming.

I glanced down at her, noting the peacefulness etched across her features. Her orange-brown hair, which rested on her shoulders, framed her face beautifully, sitting gently against her cheeks. I couldn't help but admire how her furry ears poked through her hair, a unique trait that made her all the more enchanting.

The faint glow of the moonlight overhead illuminated the curves of her face. Highlighting the softness of it in a way that made it seem to glow in the dark, and I felt a strange comfort come over me just being near her.

The way her lashes laid softly against her cheek as she lay made her look even more serene.

As warmth flooded to my cheeks, I grew even more embarrassed about our situation. To distract myself from the rush of emotions, I quickly scooped up a handful of snow and stuffed it into my mouth.

The frigidness sent a shock through me, biting against my tongue and forcing me to focus on something other than

Celine.

I chewed on the snow quietly, helping myself to another handful to make sure the chill would calm my body.

It worked, but it took every fiber of my being to avoid looking at Celine any further.

As I sat there, the twilight of the moon began to feel like it was trickling into my bones. Soon, I felt the heavy weight of fatigue settle over my eyes. The rhythmic sound of Celine's breathing mixed with the gentle sounds of wind pulled me into a state of comfort I didn't expect.

I shook my head, trying to rattle my brain awake. *Stay awake, you promised Celine you would keep watch.* I told myself.

Though, the battle against exhaustion was becoming incredibly difficult with Celine's warmth against me. Each passing second felt harder, and I could feel my eyelids staying closed longer with each blink.

Before I knew it, I succumbed to fatigue. I couldn't hold out any longer, and slipped further into the warm embrace of sleep.

No harm in resting my eyes, right? I foolishly told myself as I allowed my consciousness to fade.

It wasn't long before I felt the clutches of a nightmare fighting against my mind.

I was fully lucid during it, making it even more daunting. Trapped, I watched as my own thoughts warped into incoherent gargles and swirled around me like a living entity.

I stood in an endless expanse of fog, and the world around me was blurry and obscure. From the corner of my eye, I caught shapes—no—figures moving in the distance.

Though every time I turned to face them, they disappeared.

"Your eyes..."

I heard a whisper echo from behind me. The voice sounded familiar, yet distorted, and I couldn't discern whose it was.

I tried to call out to it, but when I did, my throat burned and ached as if the words were laced with poison.

I started coughing, but each cough burned with increasing intensity, sending the pain throughout my chest.

I doubled over, desperate for relief, but the burning only intensified.

Then, through the fog, I caught a glimpse of Celine running parallel to where I lay.

She stopped for a moment, standing there, searching for something.

Another whisper broke out from behind my ears. "You..."

I read Celine's lips as she stood there screaming my name. She was searching for me.

"Celine!" I tried to shout, but the words choked in my throat as the burning ripped through me with each attempt. My eyes watered from the stinging, and I struggled to keep them open.

I wanted to run to her, to hold her hand and escape the suffocating fog, but my limbs felt like they were being weighed down by heavy lead.

Before I knew it, I couldn't breathe any longer. The burning made it impossible to take another breath, and I laid there choking.

"Celine!" I croaked again, trying to will my arms to drag me towards her.

She turned her head, noticing me, and started running, but she wasn't moving. It was like she was rooted in place—no— it was as if I was moving further from her.

She yelled, but this time I could just make it out. "Drifted, you must fight it!"

I felt myself slipping as the remaining air in my lungs quickly ran out. I gasped, searching for any air to quench my lungs, but none came.

Then, without warning, the ground beneath me shook.

It felt like an earthquake was threatening to open the area I was lying on. I tried to pick myself up from the floor, but the grumbling made it impossible to stand.

Suddenly, the ground cracked open beneath me, fissures growing wide to swallow me whole.

As I felt myself plummeting into the abyss, two hands grabbed my arm.

I looked up to see Celine's frantic expression, her eyes wide with fear. She was holding onto me, screaming something at me, but no sound escaped her lips.

I wanted to shout back, to reassure her that I would be okay, but the burning still had its grip on my throat.

The world around us began to darken, and I felt the edges of my sanity crack like glass. I could see the intensity in Celine's eyes, and it fueled my own panic.

Then, right as Celine lost the strength to hold on to me any longer, everything went fuzzy.

I jolted awake, desperately gasping for breath.

Celine was right in front of me, her face inches away from mine as she shook me gently.

"Drifted! Wake up!" she urged.

I let out a shaky breath as the world cleared. Blinking rapidly, I tried to compose myself. I was disoriented, but safe in our makeshift camp once more. "I'm awake," I murmured, still shaken. "I'm awake."

She held the back of her hand to my forehead. "You are burning up, Drifted. What is the matter? Another nightmare?"

I nodded, trying to ignore my heart pounding in my chest. "It was... Intense. More so than usual. But I'm fine."

Her expression quickly hardened, and her eyes began darting between me and the woods.

"As much as I would love to tend to you, we must depart. Now."

I sat up straight, Celine's anxiousness sending a jolt of adrenaline through me. "What's the matter?" I asked.

"The guards, they are near," she replied, her ears swiveling on her head, trying to dial into the location of whatever was disturbing the woods.

My eyes widened, and I quickly scooted in front of Celine, kneeling in front of her as I motioned for her to get on my back. "Right. Let's get moving then."

Celine quickly positioned herself on my back. I stood up and handed my satchel to her. "Hold on tight," I told her as I felt her weight settle against me.

With a deep breath, I took off into a jog, the cold air against my face waking me up the rest of the way. I needed to put as much distance between us and the guards as possible.

"Celine," I called back to her, "Can you tell how far they are?"

She adjusted herself on my back until she was upright. She took a second to reply, presumably tuning her ears to the noise the guards were generating. "Not far, a few miles at best."

A few miles. This wasn't good. With Celine on my back, a jog was about the most I could manage. The guards would be upon us in no time.

How could they have found us so quickly?

I figured we would've had at least a day's advantage after we took that fall.

I pushed myself harder, with the snow crunching loudly underfoot. By this point, I completely tossed trying to keep our presence concealed to the side.

I felt something cold and rough brush against my side as my arms pumped.

I glanced down briefly, and because it was dark, I could barely make out what it was.

My heart skipped when I realized it was blood.

It was a small splatter frozen onto the fur of my cloak, likely from the earlier fight with the guard. I hadn't noticed it throughout the chaos of the chase, but now, as we ran for our lives, the sight of it made my stomach drop.

This must've been how they tracked us down so quickly. With my cloak sullied by the blood of the dead guard, tracking the scent would've been a breeze for the others.

I considered removing the cloak, but it wouldn't matter. If what that female guard back in the town said was true, my scent alone would be as easy to track.

The best thing that I could do now is keep on running.

I pushed myself even harder. The whole reason we were in this position was because I was careless.

How hadn't I noticed this blood earlier?

I cursed myself. Not only was I putting my life in danger, but Celine's as well.

Just as I was about to pass a large tree, something flickered in the corner of my vision.

A shadow, too quick to identify. If I weren't so distracted already, I may have noticed it in time.

Before I could react, I felt Celine turn on my back. She turned her body weight hard, knocking me off balance and pulling us toward the ground.

As I fell backwards, time seemed to slow down. I looked up in time to see the blur of a wolf's body leap right over us— its paws and snapping jaw barely missing our heads.

The wolf landed a few feet from us as I scrambled to Celine's side, drawing my sword.

The wolf turned on its heels to face us, growling in a low grumble that made my heart race even faster than it already was.

"Stay back!" I yelled out, pointing the tip of my sword straight at it.

But it didn't flinch.

Instead, its growl deepened, rising in volume as it bared its teeth even more. It began barking at us as it took slow, methodical steps closer.

This wasn't good; with this wolf keeping us busy, the other guards would easily have enough time to catch up.

"Drifted," Celine called out from behind me, her voice strained but firm.

"What is it" I replied, not daring to take my eyes off of the encroaching wolf.

Celine placed a hand on my shoulder. "You must leave me behind. I cannot walk, but you may still be able—"

"Shut up! Don't be ridiculous!" I interrupted her, the words flying out before I could stop them. "There's no way I would ever leave you to your death, Celine."

I felt her hand recoil from my shoulder for a moment before she placed it back on. "Drifted, hear me well. If you stay, both of our fates are sealed here. However, you still possess the chance to get away, to continue north towards my father."

I shook my head, gripping my sword tighter. "I'm not abandoning you. It will not happen. We're going to see this through together—no matter what."

The wolf howled, loud and insistent.

There was no doubt in my mind that it was signaling to its teammates that it had us found and cornered.

Then, behind me, a whisper came through the air, barely audible, but unmistakably clear.

"Truth..."

The sudden whisper startled me, but I kept my eyes

focused on the wolf.

Not now, damnit why now? I cursed to myself.

The same cold, disembodied voice was becoming all too familiar.

The back of my head started to throb with a light, annoying ache.

Another whisper came through, louder this time. "Unseen..."

The word smacked the back of my skull like nails dragging across stone, making the ache intensify with every second.

My vision blurred, and I squeezed my eyes shut, begging for the pain to stop.

But it didn't.

The whispers grew louder, more insistent, as if they were surrounding me.

The wolf, noticing this, took another step further, taking advantage of my moment of weakness.

"Don't get any closer!" I yelled weakly, trying to sound stronger than I felt.

I tried to hold up my sword, but the pounding in my head was too distracting.

"Eyes..."

"Pain... pain... pain!" The voiced yelled at me, and the pain surged.

I dropped my sword into the snow and clutched my head. It felt as though my brain was being squeezed from the inside out.

My temples throbbed with an intensity that made it difficult to breathe, and my hearing began to fade.

"Drifted!" I heard Celine's muffled voice from behind me.

But I couldn't respond. The pain too loud to focus on anything else.

"Make it stop..." I muttered, my voice strained as I

struggled to stay upright.

"Drifted! What is wrong!?" I heard the cries from Celine intensify as she shook my shoulders.

It was too much to handle; I couldn't take it anymore.

I quickly felt my body losing energy. My heartbeat was thundering in my skull, each pulse making the world around me spin further.

Everything was closing in on me, and my vision dimmed as I fought to keep my balance.

My knees gave out from beneath me as the ground rushed to greet me.

Before everything went black, I saw blurred movement to my right.

More wolves were approaching quickly, their shadows getting larger as they neared. Their red eyes were glowing intensely, and I could hear their barks in-between my heartbeats.

This is it, this is the end. I thought to myself as my eyes closed. *Celine, forgive me.*

CHAPTER 5

My eyes snapped open as my heart raced. I sat upright in a daze, unsure of what to expect next.

Slowly, as my eyes came to, I realized I was no longer in that snowy forest, stuck in the cold.

Instead, I was in a dimly lit room.

The air was thick with the smell of moss and earth, and there were symbols on the ceiling I couldn't discern.

I pushed myself up further in the bed I found myself lying in. The soft mattress beneath me was made of materials I couldn't quite place, possibly feathers. It was comfortable. Too comfortable.

It had thick woven leaves and moss, and the sheets had a smooth texture that reminded me of silk, but softer. I felt uneasy as I took in my surroundings. The warmth of the room felt all too unreal with everything I had been through recently.

The surrounding walls were equally as strange—made of wood, yes, but not with the kind I was used to. These walls looked as if they were crafted from bark, smooth and textured in a way that looked unnatural—or rather, too natural—as if they were part of a forest.

The soft light in the room came from the glow filtering through vines and leaves that grew out of the walls. To add to the strangeness, flowers bloomed in clusters near the corners, their petals bright and vibrant against the wooden backdrop.

I glanced around, trying to make sense of where I was. The room felt safe, but I couldn't shake the feeling I didn't belong here. My body was still heavy with fatigue, but the fear that gripped me tightly kept me alert.

I tossed the sheet off of me, and to my surprise, my usual garb was gone. I wasn't in the cloak and clothes I left home with. Instead, now I wore a soft cotton shirt. It was loose-fitting, with long sleeves that fell past my wrist, the material allowing for effortless motion. It felt different, like it was made specifically for comfort.

I looked down and saw that my pants had been changed as well. Instead of the rough trousers I was used to, I wore something softer, made from a light material. The fabric was a dull mud-brown, almost the color of dirt. The clothes looked normal enough, but I couldn't place the material used.

Where was I? Where was Celine? And what happened after the guards got to us?

A thousand questions began swirling around in my head, but one thing was certain. I needed to get out of here, find Celine, and figure out what the hell was going on.

I glanced around the room once more, looking for an exit. To the left of me was a door carved right into the face of the wall, a subtle wooden doorknob attached to it. If I was going to get out of there, that would be the only way.

As I prepared to get myself out of bed, the door swung open. And to my surprise, a familiar but unwelcome face stuck its head through the now open door. Instantly, my body froze, and my blood ran cold.

The female guard from the town in the Madlands—the one who had helped me escape from the cage—stood there, her eyes meeting mine with a gleeful expression.

I felt a chill run down my spine as my heart sank into my stomach. I must've been captured. After I passed out, the guards must've brought me back here to inflict their punishment for the death of their queen. The wolves had surrounded Celine and me, and now I was back in this hellish place.

No, I wouldn't go down without a fight.

My eyes darted around the room, desperately searching for anything to defend myself with. Surprisingly, I spotted my sword leaning against a wooden bedside table.

I quickly grabbed it and pointed it at the female guard. I had no intention of letting them have their way with me. The death of their queen must've hurt them deeply. I mean, they've been chasing us for weeks.

"Stay away!" I yelled, "If you think I'll go down without a fight, you've got another thing coming!"

The door creaked open more, and she stepped in. An enormous grin spread across her face as she looked me over, calculating and amused. Her smile grew wider as she leaned against the doorframe, seemingly unbothered by my threat.

"Oh, how eager you are to meet your end," she said, her voice lifting with amusement. "But I do so love a good chase." She pushed herself off the doorframe and took a few steps forward, bouncing on her toes.

"You need not look so grim, boy," she continued, her grin growing wilder. "It's not every day I get to catch such a feisty one. What shall we do with you, I wonder?" She tilted her head slightly, her red eyes burning. "I must say, you are making this far more entertaining than I expected."

"I mean it, stay back!" I yelled once more, trying to hide the fear that was probably etched across my face.

She paused for a moment, her eyes staying locked onto mine. She took another step closer, and I thrusted my sword at her once more. But she didn't care, chuckling softly as if I were nothing to take seriously. The mischief in her voice only intensified.

"I was expecting you would be more... cooperative, but you're so much more fun this way."

Without warning, her hand shot up, and in the light I saw a glint as her nails grew into claws. Before I could react, the sword was ripped from my hand, smacking against the wall and falling to the ground with a clatter. I barely had time to brace myself before she was on top of me, her knees pinning my arms to the bed with surprising strength.

I coughed, surprised by her speed. I tried to get up, but she dug into my arms deeper with her knees, pinning them further.

"You should know better than to think you could hold your own against me," she whispered, her voice mocking.

She brushed her claws against the side of my cheek, and I pulled my head away.

"Quit toying with me! If you're going to end my life, then do it already!" I yelled at her, annoyed that she thought to make my death a game.

Her eyes widened, and she tilted her head to the side. "If that is your will," she replied coolly.

I watched as her smile grew wider and her lips parted to reveal sharp fangs. I froze, letting the reality of what was to come next settle in. She was going to kill me, and there was nothing I could do to stop it.

She leaned in closer, her breath hot against my skin, and as she neared my neck with her mouth open, I squeezed my eyes shut, bracing for the inevitable.

Aunt Silvia, Uncle Alfarr, the twins... Celine. I'm so sorry. I thought to myself.

But as the seconds dragged, I waited for the bite, the tearing pain to pierce my flesh, but it never came.

Confused, I opened my eyes only to feel something soft and warm brush against my cheek. I blinked in disbelief.

It wasn't fangs that touched me, but lips. Her kiss lingered for a moment.

"What... what the hell" I murmured, stunned, unable to process the situation.

The guard suddenly pulled away and sat up. Then, to my surprise, she laughed, loud enough to fill the room. She was laughing so hard that she was shaking, clearly struggling to catch her breath as she held her stomach.

"You should see the look on your face," she chuckled, barely able to get the words out in between her laughs. "I could hardly keep my own straight!"

Her eyes sparkled as she wiped a tear from the corner of her eye.

I stared at her in disbelief. What was all of that a moment ago? Was this guard crazy?

The guard, noticing my stares, looked down at me. "Do not look so serious, Drifted," she added, still grinning widely. "I am not interested in taking your life."

She got up from on top of me swiftly, brushing off her clothes as she righted herself. With a playful tilt of the head, she glanced back down at me. "If you really had been captured," she said. "Do you honestly believe your captors would leave your sword within reach?"

I blinked in silence, unsure of what to say next. Was she waiting for me to drop my guard before ending me?

No—it wasn't that. She definitely possessed the power to finish me off whenever she wanted to; that much was certain. But here she was, making a joke of the situation, messing with me as if this were all some sort of game.

The guard walked by the door and stood next to it, staring at me with a smirk still plastered on her face. She raised an eyebrow and motioned toward a wooden chest across the room. "There is clothing in that chest, hurry up and get dressed, Drifted. You should not be lounging about while we have matters to attend to."

I'm not exactly sure why, but I was compelled to get up and follow her orders. Not out of fear, but solely of the fact that the strangeness of the situation clouded my judgement.

I got up, walked towards the chest, and opened it. Inside was another fur pelt, much like the one she gave me in the Madlands, a leather tunic, fur shoes, and the rest of my gear I had with me on the night Celine and I got captured.

I stared at the clothes, and then back toward the guard, who was still standing in the doorway. "I... I don't need your help getting dressed," I muttered.

"Ah yes," she replied with a playful shrug. "I suppose I should give you some privacy after all."

She turned to the door but paused before exiting, flicking her eyes back toward me. "Shout for me if you require any... assistance."

With that, she stepped out of the room, her voice trailing off as the door shut softly behind her.

I sat on the side of the bed with a sigh. I didn't know how to continue. Was I really going to listen to her as if nothing was wrong? As if none of this were strange?

I mean, what choice did I have? She insinuated that I wasn't, in fact, captive. But then why did they bring me here? I suppose there was some truth in her words. Why would they go out of the way to clothe and house me if their plans were to punish me?

My fist clenched. The more I tried to make sense of it, the less it added up. The guards had tracked me down—there was no mistaking that. It almost felt like they were preparing me for something. Or perhaps they simply needed me alive for some other reason.

Either way, I couldn't stay in this room forever.

I had to figure out what my next move would be. There was no way I could formulate a plan until I knew exactly what

I was up against.

Despite my better judgment, I wore the cloak and boots that were immensely soft. Then I grabbed the remainder of my items from the trunk before buckling my belt and sheathing my sword.

With one last sigh, I placed my hand on the doorknob, trying to steel my nerves before I walked into the unknown.

I turned the knob and pushed to door open. The bright light from outside flooded the dim room, and I squinted as I stepped into the open.

Immediately, I was greeted with a cold slap to the face that chilled my nose. Then, as my eyes adjusted to the light, I took in the awe-striking sight before me.

The area before me was enormous, a kind of cul-de-sac surrounded by equally sized wooden houses with roofs covered in snow. The houses were simple in structure, with rough-bark wooden walls and chimneys puffing faint trails of smoke. Despite the snow still blanketing the ground, there were lush vines that crawled up the sides of most houses and moss that grew along the edges of paths. The air smelled fresher here, cleaner even. A thin scent of dirt and pine with something floral.

The amount of life and growth surrounded by snow left me in awe. It was like stepping into another world— one that seemed to defy the season.

"You certainly look comfortable," I heard a familiar voice break through my focus.

I was so captivated by the sight that I hadn't noticed the guard standing a few feet away from the doorway. She stood, looking at me with a mischievous grin on her face.

"Just, Where are we?" I asked, slightly annoyed at being left in the dark about my situation.

"It is gorgeous, is it not?" the guard replied, her eyes

sparkling as she took in the surrounding sights.

None of this made sense. Back in the Madlands when I first saw this guard, she was demanding, and honestly a bit scary. The memory of her crushing the hand of one of her allies that beat me up sent a chill through my body.

But now, she was here, friendly, bubbly, even though she was annoyingly so. It was as if the violence I'd witnessed was merely a footnote in her life. There was a stark contrast between the girl, who had appeared like a force to be reckoned with, and the one standing in front of me now.

Something about this place—and her—wasn't adding up, and I was determined to get to the bottom of it.

"I guess it's nice," I answered back defensively. "But you didn't exactly answer my question."

"There is no need to be so pushy," she said mockingly, pointing a finger in my face. "I was about to get there."

She was seemingly oblivious to the tension I was feeling between us, and I had no choice but to wait for whatever answer she was going to give. I crossed my arms, tapping my foot. "Well... then, out with it."

She rolled her eyes.

"If you must know, Drifted, we are currently in the most sacred region of this world. The one and only Sylphreach."

She paused for a moment, as if expecting a reaction of awe or disbelief from me. When I didn't immediately speak, she bounced on her heels, clearly savoring my confusion.

"You are quite the lucky one, you know," she continued, now walking circles around me. "Most humans can only dream of stepping foot in this place, let alone stand here, breathing its air. But here you are... such a fortunate soul."

I stood there, now even more confused than I was before. Beating around the bush must been in her blood.

"I have no clue what you're on about," I replied to her.

Though deep down, I knew she wouldn't try to remedy that at all.

"Aye, I suppose someone like you would not,"she replied with a laugh, stopping in front and staring at me with her piercing red eyes.

"It would be great if you cared to explain. Even a little more would do wonders," I replied, staring right back at her.

She put a finger to her chin and looked up into the air, as if she were weighing her options.

"No, I do not think so," she answered, turning her back to me.

"No?" I questioned. "What do you mean, no?"

"I mean, I do not feel inclined to answer you at this very moment. Was I not clear enough?"

"And why not!" I yelled, growing increasingly more frustrated by the second.

"I am famished. It is difficult to speak when one's stomach is empty," she turned, walking away from me. "If you wish to learn anything, it would serve you well to follow."

I stood there dumbfounded, staring as she walked further away with such a casual bounce in her step. Nothing about this situation made any sense—nothing about her made sense.

But I didn't have much of a choice, did I? I could stand here and fume, but that would get me nowhere. Whatever was going on, she was the only one I knew here that could give me any answers. If I were to get my wits about me, I'd have to follow her, no matter how bizarre the situation was.

With a heavy sigh, I pushed my frustrations aside and jogged to catch up. "You'll answer my questions after a meal?" I questioned.

"Mhm," she answered simply, not giving me much else.

As we walked through the courtyard, I took in my surroundings with growing curiosity. The houses around us looked fairly similar—some smaller, some larger, but mainly similar in design. Wooden structures with thick and sturdy walls made of the same darkened bark exteriors. It looked as if they had grown straight out of the ground.

Despite the many houses around us, the streets were strangely quiet. Not a soul passed by us as we walked. Every step we took echoed on the empty road.

I couldn't keep my thoughts to myself. "Why's it so empty here?" I asked, glancing around again, hoping that someone would pop out from behind the buildings.

The guard, still walking ahead of me, let out a small, teasing laugh. "Oh, Drifted, do you not know?" She motioned to the snow on the ground. "I i's winter. Normally, people seek to stay indoors to keep warm during this time." She shot me a glance, clearly enjoying the opportunity to mock me. "I am surprised you had not noticed. It makes it difficult to wander outside, no?"

I frowned, a bit embarrassed by her teasing. "You don't have to be condescending, you know?" I replied, crossing my arms.

"Me, condescending?" she questioned sarcastically. "I can be no such thing."

"That's not really something you get to decide," I murmured back, still feeling the sting of her words.

She turned her head, glancing back at me. "Oh, Drifted, you wound me with such harsh words. But if you must know, many here stay inside during the colder months. While we are perfectly capable of being out during the winter, it is more comfortable to stay indoors."

She turned her head back forward and began looking around at the houses surrounding us. "Much like you humans, we tend to keep to ourselves when it is like this—when the snow falls and the world slows down."

There it was again, another confirmation that these people didn't consider themselves human despite their obvious similarities with us. Maybe it wasn't some strange mutation that made them sprout ears or give them the ability to shapeshift into wolves after all.

"You say humans as if you people aren't that. Then what are you?" I asked, trying to keep the curiosity hidden. If she noticed it, she would likely keep the answer to herself.

The guard raised a finger, wagging it in the air. She clicked her tongue at me. "All in good time, you are quite the impatient one, it seems."

"Impatient? You've barely told me anything at all." I said as I quickened my pace, walking next to her now.

"You shall learn more in time. But I will say this—just because we share similar form of locomotion, it does not make our kind the same."

I sighed, tossing my hands up in defeat. This must've been where Celine learned to speak so cryptically.

Wait, how could I have forgotten? Where was Celine?

"Hey! Wait a second," I yelled at the guard. "Celine, the girl who was with me before you brought me here. Where is she?"

The guard stopped in her tracks, her head turning slightly as if she had remembered something important. She raised an eyebrow and grinned. "Ah yes, the girl. Celine is her name, correct?" She paused as if she were choosing her words carefully. "She is... meeting someone special. Do not concern yourself with her for the time being."

My heart rate quickened a bit at her answer, and I raised an eyebrow. Celine was presumably safe, but where? Why wasn't she with me, and who was this person that was so 'special'? The uncertainty made my stomach twist, and I quickly walked in front of the guard, blocking her path. "What do you mean 'safe'? Where is she?" I pressed, my voice raising higher than I had expected.

She looked at me, amusement still dancing in her eyes. "It is not your concern. Worrying about her will not change anything. You should focus on yourself for the moment."

She moved around me like I wasn't even there, her steps swift enough to slip past with ease.

"You're not answering me," I muttered under my breath as I turned to join her again. "I'm not just going to forget about her."

The guard shot me a look from the side, her voice different from the usual condescending tease I was getting used to. "Of course you shall not. But there are more important matters ahead of you, Drifted. Much more than you believe you are owed."

I gritted my teeth and kept my mouth shut. For now, I'd bide my time and follow her. Whether I liked it or not, I had no other choice. But I couldn't stop the worry that was chewing at me. I'd lost Celine once before. I wasn't planning on doing it again.

The guard cut a corner of a large wooden building, and I followed closely behind her, still stewing in my own thoughts. When I rounded the corner, something made me stop dead in my tracks.

A colossal oak tree unlike anything I'd ever seen before stood tall and proud in the distance. It had an immense trunk, anchoring it to the very ground we were walking on. It looked like a guardian for this strange land. Its bark was light and weathered, its texture twisting in intricate patterns, as if the tree itself wanted to tell a story.

Its branches were vast, sprawling outwards like arms stretching to touch the sky. They stretched so far that they encapsulated the area, casting great shadows despite the sun being hidden behind the clouds. Despite the snow and season we were in, the tree's leaves were lush and vibrant, a beautiful green that defied the winter air.

"Woah... it's... massive," I muttered to myself, unable to tear my eyes away.

The guard stopped ahead of me, glancing back with an almost smug look on her face. "Magnificent, yes?" she said, spreading her arms as if to present it. "The heart of Sylphreach. She has stood for countless centuries, untouched by time or season. Even the harshest winters cannot claim her vitality."

As I stood there, marveling at the colossal oak, something clicked in my mind. The texture of the surrounding buildings, the way the wood seemed almost alive, the way the streets curved so naturally—none of it felt man-made. It all shared the same intricate patterns, the same rich tones as the bark of the tree.

I kicked away some snow on the ground to reveal the path we were walking on. Exactly as I thought, it had the same texture as the oak before us.

"That's amazing," I said aloud, though more to myself than to the guard.

She grinned, catching the awe in my voice. "Ah, you are starting to see it, Drifted."

I turned to her, my brows furrowing. "The buildings, the streets... everything here—it's all part of that tree, isn't it?"

She clapped her hands together, clearly amused by my realization. "Indeed! You catch on faster than I expected." She turned, gesturing toward the massive oak with reverence. "The Elderwood, as we call her, provides for us. She senses our needs and forms what we require from her body. The houses, the light posts, even the very ground you stand on— it's all her gift to us."

I stared at the tree in silence, struggling to wrap my head around the enormity of what she was saying. "You're telling me this tree... grew your entire town?"

The guard chuckled, clearly enjoying my disbelief. "Not only the town, Drifted. Our homes, our tools, our way of life—she has given it all to us. The Elderwood is the lifeblood of Sylphreach, and through her, we thrive."

As I scanned the tree further, I noticed small openings and arched doorways carved directly into the bark, seamlessly blending in as if they had always been there. The entrances varied in size, some large enough to fit several people at once, while others were no bigger than a crawlspace. They were scattered across the lower trunk and climbed higher until they disappeared into the canopy.

"Do people live on it?" I asked, still trying to process the enormity of it all.

The guard followed my gaze and nodded, her grin softening into something resembling pride. "Indeed, they do. The Elderwood is not just our provider but also our protector. Many among us choose to dwell within her embrace, high in her boughs or deep within her core. It is a sanctuary unlike any other."

"Is that where we're headed?" I asked, my intrigue getting the better of me.

She clicked her tongue again, grabbing my hand and pulling me down another path. "Have you already forgotten my words, Drifted? I told you my stomach calls for sustenance first. Only after I have dined might you earn your answers."

She glanced back at me with her smile widening. "Unless, of course, you are not hungry? I can arrange for you to make yourself useful in the kitchen."

I pulled my hand away and rolled my eyes. "I can follow you myself fine. Let's just get this over with."

She let out a laugh that echoed through the snowy streets, her playful energy somehow making the odd situation I was in less strange.

Before long, I saw a large wooden building in the distance. A chimney sat on the roof, and thick smoke billowed through it. I caught the scent of something great—meat, and lots of it.

As we approached the large wooden building, the tantalizing aroma of roasted meat grew stronger, filling the crisp air. My stomach betrayed me, and grumbled loudly at the smell.

The guard looked over her shoulder, snickering at the sound of my stomach. "Ah, it seems you share my plight, Drifted. It only makes sense, with you having been out for a week."

"A week!?" I exclaimed, my jaw dropping. "You mean to tell me I haven't eaten in a week?"

She stopped for a second, counting on her fingers. "Aye, that does sound about right. Maybe longer, but you must forgive me. I was not exactly keeping count."

I stared at her, dumbfounded as my stomach growled again. "You're seriously telling me I've been unconscious for that long, and you didn't think to, I don't know, make sure I wasn't starving to death?"

She waved a hand dismissively and turned to keep walking. "You are alive, no? Now, come along before you collapse. It would be such a bother to have to carry you again."

I shook my head, muttering curses under my breath as I followed her toward the smoky building. "This place keeps getting weirder."

As we neared the large opening in front of the building, the sounds of life inside became unmistakable. Chatter echoed from within, and the clinking of mugs came through with bursts of laughter. The warmth spilling out sounded inviting, but it only heightened my feeling of unease.

As the guard got ready to step inside, she stopped abruptly, spinning on her heels to face me. She placed her hands on my chest to stop me. "Before we enter, Drifted, a bit of advice."

I raised an eyebrow. "Advice?"

She leaned in closer, lowering her voice. "Do well to excuse the stares you are bound to receive. It isn't every day that my people have the pleasure of interacting with a human."

I frowned. "You make it sound like I'm some kind of sideshow."

She let out a chuckle, clearly enjoying my discomfort. "Oh, not a sideshow. More of a... curiosity. Don't take it personally. It's just that you are an oddity here."

She straightened and motioned toward the open door. "Now, do try to look less grim. You do not want to make a poor first impression, would you?"

I let out an exasperated sigh, pinching the bridge of my nose. Exactly what I needed—a crowd. And even worse, one that wouldn't stop staring.

Just my luck, I told myself as we entered the building.

CHAPTER 6

As soon as we entered the building, I watched as if in unison, noses and furry ears twitched. My stomach felt queasy as a sea of noses sniffed the air, trying to find the source of whatever smell grazed them.

Then, the heads turned to look in my direction. Dozens—if not hundreds—of red piercing eyes were fixed on me.

I stood there frozen, unsure of what to do next. These stares felt unfortunately familiar. I was stared at like this back when I first entered that town in the Madlands with Brute. But something about these stares felt different. Instead of stares of hatred. These were more curious.

Suddenly, the guard stood in front of me, intercepting the stares.

"Aye, my brothers and sisters!" She started, cupping her hands around her mouth to amplify her already loud voice further. "It is true, as I am sure you all have smelled. Standing before you is indeed a human. He is important, and he is our guest. You would do well to treat him kindly."

Nervous, I held up a hand as if that would ease the tension in the room. "Hi…"

The guard turned to me. "Well, Drifted. I cannot exactly say that is the greatest introduction I have ever heard." She let out with a snicker.

My face grew hot. "How else am I supposed to introduce myself to a large group like this?"

I heard a giggle come from somewhere in the sea of red eyes, then another followed, and another.

"This human boy is hilarious!" I heard someone shout.

Then, without warning, the entire building joined in on the laughing.

I stood there dumbfounded, my face growing even warmer. What did I say that was so funny to them?

"I believe you did just perfect," The guard replied to me with a thumbs up, though I could tell it wasn't sincere. "Now, would you please make haste? I feel as if I could eat a boar."

She grabbed my hand and dragged me across the room as it filled with more laughter.

"What did I even say?" I muttered to myself as the guard led us to a square table in the far corner of the room.

I took a seat, and the guard followed, sitting down in the wooden chair with enough force to shake the table.

"Caldryn," she yelled, waving her hand in the air. "I require your services!"

I heard some shuffling from behind a door not too far from us, and then shortly after a man walked out, adorned in a white chef's hat and a stained apron.

He was a larger man, with a belly that the apron couldn't completely cover. He had a shortly trimmed, brown—but greying—beard that he scratched with a single clawed finger. And as he approached our table, I noticed he walked with a slight limp

"Ah, I see you have decided to bless us with your presence again. Is that so, Sabrina?"

Sabrina. That must be her name. Finally, I got some kind of information, even if it didn't come from her herself.

"My dearest Caldryn. May we skip the formalities this time around, I am quite hungry." Sabrina replied with a wide, toothy smile.

The chef pulled out a slip of paper, and something that resembled a long, carved black stone and began etching with it on the page.

"And what would you have today?" He asked Sabrina.

"I shall have my usual order," she answered. "And the boy here shall have the same," she finished, pointing at me.

The chef finished etching on his paper and quickly disappeared back behind the door he came in from.

"So, your name is Sabrina?" I asked with a smirk. Happy that I was able to get a crumb of information about this place.

"Ah, yes. Did I forget to mention that before?" She answered back, raising one leg on the chair she sat in so that only one was now planted on the ground. "It must have slipped my mind."

"Yeah, I'm sure it did," I replied. "You probably would've kept it hidden as long as possible if that chef hadn't ruined it. What's with all the secrets?"

Sabrina yawned and patted her stomach. "In due time, Drifted. Have you not ever heard the phrase 'curiosity killed the rat?'"

I let out a stream of air from my nose. "It's cat."

Sabrina raised an eyebrow. "Pardon?"

"The phrase, it's cat, not rat." I replied.

"Like the feline?" Sabrina asked.

"Yes, like the feline." I answered again, with a slight chuckle this time.

"Though rats are also curious creatures, are they not?"

"I'm not refuting that, I'm just telling you what the correct saying is." I tapped on the table. Why were we arguing about this?

"Ah, yes. I do suppose that makes more sense. Though I believe I prefer rat, nonetheless."

I let out a sigh. Nothing was easy with this girl. "As you wish." I replied, resting my head in my hand.

The door the chef disappeared behind swung open again,

and out came the same man. Only this time, he was carrying two large plates piled high with what appeared to be various meats, and two large wooden mugs.

He sat the plates down on the table, and I could've sworn I felt the room shake a little.

"Enjoy," he said, dropping our mugs in front of us and hurriedly disappearing back behind the door.

In front of me, blocking out my view of Sabrina, was a large medley of grilled meats and seafood. Beef, chicken, fish, and other meats I couldn't even begin to identify.

The smell was amazing, and my stomach grumbled loudly in anticipation.

From the other side of the meat mountain, I heard Sabrina slurp up a bit of her drool. "Oh, Drifted. Is it not marvelous!" she shrieked, clapping her hands together.

"Yeah. It looks amazing... But I don't see a single vegetable on here." I replied.

Sabrina poked her head from the other side of her plate. "Ah yes.... I forgot you humans require other... Nutrition," she replied, her face struggling to hide her disappointment.

"Caldryn!" Sabrina yelled again.

The chef returned hurriedly. "Aye, Sabrina. What have I forgotten this time?" he asked.

Sabrina cleared her throat. "My dearest, Caldryn, do you happen to have any vegetables—" She paused, shuttering at the word. "For our guest here?"

Caldryn scratched his beard and looked up at the ceiling. "No, unfortunately we are fresh out!" he replied, turning and disappearing back behind the door. I know he said unfortunately, but for some reason, he sounded enthusiastic about it.

Sabrina shrugged, "Sorry, Drifted. Though, I did try. You shall have to go without your vegetables for the time being."

Without waiting for another word, she picked up a large cut of steak with her bare hands and took a large bite out of it.

"Praise the moon!" she squealed in delight. "This must be the closest thing to heaven," she added, taking another large bite of the meat.

I watched in awe and disgust as she ate. One bite of meat here, another bite of fish there, all in quick succession. She barely took any breaths in between her bites, and I started fearing she would accidentally choke to death.

Though whenever she bit off more than she could swallow, she took a large swig of whatever she was drinking from her mug.

"What is that?" I asked her, trying desperately to conceal the unease on my face.

"This," she started, raising the mug into the sky as if it were some trophy. "This is possibly one of the greatest things we adopted from your kind, Drifted. Behold, the drink known as pine!"

"Pine?" I questioned. Never hearing of that drink myself. I lifted her mug and brought it to my nose, taking in a deep whiff.

Immediately, my nose was filled with the potent scent of fermented grapes. "Do you mean wine?" I asked her, wrinkling my nose.

"What was it that I said?" Sabrina asked.

"You said pine. It's wine." I replied.

Sabrina rolled her eyes. "If I wanted a lesson on language, I would have visited our school, Drifted." She said, sticking her nose in the air.

"I was trying to help," I replied.

"Regardless, this is... What was it you called this beverage again?"

"Wine."

"Aye, yes. Wine. This is wine, A most curious concoction! Bitter, yet sweet. A liquid that dances on the tongue and warms the soul. Truly, you humans have a knack for indulgence." She took another sip, savoring it as though it were some treasure. "A wonder you don't drink this all day, Drifted."

She set her mug down, licking the purple stain from around her lips. "Anyway, Drifted. You haven't touched your meal. Are you not hungry?"

I looked down at the steaming platter. In my awe, I completely forgot to eat. The food smelled delicious, but Sabrina's eating habits left me nauseous.

Still, my stomach grumbled, as if telling me to suck it up. If Sabrina was telling the truth, being out cold with no food for a week was most likely wreaking havoc on my insides.

I looked around the table for utensils and didn't notice any. I then looked toward Sabrina's side of the table and noticed she didn't have any either.

"Hey, Sabrina. I think Caldryn forgot to give us utensils." I said to her.

Her ears perked up, and she looked at me with a bit of sausage still hanging out of her mouth. "Utensils?" she questioned.

"Yeah, you know. Like a fork and knife." I replied.

Sabrina stared at me as if I were speaking a foreign language. "Caldryn!" she screamed again.

Again, Caldryn came out from the wooden door, but this time, the door swung a bit harder. Hitting the wall behind it.

"Yes... Sabrina," Caldryn replied, shuffling over. As he stood there, I noticed he was now tapping his foot.

"Do we happen to have any... any—" Sabrina struggled.

"Utensils." I cut in.

"Aye, do we happen to have any of those items?" She asked Caldryn.

Caldryn again scratched his chin. Thinking. "The small spiked items humans hold in their hands during food consumption?" He questioned, looking at me.

"Umm, yeah, sure. I think you're describing the right thing," I answered back.

"No. We do not." Caldryn replied with a straight face. Before waiting for my reply, he turned on his heels and again left behind the wooden door.

I glanced down at my still untouched plate. The aroma was certainly enticing, but the thought of digging into the greasy meat barehanded didn't sit right with me. As I debated whether to suck it up and dig in, something unexpected happened.

Out of nowhere, Sabrina leaned forward with a giggle as her hand darted toward my plate. Before I could react, she plucked a piece of meat from it and pushed it toward my lips.

"Open wide, Drifted," she teased, her eyes sparkling. "We can't have you wasting such fine sustenance now, can we?"

I didn't have time to react to what was happening before the food was in my mouth, leaving me blinking in stunned silence.

I chewed the piece of meat, and to my surprise, it was incredible. The flavors were perfectly balanced—spiced enough to add a kick, yet not so overwhelming that it overpowered the natural richness of the meat.

It was tender, practically melting as I chewed it. For a moment, I forgot where I was as I savored the taste, letting it roll across my tongue. It was the kind of bite that you never wanted to end.

"Well?" Sabrina asked, leaning in closer with a wide smile. "Do I get thanks for rescuing your once blind taste buds?"

I nodded my head, picking up a piece of shrimp with my hands. "This is delicious!" I replied to Sabrina.

I could see why she ate the way she did now. The food practically called for it. And I had the thought that eating it bare-handed actually made it taste better, somehow connecting me with the meal itself.

Sabrina beamed at my response and continued eating with enthusiasm, tearing into her food with an energy that was now oddly contagious. I followed suit, grabbing another piece of perfectly seasoned meat with my hands. Each bite sent a pack of flavors to my tongue, and I couldn't help myself from scarfing down.

The minutes flowed as the two of us ate. Sabrina would occasionally comment on the food, making jokes as she nudged me to continue eating every time I stopped.

"You've barely touched that piece! Do not make me have to feed you again," she teased, tossing a piece of bread into her mouth.

"Very funny," I replied, patting my bursting stomach. "I can feed myself, thanks."

As the meal progressed, I glanced nervously at the wooden mug in front of me. My stomach churned as I thought about the wine Sabrina mentioned earlier. Memories of the spinning room and pounding headache I got from the last time I drank made me scared to indulge in alcohol again. Still, my throat was coated in oil from the meats, and I knew I couldn't avoid it forever. I slowly lifted the mug to my lips, bracing myself for the bitter taste I remembered.

To my relief, it was just water—cool and refreshing. I took another sip, feeling the liquid wash away the salty oil from my throat.

Sarina caught my reaction and tilted her mug towards me. "Ah, worried about my precious wine, were you? You need not have fear. I would not let you disgrace my beloved beverage with your human inability to appreciate it."

"Thanks for the vote of confidence," I replied, rolling my eyes.

The two of us continued to devour our meal, the low chatter of the people around us and the meal dulling whatever unease about this place I had. For a moment, everything else melted away, and only the sound of Sabrina's laughter and the tapping of dishes remained. It was an ease I hadn't felt in a long time.

As I got through a decent portion of my food, I leaned back in my chair, stuffed to the point of bursting. I watched in disbelief as Sabrina finished the last scraps on her plate, licking it clean. She looked unfazed by the gross amount of food she'd just consumed. A nail turned into a claw, and she used it as a toothpick, picking at her teeth as she sucked them.

"How can you even eat that much?" I asked, half in awe, half in horror.

Sabrina gave a wide smile, showing off her teeth, not free of any remnants of food. "Simple. I am not a delicate human like you. Besides, wasting meat would be a crime against the moon."

She leaned back. "Did you enjoy it?"

"Yeah, it was great," I admitted. "But now that you've had your fill, I think it's time you've held up your end of the deal." I leaned forward, resting my arm on the table. "I have some questions that need answering."

Sabrina sat back in her chair and groaned loudly, tossing her head back as if the mere thought of answering my questions was exhausting. "Ah, you humans, always so curious, so demanding." She waved a hand before locking her sharp red eyes on mine. "Fine, Drifted. You may ask your questions, and I shall grant you answers—but only if it is within my power to do so."

I narrowed my eyes at her, refusing to be thrown off by her tone. "If it is within your power?" I questioned.

Sabrina wagged a finger in my face. "Ask your questions, Drifted."

I stared into her eyes. "Alright, first question. Why do you keep referring to me as 'human' like you and everyone else here isn't one? You all look human enough to me, despite the more glaring differences."

Sabrina's grin returned. "Ah, but appearances can be deceiving, Drifted." She lifted her hands and tugged at her furry ears. "You assume we are the same because we share some traits, but in truth, my kind and yours are worlds apart."

"Worlds apart?" I raised my eyebrows. "You mean there's more than the furry ears and the whole turning into wolves thing?"

She laughed softly. "Ah, you simplify it so. Those are but surface-level differences. The distinction runs much deeper than that." Sabrina let out a shallow sigh before continuing. "We—my people—are known as Lupine. A race born not only of the world, but from the moon's very light. Our essence, our existence, is tied to forces far beyond the reach of human comprehension."

I blinked, trying to process her words. "So, you're saying your kind are... what? Spirits? Some kind of Celestial beings?"

Sabrina shook her head. "We are Lupine, Drifted. That is all you need to know for now." She leaned back in her chair, clearly pleased with herself.

I exhaled sharply through my nose, confused and frustrated by her half answer. "Lupine? So that's it? That hardly explains anything."

She waved another hand. "Patience, Drifted. There are things I am barred from answering. Ask your next question.

We must depart soon."

"Fine, then answer this—where are we, actually? And how is this place different from that stone town I met you at before... in the Madlands?"

Sabrina's expression shifted instantly. Her smirked vanished, and she I could tell she was confused. "Madlands? What do you—." She pinched the bridge of her nose with her fingers.

She straightened her posture and tilted her head slightly, narrowing her red eyes at me. "Is that how you humans refer to this area? The Madlands?" she repeated. "You dare call this the Madlands?"

I stammered slightly, caught off guard by her sudden change in demeanor. "Uh... well, I don't think anyone else knows about the Madlands besides a few people, me included. But that's what Aldhard called it."

She groaned, dragging a hand down her face as if I had just said the most absurd thing in the world. "How utterly preposterous," she muttered. "Madlands, indeed. Leave it to humans to name things in the most ungracious of manners." She shook her head, clearly vexed. "Drifted, this is Velora. The land you so insultingly refer to as the Madlands is our home, a realm far vaster than your Moonveil could ever hope to be."

"Velora," I repeated. "Okay, got it, sorry."

"Yes, Velora," Sabrina replied with a slight huff, moving a strand of her jet-black hair from her face. "It is a sacred land, consisting of three major towns and smaller outposts scattered throughout. The three are Sylphreach, Thornwallow, and Lostsummit. You have now had the dubious honor of seeing two of the three. Obviously, we are in Sylphreach now, but when we first crossed paths, we were in Lostsummit."

"I see, so what makes Sylphreach different from

Lostsummit, I mean... besides the obvious structural differences?"

Her smirk returned, though it was wider now. "The difference is that Sylphreach is the heart of Velora, it is where the Elderwood's blessings flows the strongest."

I leaned back in my chair, trying to process all the words. Sylphreach, Velora, Lostsummit. This entire area was larger than I could've imagined. Larger than anyone in Moonveil could've ever imagined. "And the other town? What is it like?"

Sabrina paused, as if taking a second to decide how much she would reveal. But before a word could escape, two small figures darted up to the table. They were children, a boy and a girl, their fur-tipped ears twitching with curiosity as they peered up at me with wide eyes.

"Hello mister!" The boy spoke up, bouncing on his toes.

Caught off guard, I scooted back in my seat before speaking. "Well hello there, little ones."

For a second, I couldn't help but think of how much they reminded me of the twins. My heart panged a bit when I thought of what they would be doing right now. Probably annoying Aunt Silvia, along with Uncle Alfarr, no doubt.

"Why are your eyes not red, mister?" The girl asked, poking at my arm.

"And where are your ears?" the boy chimed in, jumping up and down to get a better look at the top of my head.

I didn't know how to reply. I looked at Sabrina for help, but she just leaned back in her chair, clearly entertained by my discomfort. "Ah, Drifted," she said, her tone dripping with amusement. "It seems you have drawn quite the audience. They are as curious as you are."

The first child leaned closer, their nose twitching as if trying to catch a scent. "He smells weird too!" they exclaimed, scrunching up their faces.

"Hey!" I protested, crossing my arms, unsure of how to handle the sudden attention.

Sabrina chuckled. "Children, children," she said with mock seriousness, wagging a finger at them. "Mind your manners. Our guest here is human. They do not have ears like ours, nor do their eyes glow red."

The second child's eyes widened in wonder. "Human?" they repeated, the word sounding strange and foreign on their tongues. "Is that why he is so... strange?"

I sighed, pinching the bridge of my nose. "I'm sitting right here, you know?"

Sabrina let out a hearty laugh and waved her hand. "Oh, come now, Drifted. They are just curious. It is not every day they meet someone as peculiar as you."

Before I could respond, two adults approached the table, their footsteps light.

The first was a tall man, his dark brown fur-lined cloak draped over his shoulders and his wolfish ears twitching in mild embarrassment. His red eyes softened as they landed on me, and he offered a polite bow.

The woman beside him was shorter, but carried an air of authority. Her brown hair was tied neatly behind her, and her ears were barely visible under the hood of her lighter cloak.

Both had a similar tenseness to them, but their expressions were warm, apologetic even.

"I must apologize for our children," the man said, his voice deep but gentle. "They are curious—sometimes embarrassingly so."

The woman offered a small smile. "They mean no harm," she added, placing a hand on the shoulder of the boy, who squirmed under her touch. "This is the first time they have met someone who is not like us."

The boy pointed up at me, his eyes glowing. "But Mama, look, his ears are strange!"

"Enough, Silas," the woman said firmly, though her tone held no anger. She turned back to me, bowing slightly. "We hope they did not cause you too much trouble, Drifted."

I shook my head, still shocked by the sudden appearance of the family. "No trouble at all," I replied.

Her calling me 'Drifted' struck me. It wasn't only Sabrina and Celine—adults also knew that name. I wasn't sure whether to feel uneasy or honored by it.

The family offered one last polite nod before turning and walking away. The children still snuck glances at me as they were gently ushered along. I watched them disappear outside, back into the snowy streets, their voices fading away.

I turned to Sabrina. "Alright, I've let this slide long enough. Why do you, Celine, and now apparently everyone else call me that?"

"Call you what?" Sabrina asked, tilting her head.

"Drifted, what does it mean?" I asked.

Sabrina's grin returned, mischievous and infuriatingly unbothered. "Ah, so you have finally decided to ask, have you? I was beginning to think you would simply accept it as a term of endearment."

"I'm serious, Sabrina," I pressed, crossing my arms. "What does it mean?"

She tapped a finger against her lips, clearly enjoying my frustration. "It is not only a name. It is who you are—or, more accurately, what you are."

"Again with the riddles! Do you care to elaborate?"

Sabrina stood up from the table, patting off her clothes. "No time. We must leave now."

I rolled my eyes. Yet another thing to add to my ever-growing list of mysteries. "Where to?" I questioned.

She flashed a grin, her red eyes gleaming with mischief. "Why, Drifted, we are off to meet someone very important," she said. "Someone who holds answers even I cannot provide."

I raised an eyebrow at her, already dreading the cryptic journey ahead. "And who exactly is this very important someone?"

She wagged a finger in my direction, her smirk growing wider. "Ah, ah, patience, Drifted. You shall find out soon enough. Let us just say they have been awaiting your arrival with great anticipation."

I sighed, rubbing the back of my neck. "That's not exactly reassuring, Sabrina."

"Reassurance is overvalued," she quipped, spinning on her heels and heading toward the door. "Now, do keep up. It would be unwise to keep them waiting long."

Her tone shifted slightly on that last word, making my unease grow. Nevertheless, I followed her, knowing I had little choice but to see where this path would lead.

CHAPTER 7

As we stepped out of the mess hall, the sun was beginning its slow drop toward the horizon. The light hit the streets with an orange glow, making the snow sparkle like scattered crystals. The air was chilly with a faint hum of life as Sylphreach began to wind down for the evening.

The information that Sabrina dumped on me still swirled in my mind as we began walking the streets again.

I was in a land known as Velora, surrounded by people— or I guess beings—that called themselves Lupine. They had their own world with rules and structure that I couldn't begin to understand. They mingled casually like we did, held professions, and had families. But everything about them seemed so distant, so supernatural—their sharp red eyes that glinted even in the dimmest light, the natural grace of their movements, and, of course, their power to shape-shift into wolves.

I stole a glance at Sabrina as she walked beside me. Watching as her eyes caught every flicker of the setting sun. Celine first called me Drifted those months ago, now Sabrina and the other Lupine did as well. The name that started growing commonplace to me felt even more significant for some reason. But no one cared to explain it. Or maybe they had. Only not in a way that made sense to me.

Sabrina had a bounce to her step, smiling, light and carefree, as if she had all the time in the world. "Where are we headed now?" I asked, my voice breaking through the silence.

She turned to me, placing her arm over my shoulder. "To

introduce you to our special person, of course." I knew she could tell how much she was annoying me, she just didn't care.

I frowned. "Why can't you ever be forward? You know that's not what I'm asking."

"This walk would go by a lot quicker if you would be patient" she said with a wink, pointing ahead.

My eyes followed her hand to the silhouette of the massive Elderwood dominating the horizon, its branches stretching high into the darkening sky.

The closer we got, the smaller I felt, and the sight made me stop in my tracks. Whomever lived there would have to be someone of great importance. So why would they want to meet with me?

"Who is this person we're meeting?" I asked, my hands growing clammy from anticipation.

"He is the kind of person you do not want to keep waiting," Sabrina replied with a grin.

While her look was playful, I could tell that she was being serious. Whoever this man was, he wanted to meet me—Isaac, a boring kid from Lunaria. I had no idea what to expect, or what I'd even say to this guy.

Hopefully, he would give me more answers than Sabrina would.

The path sloped upward once we got to the base of the tree. The snow thinned underfoot until the ground turned to smooth, worn wooden steps. I hadn't noticed before, but this part of Sylphreach felt different—heavier, older. The air was warmer here as well, despite the cold.

As I looked into the canopy, I noticed structures scattered throughout. Wooden houses lined the towering branches of the Elderwood. At first, they looked like random shapes that blended seamlessly with the massive tree's bark and foliage.

But the further we climbed, the clearer they became.

Dozens—no, hundreds of homes were perched along branches like bird nests, connected by thick walkways and bridges that swayed gently in the breeze. Lanterns glowed softly along the rope bridges, shining through the dark of the setting sun.

"How many people live here?" I asked Sabrina.

"Oh, I am not too certain, far too many to count," Sabrina pointed to a house high in the canopy.

I looked straight up, covering my eyes with my hands. Though it was high up, I could see that the house was covered loosely in bright red flowers.

"Yeah, it's a nice place. Why are you showing it to me?" I asked, eyebrow raised.

"That is where I reside!" Sabrina replied, bouncing up and down.

I smirked a bit. "Looks... quaint,".

I was surprised her home would be anything but a madhouse.

"Perhaps someday I shall even let you visit," she said with a wink.

I rolled my eyes. "I think I'll pass on that"

Sabrina gave a mock pout before turning back to the path. "Suit yourself. But do not blame me if you miss out on the best view in Velora!"

She bounded up the steps ahead of me, leaving me staring after her, half annoyed and half wondering if she'd ever stop teasing me.

It was amazing to think that this tree had created this entire town, a living, breathing town. The branches, more than thick enough to walk across, carried Lupine figures that moved effortlessly along the bridges. Some glanced down at us, their eyes reflecting the light before they turned back to whatever tasks they were doing.

It was impossible not to be impressed—or feel out of place.

"Come now, Drifted, we have a meeting to attend!" Sabrina called over her shoulder.

She was already several steps ahead of me, her cloak swaying behind her as she ascended the stairs to the large opening in the Elderwood.

I shook my head and followed, my feet falling into rhythm behind hers. I knew that whatever awaited me at the top would be like nothing I'd ever experienced before.

The climb felt endless with the weight of anticipation pressing down on me with each step. The opening was clearer now, and I could make out carved patterns around its edges that glowed with a soft light.

When I finally reached the top, I stopped to catch my breath, my eyes immediately drawn to Sabrina. She was waiting in front of the massive opening, one hand on her hip, her signature wide smile plastered across her face.

"You took your time," she said. "I trust the climb was not too taxing on you?"

I straightened, trying to cover the unease bubbling in my stomach. "I've had worse," I said, though my voice lacked the same composure as hers.

My eyes shifted past her, drawn to the figures stationed on either side of the entrance.

Eight guards stood at the ready, four on each side, their presence impossible to ignore. They were tall, covered in cloaks of dark leather accented with woven patterns of bark and leaves. Their hoods made deep shadows over their faces, but their vibrant eyes pierced the low light as they watched me with unsettling intensity.

Each had bone daggers resting on their hips, but they

looked clean and hardly used.

I swallowed hard, my hands clenched at my sides. They weren't merely standing—they were perfectly still, like statues.

"Do not let them unsettle you," Sabrina said.

She gestured toward the guards with a faint wave of her hand. "Their purpose is to protect, not intimidate. This close to the Elderwood is sacred ground, and no one enters lightly."

"Right," I muttered, though their watchful eyes made it clear that I was being judged—whether I liked it or not.

"You have no reason to fear them," she continued, her tone remaining even. "They see what you may not yet understand. And soon, you will."

As Sabrina began walking again, I stuck close behind her, scared of being left behind with the guards.

Their silence sent shivers down my spine, though I couldn't tell if it was from fear or respect.

Just as we stepped in between the guards, to my surprise, they all simultaneously bowed.

In perfect unison, each of them lowered their heads in a deep motion. The movement was smooth, almost ceremonial, and it left me frozen in place.

"May the moon guide you, Drifted," they said together, their voices resonating in perfect harmony that filled the air.

I blinked, unsure how to respond, my eyes darting to Sabrina for guidance.

She glanced back at me, covering her mouth, trying to stifle a laugh.

"Oh, do try not to look so bewildered. They honor you, Drifted," she said. "They may believe their gestures were wasted if you do not respond."

"I—uh, should I say something back?" I stammered.

Sabrina's lips curved into a faint smile as she clasped her hands behind her back, clearly savoring the moment. "A simple nod will suffice, I think. Or," she added, tilting her head thoughtfully, "you could bow in return. Though I would suggest you try not to fall over while doing so."

I nodded stiffly, feeling my palms grow sweaty. "Uh... thanks," I muttered awkwardly. Though my words felt inadequate compared to theirs.

The guards didn't react. They didn't seem to mind my awkwardness, or perhaps they were too disciplined to show it.

They all simply straightened themselves back into position.

Sabrina chuckled softly and started walking again, her cloak trailing behind her. "Well done, Drifted. You have successfully survived your first formal greeting. Shall we continue, or would you like another chance to dazzle them?"

I sighed, falling into step behind her. "I think we should just get this meeting over with."

"Wise choice." She replied. "You shall have enough chances to practice as the days come."

I gulped. "What do you mean 'enough chances'? I have to do more of these?!"

Sabrina didn't respond. Instead, she started humming as if she didn't hear me.

"Sabrina?" I questioned her again.

Her humming grew louder.

"Sabrina!" I yelled in a hushed whisper, not wanting to embarrass myself in front of the guards.

"Ah, look, Drifted, we have arrived."

My stomach dropped, my irritation fading as I realized I'd been so focused on her that I failed to notice we were inside the Elderwood.

The sight stopped me in my tracks. We entered an enormous cavity, far larger than anything I could've imagined. The entire space felt alive, its massive walls curving upward like the ribs of some ginormous beast. The ceiling stretched so high above us that it disappeared into darkness, with only the occasional glint of light reflecting off distant surfaces giving way.

Around us, platforms and staircases spiraled up the walls, their design so seamless that it was impossible to tell where the tree ended and the structures began. Bridges of woven branches arched gracefully across the vast space, connecting levels and walkways in intricate patterns. Each detail felt organic, as if the Elderwood had grown itself into a palace of unimaginable scale.

The air was warm and carried a faint sweet scent that reminded me of blooming flowers after a spring rain. Soft murmurs echoed throughout the chamber as Lupine bodies moved along various platforms.

"Woah... it's amazing," I caught myself saying out loud, my voice trailing off as my eyes followed the paths above. I caught glimpses of grand doors set into the wood, their frames carved with intricate patterns of moons and wolves.

Who in the world could possibly be in a place like this that would want to meet with me?

"Are you sure I'm supposed to be in here?" I whispered.

Sabrina turned to me, her red eyes glinting softly in the golden light. "It is not for you to question, Drifted," she said, her voice calm and deliberate. "You are here because you must be." She tilted her head towards another opening to our right. "Now, come. We have kept him waiting long enough."

I hesitated for a moment longer, my eyes lingering on the Lupine moving above.

Then with a deep breath, I followed Sabrina, my footsteps feeling even smaller and insignificant against the grandeur of the room. Each step felt heavier as we approached an opening with a small amount of light spilling out.

The moment we stepped through, I stopped short again, and my breath caught in my throat. The space we entered was no less grand that the one we'd left, but its atmosphere was different—heavier. Pillars of twisted bark lined the walls, their surfaces also etched with flowing designs that were foreign to me.

At the far end of the room, elevated on a dais, sat a man in a massive chair carved from the same living wood as the rest of this place. I could tell that this was no ordinary chair—it was a throne, its back towering high and adorned with twisting branches that framed the figure like a crown.

Beside him was another throne, even larger and more decorated than the one he sat on. But this one was empty.

He sat slouched, one leg spread out lazily in front of him while the other rested, bent at a sharp angle. His head rested on one hand, and his fingers tapped rhythmically against the armrest as though he were lost in thought. Given the distance, I couldn't make out his features clearly, but I could tell he had a commanding demeanor.

"Who... who is that?" I whispered, leaning slightly toward Sabrina as we walked. My voice was low, but in the silence of the room, it felt like a shout.

"Hush, Drifted," Sabrina replied without looking back.

I clamped my mouth shut, swallowing the questions that threatened to spill out. Her reaction made it clear whoever we were about to meet was not someone to take lightly.

My legs trembled slightly as I moved forward, each step bringing us closer to the throne and the man waiting at its center.

Finally, Sabrina came to a stop a respectful distance from the dais. She stood tall, her usual playful demeanor subdued, as she dipped her head slightly in acknowledgment. I froze beside her, unsure whether to follow suit. The man on the throne didn't move, but his gaze shifted, settling on me.

"Drifted," Sabrina started with a slight bow. "I present to you His Grace, Prince Consort, Rowen Pellehan."

The name carried a weight that made my chest tighten, though I couldn't explain why. My gaze flicked to Sabrina, searching for some clue in her expression, but her focus remained locked on the man before us. For once, she was devoid of teasing remarks or playful glances.

"You stand before the one who speaks for all the Lupine in Sylphreach. The one who has awaited your arrival."

My arrival? I thought to myself. The very notion sent a jolt through me, but I forced myself to swallow the anxiety rising in my throat. Instead, I focused on the man—Rowen— unsure of what to say, unsure of what he expected from me.

I felt a nudge at my side and looked down to see Sabrina jabbing her elbow into me.

She cleared her throat lightly. "This is one of those moments, Drifted, where it would do you well to practice the art of introductions," she said, her voice just teasing enough to make me grit my teeth.

"Oh, uh, yes. Right," I stammered, shifting uncomfortably under Rowen's watchful eyes. "May the moon, uh... watch you?"

The words hung awkwardly, and I watched as Sabrina's mouth twitched at the corners and she covered it with her hand, holding back a laugh.

Rowen raised an eyebrow, his head tilting as he regarded me with a look that felt equal parts amused and unimpressed.

Sabrina couldn't hold back anymore. "Ah, no, Drifted," she said, still trying to stifle her laugh. "It is may the moon *guide* you. A simple greeting, truly." She looked at Rowen, dipping her head slightly. "You must forgive him, Your Highness. He is… unfamiliar with our ways."

My face felt red hot as I tried to weigh my next words. "I apologize, I'm still, uh… learning," I muttered."

Rowen finally spoke, his voice calm and deep. "Clearly," he said, though I could tell there was no malice in his tone, only a faint trace of humor. "Your name is Isaac, correct?"

I paused. How could someone of such high stature know my name? Not only that, but he used my real name.

"Yes, sir, I mean... Your Highness. That is correct." I replied.

Rowen's lips curved slightly, not quite a smile, but enough to make his expression seem less severe. "It has been a long time since I've seen another human," Rowen said. "It is... nice to meet you."

My eyes grew wide. Another human? I stared at him, the weight of the room momentarily forgotten.

In my distraction, I realized I hadn't fully taken him in before. Now, with him so close, the details stood out to me. He was not like the Lupine at all. His hair was deep brown, streaked with gray, that curled slightly at the edges. His beard, long and unkempt, matched the graying of his hair, giving him a weathered appearance.

But it was his eyes that stood out to me the most. Hazel. Warm and human. They lacked the bright glow of red that marked the Lupine, and had a softness to them, a reflection of something deeply familiar.

"You're... human?" The words escaped me before I could stop them.

Sabrina let out a snicker. "Did I forget to mention that before?"

Rowen chuckled softly. "Yes, Isaac. I am as human as you are. Have I begun taking on the appearance of the Lupine after all these years?"

I opened my mouth to speak but couldn't find a response.

What was a human doing in a place like this? Among the Lupine, no less—and not just living with them, but leading them?

Sabrina nudged my side again. "Perhaps you should close your mouth, Drifted. Lest you collect flies."

I snapped my jaw shut, glancing sideways at her. She tilted her head as if daring me to protest, but I swallowed my frustration. This wasn't the time to rise to her ridicule.

Rowen let out another chuckle, playing with his beard. "I see you've met Sabrina," he said, his tone carrying some sympathy. "You'll get used to her, or perhaps not. Few truly do."

Sabrina gasped dramatically, pressing her hand to her chest as if she had been deeply insulted. "Now, my lord, you hurt me so! Surely, I am not *that* difficult to endure."

Rowen's lips twitched, but he said nothing, the faint smile on his face speaking volumes.

"I don't understand..." I murmured under my breath. The weight of everything began to press down on me, and my words came tumbling out. "I don't understand what's going on. Why are you here? Why am I here?" I looked to Rowen now, my voice rising.

Rowen's eyes softened, and he sat forward, resting his elbows on the armrests of his throne. "Isaac," he began gently. "I know you have questions—more than I can answer in a single moment. This place, the Lupine, me..." He trailed off, studying me closely. "All of it must feel overwhelming. And it is."

I didn't respond, gritting my teeth as uncertainty bubbled in my chest.

He leaned back slightly. "I ask for your patience. We will address everything in time, but first..." He began playing with his beard again. "Let me ask you something. How is

Moonveil?"

I blinked, startled by the question. "Moonveil?" I echoed.

Why was he asking about Moonveil at a moment like this?

Rowen nodded his head. "Aye, boy. It's been so long since I've got to set eyes on my homeland."

"It's... fine, I suppose." My answer felt hollow, and I quickly added more. "Well, it's been dangerous lately. The fiends are worse than they've ever been. The woods aren't safe anymore—not even close to town. Everyone's scared."

Rowen's expression shifted subtly—his brow furrowing ever so slightly, his gaze turning inward, as if weighing the significance of my words. "I see," he murmured. His tone carried a depth that made my stomach twist, though I couldn't quite place why.

I took a breath before continuing, unsure if I wanted to keep going, but the words came anyway. "Noctiluna was brought to ruins the last time I was there; a large number of fiends stormed the town. It was... horrible"

Rowen sat up on his throne, his gaze growing more tense. "How long ago was this?" he asked.

"Not long," I replied, thinking back to the chaos that engulfed the town. "A few months, maybe. The fiends moved so fast, they came out of nowhere. People—the Kingsguard tried to fight back, but—" I stopped, the memory of the overturned streets and destroyed buildings flashing in my mind. "It wasn't enough."

Rowen exhaled slowly, his hand still stroking his beard, his eyes darkening as he processed my words. "Noctiluna was my hometown," he breathed. "I grew up among its streets, its people. To hear of its suffering..." He trailed off, shaking his head. "I can do nothing now but ask the moon to protect the rest of its people."

I felt pangs of guilt in my stomach. "I'm... I'm sorry," I

said, my voice barely above a whisper. "I didn't mean to; I didn't know."

Rowen raised a hand to stop me. "You have nothing to apologize for, Isaac," he mumbled. "The burden of Noctiluna's fate does not rest on your shoulders."

Even so, the guilt lingered. I looked down, fidgeting with my hands, before a memory came to me. "Wait," I said, glancing up at him. "The Kingsguard—before I left someone told me the town was going to receive reinforcements."

Rowen raised an eyebrow, his expression shifting to one of quiet interest. "Reinforcements?"

"Yeah," I said, nodding quickly. "I don't know if they ever came. I couldn't stay to find out. But if they did…" I hesitated, the hopefulness in my own voice surprising me. "All hope might not be lost."

Rowen's lips pressed into a thin line as he considered my words. "The Kingsguard," he murmured, as if testing the name. "They have long been the backbone of Moonveil's defenses. If reinforcements came, then I'm sure Noctiluna was spared further devastation."

"It's possible," I said, though I couldn't shake the uncertainty gnawing at me. "I… I don't know."

Rowen nodded slowly, his gaze distant again. "Hope is a fragile thing, Isaac," he said after a pause. "But it is not easily extinguished. Your words carry more optimism than you realize."

Sabrina, who had been uncharacteristically quiet, tilted her head. "The Kingsguard," she said thoughtfully. "A curious force, always so bold in their actions. But even boldness has its limits when facing fiends."

I frowned. Her words only deepened the knot in my chest. "What do you mean?"

Sabrina smiled faintly, though her tone remained

measured. "Only that the fiends are unlike any force in this world. They are not bound by courage or strategy. They are bound by something much deeper."

I wanted to question her further, but Rowen raised a hand, silencing any further remarks. "Enough, Sabrina," he said firmly, his hazel eyes locking onto mine. "For now, we focus on what lies ahead. Isaac, you being brought here is no coincidence."

His eyes shifted to another opening on the far side of the room. "Though, before we continue, there is someone else who needs to be a part of this conversation."

He gestured toward the opening, his fingers waving someone in. "Celine," he called, his voice echoing through the vast room.

My breath hitched at the name.

For a moment, there was nothing but silence, the faint hum of the Elderwood filling the quietness. Then, soft footsteps echoed from the distant hallway.

My heart thudded in my chest as a figure emerged, the soft light in the room outlining her slender frame before she stepped fully into view. The dark blue cloak I loaned her was draped over her shoulders, the hood pulled back, allowing her hair to fall loosely. Her bright violet eyes illuminated the room, shining with an intensity that made it impossible to look away.

She glanced at me briefly before directing her gaze back to Rowen.

I wanted to speak, to call out to her, but it felt inappropriate in the current situation.

Celine came to a stop a few paces from Rowen's throne, dipping her head slightly in acknowledgment. "You called, Father?" she said, her tone carrying the same calmness as always.

Celine's gaze returned to me, her expression relatively plain, but the faintest trace of a smile played at her lips.

CHAPTER 8

Father? Did she just say father?

My brain was racing. This was the man that Celine was telling me about in the forest? Her father was a king—or prince consort—whatever that meant. Regardless of the meaning of his title, he was, in some sense, royalty. That much was clear.

My gaze flicked back to Rowen, who was now studying Celine with a calm, expectant expression.

Celine's voice came through the fog in my thoughts. "Father," she said again, her tone formal, though there was a sort of warmth beneath the surface.

She dipped her head slightly, A gesture of respect that felt oddly practiced, as if she had done it a hundred times before. "You summoned me?"

"Aye, child, I did," Rowen replied. "Isaac has arrived. We all have much to discuss."

Celine's eyes flicked to me, those bottomless violet pools that always pulled me under. My chest tightened as her gaze lingered, her expression showing nothing of the emotions she might have been feeling.

What happened after I passed out in the woods?

I wanted to say something, anything, but the words lodged in my throat. Instead, I stood there awkwardly, staring at her like it were the first time we met.

"Aye, father. That would be best." Celine replied to Rowen, her eyes still locked onto mine, as if waiting for me to speak.

"Has the proverbial rat got your tongue, Drifted?" Sabrina whispered, her tone light with amusement as she stepped in front of me, her red eyes blocking my view. "Or has my presence brought you to silence? A common reaction, I assure you."

I snapped out of my daze, taking a step back. "What? No, I just—" I fumbled over my words as I searched for an explanation that didn't make me sound like a complete fool. "I just don't have anything to say."

"Nothing to say?" Sabrina chucked softly. "Was it not Lady Celine you were inquiring about earlier?" She glanced at Celine while pulling at my cheeks with her hands. "You certainly have a knack for leaving him speechless, m'lady."

I tried to pull back, but Sabrina tightened her grip. "Cut it out." I said under my breath, swatting her hand. Though it only made her grab tighter.

"Sabrina, that is enough," Rowen said, his tone stern enough to cut through Sabrina's teasing. "We don't have time for idle talk."

Sabrina raised an eyebrow before stepping back from me, still maintaining her grin. "As you wish, Your Highness."

"Isaac," Rowen spoke, turning his attention to me.

"Erm... Yes, sir—I mean, Your Highness," I replied, flustered.

Rowen studied me for a moment longer before speaking. "I will not force you to follow us, as I know this must all be very confusing for you. You have been thrust into a world you do not know, with beings far above your realm of understanding. And now, you stand in a place that is unfamiliar and daunting."

I nodded, grateful for his acknowledgement, but still utterly lost.

Rowen stood from his throne, dusting off his clothing.

"The path is yours to choose. But know this—if you wish to have any of your questions answered, or if you wish to understand why you are here, your role in all of this, it would do you well to come."

His words hung in the air for a bit, and I could feel the importance of them settling in my chest. This wasn't merely a invitation—it was a turning point, a choice that felt far more significant than anything I'd made before.

This was my chance to learn what was going on. Why I was brought here, why I had been tricked into traveling to Lostsummit.

Though at the same time, I was scared. Scared of the unknown, scared that there would be no going back after making such a decision. What was I getting myself into?

I thought back to Lunaria, back to my aunt and uncle, back to the twins. What were they up to? Was I doing the right thing being here? Would this path guarantee their safety?

Rowen stepped down from the dais, turning and walking towards the entrance that Celine had appeared from.

"Come now, Drifted," Sabrina said, bouncing on her toes. She leaned slightly toward me, clapping her hands together. "This will be fun! Perhaps the most exciting thing you have ever done!"

Before I could respond, she turned on her heel, her braided-ponytail coming dangerously close to slapping me in the face. Her footsteps echoed lightly against the wood, fading as she followed Rowen.

I hesitated, glancing toward the archway where they had gone, then back to Celine, who hadn't left yet.

I shifted uncomfortably as we stood there, just looking at each other. And for a moment, I felt like she could see every thought racing through my mind.

She shifted her gaze to me; her expression remained calm

and unreadable, but there was something in her eyes—something that silently urged me forward.

There was something in her gaze that told me she knew exactly what I was feeling—my fear, my uncertainty.

Simultaneously, we gave each other a slight nod, a gesture of agreement that felt like the only response necessary.

Celine turned, her cloak shifting around her as she walked toward the opening.

I let out a slow breath, steeling my nerves as I forced my legs to move, following behind her into whatever lay ahead.

A long, dimly-lit hallway stretched before me. Lanterns containing what appeared to be fireflies lined the corridor, emitting a soft glow throughout. Archways covered either side of the hallway, some framed with symbols I didn't understand, and others depicting different phases of the moon cycle.

From the rooms, I could hear the soft murmur of voices—low tones that blended into the hum of the Elderwood. Occasionally, a shuffle of movement or the tap of wood gave a sense of activity to the otherwise quiet atmosphere.

As we passed by the rooms, I caught glances of Lupine moving about, some turning and giving a quick smile before returning to their work

Ahead of me, Rowen walked with a steady stride. Sabrina was beside him, her fur cloak bouncing playfully with each step. She was speaking to Rowen, though it didn't appear as if he was paying any attention.

Serves her right, the blabbermouth, I thought to myself, a small snicker escaping my lips.

Sabrina glanced back over her shoulder, almost as if she could read my thoughts. She stuck her tongue out at me, pulling down the bottom of her eye with her finger in a quick motion. Before I could react, she spun back around as though if nothing had happened.

"What is wrong with her?" I muttered under my breath, quickening my pace to catch up to Celine.

"It appears Sabrina enjoys your company, Drifted." Celine spoke to me, though she kept her eyes forward.

"Yeah, right, she really enjoys annoying me more like it," I replied to her, rolling my eyes unintentionally.

Celine's lips twitched a bit. "Perhaps," she said, keeping her tone gravely neutral.

I glanced at her, waiting for more, but she offered nothing further. This was just like her—straightforward and to the point, never giving any more away than she intended. Admittedly, it was hard to ever tell what Celine was thinking.

"Hey, Celine," I started, moving briskly until I was right beside her.

"Yes, Drifted?" She responded, turning her head to look at me.

"Why didn't you ever tell me that you were royalty?" I questioned. "I mean, why didn't you ever tell me that your father was someone of such high importance?"

Celine's expression didn't change. It didn't even appear like she had to think about an answer. She faced forward again, her voice calm when she finally replied. "I did not know."

Her words stopped me in my tracks for a bit, but I quickly regained composure and caught up to her again. "You didn't... know? How could you not have known?"

She looked at me again, the deep violet of her eyes meeting mine with some softness. "As I told you before in the forest, Drifted. I never knew my father until now."

I blinked. "Yeah, but... didn't anyone ever tell you? Didn't he ever try to find you?"

"No, Drifted," She replied. Her tone was even, but I felt as if there was something beneath the surface that she wasn't saying.

Before I could press her further, Rowen and Sabrina took a turn into one of the rooms to the left.

Celine followed, and I hesitated for a quick moment, watching her walk ahead.

How could I have been so insensitive? Maybe I questioned her too much, or maybe the subject was a touchy one for her. But I just didn't understand, and maybe it wasn't my place to understand.

I took another deep breath and trailed behind her as she entered the room.

Upon entering, I noticed it was moderately sized, the wooden walls stretching and curving gently upward like the inside of a hollowed out tree.

The walls of this room were all covered in various maps, some larger, others smaller, though all seemed very detailed. Some maps depicted dense forests, winding rivers, and jagged mountains. While others showed what looked to be different towns. Symbols and markings, most of which I couldn't decipher, were scattered across their surfaces.

A long wooden table sat in the corner, polished smooth and surrounded by high-back wooden chairs. It was covered with more maps, as well as what looked like figurines carved from dark wood, their shapes resembling buildings, animals, towers, and other objects.

Torches set into the walls burned with flickering flames, and despite the room's quietness, I felt a buzz of energy in the air.

I stepped further inside, glancing at Sabrina and Rowen. They were already on the far side of the room, standing near one of the larger maps on the table. Rowen's hand rested on the edge of the map as he studied it.

Celine stood slightly in front of me, also looking around at the maps plastering the walls. She seemed as intrigued as I did, her gaze lingering a map that contained a large bear. Her fingers moved lightly over the surface as if trying to piece together its meaning.

"What is this place?" I questioned, my eyes darting from wall to wall.

"This room is known as The Hollow." Rowen spoke up, gesturing toward a chair as he took a seat in a larger one at the far end of the table. "This is where plans are formed and decisions are made."

"Is it not just the most invigorating thing, Drifted?" Sabrina explained, her eyes gleaming. Her fingers gravitated towards one of the wooden figurines, but before she could touch it, Rowen smacked her hand away. "All the plotting, all the grand schemes... It is like stepping onto the page of a storybook, no?"

I frowned, glancing around the room again. It wasn't the word I would have chosen. The heavy air, the endless maps, the tension that hung over every corner—it felt more like stepping into the heart of something serious, something larger than myself.

But Sabrina's enthusiasm was hard to ignore, even if it felt slightly misplaced.

"Sabrina, this isn't a game," Rowen said, clearing his throat.

"Of course not, my lord," Sabrina replied, giving a mock bow. "But you must admit, it's rather exciting." She winked at me as if we were somehow in on the same joke.

Rowen let out a sigh and shook his head slightly. He gestured toward the table, sweeping his hand across the array of chairs. "Everyone, take a seat. There is much to discuss."

Celine moved without hesitation, stepping next to the chair beside Rowen. She sat down with quiet poise, her back straight. I watched as her eyes focused on the large map in front of her.

Sabrina strutted to the chair directly opposite Celine. She dropped into it with far less grace, leaning back lazily and propping one leg up on the seat. She drummed her finger idly on the table's edge.

"Ooh, I cannot wait," she muttered under her breath. Her smile made it clear she wasn't going to be taking any of this seriously.

I hesitated, glancing between the chairs before finally stepping forward. I felt as if I was intruding on something I shouldn't have, and I didn't like the feeling of the heavy room on my shoulders. I swallowed the lump in my throat, made my way to the chair next to Celine, and sat down. And for a moment, I stared at the carvings on the table's surface, unsure of where to look.

I felt something on my knee and looked down to see Celine's hand resting gently on it. It was then that I noticed I was subconsciously shaking my leg.

She didn't acknowledge it, but her touch was enough to ground me a bit.

Across the table, Sabrina shot me a smirk, wagging her finger before quickly looking away as Rowen cleared his throat.

"Now that we are all settled," Rowen began, his eyes dancing to everyone at the table. "We can begin."

The room hung in anticipation for a bit, Celine, Sabrina, and I looking at each other, waiting for Rowen to start speaking.

After a few seconds, he cleared his throat again, and began playing with his beard. "Isaac."

"Yes, your highness?" I replied, looking toward him, trying to seem more confident than I was.

"You are probably wondering how you wound up here, no?" Rowen replied, locking his eyes onto mine.

"Yes, Your Highness," I replied, my mouth suddenly going dry. "That's one of the many things I've been trying to figure out."

Rowen leaned forward in his chair, rested his elbows on the table and laced his fingers together. "Then let us begin there," he said. "What do you remember of the events before you were found in this place?"

"I... I remember," My mouth paused, trying to recount the day in the forest. "I remember Celine and I were traveling after we escaped from Lostsummit. We were headed somewhere, Celine didn't know exactly where."

Rowen nodded. "Yes, continue."

I swallowed a bit, then glanced briefly at Celine, whose expression remained still, her eyes fixed on me now.

"There were guards," I continued. "They had been chasing us relentlessly for months. Then..." I paused, the memory of the fall from the cliff and getting surrounded afterwards coming back into my mind. "We tried to escape, but Celine injured her leg after a fall we took, and we couldn't make it far enough. Eventually we were surrounded, and the next thing I knew, I woke up here."

The room fell silent for a moment. Rowen leaned back in his chair now, slouching, stroking his beard as he considered what I said.

Celine was also silent, her gaze distant, almost like she were reliving that day in the woods in her own mind.

"And do you remember what happened after, or during the time you got surrounded?" Rowen asked. "When we found the two of you, you specifically didn't look the best."

I thought for a moment and shook my head. "No, nothing." I admitted. "I had a headache, and then everything went black. One moment we were cornered, and the next, I was here."

"And what of you, Celine?" Rowen turned his gaze to Celine now. "You were still able when we found you two. What do you remember of Isaac's condition?"

Celine pursed her lips and looked at Rowen.

"Drifted was... not well," she began. "When we were surrounded, he suddenly grabbed his head as though in pain. He fell to his knees, clutching his ears as if trying to block out a sound—though I could hear nothing."

Her words made my stomach twist, the back of my head throbbing with a slight pain. Hearing the events again felt like an itch in the back of my mind I couldn't reach.

"My lord," Sabrina started, but Rowen cut her off.

"Yes, Sabrina, we share the same thought."

"What thought?" I interjected, leaning forward in my seat now.

"Isaac, I believe you were soon to be afflicted with hysteria." Rowen said, his tone darkening. The sudden weight of his words made my heart skip a beat.

"Hysteria?" I repeated. My chest tightened as I tried to make sense of it. Thinking back to the many days I spent gripped with fear in Lunaria as a new person afflicted with the illness came scratching at the town's perimeter walls. "How? What do you mean?"

"What we all have been taught in Moonveil about Hysteria isn't exactly the truth," Rowen interrupted gently. "It isn't caused by coming into contact with fiends or even straying too far into the forest."

I hesitated for a moment before speaking. "So, you know what does?"

"Aye, Isaac," Rowen started. "You see, over the lands of Velora is an aura—a miasma, if you will."

"A miasma?" I repeated, frowning. "What do you mean?"

Rowen stroked his beard again. "It is an ancient, noxious fume, woven into the atmosphere of Velora. When humans like you and me come into contact with this miasma for more than a day, it alters our brain chemistry, driving us to the madness that you know very well. At first, it's subtle—confusion, unease, headaches. But as time passes, Hysteria takes hold, twisting one's thoughts, clouding their memories, and altering their mind."

"Wait, but why would something so dangerous be used against humans?" I questioned further.

"The miasma serves a singular purpose—to shield the Lupine from the outside world. To keep their existence hidden. Though it is unlikely, given the vast distance between Velora and Moonveil, it does occasionally happen that humans end up inside the bounds of Velora."

I blinked, reveling in the information that was dropped into my lap. "I see..." My voice trailed off.

Rowen nodded solemnly. "It ensures that those who find their way here cannot return with clear minds. They cannot speak of what they have seen, for their memories will betray them, and their words will sound like the ravings of a madman. It is a safeguard, Isaac, one that has protected the Lupine for centuries."

A thought jumped into my mind, and I prodded further. "Wait, but you said that it takes about a day for a human to get hysteria. I've been in Velora far longer than a day, and on top of that, you live here."

"That is an easy question to answer," Sabrina inserted. "It is because the moon has favored you," she said matter-of-factly.

I furrowed my brow, becoming even further confused. "The moon?" I asked. "What does that even mean?"

Rowen sat up straight again, taking the attention once more. "Isaac, the Lupine believe that the moon holds a... cosmic power—something beyond mortal understanding. Its light is said to guide, to protect, and to bless those it favors. It is not something someone like you or me can control, nor is it something we can seek to fully understand."

The moon favors me? I thought to myself. The words sounded absurd as my mind replayed them.

Rowen continued speaking. "After we brought you here, Sabrina transcribed a sigil on your forehead—the same sigil that I bear. It nullifies the effect of the miasma."

My eyes widened, and I reached up to touch my forehead. "A sigil?" I repeated, my hands feeling around for any kind of etching.

Rowen chuckled a bit before holding up a hand. "Don't waste your time, Isaac. It isn't something physical you can see or feel." He moved the hair from his forehead to show it was empty. "You see, it's a form of light energy, though for my own sanity, I call it magic."

My thoughts raced, and I again felt Celine's hand on my knee again. "So, without it, I would've..."

Rowen jumped in to finish my sentence.

"Succumb to hysteria. The sigil creates a barrier between the miasma and your mind, shielding you from its effects. With how far along the hysteria was when we found you, I'd say you only had two more hours before you would've been beyond saving."

My stomach dropped, a cold chill running through me as the image of myself rambling through the streets and woods disheveled vividly played in my mind.

Sabrina flashed me a smile and rested her head on her

hands. "Do not look so grim Drifted, the sigil I inscribed on you is a work of art, if I do say so myself."

I shook my head, her jokes doing little to ease the storm in my head. "How could it be that the moon favors anyone? It's just a moon. Something in the sky."

The room grew quiet for a moment, and I started to feel as if I had said something insensitive. Celine, who had stayed mostly silent until now, spoke up. "You are wrong, Drifted."

I turned to look at her, surprised by the intensity in her tone. She looked at me, her eyes unflinching and intense. "The moon is much more than that," she continued. "Far greater than you realize."

She straightened in her seat. "As I told you in Noctiluna those months ago, the moon has guided me throughout all of my journeys. Its light has shown me the way when all other paths seemed lost. It was the moon that gave me the strength to keep moving forward, even when everything around me continued to fall into darkness."

I gulped, surprised by how passionately Celine was speaking. This was rare for her.

"And I believe it was the moon that guided me to you, Drifted. It is no coincidence that our paths crossed. The favor it has shown me, and now you—is the only reason we are still together."

There was such certainty in her voice that it felt useless to argue, to tell her how impossible it all sounded. Though how could I say that now, seeing what I've seen so far in this strange place? I wondered if there might be some truth in it all.

"Believe me, Isaac," Rowen's voice broke through my thoughts. "I was in your place once. I, too, didn't believe what I was being told. I thought the stories were exactly that— stories. And yet, here I am. The truth has a way of making itself known, even to the most skeptical among us."

I looked at him, his words sinking in as I questioned everything I knew—or thought I knew.

Rowen continued. "Besides, I feel if we stay on this topic any longer you may upset someone..." He gave a head nod towards Celine while winking at me.

I glanced at Celine; there was the faintest sign of tension in the way she held herself, her hand tapping the table occasionally, as if she were getting ready to speak.

Sabrina laughed, tilting her chair back and surprisingly balancing it on two legs. "You best tread lightly with Lady Celine, Drifted. She might have you doing laps around the Elderwood for penance."

"Oh, quiet," I shot back at her, looking away. Her laugh only grew louder, echoing softly in the expansive room.

"Alright, everyone. That is enough," Rowen stated, standing up from his chair. His eyes swept over all of us. "It is late, and I believe Isaac has plenty enough to process for one evening."

I let out a shaky breath I hadn't realized I was holding. The pressure of the new information hanging over my head like a boulder.

"Sabrina," Rowen continued. "Show Isaac to his quarters. He'll need plenty of rest if he's to make sense of everything we've discussed."

Sabrina gave an exaggerated sigh, letting the chair fall back onto all four legs. "As you wish, Your Highness," she said with bow. Though she looked up at me during it with a wide grin.

Rowen looked toward Celine. "Celine, you shall remain with me. There are other matters we need to discuss before the night is through."

Celine gave Rowen a small nod as she remained seated.

She shot me a glance and placed a hand on my shoulder before she turned her attention back to Rowen. "Yes, father."

"Come along now, Drifted," Sabrina said, already on her feet and moving towards my side of the table. "Allow me to show you to your accommodations. Fit for a moon-favored one such as yourself."

I rolled my eyes and stood from my chair. Admittedly, I was grateful to escape the weight of the conversation in the room and rest my head. Even if it meant I had to endure Sabrina a little while longer.

As I followed her out of the room, I couldn't help but glance back at Celine and Rowen, figuring they had a lot of catching up to do given the time they lost.

Sabrina led me back down the long hallway, the dim light of the lanterns lighting our path again. She hummed to herself softly, clearly unbothered by anything she heard in the room previously. "Quite the meeting, yes?" she asked, glancing over her shoulder at me.

I didn't reply, keeping my eyes forward. The thought of talking about it made my head hurt more than it already did.

"Silent treatment? As you wish," she said with a shrug.

We continued down the hallway, retracing our earlier steps. The faint hum of voices and movement was still present, but definitely quieter now.

When we reached the entrance of the Elderwood, Sabrina turned left at the top of the stairs and gestured for me to follow.

The path wrapped around the massive trunk of the Elderwood and curved upward. Soon we arrived at a bridge crafted from thick, intertwining branches. Sabrina stepped onto it without any hesitation, the wood creaking faintly under her boots. "Do not dawdle," she called over to me. "This bridge is much easier to climb when you are not staring at your feet."

I followed slowly at first, trying to keep my balance, the climb feeling steeper with every step. The bridge led to a series of steps that spiraled higher into the Elderwood. The higher we got, the cooler the night air grew and the sweeter the aroma of flowers got.

As we climbed, the bridge broke off into various thick sections of flat platforms, each one wide enough to hold a handful of sizeable homes.

Here and there, Lupine moved about, their movements effortless in comparison to mine as they crossed the bridges and walked about the staircases connecting various levels. Some carried woven baskets or bundles of wood, while other gave us smiles and waves as we passed, their red eyes glinting in the dark of the night.

Eventually we reached high up into the canopy of the Elderwood, and Sabrina came to a stop.

"This," she said, with a dramatic wave of her hand as we reached the flattened section, "is what we call the High Perch. Is it not just lovely?"

I paused, glancing at the area. There were only two houses here, but the decor was breathtaking. Vines of delicate white flowers trailed along the edges of the houses, their petals bright against the darkness of the sky. Hanging lanterns swayed gently from the branches above, casting shadows of leaves on the snowy floor below.

"Not bad, huh?" Sabrina said, glancing at me with a smug grin. She pointed to the house on the left, its door carved with swirling patterns that reminded me of flowing water. "That, my dear Drifted, is where you shall be staying."

I stared at the house in disbelief. "That's... mine?"

"Mhm," she replied. "The Elderwood grew it upon your arrival."

I stepped closer, my eyes observing every inch of the home. The way everything fit perfectly together—the vines, the foliage. It was almost too perfect.

I turned to look at the other house and felt my heart sink. The dark wood, the red flowers that draped it, the slight tilt of the roof—it was the same house Sabrina had pointed out to me earlier.

I shot her a look. "Sabrina..."

Her grin widened with sharp, mischievous fangs. "Hmm?"

"This is your house... isn't it?" I questioned, my shoulders dropping.

"Guilty!" she said, giggling while clapping her hands together. "The finest home in all of Sylphreach, if I do say so myself. You have the privilege of having none other than the great Sabrina as your neighbor. How many humans get to say that?"

Well, it isn't something anyone would want to brag about. I thought to myself with a sigh. But as much as I hated to admit it, a part of me was grateful for her presence. At least I wasn't completely alone in this strange, overwhelming world.

Sabrina tilted her head. "Oh, come now, Drifted. Do not look so down." She stepped toward her door, her cloak swishing in the breeze. "You know, I was up here all alone before your home sprouted. It is almost as if the Elderwood knew we would be the best of friends!"

I raised an eyebrow, too exhausted to muster much of a response. Her cheerfulness was relentless, even at the end of such a long day.

Stopping at her door, she turned back to face me, leaning against the wooden frame. "Should the solitude of the night prove too much, know that I am but a few steps away. Do not hesitate to call upon me—though I cannot promise peace and quiet in my company."

She dipped her head slightly in a joke farewell. "Rest well, Drifted," she said as she opened her door and disappeared inside.

I sighed, running a hand through my hair as I turned toward my own door. As beautiful and serene as the house was, I couldn't shake the weight of the day's events—or the questions still churning in my mind.

I pushed open the wooden door. It moved smoothly, without so much as a creak. The first thing noticed upon entering was just how warm it was. Despite the coolness of the night outside, the air inside was extremely inviting.

The interior was modest, but crafted with the same elegance I came to expect from this place. The walls were smooth and curved, the grain of the wood running in natural, swirling patterns. Light came from a cluster of some luminous crystals set in the branches above, their glow resembling soft moonlight.

To my left was a small sitting area with a low table made of dark wood, its surface polished to a shine. A pair of chairs with woven backs were placed on either side, their cushions covered in fabric adorned with patterns of stars and crescent moons. A bookshelf lined the far wall, its shelves filled with what looked like leather-bound tomes, though I couldn't read the titles from where I stood.

To my right, a narrow doorway led to what I assumed was a bedroom. Peeking through, I caught a glimpse of a neatly made bed draped in soft, silvery linens, its headboard carved with delicate floral designs. A small nightstand stood beside it, a single lantern resting atop it.

The floor beneath me was smooth, made of the same seamless wood as the walls, but covered here and there with soft rugs that added warmth and color to the space. Their patterns were intricate, depicting forest scenes and the phases of the moon in muted tones of green and blue.

I dropped my pack near the bedroom door and wandered over to the bed, sitting on its edge. I took off the rest of my gear, letting it drop to the floor before laying down.

The events of the day replayed in my mind, each one weighing on me like boulders. How was I supposed to make sense of it all? And why me? I was simply a boy from Lunaria. What did any of this have to do with me?

I knocked my head against the plush pillows and stared up at the ceiling. The soft light from the crystals made gentle patterns across the wood. For a moment, I let my mind drift to Sabrina's parting words. Despite her constant teasing, she'd been oddly reassuring in her own way. Knowing she was next door was... comforting, though I'd never admit it to her.

Before long, my eyelids grew heavier, and exhaustion pulled me under its sweet embrace.

CHAPTER 9

A knock came at the door, waking me out of sleep.

I stirred against the fog of waking up. My eyes fluttered open, and the light of the sun streaming through the window above my bed stung my eyes. For a moment, I lay there disoriented as my thoughts struggled to clear.

Knock. Knock.

The sound came again, louder this time, and I groaned, forcing myself upright in bed.

Ugh, I bet I already know who it is, I thought.

"Sabrina," I growled. What a great start to my day. She couldn't even let me get a small break from her antics, could she?

I swung my legs over the edge of the bed, my feet meeting the cool wooden floor.

Knock. Knock. Knock. Knock. Knock. The door banged again.

"I'm coming!" I called out, my voice still thick with sleep. "Geez." I rolled my eyes as I shuffled out of the room toward the door.

"You're so annoying Sabrina, it's too early for your sh—"

When I opened the door, the words died in my throat.

It wasn't Sabrina at all.

Standing there, tall, playing with his beard, was Rowen. His eyes were fixed on mine. I stood there, shocked, unsure of how much he heard.

"Good morning, Isaac," he said with a curious look on his face. "What was it you were saying before you opened the door?"

Flustered, I stammered, "Oh... Erm. Nothing. I mean, nothing, sir—Your Highness."

I rubbed the back of my neck awkwardly. "I thought you were someone else."

Rowen raised an eyebrow, unamused. He took a step forward. "May I enter? I came to speak with you."

"Oh, yeah, of course," I replied, stepping aside from the doorway.

Rowen ducked slightly, his shoulders brushing past me as he stepped inside. He briefly scanned the room before he made his way to the sitting area. With a groan, he lowered himself into one of the chairs.

I lingered by the doorway for a moment before following him. Rowen, the Prince Consort of Sylphreach, had climbed all the way up here to talk to me? Someone of his name—his stature—shouldn't have been the one to make this trip. He could've easily sent someone else. A messenger, a guard, hell, even Celine. But here he was, sitting in my quarters.

"Sit, boy," Rowen said, his voice pulling me back to reality. He gestured to the chair opposite him.

I nodded, quickly shuffling to the seat and sitting down. I gripped the armrest as I tried to hide the nervousness bubbling inside me.

Rowen leaned back and crossed his arms before he spoke. "Last night was a lot to take in," he began. "But there is more you need to know. More that you deserve to know." He paused, his eyes sharp as they landed on mine. "Though last night I could not help but notice that you seemed... skeptical when we spoke of the moon's favor towards you."

I scratched my head. To be honest, I still wasn't convinced. "I mean, yeah," I said cautiously. "With all due respect, it's not something I'm exactly used to hearing. The idea that the moon was what saved me from hysteria... it's a lot to digest."

Rowen nodded, as if he'd expected my response. "I understand your doubt, especially for someone who has not grown up with the beliefs of this land."

He unfolded his arms. Now resting them in his lap. "And yet, I've seen it in ways I cannot fully explain, but I know it is real. It's what allowed me to survive here for thirty-six years, just as it has allowed you to endure the miasma. And it is what binds us to this land."

His eyes met mine, calm yet filled with conviction. "You may not believe it now, Isaac. That is your right. But the moon has chosen you for a reason. Whether you accept it or not, its favor will continue to shape your path."

Rowen's words settled over me, wrapping around my thoughts and refusing to let go. As much as I wanted to dismiss what he was saying, a part of me couldn't help but see the truth in it. Everything I'd seen so far went against what I thought was possible—the Elderwood, the Lupine, this entire civilization thriving beyond Moonveil, went against everything we were ever taught. I'd been raised to believe that the outside world beyond our lands was nothing but dense forest and fiends. Yet here I was.

I exhaled slowly, placing a hand to calm my shaking leg. "I guess," I started, my voice uncertain, "I can't say that it's impossible. Especially not after everything I've been through."

Rowen watched me silently.

I frowned, leaning forward in the chair. This all felt like a story you told to some wide-eyed kid before bedtime. But the more I thought about it, the more I realized this journey had been one impossible thing after another. Maybe that was the point.

I nodded, trusting that things would be revealed to me in time. "Alright," I whispered. "I won't say I fully believe everything I'm hearing, but I'll try to keep an open mind about it all."

Rowen nodded his head, a small smile growing on his lips.

"Can I ask you something else?" I said, my voice hesitant.

Rowen tilted his head slightly. "You spent your time listening to me. Ask away; you're owed that much."

"That day in the forest," I began. "When Celine and I got surrounded... How did you even find us?"

Rowen's expression turned into something resembling darkness and curiosity. "We were actually tailing you for quite some time," he admitted. "A bit before you and Celine reached Noctiluna."

"You were tracking us?" I repeated.

"Aye," Rowen continued. "It was then that we realized you had gotten in contact with Remus—or the one you knew as Brute."

Just the mention of the name angered me. My hands curled into fists in my lap as the memory of his betrayal came to the forefront of my mind. The trust I placed in him, the hope that he had been an ally—a broth... I let the thought trail off.

"Brute," I spat the name out.

Rowen observed me, watching as the anger bubbled inside of me. "Remus' betrayal runs deep," he breathed. "He is a dangerous man, one who has caused great harm both inside and outside of Velora."

I let out a slow, shaky breath, the anger still simmering beneath the surface. "So, you knew this whole time," I said, my voice low. "And you didn't think to warn us?"

Rowen's tone hardened, though he remained calm. "We attempted to intercept you when the time was right, Isaac. But Remus fought us off," he said evenly. "Had we approached any sooner and you wouldn't have believed what you were being told."

I hesitated, but he was right. At that time, I trusted Brute fully; it would've been easy for him to turn me against them.

Rowen continued, noticing my acceptance. "Sabrina had been working undercover at Lostsummit for some time, as we anticipated something would've happened to you. It was her intervention that allowed you to escape when you were captured there, if you recall."

Another vision came to my mind: the chains, darkness, the beating I took while being held captive. Then, I remembered Sabrina unlocking my cage and restoring my energy with the elixir. Because of her shift in character, I almost had forgotten it was her that day. "Sabrina... Yeah, I remember that now."

Rowen nodded. "Precisely. Her role was to gather information and act when the opportunity arose. And when the guards captured you, she acted. It was no coincidence you escaped when you did."

His gaze shifted toward a window, a thoughtful look on his face as the morning light came in stronger now. He stood slowly, his eyes shifting to the door.

"There will be time for more questions later," he said. "But for now, it is time to feast."

I blinked, surprised. "Feast?" I questioned.

"Yes, Isaac. You see, the Lupine take their meals very seriously. If we are late, I will never hear the end of it."

Before I could respond, he made his way toward the door. "Get ready and meet me back in the Elderwood. I will be waiting."

He paused briefly with his hand on the knob, turning his head to glance back at me. "Do not tarry, boy. Celine has been asking about you since daybreak."

With that, he left, the door closing softly behind him.

Celine's been asking about... me? The thought lingered in my mind. I couldn't tell if it made me nervous, curious, or something else entirely.

Shaking my head, I pushed myself up from the chair and made my way to the bedroom.

I stopped at the edge of the bed, staring down at my gear on the floor. I rubbed the back of my neck, groaning softly as I reached for my scabbard and sword.

As I continued dressing, I wondered what Rowen had meant about the Lupine taking their meals seriously. I mean, everyone likes a good meal, how serious could eating get?

I grabbed my cloak from where it hung on the chair in the main room and threw it over my shoulders. The fabric felt familiar, like a small piece of home in this foreign land.

As I made my way towards the door, I thought about what Rowen said about Celine asking about me.

Don't get too excited, I told myself. Knowing Celine, she was probably just curious as to where I was. Regardless, I felt happy that she was concerned about me, afraid that I had upset her with my remarks about the moon last night.

With one last glance at the room, I opened the door and stepped outside to greet the morning air of the High Perch.

"Oh, Drifted!" I heard a voice sing.

No, no, by the moon, please no.

I turned my head to see Sabrina waving her arms against the rail of the bridge, an enormous smile on her face. "Fancy seeing you have decided to join the rest of the hardworking beings," she said, walking toward me with exaggerated strides. "I was beginning to think you had decided to hibernate."

I pinched the bridge of my nose, already regretting stepping outside. "What do you want, Sabrina? It's too early for this."

"What do *I* want? I have been waiting for you all morning," she said, placing a hand over her heart. "We would not want you to miss such an important meal, now would we?"

"How can you even have any room in your stomach left

after how much I saw you eat yesterday?"

Sabrina gasped. "How dare you! I was simply replenishing my energy after a long day of watching you sleep. It is not my fault you eat like that of a newborn pup."

"You ate like the moon was about to fall out of the sky..." I muttered as I made my way down the bridge.

Sabrina walked beside me. "Ah, but you see, Drifted. A well-fed Lupine is a sharp Lupine. Try it one day; it may serve you well."

"I think I'll survive without eating half the table." I replied, quickening my pace.

Sabrina skipped ahead of me as we neared the Elderwood, its towering trunk even more imposing in the bright morning light. "Quickly now, Drifted. I do not enjoy the pangs of hunger."

I followed reluctantly. The warmth of the massive tree enveloping me instantly.

The sound of voices grew louder as we walked deeper into the trees, following a path that wound toward the center. Lupine moved quickly through the area. The energy felt different today—busier, more focused, like something important was on the horizon.

Sabrina led me toward a set of stairs that spiraled upward. She bounced up them effortlessly, pausing briefly at the top to look back at me. "Quick feet, Drifted. I have not all day!"

"Must you speak every chance you get?" I muttered, brushing past her as we reached the next level.

The scent of food hit me like a smack to the face. It was savory, mixed with the warm scent of freshly baked bread. Soon, a dining area came into view, a spacious chamber filled with long wooden tables and benches. Various Lupine were gathered, their voices a lively hum that echoed against the curved walls.

As I took it all in, Sabrina turned to me with a sly grin. "Oh, Drifted," she said in her teasing, tilting tone, "what luck you have. You get to practice one of those fine introductions again."

My stomach sank, and I stopped mid-step.

Great, this is just great.

The embarrassment was already creeping in. Yet another chance to humiliate myself in front of strangers.

I shifted awkwardly, trying to distract myself from the observing pool of red eyes following me. The Lupine seated at the table carried an almost regal air about them, their postures straight and stiff despite the casual setting. Their faces were drawn in subtle pouts, expressions too poised to be mistaken for sulking—like nobles who had been mildly inconvenienced.

Every detail about them felt too specific, as though the smallest thread or mark had a meaning. It was intimidating.

Even though I saw smiles on their faces, I couldn't shake the feeling that I didn't belong here.

"Do not tell me you are getting cold feet," Sabrina said, pulling me out of my thoughts. She tilted her head. "Come now, Drifted, chin up! Perhaps you shall even impress someone this time."

I let out a low groan, avoiding her gaze as we stepped further into the hall. Impress them? That was a stretch. Right now, I just wanted to get through this without making a complete fool of myself.

As we neared, Rowen, who was sitting at the head of his table, locked eyes with me. He gestured over me with a simple wave of his hand.

Sabrina, of course, didn't miss the opportunity to make things worse.

"Go on, Drifted," she said, nudging me playfully in the

ribs. "Your audience awaits."

I shot her a glare, but it didn't stop the smug smile from growing on her face. Taking a deep breath, I squared my shoulders and stepped forward, my boots thumping against the smooth wooden floor.

As I neared the head of the table, I couldn't help but notice the quiet ripple of curiosity that spread through the room. Conversations hadn't completely stopped, but I noticed the change in energy.

When I reached Rowen, I stood awkwardly for a moment, unsure whether to speak first, or for him to address me.

Thankfully, he spoke.

"Everyone," he began, and the room immediately quieted. All the attention now focused on him—and, by extension, me. "This is Isaac, our guest in Sylphreach."

His gaze traveled across the table, ensuring every Lupine present was paying attention. "As you may notice, he is human. Meaning he is a special guest, and shall be treated as such. I trust you all will show him the respect and hospitality that befits one who has been brought into our fold."

I felt my throat tighten as I realized that this was the moment for me to speak. The stares that followed were less curious and more deliberate now. As if they were assessing whether I was worthy of such praise. My palms felt clammy, and I knew there was on one thing that I could do to avoid completely embarrassing myself.

Taking a slow breath, I straightened my shoulders, crossed an arm in front of me, and took a slow bow. Carefully, I repeated the only phrase I could. "May the moon guide you all."

There was a brief silence as the words hung in the air for a moment. I thought I might've messed it up somehow. But then a few Lupine nodded in approval, their gazes softening slightly.

Then, almost as if on cue, they all turned back to their conversations, their attention shifting away from me entirely. The hum of voices resumed, as though my presence had only been a passing curiosity.

I stood there, surprised. One moment I was under the spotlight, and the next, I was practically invisible. It was relieving, sure, but the abruptness left me feeling strangely small.

I felt a tug at my sleeve and looked down to see a pair of violet eyes staring back up at me. In my embarrassment, I hadn't noticed that I was standing directly behind the seat Celine was in.

"Take your seat, Drifted," she said, gesturing toward the empty chair next to her.

I nodded and slipped into the chair. My face still warm from the introduction.

"You did well," she said, her voice so soft that I could barely hear her.

I looked at her, surprised, but the smile on her face made my hands grow even clammier. "Thanks," I said, my voice equally quiet.

Before I could dwell on it, a familiar—annoying—presence dropped into the empty chair next to mine. Sabrina plopped down and leaned on the table, tilting her head to stare straight at me. "Oh, well done, Drifted," she said in a hushed, mocking tone. "You have impressed them all with your eloquence."

As I got ready to retort, Rowen spoke up, leaning a bit past Celine to see me.

"Aye, Isaac. A fine introduction that was," he said.

"Thank you, Your Highness," I said, the tension in my shoulder easing slightly.

I looked around the long table before me and noticed the

assortment of plates on the table.

"So, what's going on?" I asked. More to myself than to anyone else.

"Breakfast," Celine replied simply.

Before I could question her further, a door at the far end of the room swung open and a familiar figure emerged. Caldryn, the Lupine chef I'd met before in the mess hall, strode into the room. His apron was tied snuggly around his waist, and his sleeves were rolled up to reveal forearms as strong as tree trunks.

Behind him, a line of Lupine, each wearing their own white aprons, followed, carrying large platters piled high with meat. The strong smell of good food filled the air, making my stomach rumble.

"Breakfast is served!" Caldryn called, his deep, booming voice cutting through the hum of conversation. The Lupine carrying the platters moved swiftly, setting the dishes down along the center of the tables. Roasted meats glistened under the light, each flanked by bowls of hearty stews and polished wooden chalices.

The energy in the room shifted again, this time to one of eager anticipation as the Lupine turned their attention to the feast being laid out before them. Caldryn clapped one of his assistants on the back. "A fine spread today, if I do say so myself!" he declared.

I couldn't help but watch as he moved with confidence, directing his team with ease. There was a warmth to him, a satisfaction in his work that was almost infectious.

Sabrina slurped up a bit of her drool as she stared at the mounds of meat in front of her. "Oh, Lady Celine, is it not marvelous?" She exclaimed, practically singing the last word.

Celine let out a slight laugh. "Aye, it does appear to be quite the banquet."

As the Lupine began helping themselves to the food, Caldryn approached our end of the table, carrying two finely arranged plates. Unlike the other platters filled with stacks of meat, these were carefully balanced with an assortment of meats, slices of bread, and an array of colorful fruits and vegetables. He set one plate in front of Rowen and the other in front of Celine with a small bow of respect.

"Your meals, Your Highness, Lady Celine," he said. "Prepared to your preferences, as always."

Rowen gave him a nod of approval, while Celine offered a quiet, "Thank you, Caldryn."

I couldn't help but stare at the vibrancy of their plates, comparing it to the tones of the meat sitting in front of me. "Wait a second," I said, leaning forward. "Back at the dining hall, you told me there weren't any vegetables left in Sylphreach."

Caldryn turned to me, his thick eyebrows raising. "I said no such thing," he replied.

"You did so!" I insisted, narrowing my eyes at him. "Yesterday, when Sabrina and I were there, she asked, and you told us you were all out."

Caldryn scowled his face, "Precisely, lad. I said we were all out." Vegetables and fruit are reserved for Lady Celine and His Majesty. They are not meant for the common table."

"Well... we aren't at the common table now. May I have some?" I asked, raising a brow.

"Apologies, Drifted," he folded his arms in front of his chest. "But I fear we are once again fresh out."

Sabrina spoke up, her mouth stuffed full of a slab of beef. "Drifted... you shall... find no... victory here," she took a large gulp. "I would suggest you surrender now."

"Caldryn," Celine said, her tone raising slightly. "Please see to it that Drifted receives the nourishment he is requesting."

Caldryn stiffened, his jaw tightening, his lips opening to protest. "My lady, will all respect—"

"Caldryn..." Rowen's voice rumbled from the head of the table.

The chef's mouth snapped shut, and he gave a slight bow to Celine and Rowen before turning back to me. "My apologies Drifted, I shall see to it that you are properly accommodated."

He motioned to one of his assistants, who then quickly disappeared to the back, returning moments later with a smaller platter containing the same roasted vegetables and slices of fruit that Celine had.

Caldryn gave another small bow. "Your nourishment as requested."

I looked down at the plate, and then up at Celine, who gave me the faintest nod. "Thank you," I said. But I wasn't sure whether I was thanking her or Caldryn.

Sabrina let out a low whistle, clapping a hand on my shoulder. "Vegetables in Sylphreach!" She raised a chicken leg like toast. "A feat to praise for generations!"

I gave her a look but couldn't help the small smile tugging at my lips as I picked up my fork.

As I picked up a roasted vegetable, Rowen spoke up again. "Eat quickly, the three of you." His gaze shifting between us. "We'll be heading to the Hollow as soon as breakfast is finished."

Sabrina groaned dramatically, tossing her head back as if she'd been gravely wronged. "Oh, can we not have a moment of peace to enjoy this fine feast?"

Rowen arched an eyebrow, his expression unamused. "You've had your peace, Sabrina. Now, we have work to do."

Celine nodded, her calm demeanor as unwavering as ever.

"Understood, Father."

Sabrina stuffed the chicken leg into her mouth. "As you wish, Your Highness," she gave me a sideways glance. "Best finish those precious vegetables."

I took another bite, picking up the pace, knowing that Rowen wouldn't wait for any of us to finish once he thought it was time to leave.

Sure enough, not long after, Rowen rose from his seat and the room quieted down. The hum of conversation halted immediately. All eyes turned to him as he straightened to his full height.

"Lupine of Sylphreach," Rowen began. "Excuse us, we must take our leave now."

The Lupine at the tables immediately stood, some placing hands over their hearts in a show of respect. Others bowed their heads slightly. It was clear there was great respect for Rowen here.

One by one, murmurs broke out across the tables. "May the moon guide you."

Rowen inclined his head toward us. "Come," he said.

I scrambled to my feet, wiping my hands on a leaf-napkin as Sabrina stood next to me, making sure to stuff a couple of more chunks of meat in her cheeks. Celine stood next, fixing her cloak as she fell in step behind her father.

As we followed Rowen near to the exit, the Lupine remained standing, their eyes lingering respectfully as we passed.

"Who are these Lupine?" I questioned Sabrina. "They all look so... important."

Sabrina swallowed her mouthful of food with an audible gulp. "Quite the observation, Drifted," she teased. "This hall is reserved for the council and their kin—those who aid in governing Sylphreach."

I placed a hand on my chin. "Like a ruling body?"

She nodded. "Indeed. While Prince Rowen has the final say on decisions, it would be far too much for him to manage every detail of the realm on his own. The council handles the intricacies, diplomacy, defense, and the like."

As we continued walking, I got another thought in the back of my head. "If Rowen is a prince—or prince consort. Doesn't that mean there should be a queen?"

Sabrina's grin dropped for a moment. "Aye, Drifted, you are not wrong. There *should* be a queen."

I frowned, noticing the shift in her demeanor.

Sabrina sighed, her gaze flickering to Rowen and Celine as they walked in front of us. "Lady Celine's mother, Queen Aylin, disappeared about seventeen years ago," she said quietly. "She vanished without a trace."

"Gone?" I echoed quietly. "How does someone like a queen up and disappear?"

"That," Sabrina said. "Is the question that has plagued Sylphreach for nearly two decades? No one knows what became of her, not even Prince Rowen."

"And he's been in charge of everything since?" I asked.

Sabrina nodded. "Aye. He stepped into her role when she vanished, taking on the customs of the Lupine almost immediately. It took a while for the council to truly respect him, but he has earned their full support."

I glanced at Rowen again, his figure turning into the Hollow. Suddenly, his composed demeanor and commanding presence felt heavier, more deliberate. He wasn't just a leader. He was someone who had endured loss and carried the weight of an entire realm on his back.

We followed Rowen inside. The intricate maps and charts engulfed us once again. The massive central table was prepared already, a new map with figurines waiting to greet us.

Rowen motioned to the seats around the table. "Sit," he said simply.

Celine moved gracefully to her usual spot at Rowen's right. Sabrina, true to form, dropped into her seat across from Celine with a loud thud, leaning back in her chair as if she owned the place. I sat next to Celine, my hands fidgeting in anticipation of whatever conversation we were going to have.

Finally, Rowen spoke, his voice calm but laced with something I couldn't quite place—urgency? Or perhaps... dread.

"The time for waiting is over," he began, his gaze lingering on the map. "What I am about to share with you all may very well determine the fate of Isaac, Celine, and the rest of Sylphreach."

CHAPTER 10

Rowen stepped closer to the table and rested his hands on its edge as he leaned forward. "What you all see here," he began. "Is Velora and all of its settlements."

I leaned forward in my chair, eyes scanning the map in front of us. It was detailed in a way that felt overwhelming at first—mountains and forests meticulously drawn— each marked with names.

Rowen's finger landed at the far edge of the map.

He paused for a second, as if waiting for us to take it in. "And this here," he continued, "is Sylphreach, our home and heart of Velora."

I nodded, letting my eyes follow the markings drawn. Sylphreach—much like Moonveil—was surrounded by dense forest, and its symbol was larger than any other.

"This," his finger shifting north of Sylphreach, stopping on a marking of thorned vines. "is Thornwallow. A land dense with thorns and foliage."

Rowen's finger then moved southwest, stopping over a jagged, mountainous symbol. "And here lies Lostsummit," he said. "Where you and Celine were captured."

I nodded again, confused as to why we were being shown this now. Perhaps Rowen wanted Celine and me to get familiar with the layout of the land?

"And while the inhabitants of this vast region are all Lupine, there is reason for the separation of living."

"Like what?" I questioned.

"Much like that of Moonveil, there is a divide between the Lupine body." Rowen looked at me, his lips scrunched as he prepared to speak.

"Isaac, tell me. What do you remember of your time in Lostsummit?" Rowen questioned, giving me the floor.

The memories of that cold, desolate, rocky place crept back into my mind. The harshness, the stares, the beatings. It was a place I would never forget.

"It was... cruel. They hated me for some reason—humans—for some reason. They treated us like we were nothing."

Rowen nodded solemnly with a blank look on his face. "Precisely. Outside of Sylphreach, the Lupine hold a different view of us. They see our kind not as equals but as a stain upon this world. To them, the world would be better off without us, and they make that sentiment known—often brutally so."

I blinked, taken aback by his words. The coldness of them stung, even if I wasn't entirely surprised after what I myself endured. "Why?" I asked, the question leaving my mouth before I had the chance to stop it. "What did humans ever do to them?"

Rowen exhaled slowly, his gaze shifting to the map as though searching for the right words. "Prejudice, fear, most likely a combination of the two. The Lupine beyond Sylphreach hold tightly to ancient grievances, some real, others imagined. They believe humans disrupt the balance of nature, taking without giving, destroying without thought. And while not all humans are guilty of such things, the perception alone is enough to breed resentment."

"But it is true, not all humans are like that, Father." Celine spoke up, glancing towards me.

"No, they are not," Rowen agreed. "But fear and anger are easier to cling to than understanding. Over time that fear festers, and brews into something more akin to hatred."

I balled my fist as Rowen's words sunk into me. "So it was some stupid grudge that made them treat me and the others that way?"

"Aye," Rowen replied. "But there is more to it than that. It was no coincidence that you were led to Lostsummit, Isaac."

I stiffened a bit and tilted my head. "What do you mean?"

Rowen pressed his hand against his lap as he began to explain. "To understand, you must know the history of Velora and of Sylphreach itself."

I nodded, ready for the story that was to come.

"Before you were born, before Lostsummit and Thornwallow ever existed, there was a council member in Sylphreach by the name of Cassius."

Rowen paused for a brief moment, looking at the map as if gathering his thoughts. "Cassius held views of humans that were... less than favorable. His rhetoric was strong and struck fear into the hearts of many Lupine. Over time, he amassed a following who shared his disdain for humanity, who believed this land would fare better without our kind."

The temperature in the room dropped as Rowen spoke, his words painting a vivid, grim picture.

"I was there for that! Though... I was rather young." Sabrina shouted, but Rowen shot her a look, and she immediately covered her mouth with her hand.

Rowen continued, "The tension spread throughout Velora like wildfire, fracturing the bonds of its people. Cassius' influence was strong, and his following grew by the day. But then... irony showed its cruel hand."

"In a twist, Cassius committed what is known as a cardinal sin among the Lupine. He fell in love with a woman—a human woman."

"Cardinal sin... human..." I muttered, "but wait, your highness, wasn't it a Lupine queen that married you? How is it a cardinal sin to fall for a human?"

Rowen tilted his head in a slight nod. "It is true that I am consort to a Lupine, Isaac. But this right is reserved for the ruling queen and the ruling queen only."

I frowned a bit, thinking of how unfair that sounded. But I wasn't going to go and judge a culture that I didn't myself understand fully.

Rowen cleared his throat before continuing. "The woman Cassius loved reciprocated his feelings, though there was one glaring issue: Cassius already had a family. A wife and son of his own."

"Once it was found out, Cassius was immediately exonerated. The council stripped him of his title, and he left. But he did not leave alone. His family followed, as did many of his supporters."

"I was there for that as well!" Sabrina chimed in again with her hand raised, nearly falling out her chair.

Rowen slowly turned his head toward her with a brow raised in annoyance, and her hands lowered slowly as her ears flattened against her head.

"But why would anyone go with him, knowing that he went against what he preached?" I questioned.

"Only a select few of higher-up council members knew the true story. Once Cassius figured he would be cast out, he orchestrated his exit before that story could be revealed. His family, in order to save face, reluctantly followed. To the public, he framed his departure as an act of protest, a stand against the council's leniency toward humans."

"A foolish man's greed affected the lives of so many..." Celine added. "His followers—blinded by his charisma— believed he was a martyr for their cause."

"Why didn't anyone try to stop him?" I pressed.

Rowen exhaled slowly. "We did what we could, but the damage was already done. His departure fractured Sylphreach in ways that could not be mended. Those who followed him became the foundation of Lostsummit and Thornwallow, their beliefs evolving and hardening over the years. What began as a single man's actions has since become an unyielding divide—a legacy of mistrust and hatred."

"I see, but... I don't exactly understand how this ended up with me being tricked into going to Lostsummit." I questioned with a frown.

Rowen breathed in through his nose deeply and then exhaled just as long. He leaned forward in his chair, taking on a stance that felt ominous. "Well, you see, Isaac, the woman that Cassius fell in love with—the human who became the catalyst for the divide in Sylphreach—was your mother, Alara."

I felt goosebumps come over my body in a wave. The words hitting me like a thunderclap. "What?" I whispered. "My mother?"

Rowen nodded solemnly. "Yes. Alara was a remarkable woman—strong willed, compassionate, and unshakable in her convictions. Cassius believed their love was unbreakable, and in his naivety, he cast aside his wife and child, believing Alara to be the end all of his life."

I sat there stunned. My stomach felt queasy, and a small bead of sweat formed right above my brow. "Though, as seemingly the world sought to make an example out of Cassius itself, Alara met your father, Malikai. She left Cassius soon after and built a new life for herself in Lunaria."

I felt like any moment I could vomit, the world around me seemed to phase in and out and warp.

"Why she left him? I'm not sure. Maybe Cassius' anger poisoned everything around him, including their love. Or perhaps she simply preferred a quiet, reserved life with your father."

The room fell into a heavy silence, the weight of the story hanging over us like a storm cloud. Then Sabrina broke the quiet.

"How poetic," she said, her tone light but edged with irony. "Cassius, abandoning the ones who loved him, only to be abandoned by the one he loved."

She crossed her arms in her chair, pondering. "Tragic, really. A tale fit for a song, though I doubt he is enjoying the ending."

"Aye," Rowen replied to her. "Unfortunately, Cassius' fall is not the end of this story. It is merely the beginning of the events that led you here."

How could there be more than this? I questioned myself.

I must've been making a face because I felt Celine lay a hand on my shoulder. "Perhaps we hold off on the rest, Father. This must be all very hard on Drifted."

Rowen shook his head. "No, Celine. As much as I would love to spare Isaac the details. It is pertinent he knows this information."

Celine gave me a look, her eyes expressing a bit of the sorrow I was feeling.

I shook my head, "It's alright, Celine. I'll be alright."

Rowen nodded once, not wasting anytime. "The woman Cassius cast aside did not crumble under the weight of his betrayal. Quite the opposite. She flourished from their fractured bond, stronger and more vengeful than ever."

"After her own exile from Thornwallow, she formed her own faction, built her own town—the very one you found yourself in, Isaac. She became Queen Maura of Lostsummit, and as her Umbra, she chose her son. A young Lupine by the name of Remus."

My eyes widened, and I leaned forward on the table, gripping the edge. "Wait... you mean—"

"Yes, Isaac," Rowen interrupted. "The queen you slayed in Moonveil was this Maura, and the man who betrayed you was her son, Remus."

"But... why me? What do I have to do with any of this?" I yelled, rage filling my lungs.

How had my life turned into this—a story of betrayal, bloodlines, and vengeance, all tied to a history I never asked to be a part of?

I shook my head, trying to wrap my mind around it. "I mean... I don't understand why any of this happened. What did I do to deserve any of what happened?"

"You did not," Sabrina answered. "Though to Maura, your family was a reminder of Cassius' betrayal. And to Remus, I am sure your family is reminder of the life he once had with his own."

"And this is why we must keep you here," Rowen added, crossing one leg over the other.

I looked up, realizing I was staring down at the table with a blank stare. "Keep me here? Like in Sylphreach."

"Aye," Rowen replied. "You see, after the fall of Queen Maura by your hands, Remus has gone missing. His whereabouts unknown. And while this is definitely concerning, it is not the most pressing issue."

"What do you mean?" I asked, my voice shaky.

Rowen's eyes narrowed and his voice dropped, possibly trying to ease the gravity of his words. "Cassius will not allow the death of his wife—former or not—to go unanswered. To him, it is not about vengeance. It is about power, reputation. He will come for you, Isaac; that is one thing I am certain of."

I felt my chest tighten, the air around me growing heavier with each word. "So, that's it then?" I said, my voice trembling despite my attempt to stay composed. "I'm just some piece in a game I didn't even know was being played? And now, because my hand was forced, Cassius is coming for me?"

The thought made my stomach churn, and my face grew hot from my frustration bubbling over. Then another thought came to me, and the realization struck deep.

"He wants to get rid of my... family," My eyes grew wide and I stood up hastily, almost knocking the chair over behind me. "I can't stay here! If Cassius hates my bloodline, then he'll target the only family I have left!"

Aunt Silvia's warm but stern face flashed in my mind, her keen eyes always catching when I tried to slip away unnoticed. Uncle Alfarr's boisterous laugh followed, his voice teasing me about my "paperweight" of a sword. And the twins, Marciana and Marcellus—so full of life, their endless energy both a blessing and a curse. I could see their mischievous grins as they plotted some new way to drive me mad.

The thought of harm coming to them sent a chill throughout my body. "I have to go back!"

Rowen calmly raised a hand, his head tilting down slightly. "Isaac," he began, his voice firm, "we anticipated this. Your family's safety has not been overlooked."

I stared at him, waiting for more.

"Even before your arrival here," he continued, "we have had Lupine stationed around the clock in the woods near Lunaria, operating in secret. They are keeping watch and ensuring no harm comes to your family."

My thumping heart settled a bit at his words.

"You have my word that I am doing everything in my power to protect them. But your presence there would only draw more danger. Cassius is not a man to act rashly—he is measured. I am sure he is waiting for his opportunity to catch you alone."

I shook my head slightly, the guilt of the situation still prevalent. "So, what am I supposed to do here?" I questioned,

"Stay here and wait for him to strike?"

Rowen shook his head. "You will not remain here idly, Isaac," he said. "In the unfortunate event that Cassius finds a way to reach you, you will be ready."

I thought back to the immense struggle of a fight I had with Queen Maura in Lostsummit. If it weren't for Celine, I wouldn't have made it out of there alive. If Cassius was any bit of a fighter as she was, I would have no chance.

"Ready? How so?" I questioned, my eyebrows raised

"You will train here, fighting alongside the Lupine, learning from their ways. We will hone your skills and prepare you for a day I hope never comes."

There was a quiet conviction in his words that sparked something in me. "This is not a punishment or a burden," he continued. "It is a chance to grow, to become more than you are now. If that day comes, Isaac, you will not face it incapable. I promise you that."

I swallowed hard as his statement settled over me. Training under the Lupine... the thought was daunting, but if it meant protecting my family, protecting myself, I couldn't turn away from it.

The gaze of everyone in the room lingered on me, as if searching for the resolve they would hope to find. I didn't know what to think—what to feel. Maybe this was the most logical choice I could make. It was true that in my current state I was in no way ready to take on this challenge alone.

If everything I heard here was true, I was going to need all the help I could get.

"Okay," I said, giving the room a look over. "Whatever it takes, I'll do it."

Rowen inclined his head, a curt smile growing on his lips. "Good. Then, your training begins later. Take some time for yourself until sundown, Isaac. You will need it."

Sabrina stood abruptly from her seat, clapping her hands frantically. "Oh goodie! This is going to be so much fun!" she said as she bounced on her toes. "I simply cannot wait to whip him into shape!"

My stomach dropped. "Wait... will she—"

Rowen raised his hand to stop me, easing my worries. "Do not worry, Isaac. She will not be the one to train you."

Rowen sighed, throwing a glance in her direction. "Sabrina, his training will be overseen by more than just your... enthusiasm."

Sabrina stopped bouncing, her shoulders sagging. "I see... no matter... it will still be fun, nonetheless."

For a moment, I actually felt a bit sad for her. But before I could dwell on it, I felt a gentle tug on my sleeve. Turning, I found Celine standing quietly beside me, her eyes meeting mine.

"Drifted," she said softly. "Do not feel as if you must do this. Whatever choice you make, I shall see it through with you."

At first, I could only stare at her. The weight of her conviction wasn't something I expected would hit me so hard. But I wasn't surprised. Since we've met, Celine has always looked out for my best interest, constantly sticking by my side.

I gave her a smile and a nod. "No, Celine. I'll be okay. This is something I must do."

She returned my nod, though she didn't seem entirely convinced, and for a moment, she stared at me, as if waiting for me to change my mind. "As you wish, Drifted."

Rowen stood, giving everyone a glance. "Alright, everyone, this meeting is adjourned... for now."

He turned to me, giving a thoughtful look. "I know that since you've got here, you've only been provided life-changing news and burdens. Though I assure you, Sylphreach is more than a place to obtain bad omens. In time, you may find it to be a place of solace."

I hesitated for a moment. The idea of finding peace in a place like this, foreign—different, felt almost impossible. But something in his tone gave me a glimmer of hope.

I sighed. "I hope you're right."

"Aye, as do I," Rowen replied.

He turned his attention to Sabrina. "Sabrina, the day is still early enough. Why don't you give Isaac and Celine a tour of the Elderwood?"

Sabrina stood up dramatically, placing her feet together and giving Rowen a salute. "Your wish is my command, Your Highness."

As she came to our side of the table to drag me along, I raised my hands, taking a step back. "Thank you, Your Highness. Though, I think I'd rather return to my quarters for now," I said, trying to choose my words carefully.

Rowen regarded me for a moment, his gaze calm. Then he nodded. "Of course. Take the time you need, Isaac. This is not an easy path for you to walk; reflection will serve you well."

Sabrina pouted, crossing her arms. "Bah! Such a killjoy."

I managed a weak smile, but my heart wasn't in it. "Sorry, Sabrina. Maybe next time?"

I turned to leave, and I could feel Celine's gaze following me, but she said nothing. For now, I needed space, a chance to piece together the fragments of the world I'd been thrown into.

My thoughts were already beginning to swirl as I stepped toward the hallway leading out of the Hollow.

The air shifted as I left the room, with low murmurs of conversation fading behind me. I ran my hand along the textured surface of the bark as I walked, the ridges and grooves surprisingly warm to the touch. The silence here was comforting, but it also left me alone with my own thoughts.

Before long, I found myself in the grand central chamber of the Elderwood. I tried to take some of the sights in— murals on the walls depicting scenes of Lupine history— battles, celebrations, and moments of unity.

As much of a marvel it was, it felt inadequate amidst the grandeur of history I didn't belong to.

Shaking off the thought, I made my way to the exit, and then to the main entrance of the Elderwood. As I stepped through, the world outside greeted me with a rush of fresh air.

As I took the corner, the bridges came into view. I stepped on the first one, and the plank creaked softly under my weight.

As I ascended, I took a look over the edge of the bridge. The forest floor was a patchwork of shadows and faint glimmers. I looked up, watching the towering canopy that to stretched endlessly.

With a sigh, I continued walking.

Eventually, I reached the High Perch. I paused at the entrance of my home, glancing back at the network of bridges behind me.

With another deep breath, I stepped inside. But as soon as the door close behind me, a wave came crashing down on me all at once. Almost immediately, my throat felt dry, and though I tried to swallow, no spit came.

My chest tightened, and I couldn't seem to draw in enough air. Each breath started coming quicker than the last, but they were shallow and frantic.

My hand instinctively shot to my chest as stumbled into the main area, knocking over a chair as I reached for it.

I doubled over, clutching at the fabric of my tunic as I

begged my lungs to calm, but nothing helped. The edges of my vision blurred, and a faint ringing crept into my ears.

Each breath felt harder to take, as if the air were thinning. And soon after, my vision blurred.

The last thing I remember was the sound of my heart pounding relentlessly, a drumbeat of worry that refused to be ignored.

CHAPTER 11

I rose abruptly, dazed and confused. My body was still aching from where I lay sprawled on the wooden floor. Looking around, I tried to make sense of my surroundings.

It took me a moment to remember that I was in the main area of my quarters, the overturned chair beside me bringing back to memory the panic.

I groaned as I pushed myself up from the floor, using the wall beside me to maintain balance. My head felt heavy, like I'd been underwater too long, and my chest still hurt from the thumping of my heart.

I looked toward the small circular window across the room. The light from the sun coming through had dimmed immensely. It was clear some time had passed, though I couldn't say how much.

I rubbed my eyes, my thoughts still a hazy swirl, and leaned back against the wall. The only sound that I could hear now was my own uneven breathing as I tried to piece together the fragments of my memory.

Suddenly, a knock banged at the front door.

I flinched at the sound as my eyes darted to the door.

"Oh, Drifted. Do open up the door!" Sabrina's voice rang from the other side.

A groan slipped from my lips as I let my head fall back against the wall. Of course, she'd be here. Just when I needed a minute to collect myself.

Pushing myself off the wall, I stumbled slightly as I made way toward the door. "Alright, alright," I muttered under my breath.

I shuffled over, irritation simmering enough to overpower the lingering daze in my mind. Reaching the door, I hesitated for a moment, then opened it.

I stepped back in surprise at what I saw.

Standing in the doorway was a large man, his broad frame filling the entrance and casting a shadow into the room.

He was tall, clad in the usual Lupine attire—thick, dark leather with intricate patterns woven throughout. His high boots were scuffed, and a long-hooded cloak was draped over his shoulders, its edges frayed as though it had seen many journeys.

On his face he bore the tattoos the Lupine in Lostsummit did. A series of three lines was etched across his forehead, bold and blue, right above his eyes. They gave him a stern, almost menacing appearance, and the way his gaze bore into me gave me goosebumps.

I straightened instinctively, trying to make myself appear larger. "Can I help you?" I asked, my voice betraying my attempts to seem intimidating.

Suddenly, Sabrina pushed her way through the large Lupine's frame, squeezing herself into the room. She brushed past him with exaggerated effort, smoothing out her clothes as she stepped inside.

"I hope that you enjoyed your break, yes, Drifted?" Sabrina asked me, tilting her head.

"Yeah... I mean, sure?" I replied, still staring at the large Lupine. "But what's going on here? Who is this?"

Sabrina clapped her hands together as if she'd been waiting for the question. "Ah, yes! Let me introduce you." She took a step near the towering Lupine and slapped a hand on his arm. "This big oaf is Lood. He is the one in charge of training you."

Lood grunted—a loud and guttural sound. Even though it

wasn't directed at me, I recoiled.

Sabrina leaned toward me to whisper in my ear. "Do not mind him. He seems like quite the serious one, but he is a giant softy."

I glanced at Lood, who was now looking at Sabrina with an intense, almost angry look.

Softy, yeah right. I thought.

"He looks like he's debating whether he wants to bury me." I replied to Sabrina with a mutter.

Sabrina laughed, throwing her head back. "Oh, Drifted. If that were his intent, you would know, and it would be swift. Lood does not waste time on the inconsequential."

"Inconsequential...?" I echoed, narrowing my eyes before realizing she was speaking about me. "Hey, what the he—"

Sabrina cut me off. "Anyway," she said, redirecting the conversation. "You should feel honored. Lood is quite selective of his responsibilities. He trains only those he believes worthy... or, of course, those the prince consort demands of him." She said the last part quickly, as if not wanting me to hear it.

Lood stayed silent as his eyes flicked to me.

I raised my hand slowly, waving it at him. "Hello, Lood. It's nice to meet you."

He didn't reply, his body almost as still as a statue. Then he let out a low grunt—a sound that wasn't quite a word but felt like some sort of acknowledgment.

I blinked, unsure of how to respond. "Uh, alright then."

"Hurry now, Drifted, there is much to do and you are already late to training!" Sabrina said as she took my hand, leading me towards the door.

As we neared, Lood shifted his body, allowing only the tightest gap to squeeze by him.

"You have kept Lood waiting far too long," Sabrina said,

practically dragging me along. "If it were not for me, he would have torn your door down."

I glanced back at Lood, who still hadn't uttered a word to me, as he followed, lumbering behind us. His gaze was fixed on us, and I couldn't tell if he was annoyed or just naturally intimidating.

"Uh, thanks for not letting that happen, I guess," I muttered, taking my hand back from Sabrina. I wasn't entirely sure about how much of her comment was a joke, but looking at Lood, I was inclined to take her seriously.

The bridges creaked faintly—loudly for Lood—as we descended back toward the Elderwood. There was a mist in the air that hung thickly, swirling gently around our feet.

"Hurry now," Sabrina said as she gestured toward a fork in the bridge ahead, leading us toward a different path than the one I was used to. This path curved away from the front of the Elderwood and wound down toward the back. Behind us, Lood's heavy steps thudded rhythmically, and for some reason that kept my nerves on edge.

"Where are we going?" I asked Sabrina, trying to look down the path. The bridge twisted sharply, covered by thick branches and large leaves, so I couldn't see much.

Sabrina glanced over her shoulder at me, her expression unreadable but composed. "You shall see soon enough, Drifted," she breathed, offering no further explanation.

I frowned but didn't press further, knowing it would get me nowhere with her. The path beneath our feet changed, the wood narrowed and curved downward in spirals that seemed to grow more intricate the farther we went. Vines from the surrounding trees and branches wove through the railings of the bridge, their dark green tendrils wrapping around the structure as if anchoring it to the forest itself.

Sabrina slowed her pace as we reached behind the

Elderwood. Peering ahead, I could now see that the bridge we were on led to a platform and opening.

"Not too much further now," Sabrina finally said. As she led us towards the opening.

The opening was a gaping archway with smooth rounded edges that made it seem like the tree had willingly opened itself to create the passage. Hanging in front of the opening were thick vines, obscuring the inside.

Sabrina stopped right before the entrance, gesturing with a sweep of her hand. "Here we are!"

I stepped closer, trying to peer into the archway. But Sabrina stepped in front of me, holding out her arms.

"Ah, ah, ah, Drifted," she said, wagging a finger in my face. "We must wait for His Highness and Lady Celine before entering."

I frowned, taking another step closer toward her. "I see. So, Sabrina, answer me this."

"Yes, Drifted?" she replied, tilting her head slightly as she looked up at me.

Before she could blink, I reached and grabbed one of the furry ears atop her head, holding it open by pulling it up. Then, with no warning, I yelled into it. "Then why did you rush me down here just to sit around?!"

Sabrina recoiled, shaking her head as her eyes widened in surprise. "Drifted!" she exclaimed, stepping back and swatting my hand away. Her ears twitched wildly as she straightened her cloak. "Such conduct is unbecoming!"

I crossed my arms, staring at her. "And dragging me all the way down here isn't?"

Sabrina sighed, shaking her head again, though I could see the smirk grow on her face. "It would be distasteful for Prince Rowen to get here before us. Do you know nothing about etiquette?"

Behind us, Lood let out a series of low grunts, though whether it was annoyance or amusement, I couldn't tell.

Sabrina stomped a foot on the floor as she turned her head quickly toward him. "Do not laugh at this, Lood. We do not condone such actions."

Lood remained silent, though the quiet rumble of another grunt betrayed him.

Before I could comment, Sabrina's gaze shifted past me, and her expression softened as she clasped her hands together. "Ah," she said, her tone formal, "they have arrived."

I turned to follow her gaze and saw Celine and Rowen descending the bridge toward us. Celine walked with her usual grace, her unmistakable orange-brown hair blowing gently in the wind. Beside her, Rowen moved leisurely.

As they got closer, I felt my shoulder tense slightly. Whatever this training was, I could tell the time for delays had officially ended.

"Your Highness, My Lady," Sabrina said as she and Lood bent over into bows.

Awkwardly, I did the same. Though I was a touch too late on the delivery.

"Drifted, are you well?" Celine asked, standing next to me as I came up from my bow.

"Huh? Yeah, I'm alright, Celine," I replied to her, tilting my head in confusion. "Why?"

"Not now, but earlier," she said, her expression portraying much concern.

I was caught off guard, her gaze felt piercing, as if she could see right through me. I felt a bit of unease, wondering if she actually could have known about the panic I had in my room earlier. The one that left me crumpled on the floor. Impossible, I thought to myself, waving away the thought. There was no way she could have known.

"Yeah, I'm okay. Trust me," I answered. I was fine, and I didn't want Celine to worry about me over something so trivial. Whatever she suspected, I wasn't ready to explain it, not yet.

Celine's attention lingered on me for a moment longer, and though her expression remained calm, there was something in her eyes that made me shift uneasily. Then, she nodded and turned her attention back towards Rowen. "Very well," she whispered.

"Celine, Isaac," Rowen started, twisting his beard and standing in front of the archway. "What the two of you are about to experience will not only be a test of skill—it will be a test of will, of heart, and of your capacity to endure."

I shifted my weight as I looked toward Celine, who was staring at Rowen intensely. It was obvious she was far more prepared than I was for whatever was about to come.

Rowen's eyes swept over both of us, his expression calm but firm. "Before we proceed, I ask you both—are you ready?"

I hesitated, feeling the heaviness on my shoulders. Ready? How could I be ready for something that hadn't been fully explained? I glanced at Celine again, who gave the faintest nod. "Yes, father." She replied.

I swallowed hard, knowing I had to follow suit. "Yes, Your Highness," I said.

Rowen tipped his head, seemingly satisfied with our responses. "Very well," he said, turning toward the archway. "Then, let's not waste any more time," Rowen finished as he moved the vines and disappeared behind them.

Celine glanced at me once more, and then followed.

Sabrina walked forward and then turned back to me with a smirk. "Do try not to trip over your own feet, Drifted," she said as she too walked into the archway, leaving me behind with Lood.

I stood there for a moment, staring at opening. My feet felt rooted to the spot as I tried to prepare myself to enter. Before I could muster a step forward, I felt the ground move from beneath me.

"What the—?" I blurted out, looking down to see my legs dangling helplessly. A low grunt rumbled behind me, and I twisted my head to see Lood's massive hand gripping me firmly by the back of my tunic. Without a word, he carried me toward the archway like I weighed nothing.

"Hey! Put me down!" I squirmed, kicking my legs. "I can walk by myself, you know!"

Lood didn't respond, nor did he even flinch at my struggling.

"This is ridiculous," I muttered, trying to pry his hands from my tunic. "Lood. I can—"

My words cut off as we passed through the vines, the bright glow of the chamber suddenly enveloping us. Lood finally released me, dropping me to my feet. I stumbled slightly, brushing myself off and shooting him an annoyed glare. "Thanks for that." I muttered.

He didn't respond and kept his eyes fixed forward. I turned to take in the area and was immediately stunned.

The chamber was vast, a large circular expanse of polished wood that stretched out. The walls curved upward into massive, arching beams that interlocked above, forming a dome-like canopy of branches and vines.

Around the edges of the arena were rows of what looked like natural wooden benches, rising in tiers that encircled the space. The entire space felt deliberately crafted to hold an audience—like we'd stepped into some kind of worn colosseum.

"This... is where we are training?" I asked under my breath.

Behind me, Lood let out another low grunt. Possibly in agreement. Ahead, Celine and Sabrina stood near Rowen, their figures dwarfed by the sheer size of the space. Whatever this place was, it was clear it was more than just for training.

"Step forward," Rowen said, his tone as commanding. "This place has served as a proving ground for generations of Lupine warriors. Many of Sylphreach's finest have honed their abilities here, tested under the guidance of those tasked with shaping them into something more."

As we approached, I couldn't help but glance at Lood, who remained silent. His eyes were immensely dark, and the added tattoos on his face didn't help soften his appearance any. I shuddered slightly.

"Your instructor," Rowen continued, nodding toward the towering figure, "is Lood. He will push you to your limits, and then further still. His methods are harsh, but necessary. If you wish to endure what lies ahead, you will listen to him without question."

Lood stepped next to Rowen and crossed his arms. He kept his expression stern as he looked down at Celine and me.

"Lood does not train the weak," Rowen continued. "If you are here, it is because you have potential. But potential alone is useless if you lack the will to forge it into something greater."

I looked toward Celine, who stood tall and calm. I straightened my back, trying to mirror her confidence, but I wasn't sure I had succeeded.

"You shall follow Lood's instruction to the T," Rowen continued. "You will not complain. You will not falter."

I gulped as Rowen spoke. Why was he so good at making everything sound so life-altering?

Sabrina, standing off to the side, tilted her head, looking at me. "Do not look so sour, Drifted," she said giggling. "If you survive—and that is a large if—you shall thank Lood later."

I ignored her as Rowen stepped closer. "The two of you will begin with a preliminary of some sort," Rowen continued. "Lood will observe you engage in a sparring match. This will allow him to gauge your capabilities and determine a training regimen best suited for you."

My stomach churned slightly. Sure, I used to spar with my father when he was teaching me the sword. But that was against someone I was comfortable with.

"Who will we be sparring against, father?" Celine asked Rowen.

Before he could answer, Sabrina stepped forward, rolled her shoulders back and pointed an index finger on each hand at herself. "Who better to test you two than I?" she said with a faint smirk.

Oh moon, please, anyone but her. I thought, already dreading the inevitable.

Rowen nodded once. "Yes, you two will be sparring against Sabrina. Do not let her carefree demeanor fool you. Sabrina is one of the most capable Lupine I know. Do not underestimate her."

"Hear that, Lood?!" Sabrina yelled, jumping up and down. "His Highness referred to me as 'capable'. Far better than any praise you have ever received." She stuck her tongue out at him.

Lood shot her a dirty look and let out a rumbling grunt. The sound was enough to make me uneasy, but Sabrina looked entirely unbothered, if not amused.

"Isaac will spar with Sabrina first," Rowen said, making his way toward the side of the ring.

"Wait.... me first?" I stammered, getting nervous by the second. I turned to Rowen, trying to keep the fear out of my voice. "And what am I supposed to fight her with?"

Rowen paused, glancing back at me. "Yes, I suppose you are right."

He moved toward a wooden barrel near the edge of the arena. Digging into it, he pulled out a wooden shield and sword.

With a casual toss, he sent the shield spinning through the air toward me. "Catch," he said.

I fumbled for a moment but grabbed it before it hit the ground. The sword came next, less dramatically this time, landing in my hands.

"Great," I muttered under my breath, looking at the makeshift gear. "This'll definitely keep me from getting embarrassed."

I looked at Sabrina, who was still empty-handed. "What about your gear?" I questioned her.

"Oh, do not worry about me, Drifted," she gave me a glare and flashed a fang-ridden smile. "I will not require them."

Her confidence sent a shiver down my spine, but I shook my head, trying to dispel any doubts. "Of course not," I muttered, half to myself. Clearly, she intended to make this as humiliating as possible.

Lood and Celine made their way toward Rowen, who was now standing on the sidelines.

After a short while, Rowen nodded toward me. "Take your stance, Isaac. Show us what you're capable of."

Not much, I thought.

I swallowed hard and adjusted the shield on my arm and gripped the sword tightly. My palms were already sweating. Sabrina's red eyes gleamed with excitement, and I couldn't help but feel like prey standing in front of her.

"Do not worry, Drifted," she said, her tone obviously teasing. "I shall try not to break you too quickly."

Well, here goes nothing.

I took a deep breath, trying to force my mind to focus, as I raised the shield and sword. My stance felt awkward, but it was the best I could muster under pressure. Across the arena, Sabrina bounced on her toes, preparing herself for the match.

Rowen took a step forward and lifted his hand. The chamber grew quiet with the faint hum of crickets chirping the only sound to fill the air. My heart pounded as I waited, every second stretching into what felt like an eternity.

Then, with a swift motion, Rowen dropped his hand. "Begin," he said.

Before I could even process the command, Sabrina was already moving. She lunged forward, closing the distance between us with alarming speed. I barely raised my shield in time to block her strike, the force of it reverberating up my arm. The impact left me stunned for a split second, long enough for her to shift her weight and swing again.

Her next punch came equally as quick, aimed at my shield. The blow was forceful, more than I'd expected, and I stumbled back, struggling to keep my footing.

"What is the matter, Drifted?" Sabrina said as she rushed me again. "Do not tell me that the shield is too heavy for you."

Another punch slammed into the shield, followed by another, each one faster than the last. My arm was already beginning to ache from the repeated hits, and I could feel myself being pushed further and further back.

"Come now," she continued, her voice maddeningly annoying. "Surely the great Drifted can manage more than cowering behind a plank of wood."

I gritted my teeth, trying to counter with a swing of my sword, but she darted to the side with a smirk, easily avoiding the slash. "Oh, that was adorable," she said, laughing softly. "But you shall have to do better than that."

Another punch slammed into the shield, and I nearly lost my grip. The force behind her strikes was surprisingly strong, and her speed made it impossible to predict where the next one would come from. I barely had time to tense before she was on me again.

"Do you plan to fight back at all, or shall we call this a victory for me already?" Sabrina taunted, her fanged grin flashing as she delivered another series of blows.

I stumbled back again, sweating profusely as I tried to control myself. Every move I made felt one step behind hers, and her teasing only added to the frustration mounting inside me. This wasn't a fight—it was a game to her, and I was the piece she was toying with.

Suddenly, Sabrina's fingers close around the edge of my shield. I panicked as I tried to pull it free, but her grip was like iron.

"What shall happen if we lose this plank? Hmm?" she said smoothly.

She flipped into the air with such elegance that left me stunned. The shield tore free from my grasp, and for a second, I lost sight of her as she soared over me.

The next thing I knew was the shield hurtling back at me. Right as I looked up, it slammed into my head with a thud. I stumbled backward, clutching my temple as pain spread throughout my skull.

I blinked, trying to clear the dizziness, and gritted my teeth. This was infuriating. And I knew she wasn't even trying yet.

As I rubbed my head, Sabrina was already moving again, barely giving me a moment to recover. I saw her move out of the corner of my eye and instinctively I raised my sword, hoping to deflect whatever was coming.

It didn't matter.

With a swipe, Sabrina's clawed hand struck the edge of the

wood, sending it flying from my grasp. Then, before I could even tense my body, she drove an open palm into my stomach.

"I do hope you did not have too large of a meal before this spat, Drifted," she said, walking circles around me.

"Just shut up already...." I groaned under my breath, still clutching my stomach.

"Apologies," Sabrina replied, leaning in close to my face to hear me better, "what was that you said?"

My head came up, eyes a mere inches away from mine. "I said shut up already!" I yelled, using the moment to lunge forward.

Before she could react, I grabbed her shoulders and drove my forehead into hers with as much force as I could muster. The impact sent a hot jolt of pain through my skull, but it was worth it. Sabrina staggered back, her smirk dropping for the first time. As she reached up and rubbed her forehead.

"Talk about using your head," she said with a frown. "Turns out you do have some fight in you after all."

My chest heaved as I straightened, gripping my sword tightly. "Yeah," I said, my voice firm despite the ache in my head. "I do."

Sabrina's grin returned as she righted herself. "Good," she replied, her tone dropping to something more serious. "Let us see how long you can keep it up. I intend to make you pay for that strike!"

She darted forward again; this time she was even quicker than before.

I raised my arms to block, but she anticipated it quickly, stepping to my unguarded side.

"Faster, Drifted!" she taunted as she slammed her boot into the side of my ribs.

I went sprawling across the wooden floor, skidding to a

stop. I clutched at my ribs as I struggled to regain my breath.

"Come on now," Sabrina said, already next to me, grabbing me by my tunic. "You were so bold a moment ago. Where is that flame now, Drifted?"

I didn't have a chance to answer before she delivered a blow to my cheek, sending sparks flying between my eyes. Pain exploded across my face, and my head snapped to the side.

Before I knew it, she was on top of me, straddling my chest, her knees pinning my arms down. She grabbed my tunic and connected another fist with my cheek again, and then again.

Each hit sent a fresh wave of pain throughout my skull, and my vision clouded. I tried to twist free, but her claws were embedded deep within the fabric of my clothing.

"What shall your next move be, Drifted?" she said, her voice tinged with some sort of cruel amusement. "Surely your plan was not getting struck the entire time?"

I grit my teeth, barely managing to turn my face away from the next hit, though it still glanced off my jaw. My mind raced, trying to find an opening, any chance to stop her, but she was too fast, too strong, and I was pinned with no way out.

Sabrina's smirk widened as she reeled back another punch, her red eyes glowing. "This should burn that light in your eyes," she said, her tone dripping with mockery.

And then, her fist began its descent.

CHAPTER 12

I slowly opened my eyes.

I was braced for the sting of Sabrina's fist. But, surprisingly, it didn't come.

Instead, I was greeted with the sight of Sabrina still on top of me. Though someone had stopped her assault, catching her wrist in their hands. It was Celine.

"I do think that is quite enough, do you not agree, Sabrina?" Celine asked her. Her voice was calm, but there was definitely a hint of authority to it.

Sabrina turned her head slowly, and for a moment, the room felt impossibly still. Then, with a smile, she relaxed her arm.

"Aye, Lady Celine," she started. "I do suppose that is enough training for Drifted."

"Indeed, it is," Celine replied, releasing Sabrina. "Now, kindly remove yourself from him."

Sabrina grinned, leaning back as she propped herself on her knees. "As you wish, Lady Celine," she said, rising to her feet with an exaggerated flourish.

I groaned as I tried to sit upright, my ribs and face throbbing with pain. Celine offered me her hand, and I hesitated before taking it.

"Are you well, Drifted?" she asked, helping me on my feet.

"I've been better," I muttered, wincing as I straightened up. "But I had her handled, Celine."

She gave a look that suggested otherwise, but said nothing else.

Sabrina, standing a few steps away, stretched her arms lazily, a smile growing on her face. "You looked to be on the brink of collapse, Drifted," she said, her words being anything but gentle. "Were you not, perhaps, planning to fight back? It is quite fortunate I spared you."

I shot her a look, my pride feeling more hurt than my ribs. "I'd never give up to you, even if it killed me," I muttered, though I wasn't sure how true that was.

Sabrina tilted her head slightly. "Ah, such bold words for one so thoroughly bested. But take heart, Drifted. I find your resilience almost charming."

I scrunched the corner of my lip and forced my eyes away from her. Instead, I turned my attention to Rowen and Lood. Their looks were unreadable, and I couldn't decipher whether they were judging me or not.

Before I had enough time to dwell on my shortcomings, Rowen's voice cut through the air. "That will suffice for now," he said. "Isaac, Step aside, for we shall now proceed with Celine and Sabrina."

I nodded and made my way towards the edge Rowen and Lood were standing at. Though not before Sabrina took another dig at me.

"Very well, Your Highness," she began. "Though I do wonder if Lady Celine will fare better than our dear Drifted."

I turned around to counter, but Celine stepped forward, as if unbothered by Sabrina's taunts.

"You may find that I am full of surprises, Sabrina," she said calmly. "Shall we begin?"

Rowen nodded, gesturing toward the center of the arena. "Take your places," he instructed. "Lood shall observe once more, and this will conclude the preliminaries."

Sabrina strutted to her position and turned on her heel dramatically to face Celine. "Come then, Lady Celine, let us see what surprises you bring," she said, giving Celine a bow.

Celine stayed silent, getting into a moderate stance, one hand in front of her with an open palm and the other planted at her waist.

I stood on the sidelines, clutching my sore ribs while anticipation grew as the two faced off. The air between them crackled with energy as they stared at each other. Sabrina's smirk was playful, but there was an edge of challenge in it, while Celine's focused face hinted at a level of skill that made me uneasy for Sabrina, of all people.

Rowen took a step towards the ring and lifted his hand in the air once again. Then, without a word, he dropped it.

Sabrina moved first, her speed incredible as she darted forward, closing the gap between her and Celine.

Celine, however, remained still. Focused as she waited for Sabrina to close in.

Sabrina threw the first strike. It was a swift, open palm aimed directly at Celine's jaw. Her movements were smooth as she twisted her body to put enough momentum behind the blow.

But Celine reacted just as quickly, raising a hand to deflect Sabrina's. The entire movement looked effortless when compared to me blocking with a shield.

The smirk on Sabrina's face widened as she spun on her heels, using the momentum from the deflection to swing her leg in an arc toward Celine's head. The speed of the kick made my chest tighten—I barely had time to process it before it was already in motion.

Celine ducked, and the kick whizzed over her head, missing by mere inches. She immediately shifted her weight and propelled herself to the side, getting out of harm's way.

But Sabrina was quicker, and she stopped herself mid spin and raised her leg in the air. Then, without hesitation, she slammed it down toward Celine like a guillotine

Celine quickly raised both arms in a cross above her head, blocking Sabrina's attack. The impact shot through the arena, the sound like pieces of wood colliding.

Smoothly, Celine turned her wrist, maneuvering her hands to grab hold of Sabrina's ankle. Then she pushed upward, trying to throw Sabrina to the ground.

But Sabrina reacted instantly. Twisting her body to catch herself with both hands on the ground, her palms slamming against the wooden floor. Using the momentum, she kicked her free leg upward, aiming it at Celine's face.

Celine released Sabrina's ankle, throwing her head back in time to dodge the incoming strike. The air from the kick was audible as she stepped back to reset her stance.

I couldn't help but feel inadequate at the intensity and finesse they were fighting at. And to top it all off, they were both unarmed—no swords, no shields.

"Man... imagined if they had weapons," I muttered under my breath.

Rowen cleared his throat and then spoke. "That wouldn't be possible. Well... Not for Sabrina, at least."

I tilted my head at him. "What do you mean?"

He turned to face me fully, his hands clasped behind his back. "The Lupine are a naturally skilled race," he began. "Many of them are born with an innate talent for hand-to-hand combat, a gift they cultivate from a young age."

He glanced at Celine and Sabrina, who were again circling each other. "However, that talent is limited to what you see before you. They lack the same aptitude for wielding weapons, swords, axes, even bows—it does not come naturally to them. No matter how much effort they put into learning the skill, the results are... lackluster, at best."

"But wouldn't adding weapons make them even that much

LUPINE

stronger?" I questioned.

Rowen shook his head. "It's not that simple, Isaac. The Lupine rely on their reflexes to fight. Their hands are their weapons. Their strength, speed, and precision are extensions of their very being. Introducing tools separates them from that connection, dulling what makes them effective. It is simply not in their nature."

He paused. "Now, with Celine being half Lupine. She may possess the ability to wield weapons, but she will never fully feel proficient handling one."

Geez, the Lupine truly are on another level. I thought to myself.

"The most you will see a Lupine carry is a dagger, and even that is mainly kept for show." Rowen finished.

I looked back at Celine and Sabrina, pondering his words. Rowen was right—there was a rawness to their combat that no weapon could replicate. Watching them was almost like watching art, and admittedly, it was humbling to witness.

Sabrina, who was strutting circles around Celine with a playful smile, suddenly stopped and reached for the clasp of her cloak. She unfastened it, and let the garment slide from her shoulder, dropping to the ground before she stepped away from it.

"Shall we make this a bit more interesting, Lady Celine?" Sabrina asked, her classic mischievous tone seeping through. "I believe it is time we cast aside the pleasantries and test our true limits."

Celine stayed silent, crouching down into a lower stance.

Sabrina looked to Rowen, her smile growing even wider as she bounced with excitement. "Shall we, Your Highness?" she asked.

Rowen nodded in approval. Though of what, I couldn't begin to decipher.

"Oh, goodie!" Sabrina yelled, clapping her hands. "Do not

hold back, Lady Celine. I certainly shall not."

Suddenly, Sabrina straightened, the playful look in her eyes disappearing. Then, without warning, her body began to shift. The transformation was fluid, almost seamless, and yet utterly mesmerizing.

Her arms and legs shortened, taking on a beast-like structure as her fingers and toes tapered into sharp claws that reflected the light of the arena. Fur rippled across her skin, a deep dark black that matched the color of her once braided hair. Her face elongated, her nose and mouth melding into a long wolf's muzzle as her ears grew more pointed atop her head.

Her hands and feet disappeared entirely, replaced by powerful, clawed paws. Her entire frame reshaped itself seamlessly into that of a wolf—elegant yet intimidating. A long tail swished behind her, and her glowing red eyes felt even more intense, now gleaming with feral intelligence.

The whole process was almost instantaneous, but time felt like it slowed as I watched. She now stood as a full-fledged wolf, her body low and taut with energy as she took a step forward toward Celine.

Sabrina let out a low growl that somehow still had the same teasing cadence as her voice did in human form. Something that I could only imagine meant that they could once resume their sparring.

Celine let out a deep breath as she prepared herself. Her open palms and composed posture were gone now, replaced by a defensive stance that showed her understanding of what was to come. She was ready, but even I could see the subtle change in her demeanor. She knew that this would be a whole new level of challenge.

Without warning, Sabrina launched herself forward. Her movements were a blur, her speed even more astonishing in this form. Almost quicker than I could blink, she was upon Celine, snapping and lunging with great ferocity.

Celine managed to sidestep, but Sabrina landed on the floor and her body sprung up again almost immediately. Celine barely had time to react, shifting backward with a series of quick, fluid jumps as she dodged.

Even though Celine was quick, she was barely keeping ahead of Sabrina's pursuit. There was no room for Celine to counter, only desperately try to keep moving. But even I knew that it wouldn't last long.

Then it happened—a single misstep. As Celine took another jump backward to avoid a lunge, her ankle rolled slightly. It wasn't much, but enough to disrupt her balance. She lost her footing for the briefest moment, and Sabrina saw the opportunity.

With a growl, Sabrina lunged forward, a black streak as she drove her head into Celine's midsection. The impact was loud, sending Celine flying backward. She hit the floor hard, rolling several times before coming to a stop near the edge of the arena.

I winced as I watched her try to push herself up, a hand clutching her side. The look of determination burned in her eyes, but there was no use—she took the full brunt of the blow.

Celine attempted to stand again but immediately fell to one knee.

Sabrina moved on top of her, standing tall and imposing. Lowering her head, she let out a low growl.

The message was clear. The match was over.

Rowen stepped forward. "That is enough, Sabrina."

Sabrina's growl softened and then, with a flick of her tail, she stepped back, giving Celine enough space to get up.

Celine pushed up slowly, her hand still pressed against her

side, though she did her best to hide any pain. There was no anger or frustration coming from her, only an acceptance of her defeat. I couldn't help but marvel at her resilience. Even though she hid it well, it must've been hard for her to take the loss.

Rowen stepped further into the arena as he gestured for us to gather around him. "That is enough sparring for now. The preliminaries have concluded."

Sabrina walked over to her cloak that was on the ground and grabbed it in her mouth before walking her way towards Rowen, sitting down with her tail wagging against the floor.

Celine walked over to join us slowly, still clutching at her side.

"Lood has observed enough," Rowen continued, looking over all of us. "He has gathered all the information he requires to proceed."

I looked at Lood, who still stood silently. Though even he didn't say much, his eyes appeared to take in everything. It made me shiver at the thought of what information he could possibly have gathered from watching us.

"Your performances have been sufficient," Rowen added. "From here, Lood will push you beyond your limits. Be prepared."

Sabrina placed her cloak on the ground and wrestled her wolf body into it, placing her muzzle and head through the hood. Then, she let out a soft huff, and her form began to shift back to its humanoid shape under the cloak. "Well, that was invigorating," she said as she stretched her arms above her head.

Easy for you to say, I thought to myself, a frown on my face. My stomach felt queasy with the anxiousness of what was to come. If this was only the beginning, I wasn't sure if I'd survive.

Rowen looked towards the exit of the arena, and then back towards us. "All of you, it is late. Return to your quarters. Tomorrow will be the first real day of training."

With that, Rowen turned and made his way toward the exit.

Lood looked over Celine and me and made a low grunt as he turned to make his way out of the arena. For someone of such few words, I found myself thinking of how big of a personality he had.

Sabrina approached Celine and gave her a low bow. "My dearest Lady Celine, I do apologize if I was too forward in our sparring session," she said, surprisingly dropping her usual sarcastic tone. "It was only the wish of His Highness that I pushed you to such an extent, I would not have thought to do so otherwise."

Celine gave Sabrina a nod, a tiny smile growing at the corners of her lips. "No, Sabrina. You did only what was necessary for the sake of analysis. I hold you no ill feelings."

Celine's consistent attitude was something that I could only dream of having. Even more surprising was Sabrina's sudden shift in demeanor. I hadn't seen her speak with such respect to anyone like this, except for Rowen.

Sabrina turned to me, and her usual sly smile quickly plastered her face again.

"Only if I could say the same for you, Drifted," she started, now getting in my face. "My only regret is that I did not get the opportunity to push you harder."

I moved my face away from hers, taking a large step back. "If you went any harder, I'm not sure I'd still be standing here." I replied.

Sabrina let out a laugh before turning around and facing the exit. "Aye, I do suppose you are correct." She walked toward the exit and took a look over her shoulder.

"Nevertheless, I will be seeing you tomorrow, Drifted" She flashed a fang as she made her way through the vines.

I let out a low sigh, only now realizing how much being around her put me on edge sometimes.

"Shall we depart, Drifted?" Celine suddenly spoke up.

I straightened my body too quickly, and the pain in my ribs flared up, causing me to wince. "Yeah... Sure, let's leave."

We made our way towards the opening and passed through the vines. I was surprised to see how dark it had already gotten.

Celine and I made our way back up the spiraled bridge in silence, both of us walking slightly awkwardly because of our injuries.

When we got to the top, I realized it was time for us to split up. But something dawned on me—I still didn't know where Celine's quarters were.

"Hey, Celine," I started. "Where have you been staying this whole time?"

Celine looked towards the main entrance of the Elderwood.

"My sleeping arrangements are not too far from Rowen's," she replied. "You have not seen it yet?"

"No, I haven't. It's not a big deal. I just realized I didn't know where you disappeared to every night."

I stretched, trying to work the pain out of my ribs.

"Well, see you tomorrow!" I said, giving her a smile before turning toward the bridge that led up to the High Perch

She looked up at me, hesitating for a moment, as if weighing her words.

"Drifted, it is important that you know where my quarters are... in the case something were to happen."

I paused, stammering as I was unsure how to answer. "S-s-something like what?"

Celine's gaze softened as she straightened herself slightly. "It will do us both well if we are prepared for anything possible," she said calmly. 'Should there be a time when we are separated, or if something unforeseen occurs, I would rather you know where to find me than risk wasting precious time."

Her reasoning made sense, but something in Celine's words stuck out to me. She appeared calm enough, but there was a hint of something else there that I couldn't place my finger on—anxiousness?

"O-okay," I managed, nodding slowly. "Lead the way, then."

Celine gave me a small nod, letting go of my hand as she turned toward the main entrance of the Elderwood. I thanked the moon under my breath as I followed her, grateful that she wouldn't notice how clammy my hands were getting.

The walk was quiet, the only sounds coming from the faint rustling of leaves and the gentle creak of the wooden steps beneath our feet. We started up the main staircase—the same one that led to the dining area. This area was normally busy, but tonight, the atmosphere felt different—more quiet.

However, unlike that morning, we didn't stop where the staircase forked toward the dining hall. Instead, Celine continued upward, leading me to a higher level that I hadn't explored before.

The steps narrowed slightly, curving inward as they wound closer to the top of the massive tree. Through small openings in the walls, I could catch glimpses of the outside—glowing moonlight filtering through the dense canopy of branches, illuminating the spiraling bridges below. It was breathtaking in its own quiet way, but I didn't have time to admire it fully.

Celine moved with graceful steps despite the pain she must've been feeling from her injuries. I tried to mimic her, but my ribs screamed with every move.

Finally, we reached a small landing near the top of the Elderwood's interior. A wooden door, framed by curling vines and faintly glowing moss, greeted us.

"This is where I reside," she said whispered, turning to face me. Again, that subtle tinge of anxiousness I noticed earlier slipped through her voice. "Should you ever need to find me, now know the way."

I took a moment to memorize the path we had taken, glancing back down the spiraling staircase that now appeared so far below. "Got it," I said, nodding. "Thanks for showing me."

I turned to leave, but mid-step, Celine grabbed my arm, sending a fresh wave of pain through my ribs, and I winced despite my best attempts to hide it.

Her eyes squinted as she let go of my arm, her eyes reflecting her worry. "You are hurt from earlier." She said, her tone now firmer. "Come, I shall tend to your wounds."

"What? No, no, I'm fine." I stammered, feeling my face heat up as her words caught me completely off guard. "It's nothing, really. Just a little sore, that's all." I tried to laugh it off, but each breath of air made my ribs sting more.

Celine tilted her head. "Drifted," she said. "Your discomfort is evident. There is no need to feign strength before me."

My face grew even hotter, and I instinctively stepped back, holding my hands up. "I—I mean, it's not that bad. I can manage. You really don't have to—"

She stepped in closer, cutting off my rambling with a raised hand. "Enough," she said. "Come with me."

She gently took hold of my arm, carefully this time, and guided me through the door into her quarters.

As we stepped inside, I paused, my eyes widening at the

sight before me. The room was magnificent; far greater than I could've imagined, fitting perfectly for someone of her royal title.

The walls of her living quarters were smooth, seamless with the natural grain of wood. Vines adorned with small, glowing flowers climbed the walls and covered the area with an ethereal glow. The ceiling shot up high above, resembling the canopy of a tree, with carvings of stars and the different phases of the moon.

As we moved into the next room, a circular bed sat draped with silk fabrics in shades of deep blue and silver. It rested on a platform of polished wood that rose organically from the floor, its edges also covered in carvings of wolves and trees.

I looked around in complete awe. "Woah... this is where you've been staying?" I asked, trying to keep my voice low.

"Yes," she replied softly.

Celine guided me to a small seating area that was arranged near a large window that had a breathtaking view of the moonlit forest below.

"Wait here, Drifted," she said. "I shall tend to your wounds."

I hesitated before taking a seat. "This really isn't necessary." But I knew arguing would be pointless.

Celine didn't respond. She turned and left the room, disappearing behind another door, leaving me alone with my thoughts.

Calm down, Isaac. I told myself, trying to control my breathing.

But for some reason, I couldn't shake my nervousness. It didn't make sense—it wasn't like this was the first time we'd been alone together. Hell, we'd spent a lot of time on the run from Lostsummit together.

Yet somehow, this felt different. Maybe it was because the

circumstances had changed. When we were running for our lives, there wasn't time for awkwardness. Our every moment consumed by the need to survive. Now, with the danger behind us, everything made me more aware of her presence.

I rubbed the back of my neck, looking around the room, trying to distract myself from my thoughts.

Right as I felt my nerves settle, the door creaked open, and Celine entered the room again. She was carrying a wooden bucket of steaming water in one hand and a small tray balanced on her other arm. She placed the tray on the table in front of me, showing a bundle of folded bandages, a jar of some kind of balm, and other supplies.

I sat up straighter to fix my posture. "You didn't have to go through all of this trouble," I said.

Celine glanced at me as she set the bucket down on a lower table. "You are injured, Drifted," she said evenly. "It would be irresponsible of me to leave you untreated."

Celine knelt by the table, dipping a cloth into the steaming water before wringing it out. She then placed the warm cloth against my cheek.

The pressure hurt at first, but the warmth eased the sting almost immediately. "Stay still," she said softly.

I did as she instructed, but my face burned—not only from the cloth.

She stayed quiet for a moment, and then she spoke. "This calls to mind our time at the inn, the one in Noctiluna," she said, glancing at me before returning to my cheek.

I chuckled, the memory resurfacing immediately. That inn—that cramped, dimly lit room we stayed in after she rescued me from the Grimroots.

"You were far worse off then," she continued, dipping the cloth back into the bucket and wringing it out. "Yet you still tried to refuse my assistance."

I let out a nervous chuckle. "Yeah... I remember. You didn't exactly give me much of a choice, though, did you?"

Celine's lips curved into the faintest smile. "Had I waited for your approval, you may well have bled out in the night."

I couldn't help but laugh quietly at the memory as Celine took a bit of balm, rubbing it on my cheek. Then she took out a bandage and placed it on gently.

"Lift your tunic," she said simply.

I nearly fainted. "W-what?"

"Lift your tunic," she repeated, her tone a lot calmer than I was feeling. Her violet eyes met mine, and I deflated under her gaze.

"Really, Celine, It's nothing I—"

She cut me off. "Your ribs, they are injured as well."

Her hand hovered toward the hem of my tunic, and I nearly fell out the chair. "No—wait! I can do it myself!"

Reluctantly, I slowly lifted my tunic, looking toward the ceiling as sweat covered my forehead. As the fabric rose, I revealed the dark bruises covering my ribs, their different hues reminding me of the blows I'd taken at Sabrina's hand. I heard a small inhale from Celine as she took in the sight.

"As I suspected," she said, dipping the cloth into the steaming water again. She wrung it out, carefully folding it before pressing it against the worse of the bruises.

"Mention injuries like this to me sooner, Drifted," she said. "There is no wisdom in enduring unnecessary pain."

"It's not that bad," I muttered back. The sting from her pressing the cloth into me harder made it clear she wasn't convinced.

Celine applied the balm to the bruises in the same fashion that she did my cheek. When she finished wrapping a bandage around my torso, she stood and gathered up the supplies in her arms.

I relaxed, assuming we were done, when Celine moved toward her bed. Without a word, she sat on the edge and removed her cloak, letting it fall to the ground beside her. Then, to my confusion, she lay back slightly and began lifting her own tunic, revealing a pattern of bruises across her side. The sight made me burn up instantly.

I turned my head, my eyes widening. "Celine, what are you doing?!" I questioned.

"Drifted," she said simply, "you will now tend to my injuries."

"W—wait, me? Shouldn't we call someone else for this? Someone more... appropriate, like an aide?"

"There is no need," she said as she turned on to lie on her side. "You are here, and I trust you to handle this task."

I swallowed hard, glancing at the supplies near her. I stood up, my legs wobbly as I took a step toward her. "Uh... right. Okay. I guess I can... try."

Celine closed her eyes. "You need not be hesitant, Drifted. The process is straightforward."

That's not what's making me hesitant, I thought, as I awkwardly picked up the cloth and dipped it into the water. I could hardly keep my hands from shaking as I lifted it toward her side.

"Press the cloth gently against the bruised area. Do not linger too long on any one spot, as the warmth must be evenly distributed," she said.

I nodded, using my free hand to stabilize the other. I placed the cloth gently on her side. She didn't flinch, but I couldn't help but feel self conscious.

"Good," she murmured. "Now, once the area has been warmed sufficiently, apply the balm. Use only a small amount and spread it evenly."

I followed her instructions. Dipping my fingers into the jar of balm and carefully applying it to her bruises.

I worked on her back quietly, trying to make sure the balm was applied evenly throughout her bruises. "What next?" I asked, trying to keep my voice calm.

"Wrap the bandage securely, but do not restrict movement," Celine instructed, motioning toward the fresh bandages on the table.

Celine sat up as I reached and grabbed a bandage. When I got back into place, I couldn't help but look at the way her frame curved

I shook my head, forcing myself to focus. Gently, I began wrapping the bandage around her torso, being mindful of her guidance. When I tied it off, she pulled her tunic down and sat up fully.

"You have done well," she said. "Thank you, Drifted."

I let out a breath and leaned back against her headboard. "Yeah... no problem."

To my surprise, Celine leaned against me, her head lightly resting on my shoulder. I stiffened, unsure of what was happening.

She must've felt my nervous shaking.

"You need not be so nervous. You performed adequately."

I couldn't see her face, but the way the words came out suggested she was smiling—or as close to a smile that she could manage.

That's not what's making me so nervous! My brain screamed.

"I shall rest for only a moment," Celine muttered.

Before I could respond, her breathing had already evened out, and I realized she had fallen asleep. Her warmth radiated against me, and for a moment, it reminded me of the night we spent in the freezing woods, relying on each other to stay alive.

Man, that training must've taken a lot out of her. I thought to myself, though the same could easily have been said for me.

I tried to keep myself composed, but my heart was pounding. Despite the awkwardness, there was something undeniably comforting about her presence. Slowly, the weight of the day began to catch up with me, and I found myself succumbing to the warmth and stillness. My eyes grew heavy, and before I knew it, I had fallen asleep as well.

CHAPTER 13

A knock came at the door, persistent and hollow, as though whoever stood on the other side had been waiting far too long. I stirred beneath the thin blanket draped over me, trying to blink the sleep from my eyes, though the dull weight of sleep kept them mostly sealed. Another knock—louder this time—pulled a groan from my throat.

"Alright, I'm coming," I mumbled, swinging my legs off the edge of the bed. I half-shuffled, half-stumbled across the creaking wooden floor, noting that everything in my quarters were ordered differently. I reached the main living room and my hand fumbled with the latch until the door opened with a creak.

Standing there was the Prince Consort, Rowen.

He stood perfectly still; his fur cloak hung neatly at his sides. There was his usual calm and stoic look on his face; save for the single brow arched high on his forehead. He said nothing.

I blinked at him slowly. "Good morning, Your Highness," I said, my voice still scratchy from waking up. "Sorry, have you been standing out here for lon—" I stopped mid-sentence as his eyebrow twitched higher on his forehead.

I frowned, unsure of his facial expression, before it hit me. I turned to face the room behind me. The walls, the furniture, hell, even the smell. It was all... different.

My stomach dropped. I wasn't in my living quarters. I was at Celine's

"I... I, umm," I stammered, unsure of what excuse I could use to get myself out of this situation. "I'm... not in my own quarters, am I?"

Rowen's lips twitched before he spoke. "No," he said finally. "You are not."

I scratched the back of my head as my face continually grew warmer. "It... Celine, she was just--"

Rowen's gaze left me and was now focused behind me.

"Good morning, father," I heard Celine's voice come from behind. I turned slightly to see her giving Rowen a bow. She offered only a faint stare in her deep violet eyes, nothing that portrayed the turmoil I was feeling.

Of course, she looked completely unfazed.

Rowen's eyes narrowed as he turned his attention back to me. "I see," he said slowly, though his voice carried a steely undertone. "And why, pray tell, is Isaac answering your door this morning?"

"I... uh..." I stuttered, heat spreading to the tips of my ears. "I fell asleep. That's all. I—"

"Drifted, and I tended to each other last night," Celine interrupted. "After, it appears that we had fallen asleep."

Tended?!

My jaw dropped to the floor. I looked at Rowen, who, for once, looked almost perplexed. He looked back at me, his eyes darkening enough to make me feel like I was being slowly dissected.

Why in the MOON would she phrase it like that?

I scrambled to find my voice, my face burning so hot I thought It might catch fire. "No! N—she didn't mean it like that, whatever *THAT* might be!" I flailed my arms frantically between the two of them, my words tumbling over themselves. "I—well, we—after the sparring session—erm, we helped each other! And then afterwards—"

"Drifted," Celine interrupted me, placing a hand on my shoulder. "Are you ill? Why can you not seem to speak clearly this morning?"

"I—no, I'm fine!" I blurted out, stepping slightly out of her reach. "Perfectly fine! I'm just having a difficult morning, is all, you know?"

"A difficult morning?" she questioned, tilting her head at me. "You have only just awoken. Perhaps I shall tend to you some more?"

Moon's mercy. She's trying to get me killed!

Rowen now placed a hand on my shoulder, his grip stronger than I imagined it would be. "Speak, boy. What is the meaning of this?" He questioned me, squeezing harder.

"Father, you need not concern yourself," she said smoothly, clasping her hands in front of her. "Isaac merely assisted me last night. I suffered a minor injury, and we both agreed rest was the most practical solution."

I blinked at her. That was so much better than 'tended to each other!' Why couldn't she have led with that?

Rowen's eyes narrowed ever so slightly, the faintest twitch of his jaw betraying his skepticism. "Is that so?"

"Yes," Celine replied, unshaken. "You may question me further if you wish, though I assure you my words are the truth."

Rowen stared for a while longer before starting to play with his beard again. Then, his grip on my shoulder relaxed, but only slightly.

"You are sure your intentions were... honorable, boy?" He asked me.

"Yes!" I nearly shouted. "Completely honorable! In fact, I would say the most honorable! I mean, I wouldn't think of— not that—"

"Drifted," Celine interrupted again. "Calm yourself. You are beginning to sound unwell again."

I turned to her, eyes wide. "You're not helping," I hissed

under my breath.

"I do not see the issue." She replied.

"Enough," Rowen interrupted, cutting through our bickering. "This discussion will wait for another time."

Rowen gave me a glare, and I clamped my mouth shut immediately.

"You are both late," Rowen continued. "Isaac, I went to your quarters and did not find you there. So decided to see if Celine had any idea of your whereabouts... how fortunate I was able to find you *both* here."

I glanced down at my feet, feeling the sarcasm in his words. He continued.

"Lood is waiting for you two at the arena. You will eat quickly and make your way there without further delay."

"Yes, Your Highness," I muttered, my head dipping down even further.

Celine offered him a slight bow. "Understood, Father. We will keep Lood waiting no longer."

Rowen's gaze lingered on me for a moment longer—long enough to make me squirm. "See that you don't," he said calmly. Without another word, he turned and left.

I slumped forward, bracing my hands on my knees as I exhaled a long breath. "Why would you say it like that?" I groaned, glaring up at Celine. "Tended to each other? Really?"

Celine's calm gaze met mine, completely unapologetic. "It was accurate, was it not?"

"Yes, but it sounded—" I paused, shaking my head. "Never mind."

Celine didn't answer. She tilted her head to the side.

I stared at her. "You're impossible."

"Come," she said, taking my hand. "We will eat quickly and proceed to the arena. It would be unwise to test Lood's patience further."

I groaned again as I trailed behind her. Breakfast felt like a mountain to climb, and Lood waiting for us at the end of it wasn't exactly the motivation I needed.

Celine led us down the staircase, her hand still lightly holding mine as I trudged behind her.

When we reached the dining area, it was quiet. The long wooden tables that usually buzzed with chatter were now cleared of plates and cups, the only signs of activity being the faint smell of cooked meat lingering in the air.

"It appears we were too late," Celine said, glancing back at me with a slight frown.

"Hey, that's alright," I replied to her. "Maybe we can stop by the mess hall later on?"

A familiar voice called out from the far corner of the room.

"Ah, if it is not Lady Celine and Drifted."

I turned to see Caldryn, leaning casually against a stone hearth. His arms were crossed over his potbelly, and his chef's hat was stained, like usual.

"Caldryn," Celine greeted him. "I presumed you would have already left the Elderwood for the day."

Caldryn chuckled, pushing off the hearth and fixing his apron. "Just about to, My Lady," he replied with a bow. "We have been finishing packing supplies to head up to the mess hall and prepare for the midday meal."

At that exact moment, my stomach growled loudly enough to echo in the empty dining area. I winced, rubbing the back of my neck as I muttered, "Sorry… we, uh, missed breakfast."

Caldryn's bushy eyebrows lifted slightly, and he gave a hearty laugh. "Missed breakfast, did you? Well, are you two not lucky? We have not packed up everything yet." He gestured toward the kitchen door behind him. "Sit yourselves down. I shall whip something up quickly."

I blinked, surprised by his offer. "Really? That'd be great—

thank you!"

"Think nothing of it," Caldryn said, already bustling off toward the kitchen. "It would not do well to send off Lady Celine with an empty stomach. You, Drifted, are just lucky to have tagged along."

"Hey!" I yelled as he disappeared behind the door.

"It seems fortune is on our side this morning, Drifted," she remarked, taking her usual seat.

"You mean your side," I muttered as I slid into the seat next to her.

After a short while, Caldryn returned, balancing two plates with eggs, slices of bread, and a few slabs of smoked meat. He sat them down, wiping his hands on his apron as he grinned.

"There you are. Eat up quickly, you two. I heard Lood is in charge of training the both of you, and I would rather not be blamed for your tardiness."

"Thank you kindly, Caldryn," Celine said with a nod.

"Yeah, thanks!" I added, ignoring the way my stomach growled at the sight of the food.

Caldryn's gaze flicked toward me, his grin widening slightly. "That growl is enough to wake the whole Elderwood," he remarked, crossing his arms as he leaned against the table. "Do you always wait until the last possible second to eat?"

I picked up a slice of meat, my mouth salivating as it glistened. "It's not like that. I... overslept."

"Hmm," Caldryn mused, raising an eyebrow. "Oversleeping, missing meals, late for training... You shall fit right in with the Lupine yet."

Celine tossed a subtle glance in my direction. "Eat quickly, Drifted. We are already late as it is."

She picked up her fork and began eating her meal quietly,

but quickly.

I followed her lead, though I ate less elegantly than she did. Caldryn lingered for a moment, as if contemplating whether to say more, before finally straightening and fixing his apron.

"Well, I best leave you to it," he said, stepping back toward the kitchen door. "Lood's patience is not known for its longevity."

Celine gave Caldryn a nod, not looking up from her plate.

"Thanks again," I added, shoving the bits of egg in my mouth to the side with my tongue.

Caldryn's grin returned as he paused at the door. "Do not thank me just yet, Drifted. You shall need more than a full stomach to get through today." With a short wave, he disappeared behind the door.

Celine remained silent as she finished the rest of her meal. I hurried through mine, more focused on avoiding any more scolding for the day.

Once I scraped the last bit of food from my plate, I leaned back with a sigh, glancing at Celine, who was already beginning to stand up.

"Let us move," she said, placing her utensils neatly on top of her plate.

I groaned, standing and stretching my back. "I'm just ready to get this over with."

Celine fixed the clasp of her cloak. "Then we should not delay." Without another word, she turned and began making her way toward the exit.

I followed, my footsteps echoing softly in the hall as we descended the staircase and exited the Elderwood.

The path leading to the arena was the same as before, winding through the outskirts of the Elderwood's sprawling roots.

As we walked, I stared at Celine. Though we haven't been in Sylphreach for long, I noticed there was a change in her overall demeanor. I wasn't sure what it was exactly, but it felt vaguely positive. Somehow, she seemed less... stressed? Maybe it had to do with the fact she didn't have to wear her hood constantly.

"So," I began, breaking our silence, "what do you think Lood has planned for us today? More sparring?"

"Perhaps," Celine replied. "Or perhaps something more... instructive. We will see soon enough"

We rounded the final bend of the spiraling bridge, and the vine-covered opening of the arena came into view. A figure was already waiting by the entrance, and even from this distance, the sheer bulk of him was unmistakable.

"Lood," I muttered under my breath, feeling my shoulders tense.

Celine looked over her shoulder at me. "Remember," she said, "this is not merely a test of your strength, Drifted. Remain focused, and you may yet earn his respect."

"Great," I said, squaring my shoulder and taking a deep breath as we got closer. "No pressure or anything."

As we got closer, Lood's figure somehow looked even larger. He stood motionless, his broad frame outlined against the backdrop of the Elderwood. His arms were crossed, and his crimson eyes fixed on us with an intensity that made me feel smaller.

"Erm, good morning, Lood," I said, forcing my voice to sound calm.

Of course, he didn't reply. Instead, he let out a grunt, barely sparing me a glance as he turned toward the wall of vines behind him. With a single motion, he extended one massive hand and parted the vines to reveal the entrance.

I hesitated, glancing at Celine. She stepped forward

without a word and entered through the opening.

I swallowed hard, forcing my feet to move. As I stepped closer, Lood's gaze flicked to me for a brief moment before he turned back to the vines, sealing the entrance behind us once we were through.

Off to the side of the arena, I noticed that Rowen was already waiting. Though, interestingly enough, I didn't see Sabrina anywhere. I figured she would take great enjoyment in seeing Lood whip me into shape. Her absence felt... strange.

Celine stood in the center, waiting, her posture relaxed but poised. I took my place beside her, my heart pounding as I resisted the urge to glance back at Lood.

Rowen's gaze turned to me briefly before returning to Celine, and I couldn't help but feel like I was being silently measured. Whatever was about to happen, he was clearly here to witness it.

Lood stepped forward, his boots crunching against the dirt as he came to stand a few paces in front of us. His rough eyes moved between the two of us before settling on me.

"Today's lesson," Rowen boomed from the side of the arena, "will test more than your strength. It will test your ability to adapt, to change."

I swallowed, glancing briefly at Celine, who remained composed. Rowen turned his gaze to me, and I felt the air grow heavier.

"As we did yesterday," Rowen continued, "we will begin with you, Isaac."

I exhaled shakily, nodding as I turned toward the weapons barrel. I saw the same wooden short sword and shield from the previous session and began walking toward them, already strategizing in my mind the best way to face whatever they had planned.

"Stop," Rowen's voice shot out.

I froze mid-step, turning back toward him, confused.

"You rely too heavily on your sword and shield," Rowen said. "So much so that when they are no longer in your possession, you become helpless. Today, you will learn to stand on your own."

My stomach twisted at his words.

"I..." I started, my voice faltering as I processed what he was saying. "You want me to fight without a weapon?"

Rowen didn't flinch, his tone strong. "As I told you yesterday, Isaac. The Lupine are so skilled in fighting because they lack the ability to wield the weapons we humans rely so heavily on."

He paused and looked at Lood, who then walked over to move the barrel of weapons out of the way. "And yet, they thrive. They turn this limiting feature into a strength. You too must learn how to do this."

Rowen then motioned for me to step back toward the center of the arena. "You will fight with the tools you were born with—your mind, your reflexes, your instincts. Until you learn to trust these, you will always be at a disadvantage."

My palms grew slick with sweat as I walked back toward the center of the arena. I shuffled into some sort of position. My feet felt awkward, and my legs even worse. I shifted my weight from one foot to the other, trying to find a stance that felt right, but nothing did. My hands twitched at my sides, feeling around for the hilt of an absent sword.

I wasn't a fighter—not really. I'd trained, sure. But my father had drilled the basics of swordplay into me from a young age. Footwork, strikes, parries—it was always about the blade. But this? Fighting with nothing but my fists? This was new. Lood got into position. Placing one open hand near his chest and then extending the other arm slight out in front of him. It was then that I realized I would be fighting him.

I gasped unintentionally.

"Wait!" I blurted out in a panic. "I'm fighting against Lood?!"

"You are," Rowen replied.

I took a step back, shaking my head. "No, no, no. There's got to be a mistake! Look at him!" I gestured wildly toward Lood, whose stance hadn't budged an inch. "He's... he's built like a bear! He could crush me with one hand!"

"Do not worry, for this lesson, I want you to only focus on landing a hit on Lood," Rowen replied.

That felt better, if only slightly. Still, I was nervous to approach Lood, just the sight of him rooted me in place. It made me sweat. All I wanted to do was stay as far from him as possible.

"Isaac," Rowen's voice broke the silence. "You hesitate. Do you fear him?"

"No!" I answered back instinctively.

Yes, my mind immediately corrected.

Rowen raised an eyebrow. "Then act. Or do you believe strength lies only in steel?"

I swallowed hard, forcing myself to take a shaky breath. *Act, huh? Easier said than done.*

I glanced at Lood again. He hadn't moved an inch, hadn't even blinked. His posture remained solid.

The knot in my stomach grew tighter.

Taking another breath, I planted my feet a little wider apart. I lifted my hands slowly and curled them into fists, the motion feeling awkward.

"Drifted!"

Celine called out from the sidelines. I turned my head toward her, startled, and for a moment she just stared at me.

Then, she gave me a nod—small, something others would've seen as insignificant—but it and an effect that somehow made my feet feel lighter.

I shook my head, a small grin tugging at my lips. *Oh, what the hell,* I thought.

Without giving myself another chance to change my mind, I pushed off with my back foot and rushed toward Lood, my fist raised, and my heart nearly beating out of my chest.

As I closed the gap, I pulled my arm back, aiming an awkward punch at his chest. My form was all over the place, my weight unbalanced, but it didn't matter—all I had to do was land one measly hit.

Before my fist even got close, Lood's arm moved. With an open palm, he slapped my hand to the side with such force that it threw me off balance. My punch flew wide, and I stumbled, nearly losing my footing.

"Focus, Isaac!" Rowen yelled at me.

Lood didn't follow up with an attack—he reset his stance, watching me like I was some clumsy animal.

I straightened again, my arm stinging from the slap. But it wasn't only my arm that hurt, it was my pride.

I squared my shoulders and raised my fists again, this time trying to regulate my breathing. *One hit. Just one measley hit.*

I lunged forward, this time, swinging my right fist wide, aiming for his shoulder. But before I could connect, Lood leaned back, the motion so smooth and effortless it made me feel like I was moving in slow motion. My fist shot right past him, hitting nothing but air.

Stumbling slightly, I planted my feet and tried again. This time, I aimed for his ribs. Again, Lood shifted his weight, stepping to the side with such fluidity that should've been impossible for someone his size.

Frustration bubbled up inside me, my breaths coming faster as I swung again, this time a quick jab aimed at his stomach. Lood swayed back to avoid the blow, his unblinking eyes still fixed on me, as if mocking my every move.

"Damn it!" I growled under my breath, throwing another punch—then another. My fists lashed out wildly, each swing more desperate than the last.

Lood didn't retaliate. He didn't even raise his hands. He easily sidestepped and leaned out of the way.

I could feel the heat rising in my face and my arms beginning to ache from the wasted attempts. My punches became sloppier, wider, as I tried to catch him off guard, to land something.

"Conserve your energy, boy!" Rowen barked at me. "Control your movements, or you will tire yourself out before you even begin!"

But I couldn't stop. I swung again, aiming for Lood's jaw, but he grabbed my arm out of the air. Using my momentum against me, he turned me around and pinned my arm behind my back.

He shoved me away, and I nearly tripped, catching myself at the last moment.

My cheeks burned as I turned to face him. He was still standing there, calm as ever, face blank. He didn't even look like he was trying.

A surge of anger crashed over me, almost instantly engulfing me. My fists clenched at my side, and I spun on my heel, charging straight toward him.

I swung wildly, no destination in mind. Lood's hand moved again, slapping my arm aside as if brushing away a fly. I didn't stop. I swung again, this time with my left, only for him to deflect it with the same effortless toss.

I threw punch after punch—sloppy jabs, rough hooks, anything I could think of to break through his guard. Each time, his massive hands swatted my arms away.

"Damn it!" I yelled, throwing another punch toward his

chest.

Lood sidestepped, grabbing my arm mid-swing. Before I could even register what was happening, his other hand clamped around my wrist, and the next thing I knew, my feet left the ground.

I let out a strangled yelp as I was lifted into the air, my entire body flipping upside down. My arms flailed uselessly, my head spinning as blood rushed to my face.

CHAPTER 14

From upside-down, I could see Rowen watching me from the sidelines, his face giving away a hint of disappointment.

"Isaac," Rowen called out. "Do you not see the folly of your rashness?"

"Yeah," I started, my voice weakened with the blood rushing to my head. "I'm starting to see it now."

With a slow motion, Lood lowered me down and let me go. I stumbled to my feet unsteadily before catching myself.

I dragged my hand down my face, trying to shake off the humiliation. "Alright," I said, exhaling heavily. "That's enough for one day, right?"

I started to walk back to the sidelines when Lood grabbed my arm, pulling me back.

My eyes darted between Lood and Rowen, hoping for an explanation to help clear my confusion.

"You are not done, Isaac," Rowen said, his voice firm. "You still have yet to land a hit on Lood."

My heart sank at the realization I would have to keep this up. I was already tapped out from the last expenditure of energy.

"Your Highness, I—"

Rowen raised his hand to cut me off. "The lesson is not over until you succeed. The mark of a fighter is not how often they fall, it is how reliable their resolve is."

I turned to Lood, who was still holding my arm. And for a moment, I could've sworn I saw the resemblance of a smile growing on his lips.

I groaned, leaning and resting my hands on my knees.

Great. I thought to myself.

"Compose yourself, boy," Rowen's voice came through again. "Focus on what you have learned so far."

As much as I wanted to listen to his wise words, looking at Lood made the task seem impossible. I mean, somehow Lood was built like a mountain but flowed like water. It made no sense.

I straightened my posture and slapped my cheeks lightly with my hands.

Taking a shaky breath, I rolled my shoulders and raised my fists. "Alright," I muttered to myself. "Let's try this again."

I pushed off my back foot, rushing toward Lood, my eyes locked on his chest as I got close.

Stay focused, I reminded myself.

As I got within striking range, I shifted my weight forward and threw a punch, aiming straight for the center of his chest. The strike felt more controlled, more purposeful than before.

But it didn't matter.

Lood's hand moved like a whip, slapping my hand to the side hard. The impact jarred my arm, throwing me slightly off balance, but I quickly regained my footing.

I gritted my teeth as I felt the usual rush of frustration bubbling within me. But I forced it down, taking a step back and raising my fist once more.

"Good," Rowen's voice called out from the sidelines, calm but firm. "You are beginning to learn. Now, do not lose focus. Precision over power, Isaac."

I nodded slightly and pushed off once again, this time aiming for Lood's face.

Right before my punch connected, Lood shifted his weight, dodging out of the way.

"Shift left!"

Celine yelled out suddenly. The words hit me like a spark

and, without thinking, I twisted my body mid-motion, my right arm pulling back as my left swung forward in a wide hook.

The punch came close—closer than anything I'd managed all day—but as it got near Lood's ribs, he quickly caught it in his hand, His palm hit my wrist, and he redirected the blow, sending me off course.

I recovered quickly, my heart pounding. *I almost hit him.*

Turning toward the sidelines, I locked eyes with Celine, who had her hands clasped in front of her.

From the corner of my eye, I noticed Rowen's gaze flick toward her. He stared at her for a moment, but said nothing. Then, he turned his attention back to me as though the moment hadn't happened.

I raised my fist again, still processing the punch that almost landed.

I stepped forward, the ache in my arms and legs dulled by the small glimmer of hope Celine's guidance gave me.

Lood remained in his defensive stance. The arena felt quieter now, the tension in the air palpable.

"Keep your weight balanced, Drifted," Celine's voice called out again.

Her words pulled me back to a memory—our first encounter in the woods, the chaotic battle against the Dreadbeak. Back then, she'd guided me through the fight, just like she was doing now.

I rushed toward Lood again, this time leading with a left jab. He adjusted his stance right before the jab came out.

"Feint right, but keep your momentum," Celine instructed again. "Then swing low with your left."

I nodded to myself, following her command. I stepped right, throwing another quick jab that I knew wouldn't connect, but it was enough to make Lood turn in response.

Before he could fully brace himself, I swung my left fist low, aiming for his side.

Lood's hand moved swiftly, intercepting the punch, but this time, he didn't have the same ease as before. The impact of his block reverberated up my arm, and I couldn't help but feel a small surge of accomplishment.

"Now, shift back, then strike high!" Celine yelled.

I turned my weight, stepping back quickly, then pivoted quickly, throwing a punch aimed at his shoulder. Again, he intercepted it, but the deflection came later this time, less effortlessly.

I took another quick step back, my fists raised as I sized him up. My breath was heavy, and my arms trembled, but my mind was starting to catch up.

This time, I stepped forward with a plan in mind. I pulled my right hand back for another punch. Lood's body shifted almost imperceptibly—his weight tilted to the left, his stance turned slightly.

I froze mid-motion, stopping the punch before it even began. Lood returned to his neutral stance as if nothing had happened, but I'd seen it.

Aha! I knew it. I thought to myself

He wasn't reacting to my punches. He was anticipating them; moving to counter before the strike fully came out.

"He's predicting my moves before I make them..." I muttered to myself.

"Correct!" Celine yelled out again. "Lood is adept at reading patterns and tells. He moves before your attack begins because you show him your intentions."

I frowned as I looked at Lood. Realizing that the entire time I'd been telegraphing my attacks.

"Focus on minimizing your movements," Celine continued. Do not let your body betray your plan."

I nodded, though it was easier said than done. My arms were tired, and my legs felt like lead, but I forced myself to steady my breathing.

This time, I stepped in carefully. I feinted with my left again, but instead of committing, I shifted quickly, throwing a low right hook.

Lood's eyes flicked to my right hand, and he moved to deflect it—but he hesitated slightly, almost too late to block it.

"Good," Celine said, her tone calm but encouraging. "Now maintain your control."

I jabbed with my left at Lood's face. His rection was instant, ducking low to avoid the strike. That's when an idea sparked in my mind—something instinctive, something I hadn't thought to try before.

As Lood ducked, I clasped my hands together mid-motion, turning the punch into a hammer. With all the force I could muster, I brought my clasped fists down toward him in an overhead strike.

Lood reacted just as quickly, his massive hands shooting up to block the attack. He caught my hands in his own, his grip strong like iron.

But then I did something I hadn't done the entire fight.

I threw a kick.

Using the momentum from our locked position, I shifted my body and swung my leg toward his side. Lood's eyes widened ever so slightly, the first real crack in his demeanor. He tried to move out of the way, but it was too late.

My foot connected with his ribs, the impact reverberating up my leg. Lood staggered back a step—not much, but enough to make me realize what I'd done.

For a brief moment, everything was silent.

"Good," Rowen's voice broke through the quiet. "Well

done, Isaac."

I stumbled back, catching my breath, my fists still raised. My chest heaved and my heart raced, but a small, incredulous grin grew on my lips. I'd done it. I'd landed a hit.

"Yes!" I cheered, the word bursting from my chest as I jump in celebration.

But the moment my feet hit the ground again, my legs buckled beneath me. The exhaustion that my adrenaline kept at bay snuck up all at once, and I toppled backward, landing flat on my back on the dirt.

The impact knocked the air out of my lungs, but instead of groaning, I started laughing weakly.

"Drifted!" Celine called out to me as she rushed over. She knelt beside me; her face covered in concern. "Are you alright?"

Laughing, I waved a hand weakly. "I'm fine! I'm fine!" I said between breaths. "I can't believe I actually hit him!"

A small smile grew on her face as she stared at me. "Aye, you did."

I pushed myself up into a sitting position, and without thinking, I grabbed her shoulders. "Celine," I said, my voice full of gratitude, "you helped me see what was happening. I would've just kept throwing punches like an idiot all day if it weren't for you!"

Before she could respond, I pulled her into a hug, wrapping my arms tightly around her. "Thank you," I said, my voice slightly muffled by her cloak.

For a moment she didn't respond, and I realized I may have overstepped. I loosened my arms and pulled back.

Her arms wrapped around me.

"It was your own strength that carried you through, Drifted," she whispered. "I merely helped you locate it."

From the corner of my eye, I noticed Rowen watching us.

Embarrassed, I quickly pushed myself off of Celine, clearing my throat. "Well, I couldn't have done it without you."

Celine stood up with a nod, brushing the dirt off her cloak as she held out a hand to help me up.

Once on my feet, I heard an annoyingly familiar voice come from behind me.

"What, pray tell, did I miss?"

I groaned as I turned to see Sabrina leaning casually against one of the arena's trees. Her arms were crossed loosely, and a wolfish grin was on her face.

"Sabrina..." I muttered, slouching over. "What an honor to have you join us."

She tilted her head. "Why, Drifted, your greeting lacks warmth. Were you not, perhaps, eager for my return?"

"No," I replied flatly.

Her gaze flicked to Lood, then back to me. "It appears you have been through quite an ordeal. Judging by the dirt on your back and the delightful expression of fatigue on your face, I dare say Lood has not been kind to you."

"I don't think 'kind' is in his vocabulary," I muttered under my breath.

Sabrina stepped closer, her smile widening slightly. "And yet, here you stand, victorious... or nearly so. You continue to surprise me, Drifted."

"Thanks, I guess," I said, though I couldn't keep the sarcasm out of my voice.

"That is enough, everyone," Rowen announced. "It is now Celine's turn. Clear the arena."

Celine gave me a nod before turning toward Lood, who was still standing in the center of the arena, steady as ever.

I took a step back, suddenly aware of how sore and shaky my legs felt. Sabrina walked beside me, her eyes fixed intently on Celine.

"Now this," Sabrina murmured, "should be entertaining."

I groaned as I hobbled toward the sidelines. Leaning on one of the wooden benches, I turned my attention back to the center.

Celine was already standing opposite Lood, her posture relaxed but readied. She showed no signs of nerves or hesitation. Watching her, I couldn't help but feel a bit of envy.

Rowen stepped closer to the center, looking toward Celine. "It is clear," he began, "that you are in tune with your instincts, Celine. They guide you well, allowing you to avoid danger with a speed few can match."

Celine turned her head to Rowen, listening.

"However," Rowen continued, "in your sparring with Sabrina, you rarely used those instincts to counterattack. You moved to evade, to defend, but never to turn the tide of battle."

Sabrina let out a soft laugh from beside me, her red eyes glinting with amusement. "She did well enough," she murmured, her tone playful. "Until, of course, I shifted."

Rowen ignored her. "When Sabrina took on her Lunar form, Celine, you were easily outmatched." His words weren't harsh, but they carried a weight that hung in the air.

Celine nodded her head slightly in acknowledgment.

"Therefore," Rowen said, his voice firm, "the rules for this session will differ. You will still be required to land a hit on Lood. However, you will also face him in his Lunar form. Also, Lood will not simply defend, but he shall pursue you as well."

My eyes widened, and I shot a loot at Celine. She didn't flinch, her calm demeanor holding steady, but Rowen's words scared me. *Pursue?*

"Lood, in his Lunar form?" I muttered under my breath, glancing nervously at the towering figure.

Sabrina leaned in slightly, her voice low and teasing. "Oh, this should be delightful—I cannot wait!."

Rowen's eyes flicked toward us for a moment, silencing any further commentary. He returned his attention to Celine. "Do you understand the task?"

"Yes, Father," Celine replied. "I am ready."

Rowen inclined his head slightly. "Then let us begin."

He turned toward Lood. "Lood."

Without hesitation, Lood stepped forward as a ripple of energy seemed to pass through him. Much like Sabrina, his body shuddered, and muscles rippled beneath his skin. Fur sprouted from his body, a deep, stormy gray that shimmered lightly.

Before I knew it, he was now a large wolf, growling low as he stared down Celine. He was much larger than Sabrina was in her Lunar form, his muscles easily pronounced under his fur.

Just the sight of Lood in his human form made me nervous; I couldn't even begin to imagine his strength in this wolf one. I gulped, worried about Celine's safety, even if this was a controlled sparring session.

Celine's stance remained consistent, and, surprisingly, she showed no fear even though she was faced with the enormous wolf that was now Lood. How did she always manage to stay so calm?

Rowen lifted his hand and then dropped it. "Begin."

Lood moved instantly, his massive body blurring with speed I didn't think was possible for someone his size. He darted toward Celine in a low crouch, closing the gap between them in mere seconds.

Celine moved in anticipation, and she sidestepped his initial lunge. But Lood twisted mid-stride, pivoting tightly to keep her in his sights, forcing her on the back foot.

Lood dashed again, his head low, as to headbutt Celine. Celine again floated out of the way, but instantly Lood was back on her. It was clear his plan was to give her as little room to breathe as possible.

"Do not let him dictate the flow of the fight!" Rowen's voice rang out. "Stay composed, Celine, and find your opening."

Lood's movements were relentless, each lunge and swipe flowing into the next seamlessly. Celine twisted to the side, narrowly avoiding a powerful swipe of his claws, her cloak billowing behind her. As she ducked as Lood lunged again, his massive frame flying over her.

Celine was trying to stay out of Lood's reach. But Lood pressed on wildly, his sheer size and speed giving her no chance to find her footing.

Lood's ears flicked and swiveled at every sound, his nose twitched, drawing in every scent in the air. It was as if the entire arena spoke to him, and he understood every word.

During my session, when Lood had been impossibly quick, easily deflecting every clumsy attempt I made to strike him, there had been a sense of restraint in his movements. He was controlled, almost mechanical.

But here, in his Lunar form, he was something else entirely. He moved with freedom that felt wild yet deliberate, less restricted than he'd been in his humanoid state. It was as though a weight had been lifted from him. In this form, thought or strategy didn't burden him—he simply was.

Lood skidded to a stop, coiling his body with tension. Then, with a powerful spin, he used his hind legs to kick up a cloud of dirt from the arena floor, swirling debris in the air.

Celine reacted, her eyes closing momentarily against the dust.

"That is not good," Sabrina murmured beside me.

It happened in an instant. Lood rushed forward, using the brief distraction to get right next to Celine. Lowering his head, he rammed into Celine's stomach, the hit clearly audible.

The impact sent her spiraling through the air with her cloak wrapping around her. She hit the ground with a loud thud, sliding across the dirt before coming to a stop.

My stomach sank, and I rushed forward. "Celine!"

Celine slowly pushed herself up, her arms trembling under body. Her breaths were ragged, and her usual calm expression transformed into one of agony. Dirt clung to her cloak and face, and she winced as she tried to straighten herself.

"I... I am fine," she said. Her eyes met mine, and though they lacked their usual steadiness, I could still see the determination burning behind them. "I am fine, Drifted."

I wasn't convinced. "Celine, you—"

"I am fine," she repeated, her voice shaking slightly, but she pushed herself to her feet. One hand moved to her side, pressing gently against her torso. She straightened slowly, her movements stiff, but her eyes stayed locked on Lood.

Without hesitation, Celine rushed forward. Her steps were uneven at first, but she quickly gained speed as she charged.

But it was pointless.

As she got in range, ready to attack, Lood watched, his eyes tracking her every movement. As she reached striking distance, he moved.

With a fluid step, Lood avoided her entirely, skirting to her side. Before Celine could recover, he lowered his head again, ramming into her left side with another brutal headbutt.

She sprawled across the dirt floor again, her body tumbling awkwardly before stopping. Dust billowed into the air, and for a moment, all I could hear was the echo of the collision.

I clenched my fists at my sides. There was no way she could keep taking hits like that.

"Celine!" I shouted, again stepping toward the edge of the arena, but she didn't move.

"Quiet, boy!" Rowen yelled out at me. His gaze snapped to me sternly. "She does not need your pity, nor does she need the mercy of Lood."

I froze.

"What she needs," Rowen continued, "is to rise on her own. To face this challenge as it is meant to be faced, and nothing more. Do not dishonor her by attempting to intervene."

I fell silent, his words leaving me stunned. A part of me felt conflicted, arguing against the words of Celine's father, so I stayed quiet. Instead, I turned my gaze back to Celine, who was still on the ground, motionless save for the slight rise and fall of her chest.

I clenched my fist tighter, my nails digging into my palms. I'd seen her face impossible odds before. Seen her stand tall when I was so close to faltering. But this...

I'd never seen her pushed so low.

As I started losing hope, I caught a flicker of movement. Celine's hand twitched against the dirt. I held my breath as her eyes fluttered open; their violet depths filled with pain.

Slowly, she pushed herself up again, her arms trembling.

"Celine," I breathed, hope flaring in my chest.

But Lood didn't wait.

Before she could fully stand, the massive Lupine darted forward. Soon enough, he was upon her, lowering his head and ramming straight into her stomach again.

I watched in shock as the air left Celine's lungs, a strangled gasp leaving her lips as her eyes widened.

She crumpled to the ground, clutching her stomach. Dust rose around her as she lay motionless.

"I can't just stand here," I muttered under my breath,

barely audible.

Sabrina's voice, quiet yet stern, interrupted my spiraling thoughts. "And yet, you must."

I turned to her, my frustration spilling over. "How can you say that? Look at her! She—she needs—"

"Strength does not grow in the shadow of others, Drifted," Sabrina said, her tone calm. "Do you think so little of her that you believe she cannot rise from this?"

"That isn't the point!" I yelled back, struggling to keep my emotions at bay.

"That is exactly the point," Rowen interjected, grabbing me by my collar and pulling me closer until I was face to face with his piercing eyes.

"You let your emotions cloud your understanding," he said. "If Celine cannot find a way to rise on her own, she will fall—not only here, but in any battle she is destined to face."

I opened my mouth to argue, but Rowen didn't give me the chance.

"If Celine refuses to take her Lunar form," he continued, "she will never be able to outmatch Lood. Or any other Lupine for that matter. This is a lesson she must learn."

My eyes widened as the realization dawned on me.

"You think she's avoiding it on purpose..." I muttered aloud without meaning to. Both Rowen and Sabrina looked at me in confusion. "Celine... she doesn't know how to take her Lunar form."

Rowen's brow furrowed, his eyes narrowing as he stared at me. "That is impossible," he said, letting go of my tunic. "From birth, the Lupine are instinctively aware of how to transform. It is not something they must be taught. Even with Celine being half Lupine, this should be innate to her."

"Well, it isn't," I said, trying to keep the annoyance out of my tone. "The only time I've ever seen her transform was back in that fight in Lostsummit with Maura."

Rowen looked toward Celine, his eyes saddening slightly.

"After that," I continued, my voice growing steadier, "there were moments when we were in danger. Times when taking that form could've saved us both." I swallowed hard, the memory of that harrowing escape flashing in my mind. "When we were running from Maura's guards, surrounded, and had no way out... she couldn't transform. She told me she didn't know how."

Sabrina took a step toward me, a look of genuine surprise on her face. She tilted her head slightly. "Drifted, are you sure of what you are saying?"

"I am," I replied. "It's not that she's refusing to take her Lunar form. It's that she can't."

Rowen took a step back, stroking his beard. The rare look of unease on his face made this situation feel somewhat heavier.

Sabrina got in my face, demanding attention. "Drifted," she said after a while, "tell me everything about what transpired when you and Celine fought Queen Maura."

I hesitated, glancing at Celine's still body in the arena before shifting my eyes back to Sabrina. Her expression was taut, the teasing edge gone from her eyes. I couldn't help but wonder why she was so worried about that at a time like this.

"I... honestly, I don't know exactly when it happened—the transformation," I began. "I was preoccupied with Maura tearing into my arm with her fangs."

I subconsciously rubbed the spot where the wound had been, the memory still vivid, though the area was mainly healed. "Celine wasn't far from me, though. There was blood—so much of my blood everywhere."

Sabrina nodded slightly, her eyes narrowing as she absorbed my words. "Continue." she urged.

"Well, right when I was on the brink of giving up. I looked back, and there she was—Celine in her Lunar form. I don't know when it happened or how."

Sabrina placed a finger on her chin, her expression thoughtful, almost calculating. She glanced at me for a moment, then stepped closer.

"Pardon me, Drifted," she said, her voice unusually formal.

"Pardon you?" I repeated, confused, but before I could say more, she grabbed my hand.

Her grip was firm, and before I could pull away, her head dipped, and I felt the sharp sting of her fangs sinking into the flesh of my palm.

"Hey! What the—" I started, but she pulled back just as quickly as she'd bitten me. A thin line of blood welled up from the puncture marks, and she pressed her finger against it.

"What was that for?" I asked, wincing as I cradled my hand, but Sabrina didn't answer. Her focus was elsewhere, her eyes fixed on Celine.

Without hesitation, Sabrina turned and rushed toward Celine. She knelt beside her, and before I could process what was happening, she stuck the bloodied finger in Celine's mouth.

I froze, my mind scrambling to make sense of the situation. "Sabrina... what are you—?"

Before the words had fully left my mouth, Celine's eyes flew open.

An intense gasp escaped her as her body jerked violently, her back arching off the ground. Ripples coursed through her, starting at her head and spreading down, her entire body jittering.

"Celine!" I shouted, my voice cracking as I stepped forward, but I stopped short, rooted by the sight before me.

Her body tensed, her fingers clawing at the dirt as strained noises escaped her lips—half gasps, half growls. The sounds grew deeper, more guttural, as her body shifted.

Her frame expanded as her orange-brown hair spread across her body, turning into a dense coat of fur. Her fingers elongated, nails sharpening into claws that dug into the earth beneath her.

She sat up suddenly, her movements jerky but powerful, the growls escaping her throat now fully Lupine. Her face elongated, her features contorting into a fierce snout.

I couldn't move or breathe as I watched the transformation take hold. The Celine I knew was gone, replaced by a towering, massive wolf with fur that glistened.

The air grew heavier, her presence now dominating the space as her piercing, glowing eyes locked onto Lood.

And then, she let out a loud howl that sent a chill through me, a sound that made the entire arena quiver.

CHAPTER 15

The air in the arena was thick with tension, the quiet broken only by the faint rustle of leaves and the sound of Celine's steady growls. She stood there, towering in her Lunar form, her orange-brown fur bristling, and her eyes glued to Lood.

I could hardly breathe as my mind raced to catch up with what had happened. Sure, I'd seen Celine in this form once before. But back then, the rush of escaping from Lostsummit muddled everything.

Sabrina took a step back from Celine, looking up at her size. She hesitated for a moment before speaking as her eyes flicked to Rowen.

"Your Highness, this means—"

Rowen held up his hand, signaling her to stop speaking.

For a while, he stood there, staring in awe at Celine's new form. The astonishment in his expression was unmistakable, but there was something deeper, harder to place. Was it fear? Curiosity? Concern?

I could tell something was running through his head, but whatever it was, he kept it carefully concealed behind his composed exterior.

Finally, Rowen straightened, clearing his throat. "The training session is over. Sabrina, do escort Isaac to his quarters."

Sabrina nodded her head while giving a slight bow. "As you wish, Your Highness."

"Wait, what do you mean?" I asked, gesturing towards Celine. "What about Celine? What's going to happen to her?"

Sabrina got behind me, placing both of her hands on my shoulders as she pushed me towards the exit.

"Do not worry your scatter-brained head; Lady Celine will be quite alright."

I planted my heels, trying to resist her push by dragging them against the dirt. "Sabrina, cut it out."

"As much as I admire your persistence," she interrupted, leaning in slightly, "you are not needed here right now."

As I hesitated, Rowen turned his head to me abruptly. "Go," he said firmly, leaving no room for argument.

I clenched my fist as I reluctantly let Sabrina lead me through the exit. As I turned back to look at Celine in her massive new form. Her growls faded, replaced by a steady stream of air from her muzzle.

As I took another step, her head shifted slightly, and her glowing eyes met mine.

And then she let out a low whimper.

I must've begun resisting again because a pinch came at my side.

"Come now, Drifted," Sabrina said. "Do not make me carry you out like a misbehaving pup."

I gritted my teeth and continued walking. Knowing that Sabrina would love the opportunity to humiliate me like that.

We stepped out of the arena and into the chilly night air. The moon already hung high above us, covering the entire town in a pale glow. I shrugged Sabrina's hands off my shoulders and turned to face her.

"What the hell is going on?" I demanded. "Why is everyone acting so strange about Celine's shift?"

Sabrina tilted her head with a smile on her lips. "Strange, you say?" She chuckled, brushing a strand of her jet-black hair from her face. "I think we are acting rather normally, given the circumstances."

"The circumstance?" I questioned. "Quit playing games with me, Sabrina, you know something, and so does Rowen. I deserve to know what's going on as well!"

Sabrina leaned against a nearby tree, crossing her arms as she regarded me with an amused twinkle in her eyes. "What I know is that it will do you well to get some rest in preparation for tomorrow."

I took a step closer, my fists clenched. "Sabrina."

She chuckled softly, her smile widening. "Oh, I do enjoy when you get all serious. But alas, some things are best left unspoken."

"You all can't keep leaving me in the dark like this and expect me to go along with it!" I snapped back at her, my fist clenching so tight my palms stung.

Sabrina's smile dropped, and her dipped slightly as she looked away. For a moment, her playful demeanor retreated. For once, it felt like my words had struck a chord—or maybe she was tired of my persistence.

"Sabrina," I pressed, my voice growing quieter. "Please... help me understand what's going on."

Sabrina looked up at me once more. "Drifted, there are things you are not yet ready, not yet able to understand. This... is one of them."

I took a step closer, unwilling to let her dodge the question again. "Ready or not, I should know. Celine, she's my—"

"Your what?" Sabrina interjected. "Your responsibility? Your burden to bear? Or are you implying something else entirely?"

I hesitated, taken aback by her words. "No, no, that's not—" I stammered.

"Then I suggest that you allow for Lady Celine to find her own way, just as you are meant to find yours."

I shook my head, opening my mouth to argue, but I

couldn't find the words. I unclenched my fist and let out a shaky, frustrated breath, turning my eyes away from her.

Sabrina pushed herself off the tree and stepped past me, her hand brushing lightly against my shoulder as she moved toward the bridge. "Come along, Drifted," she said, her tone becoming playful once more. "I would not want you getting lost."

Begrudgingly, I allowed my feet to move as I followed her up the bridges and further away from the arena.

The walk to the High Perch was silent. Sabrina led the way while I trudged behind her, my mind still replaying the events of the day.

Celine's transformation, Rowen's commands, Sabrina's cryptic deflections—it all churned in my brain like a storm I couldn't calm.

Sabrina glanced back at me. "Have you nothing to speak about?" she questioned. "This walk could go by much quicker."

I didn't reply.

"Ah, giving me the silent treatment, are ya'?" She said before turning her head back forward. "Suit yourself. I tend to enjoy the sound of my own footsteps."

The silence between us stretched as we continued, her occasional glances doing little to pull me out of my thoughts.

Eventually, we got to our living quarters, and I quickly walked toward my door, eager to give myself the alone time I needed.

My hand was on the latch when Sabrina's voice stopped me.

"Drifted," she said, her voice devoid of its familiar lightness.

I paused, but kept my head forward, refusing to turn in acknowledgment.

"Do understand that what is to come is for the betterment of the both of you," she said, "For you and Lady Celine."

I let her words simmer for a short while. They were heavy with a meaning that I couldn't even begin to grasp. Then, without replying, I pushed the door open and stepped inside, closing the door behind me.

I pushed off the door and moved toward the bedroom. Every step felt like lead weighed them down as the exhaustion of the day pulled at them. By the time I reached the mattress, I had no energy left to do anything but collapse into it, sinking into the thin fabric.

I lay there for a while, staring up at the ceiling, trying to get myself to fall asleep. But no matter how much I tried, it wouldn't come.

My mind refused to rest, spinning endlessly over everything that had happened. Celine, Rowen, Sabrina, even Lood, kept popping up.

And then there was the situation with my blood.

I turned my head toward the moonlight filtering in through the window, my brow furrowing as the memory replayed itself. Sabrina had taken my blood without hesitation and then rushed to Celine. Seemingly, this was the spark of her transformation.

Why?

How?

What was it about my blood that had triggered her change? Was it only my blood? Or would anyone's blood have had the same effect? And why had Sabrina seemed so sure it would work?

The more I thought about it, the more my head hurt.

I turned onto my side and pulled the blanket over my head. Sleep still wouldn't come. Every time I closed my eyes, I saw the stares of everyone who was in the arena. Eyes that carried a secret.

I tossed and turned, trying to count sheep in my head, but nothing brought the deep embrace of sleep. My body screamed, but my mind stubbornly ignored it. Caught in an endless loop of questions and half-formed theories.

Hours slipped by unnoticed, the dark sky outside my window slowly lightening with the soft colors of the approaching dawn. Before long, I realized the faint line of sunlight filtering into my room. My eyes stung with fatigue, and my head pounded from the lack of rest, but there was no use in trying any longer. Morning had come, and I'd stayed awake through the entire night.

Dragging myself out of bed, I shuffled toward the window. I looked below as various Lupine were already beginning to shuffle, getting ready to start their days. A new day had already begun, and I knew I wasn't prepared enough to face it.

Suddenly, a thought flickered into my mind. Celine would most likely be at breakfast, and I could speak to her there about what happened in the arena last night. Figure out what happened after they forced me to leave.

With a newfound urgency, I quickly got myself ready and rushed toward the door, determined to find answers. But as I opened it, I froze. Standing there, large and imposing, was Lood. He filled the entire space, looking down at me with his rough red eyes.

For a moment, neither of us spoke or made a sound.

Then, Lood grunted, the sound rumbling deep from within his chest. It was as close to a greeting as I'd ever gotten from him. I blinked, my mouth opening and closing as I fumbled for words.

"Uh... good morning?" I finally managed to get out.

He didn't respond.

"I was just... heading to breakfast," I said, nervously

scratching my head.

He let out another grunt, this one shorter, almost dismissive. Then, silence stretched on and I shifted uncomfortably, unsure of whether I should try to move past him or wait for him to step aside.

"Do you... need something?" I asked cautiously.

Lood's eyes narrowed slightly, but he finally stepped to the side, holding his arm out as if gesturing for me to start moving.

I hesitated briefly before stepping out into the open area. As I walked, I noticed Lood following close behind me. I looked over my shoulder slightly.

"Are you following me?" I questioned.

He didn't respond.

I continued speaking, nervously trying to get him off my tail. "Are you hungry as well?"

He didn't respond.

With a sigh, I picked up my pace. Every so often, I glanced back, only to find Lood trailing me with an unchanged expression, his silence as heavy as his presence. The Lupine I passed along the way offered nods or quiet greetings, though their eyes often flicked curiously between me and my now enormous shadow.

The closer I got to the Elderwood, the more my nerves began to build. I was sure Lood following me so intently was no coincidence. Whatever awaited me there, it was unlikely to be a casual breakfast conversation. But that wasn't going to deter me from finding out some answers.

I climbed the wide, spiraling steps that led up to the floor of the dining hall. The fatigue from the sleepless night made my steps feel heavier, but I trudged on. The sound of my boots echoed faintly against the wooden steps, joined by the heavy thuds of Lood's footsteps behind me.

As I reached the top, the faint murmur of conversation

filled the air. I stopped at the top of the stairs, preparing myself for the questions I'd ask Celine. A smile grew on my face, knowing she wouldn't leave me in the dark as Rowen and Sabrina had.

As my eyes scanned the room, I took in the sight of the patrons seated at the long wooden table, their conversations blending into a garbled mess. My gaze moved toward the usual spot where Celine, Rowen, and Sabrina sat together. But to my surprise, the area was empty.

I stood there for a moment, unsure of what to make of their absence. How could they all not be here? The thought of speaking to Celine had been my driving force, and now that she wasn't here, my feeling of unease grew deeper.

Out of the corner of my eye, I spotted Caldryn. His arms were covered with a tray of dishes as he made his way toward a group of Lupine sitting at the table. I hurried over to him.

"Caldryn," I called softly, trying not to draw too much attention. He glanced at me, his brow raising slightly.

"Ah, if it is not the Drifted," he said with a nod. "You are up early this time, yes?"

"Have you seen Celine?" I asked quickly.

Caldryn shook his head, the corner of his mouth raising. "No, I have yet to see Lady Celine today. Or His Highness or Sabrina, for that matter."

My head dropped slightly at his response. "Thanks," I muttered, my voice hollow.

I suddenly became aware of the way the patrons at the table Caldryn was serving were watching me. Their eyes were curious, perhaps even slightly wary. Remembering my manners, I gave them a small bow.

"May the moon guide you," I said, the formal phrase feeling stiff on my tongue. The patrons nodded in return, their expressions softening.

Straightening. I turned and slowly made my way back toward the exit of the dining hall.

As I neared the opening, Lood stepped in front of me, blocking my path. He didn't utter a grunt, but he raised a hand, gesturing for me to follow him.

I hesitated, worried about Celine's whereabouts. Though whatever he had to show or tell me felt important. Wordlessly, I nodded and fell in step behind him.

Lood led me out of the Elderwood. He didn't speak, and I didn't dare break the silence, the weight of his presence was enough to keep my questions at bay for now.

We descended the wide path until the familiar sight of the arena came into view.

Of course, I thought to myself. The rest of the group must already be there, perhaps waking up early to continue training.

The thought sparked some life in me and pushed back the dread that clung to me the entire morning. My steps quickened, and soon I found myself practically speed walking to the arena entrance.

But as I reached the entrance, my enthusiasm was quickly snuffed out. I stepped inside to find the arena eerily quiet.

I looked around, my eyes trying to scan every corner. It was empty.

"Hello?" I called out, my voice echoing against the wooden walls.

Of course, there was no reply. Only the sound of Lood's footsteps broke through as he walked behind me.

"Where is everyone?" I asked under my breath.

I turned to Lood, who stood there looking down at me. "Where is everyone, Lood?" I questioned again, getting slightly frustrated.

I huffed as I realized it was pointless questioning the big oaf. I hadn't heard Lood speak since meeting. What made me think he would answer me now?

I let out a sigh, shaking my head. "Never mind..."

"They are preoccupied," I heard a deep voice say. "They are not here."

I froze for a second as my eyes locked with the source of the voice. It was Lood—the same silent, daunting Lupine that only conversed in grunts and groans.

"You... you can speak?!" I yelled out, raising my arms in an exaggerated manner.

Lood folded his arms. "Yes," he replied.

"Well, you haven't uttered a word since I've met you!" I answered back.

"Is silence not as powerful a form of communication as speech?" Lood questioned back.

I tilted my head slightly, raising an eyebrow. "No?"

"Do not mistake the absence of words for the absence of understanding. I observe. I listen. I speak when necessary."

Confused, I opened my mouth to speak, but honestly, I didn't know how to reply to his unflinching scrutiny.

"I do not need to ramble constantly like that chatterbox, Sabrina," he continued. "Let this be a lesson to you, Drifted. There is purpose in my words."

Lood stepped away from me. "You should prepare yourself," he said, walking toward the center of the arena. "Your training session will begin soon."

I nodded slowly, but then shook my head as I realized my question hadn't exactly been answered yet. "Wait," I called out. "What about everyone else? Is Celine not training anymore?"

Lood turned his head slightly, locking his eyes onto mine. "Celine is undertaking her own specialized training," he replied, clearing the dirt ground with his boot. "As will you as well."

His words only deepened my confusion, but I could tell he was getting annoyed having to speak so much. As I tried to speak again, Lood raised his hand, silencing me without a word.

"Your path is your own, Drifted. Now, prepare yourself."

As I walked toward the center of the arena, I couldn't shake the questions swirling in my mind. Everything had become more secretive since Celine's transformation. What had changed so drastically? Why did it feel as though they were intentionally keeping me away from her?

My thoughts churned as I passed the arena floor. *Specialized training.* The phrase echoed in my mind. Why now? Why the sudden divide? There were barriers being placed between us, barriers I didn't fully understand.

I kicked up dirt, trying to quell the anxiety in my chest. Nothing made sense, and the lack of details provided by anyone was beginning to wane on me.

I was pulled back to reality by the sound of Lood's heavy footsteps getting louder as he approached me. He stopped a short distance away.

"Pay attention, Drifted," he said, his voice firm. "This training will not be as it was yesterday."

I straightened. "What do you mean?" I asked cautiously.

"Yesterday's sparring revealed much," Lood began. "You rely too heavily on the calls of Lady Celine. While it is commendable to trust in one's comrades, such reliance must be an addition to your own strength, not its foundation."

I blinked. It never felt like anything was enough for the Lupine. Here I thought working as a team was a positive, but Lood made it seem as if I were doing something wrong.

"What's wrong with relying on each other?" I questioned him.

"Teamwork is vital, yes, but it should enhance your

abilities, not mask your weaknesses. What will you do when there is no one to call instructions to you? No one to guide your steps or warn you of danger? You must learn to stand as your own pillar."

His words stung a bit, but I knew they weren't meant to hurt my feelings. There was a truth in them I couldn't deny, even if I wanted to. "So, what's the plan?" I asked, swallowing my pride.

Lood nodded slightly, as though approving my willingness to listen. "Today, you will fight as you are, alone. No voices to guide you, no one to warn you of your missteps. No weapon or shield to hide behind. You will learn to rely on your instincts, your awareness, and your own ability."

"So, the same regimen as yesterday?" I questioned. "Trying to land a hit on you again?"

"No, Drifted," he said, something resembling a smile growing on his lips. "This time, you will not be attacking. This time, it shall be you who defends."

Before I could question it, Lood crouched down and shifted. His form contorted, and in a seamless, quick transformation, he was now in his wolfish Lunar form. The same powerhouse that exhibited speed and finesse during his sparring against Celine.

I took an involuntary step back, caught utterly off guard. My heart began pounding in my chest as the wolf before me let out a low growl.

"Now wait a second, Lood! You don't honestly expect me to defend myself against you like this, do you?!" I yelled.

Before I could prepare myself. The lesson began.

CHAPTER 16

I dove toward the floor as Lood's large, gray-furred body went soaring over my head.

As Lood turned, I saw the wild look in his red eyes—a look so primal, so raw and feral it made my legs feel like jelly.

I barely had time to get up as he prepared for his next strike. His claws sliced through the air where I had just been a second earlier, and I went tumbling to the ground in a desperate attempt to distance myself from him.

I scrambled up from the loose dirt, my boots scuffing the ground as I tried to regain some balance. Every thought in my brain told me to run, but I knew there would be no escaping him. The trees that lined the edges of the arena would offer no safety from a Lupine who could so easily sniff out my scent.

I looked at Lood again. Even though this was a training session, there was such ferocity and power behind his attacks. Every time he took a step, the thick muscles beneath his fur pumped, easily pronounced. I tried to steady my breathing as Lood got closer. Freaking out at a moment like this could be deadly.

Slowly, Lood circled me, and I, not trying to give him my back, began circling in the opposite direction. My pulse thudded so loudly in my ears that it almost drowned out the soft scrape of his claws against the ground.

He was testing me. Probing for weakness.

With a low growl, he feinted to my left. I jerked away, boots slipping on the loose dirt, realizing the move was a ploy. He just wanted to see if I'd overreact—and I did. I quickly inhaled through my nose and exhaled through my lips. Losing my composure would only make me sloppy.

Lood charged again. This time, I stepped in, aiming to slip past his attack and tap him—a light blow to remind him I wasn't going to go down without a fight. But he was too fast; he twisted and swatted my arm away with a force that made me grit my teeth. Pain shot up from my forearm and settled in my shoulder as I stumbled back.

A quick glance showed a fresh tear in my sleeve from where his claw had nicked, but thankfully, I was still in one piece. Despite the sting of the bruise I would definitely feel by morning, I still felt determined. This was why we were training—to learn what I was capable of, to push myself to my limits.

I clenched my teeth, trying to ignore the pain in my arm as Lood charged again. Even more relentlessly than before. I sucked in a breath and planted my foot in the dirt. If I didn't want to get pummeled, I needed to be ready.

But all of my thoughts kept drifting back to Celine. Their constant evasions, their awkward silences and half-answers in response to questions about her... it fanned a fiery flame in my chest. If they wouldn't tell me, I'd find a way to force the issue. Maybe my best way forward was to prove I was stronger than they gave me credit for.

I let the frustration rise as my muscles burned with energy. As Lood lunged with his claws raised, I stepped into his attack. At the last second, I spun to his side, angling my shoulder into his ribcage. The jolt slammed through both of us, and it sent me to the ground.

I looked up in time to see Lood staggering as he landed, a low growl rumbling in his throat. *Good*, I thought to myself. If he wanted to charge me again, let him. I'd use every ounce of pent-up anger to stand my ground.

Lood shook his head once, as if to clear it, and I caught a hint of respect in those wolfish eyes. Another low, guttural growl followed, not angry—more like an acknowledgment. For a moment, neither of us moved, as the sound of my harsh breathing filled my ears. My shoulder ached from slamming into him, but I shook it off.

I pushed myself to my feet as I watched Lood lower himself to the ground. Without warning, the thick fur on his body rippled. He dug his claws into the dirt, and I saw his muscles bunched up. I wasn't sure exactly what was happening, but it appeared things were about to amp up.

I squared my stance, trying to keep my voice steady. "Alright, then," I muttered under my breath. My boots squeaked as I repositioned myself, bracing my body.

There was no question in my mind: I'd take everything Lood could dish out. It was the only way to prove I was strong enough. Then, and only then, would they stop treating me as if I were weak.

Lood huffed, sending a small cloud of dust swirling around his muzzle. Then, in one swift movement, he pounced at me, his jaw open.

I wanted to dodge out of the way, but my legs felt sluggish compared to his movement. I knew there would be no way to dodge in time, so at the last possible second, I thrust my arm up to shield myself.

Pain exploded as Lood's fangs clamped down on my forearm. A sharp gasp came from my throat, the bite rattling my senses. My vision blurred for a moment, but I managed to stay on my feet as I bit down to stop any scream from escaping. The force of his bite pushed me back, and I could feel his hot breath on my skin.

For a split second, our eyes met—mine wide with alarm, his narrowed with intensity. *This is just training. He's not trying to kill you, Isaac.* I told myself. But the pain was real, and his strength felt overwhelming.

I braced my free hand against his shoulder, trying to ease the pressure on my arm. His jaw clamped down even harder, and his growls vibrated through my bones. I kept any fear from bubbling up to the surface. If I couldn't handle this, no one would ever see me as their equal, especially not Lood.

I dug my heels deep into the dirt and pushed back with every ounce of will I had. Lood planted his back legs, resisting my efforts. I gritted my teeth, cursing in my head. There was no way he was going to let me free without a fight.

I raised my hand, balled it into a fist, and lashed out at the side of his face. I held back a little, not wanting to hurt him. But the second my knuckles connected with fur and muscle, Lood growled and bit down harder. Pain shot through my arm, and I almost dropped to one knee.

I raised my fist again and sent another strike to the side of his head. Lood shook his head viciously, and my eyes watered from the pain. It was clear this would continue until I could show him I was serious. Until then, he'd never stop.

Steeling my nerves, I summoned whatever strength remained in my trembling body. I sent another fist onto the top of his head. The blow stung, but I drew my fist back a second time. I yelled, and swung my fist straight into his snout, putting as much force behind it as I could without losing control.

Lood's jaw loosened in shock, and I felt my pinned arm slip free, burning with pain and slick saliva. I took a step back, clutching my throbbing forearm, heart pounding so hard that I could feel it pulsing throughout my fresh wound. Lood shook his head, blinking in a daze from the hit. The moment hung there for a second, while I waited to see what he would do next.

Lood crouched down, and I watched as the fur along his arms receded and his muscles rapidly began to shift into skin. He straightened, still breathing hard, his face contorting with the last traces of the transformation.

After a short while, Lood was back in his humanoid form—tall, broad-shouldered, and... completely nude. Heat flared across my cheeks, and I whipped my head away, suddenly embarrassed.

"You fought well," he said, his voice rough from the change. "That is precisely the resolve I sought to see from you."

"Erm, thanks," I mumbled, keeping my eyes glued to the ground.

"What ails you, Drifted?" Lood asked, taking a step toward me. "Blood does not make you lightheaded, does it?"

I took a step back, trying to maintain some distance between us. "No, no—it isn't that..." I looked toward the roof of the arena. "This isn't exactly the most comfortable position to be in."

Lood let out a short exhale. "Ah, you mean the state of bareness that I am in?" he questioned. "When the Lupine shift into their Lunar forms, everything comes off. Naturally, when we shift back, we are like this."

I turned my back to him, and a quick image of Celine shifting back into her human form from her first transformation flashed through my mind. I blushed harder. "Ah... Yeah, I see."

I heard Lood's footsteps move away from me, and I took the risk of a quick glance to see where he was going. He knelt beside a large leather knapsack and began rummaging through it.

After a short while, I felt something soft hit the back of my head.

"Aid to that arm of yours," Lood said, nodding at my wound. "If you can fight through a bite like that, maybe you are finally ready for more of a challenge."

I glanced down to see a small roll of gauze lying at my feet. I crouched down and picked it up, trying not to jostle my bitten arm any more than necessary.

I unwound a strip of gauze and wrapped it around my forearm, wincing whenever the fabric pressed too tightly on rawer portions. I did my best to tie it off one-handed—though I knew my makeshift job looked clumsy. Still, it would be enough to keep the wound contained until I could tend to it further.

A rustle of cloth behind me caught my attention. Before I knew it, Lood was standing next to me again, and this time I didn't need to shield my eyes. He wore a loose shirt and rough trousers, both a bit rumpled from being shoved in the knapsack, but it was more than enough to soothe my earlier embarrassment.

He jerked his chin at my bandaged arm, voice still low and rough. "That is a start. But you best change that dressing soon. The bite may fester."

"Ah, don't worry too much," I replied, raising my injured arm with a smile. "I tend to heal pretty quickly."

Lood eyed me for a long moment, as if weighing to say something else. Finally, he nodded. "I see."

A loud whistle cut through the clearing behind us. Instantly, my shoulders tensed. Whatever relaxation I'd felt surviving the spar vanished in an instant.

"Oh, Drifted!" a voice called out.

I let out a long sigh. Unfortunately, I could recognize Sabrina's voice anywhere.

I turned around slowly, my shoulder sagging. I was ready to tell her off, but as my eyes fell on her, a thought shot through my mind: she could tell me more about Celine.

Sabrina sauntered toward me, a sly grin on her lips.

"I caught the tail end of your little tussle," she purred, hands perched on her hips. "It appears you are not as hopeless as I had once thought."

Her eyes moved to my bandaged arm, and she began unraveling it. "But your skill at patching yourself up is still as hopeless," she teased, already tugging at the strip of gauze. "Let me see the mess you have made here."

I winced as she pulled a little too hard, but she didn't notice—or she did and chose to ignore it. She unraveled my sloppy attempt, exposing the fresh bite marks underneath. I tried not to flinch, but the cool air brushing against the wound was painful.

"Hush," she said as I sucked in a breath. "If you are going to square off against a Lupine, you must better learn how to handle the aftermath."

She rummaged in a small pouch at her hip, withdrawing a roll of clean bandages. I opened my mouth to protest— something about being perfectly capable of taking care of myself—but bit my tongue when I caught the look in her eye.

Sabrina pressed a fresh pad of gauze over the wounds and wound the bandage snugly around my forearm, far better than I had. "You gave Lood a decent fight," she said. "I would say that is proof enough you are not as fragile as everyone thinks."

"Thanks," I murmured, flexing my fingers as she tied off the bandage. My skin still throbbed, but at least now it felt more secure.

She gave my dressing a light pat. "There, now say goodbye to Lood for the night. We must go meet with Prince Rowen."

I tilted my head, confused by her words. "Wait—Prince Rowen? What for?" I asked.

Sabrina let out an exaggerated sigh. "Bah! Must you question everything, Drifted?" She asked, tossing her hands in the air. "You shall find out once we get there."

I hesitated, placing my hands on my hips. "I'm done following you blindly, Sabrina. Either tell me why we're going or go alone."

Sabrina turned on her heel, her long braid coming close to smacking me in the face. She threw her hands up in defeat. "As you wish, Drifted. If you do not wish to find out more about Lady Celine, I will not force you."

My hands dropped back to my sides. I wondered if she was bluffing, but I couldn't risk it.

I exhaled through my nose. "You know that's not fair."

Sabrina flicked her braid over her shoulder. "It is up to you, Drifted. Stay here and sulk—or follow me."

With that, she walked toward the exit of the arena.

I shot a look at Lood, who gave me a half shrug.

I looked back toward Sabrina, who was halfway out of the arena already.

"Fine," I said, swallowing my pride for the moment. "Let's go."

Sabrina snorted softly, as if pleased. "I knew you would see reason," she yelled back, beckoning me to follow.

I followed behind her as she began skipping up the spiraling bridge.

By the time we reached the Hollow, my legs felt like lead because I tried to keep up with Sabrina's pace. She led me through the dimly lit corridors as I prepared the questions I had for Rowen in my head.

Eventually we reached the Hollow and, upon entering, I saw that Prince Rowen was already seated at the large circular table. He glanced up at us as we approached, his face straight.

I looked around and noticed there was no sign of Celine.

228

Sabrina hadn't spoken a word about her the entire walk, and each unasked question churned in my gut.

"Come in," Rowen said. He waved his hand toward the chair that was directly across from him. "Take a seat, Isaac."

I stood in the doorway for a moment. Then, remembering my manners, I dipped into a slight bow. As I straightened, Rowen gave me a nod in acknowledgement.

I stepped forward, pulling out a chair. I felt Sabrina move off to the side, but I kept my focus on Rowen as I sank into the seat.

Rowen looked at my bandaged forearm as it rested on the table. A faint crease formed on his forehead. "Lood seems to be taking it quite rough on you, Isaac," he observed, keeping his voice calm.

I glanced at my arm and quickly folded it against my side. A nervous chuckle slipped out of my lips. "He's trying to toughen me up," I said, forcing a grin. "I'll be alright."

Rowen's lips pressed as if he wanted to question further. But he only offered a curt nod. "Good," he said, interlacing his fingers together. "It wouldn't do well to have you maimed."

I could feel Sabrina moving behind me, probably making faces or bunny ears above my head, but I refused to turn around. If Rowen was about to reveal something—anything—about what was happening to Celine, I needed to keep my focus.

Rowen leaned forward and started playing with his beard. "Usually, Isaac," he began. "I have questions of my own for you before permitting you to voice yours. But tonight..." he spread his hands slightly in a gesture of concession. "Tonight, I'll give you the floor first."

I blinked, suddenly at a loss. This was the moment I'd been preparing myself for—my chance to find out what was going on—but all my carefully rehearsed questions vanished.

"Uh..." I began, turning my head around slightly to look at Sabrina standing behind me. Of course, she didn't offer any help and only offered a teasing grin. An uncomfortable silence stretched, and I could practically hear my own heartbeat.

Finally, I blurted out the one name that had been echoing in my mind. "Celine."

Rowen tilted his head and then folded his arms and leaned back in the chair. "Yes," he muttered. "Celine, my daughter. I suspected she would be at the core of your questions."

Rowen let out a sigh and shifted in his seat. "Celine is well," he said. "You needn't worry about her safety."

My shoulders relaxed, but only slightly. "If she's fine," I started, "then why does it feel like I'm being kept away from her?"

Rowen made sure to lock his eyes with mine. "Because you are."

I frowned at his blunt response. "But why?"

"Because Celine's Lunar form is... different," he said, measuring the words. "Not in the sense that she can't shift like the other Lupine, but rather in the manner by which she transforms."

For a moment, I sat there recalling the night Celine shifted. It all happened so fast—too fast for me to grasp what truly occurred. "What do you mean?"

Rowen inclined his head. "Do you recall how that transformation took place?"

I hesitated. "I'm not... entirely sure," I admitted. "It seemed like... I mean—" I swallowed. "After Sabrina took a bit of my blood and gave it to Celine?"

A subdued murmur left Rowen's lips, almost a hum of acknowledgment. "All Lupine can take on their Lunar form at will," he said, fingers tapping lightly on the table. "Celine, however, appears bound to a different catalyst. Your blood."

My chest tightened, but I still didn't fully understand what I was hearing.

Rowen continued, "Not only is her transformation abnormally triggered, but her Lunar form is unlike any we've seen before—in size and ferocity. You've witnessed it yourself, have you not?"

I nodded. Celine was much larger than even Lood in his Lunar form. "I... Yeah. She was massive."

Rowen leaned in again. "This is precisely why we've kept you two apart. We need to confirm our suspicions about her transformation—why is it that your blood seems to act as the start—and then figure out the rest of the unknowns."

I shook my head in confusion. "Unknowns? What more could there be?"

Rowen looked at my wounded arm and then back up at me. "For one thing, we've observed that once she holds her Lunar form, she collapses the moment she shifts back. Since yesterday, Celine has been resting, nothing can stir her. How much strain is her transformation putting on her body?"

Rowen paused before continuing. "Then, there's the question of what if Celine loses her composure in this form, who could stop her? Her size alone out-measures every Lupine I've ever encountered. Suppose she rampages—there might not be a single one of us capable of containing her."

I leaned forward quickly, admittedly I was upset at his suggestion Celine would ever do something like this. "That's impossible. Celine would never hurt any of us!"

"Can you guarantee that?" he asked, his stare turning cold. "One hundred percent?"

I opened my mouth but found nothing to say in the face of that question. Of course, I believed in Celine with every fiber of my being. But the seed of doubt had already been planted.

Rowen didn't let the silence stretch long. "And if, by some cruel twist, she did lose herself," he continued, "if she threatened the safety of Sylphreach... would you be willing to be the one to cut her down?"

My heart thudded against my ribs, and I fought the urge to recoil at his words. The idea of raising a hand against Celine— of ever having to face her that way—made my blood run cold. But Rowen didn't look away. He wanted an answer, no matter how much it shook me to my core.

I lowered my head, unable to push out the words that sat stuck in my throat.

"I didn't think so," Rowen said, releasing a breath.

I heard to soft creak come from behind me, and suddenly Sabrina was beside me, easing herself into the seat. I didn't look up at her, but I felt her hand pat my head.

"There, there, Drifted," she murmured. She was poking fun as usual, but her touch was surprisingly grounding.

I kept my eyes on the grain of the table and started running my finger around it. Could I really take down Celine if the time ever came? I shook my head, trying to clear my head. *No, not a chance.* I thought.

Rowen spoke up again. "Rest assured, we're taking every precaution," he said, as though addressing both me and Sabrina. "We're monitoring Celine's wellbeing very closely. If there's even a hint of trouble, we will be ready."

I glanced up, finally forcing myself to meet his gaze. He watched me steadily, a faint crease growing on his brow. "Until we learn more," he went on, "we'll need to maintain our current arrangements. I know it may seem harsh, keeping you two apart... but we cannot risk her health—or anyone else's safety."

A dull ache throbbed in my chest at the thought of Celine

somewhere behind closed doors, under constant surveillance. But part of me understood his logic, however begrudgingly. This was about something bigger than my own wants.

Sabrina squeezed my shoulder. For once, she didn't offer a joke. She just let Rowen's words settle over the room.

Rowen stretched before settling back in his chair again. "Now, I have a question for you, Isaac," he said.

I gave a nod. "Yes, Your Highness?"

"We're in the midst of gathering all possible information about Lostsummit," Rowen continued. "We're hoping to uncover anything that might explain Celine's transformation—especially since, from your account, that's where it first happened."

I gave Rowen another nod. "Yeah, as far as I know."

"Well, we need a way to travel into Lostsummit relatively undetected. Ever since Celine and you caused that ruckus, it's been difficult to get any of our spies in there as we had before."

I rubbed the back of my neck and let out a nervous chuckle.

Rowen spoke again. "When you and Remus ventured to Eclipsia," he went on, "as I said before, we had scouts following you at a distance—keeping watch on you two." He pressed his lips together. "Yet, only a couple of days later, Sabrina reported seeing you two in Lostsummit. Such a journey should have been impossible, given the distance. How did you two get there so quickly?"

I looked up for a second, recalling the trip Brute and I took. "Well, we actually had some help," I said, clearing my throat. "While I was there, Brute introduced me to a man named Aldhard. He was a scientist—I think. He spent a lot of time studying and training Dreadbeaks, teaching them how to listen to human commands."

I could sense Rowen's interest piquing as I went on.

"Aldhard showed us how to ride them. And we flew them all the way to Lostsummit."

Rowen shoved his chair back and stood, both palms on the table. "You mean to tell me you actually rode a fiend?!" he blurted out in disbelief. "And the two that you both rode. Where are they now?"

I gave Rowen a frown. "Well, you see. Once we got to Lostsummit, Brute... killed them."

"Damnit," Rowen cursed, sucking in air through his teeth. He raked his hand through his beard, and for a moment it looked like he was fighting the urge to pace. "Being able to fly directly into Lostsummit would make things infinitely easier for the scouts."

An idea struck me, and I raised my chin. "Why don't we bring Aldhard here? To Sylphreach?"

Rowen's eyes narrowed thoughtfully, as though turning the suggestion over in his mind. I pressed on. "As far as I saw, Aldhard's a good man. I'm sure he'd be willing to help us."

Before I could continue, Sabrina let out a squealing, excited laugh. "Drifted! That sounds like a grand idea," she exclaimed, getting her face way too close to mine for comfort. "Oh, Your Highness, please agree. Imagine if that man taught us how to control those otherwise useless fiends. We could have an entire flock of the beasts."

Rowen folded his arms, deep in thought. "If that man—Aldhard—can truly teach us to master such creatures," he said slowly, "then he'd be an immensely valuable ally to the Lupine."

I cleared my throat. "The only problem is... he's currently locked up deep in Eclipsia."

Rowen waved his hand absent-mindedly; his eyes fixed on the table. "You needn't worry about that. We will handle the logistics of the task."

Rowen then suddenly looked up at Sabrina. "As for you, get ready to move. Take a group with you—you'll leave for Moonveil tonight."

"Wait, tonight?" I blurted. "You're sending out a group of scouts already?"

Rowen gave a single nod. "Time is of the essence, Isaac. If we're serious about making contact with Aldhard, we can't afford to waste any time."

"Well, I suppose I should go get my gear together," I said, standing up from the table.

Rowen raised a hand. "You," he started. "Will be returning to your quarters. Lood will be looking for you in the morning to continue your training. You've got a challenging few months ahead."

Sabrina started clapping her hands in excitement. "Cheer up, Drifted," she said, flashing me a large smile. "Once you are trained up proper, you shall come running with us on all the fun hunts, yes?"

Rowen made it clear. I wouldn't be joining them tonight or anytime soon. That left me stuck here, under Lood's not-so-gentle watch. But maybe that wasn't exactly a bad thing. At least this way, I would be able to be here for Celine in case she needed me.

Still, I couldn't help feeling left out as I trailed behind Sabrina as we headed out of the Hollow. My thoughts churned with anticipation, knowing that by the time I saw Celine again, everything might be different. But if there was one thing I'd learned since arriving in Sylphreach, it was that I couldn't afford to give up. Not on Celine, and not on myself.

I just hoped that by the end of this all, I'd finally be ready for whatever awaited me—and for whatever path was ahead of Celine and me.

CHAPTER 17

The days had blended into one long blur of bruises and aching muscles. What began as an awkward attempt to hold my own against Lood slowly transformed into something that I could almost call progress. Almost.

Before I knew it, the months had slipped by with non-stop training. The initial sting of constant failure driving my training had dulled and got replaced by determination that kept me on my feet, even when every fiber of my being told me to quit.

I wasn't anywhere near besting Lood—not even close. But I could see the changes. My movements and reactions grew quicker. The awkwardness in my punches peeled away and grew confident. I still found myself flat on my back by the end of every session. Yet, I picked myself up every time, feeling a little less hopeless.

It wasn't only the cuts and scrapes that marked my growth. It was the way my fists moved with a confidence they hadn't before, the way I could anticipate Lood's strikes a fraction of a second sooner. Sure, it wasn't enough to win, but it was enough to remind me I wasn't wasting my time.

I stopped seeing Sabrina after she left on her expedition to bring Aldhard to Sylphreach. The sound of her voice and wit were something that I strangely missed.

Rowen, too, had all but vanished. The last time I'd seen him was that night in the Hollow. Whatever plans he was tangled in now, they didn't involve me at all.

And then there was Celine. I hadn't seen her since that night in the arena, not even in passing in the halls. It concerned me more than I wanted to admit, her absence something I never really got used to. But as the days continued, I learned to push those thoughts to the back of my mind. There was nothing I could do about it, and dwelling on her absence wouldn't make her appear any sooner.

I stood up and started preparing myself for the day. The soreness in my muscles had become commonplace. Lood was likely already waiting for me at the Dining hall, waiting for us to eat and then begin our session.

After grabbing my gear, I stepped out into the open air of the High Perch. The morning light was soft, and I stretched my muscles against the cold air. I paused for a moment, leaning on one of the rails. The view from the Perch was as vast as usual.

As I gazed out, my eyes caught movement near the main entrance to the Elderwood. A group of Lupine were making their way toward it in a tight formation. At the center of their procession, were two hooded figures. From this distance, I couldn't make out much detail, but there was definitely some significance to their escorts.

I watched as they disappeared underneath the canopy of the Elderwood. Curiosity flickered in my mind, but I shook it off. Whatever was happening, it wasn't my concern.

With that, I turned and started heading down toward the arena, where Lood's inevitable lessons awaited.

The path took me past the entrance of the Elderwood. As I approached, I noticed that the group I had seen from the High Perch had stopped just short of the entrance. The Lupine stood in a loose semicircle, their attention focused on the two hooded figures. They were in conversation, though their words were too low for me to catch.

I turned away, determined to mind my own business, though the scene tugged at my curiosity. As I was about to continue down the path to the arena, a familiar voice called out to me.

"Drifted!"

I froze, turning toward the sound. I looked to see Sabrina jumping up and down, waving her arms in the air, a hood obscuring her face slightly. She waved me over with a smile.

"Well, if it is not my little sparring champion," she said. "This way, you will not want to miss this."

"Sabrina?" I questioned, walking toward her. "What's going on?"

Instead of answering, she grabbed my hand and pulled me toward the group near the Elderwood. "Oh, just you wait until you see what goodies I have brought," she said.

We pushed through the gathered Lupine, Sabrina ignoring the glances we were getting. As we neared the center, I could see one of the hooded figures standing taller than the other, their face covered by the hood on their heads.

Finally, Sabrina stopped and released my hand, turning to face me in a dramatic fashion. "Drifted," she declared, drawing out the words. "Behold the culmination of my greatness. I bring to you... one of your own. Ald... Aldhorn? No, wait—Aldhard!"

The figure turned to face me, and I saw a smile grow on their lips. Then, pulling back the hood of his cloak, Aldhard's face came into view. His expression was as composed as it was back in Eclipsia, and he gave me a slight nod.

"Isaac," he greeted, his voice warm. "It's been a while."

"Wha..." I trailed off, caught off guard. I'd known they were going to bring Aldhard to Sylphreach—it was the entire point of Sabrina's expedition—but I hadn't expected to see him here so quickly. Honestly, I hadn't even realized exactly how much time had passed since they left. The trek to Moonveil would've been at least a month, probably more.

"You're... here?" I said, "Already?"

Aldhard raised an eyebrow, a faint look of amusement on his face. "Aye, apparently they had no trouble sneaking me out of Eclipsia," he said. "Your friends here are quite resourceful."

I glanced at Sabrina as she bumped my side with her hip. "Resourceful? Try brilliant," she said, crossing her arms. "No guards, no alarms—you should have seen me, Drifted. I was flawless."

I ignored her as a soft mumbling interrupted the moment, drawing my attention to the other figure that stood beside Aldhard. The person turned to reveal a hooded woman. She was small and frail, with dark, matted hair peeking out from beneath the edge of her hood. Her thin frame looked almost too fragile to be standing.

Before I could ask, Aldhard chuckled, his voice light. "Ah, that's right. You've never met her." He gestured toward the woman. "Isaac, this is my mother... Elvara."

The woman looked up then, her eyes keen despite her delicate appearance.

She was saying something I couldn't make out. The words were muddled and quiet, almost like she were speaking to someone who wasn't there. Though to make the situation less awkward, I gave her a polite smile.

"It's nice to meet you, ma'am," I said gently, dipping my head.

Her mumbling paused for a moment, her eyes narrowing as they focused on me. Then, her lips twitched into a small frown, and her ramblings began again.

"So pure," she murmured. "Your eyes... so pure, like light... light. Eyes unseen, yes... unbroken... yes."

I stood there, unsure of how to respond. Aldhard stepped in, placing a hand on my shoulder.

"The Hysteria has taken its toll over the years. I'm not sure she'll ever be the same," he said with a sigh.

Elvara continued to murmur, but I could tell her attention wasn't with us anymore. Glancing at Aldhard, I didn't know if I should press the issue. Instead, I opted for a simple nod.

"Well... I'm glad you two made it here safely," I said, trying to fill the air.

Aldhard gave me a nod as he glanced around. His eyes lingered on a Lupine next to him. He studied the Lupine, looking over the features that marked them so different from us humans.

"I must admit," he began, creases growing on his forehead. "I don't understand... this place. These people." He paused, scratching his chin and then looking up at the sprawling canopy of the Elderwood. "Their eyes, their... ears—it's unlike anything I've seen before. It's both fascinating and unsettling."

I wasn't surprised that Aldhard wasn't completely blown away by the Lupine as I was when I first met them. After all, he was a man of science, he's probably seen his fair share of strange and unordinary. "It takes some getting used to," I admitted. "But they've been good to me. And... well, they'll be good to you both as well." I said, gesturing to him and his mother.

"I don't doubt your word, Isaac," Aldhard replied. "But I can't say I understand their reasoning for bringing us here. That's the part I'm struggling with."

I opened my mouth to answer, but before I could respond, a voice called out from the entrance of the Elderwood. "Perhaps I can shed some light on that."

I turned to see Rowen stepping out from the opening, his cloak flowing behind him.

The Lupine all gathered nearby and immediately dropped

into low bows, their voices harmonizing as they spoke their familiar phrase: "May the moon guide you."

Rowen acknowledged them with a nod before focusing his attention on Aldhard. "Aldhard," he said, "welcome to Sylphreach. I understand you must have many questions about your presence here. If you'll follow me, I'll do my best to answer them."

Aldhard stood silent for a second, possibly trying to gain his bearings. Then he gave a slow nod. "Very well," he replied. "Lead the way."

Rowen then looked at Sabrina and me. "You two. You will be joining as well."

Sabrina began jumping up and down before I could even respond to Rowen. "Oh, goodie! Isn't this grand, Drifted? We get to hear all the engrossing news!"

"Yeah... I guess," I replied, dreading the extra work that Lood was going to put me through for being late. But there was no way I could deny a direct order from Rowen.

As we entered the Elderwood, a female Lupine approached us. She stepped in front of Elvara, speaking to her in a soft voice. "Come, I will show you to your quarters," she said, dropping her head slightly as a gesture of respect.

Elvara blinked, her murmurs stopping for a second as she stared at the Lupine. The female Lupine took her hand and then began trying to usher her away.

Aldhard quickly stepped up, grabbing his mother's hand and pulling her back with a wild look in his eyes. "Do. Not. Touch. Her," he said, his voice as sharp as a blade.

The female Lupine paused, and she quickly retracted her hand, giving another courteous nod. Sabrina stepped in, her hands raised. "Aldhard, I assure you that your mother will be quite alright. We take care of our own here, and that includes our guests."

Aldhard looked between Sabrina and the other Lupine woman, his grip on his mother's hand tightening. His eyes then shifted to me, looking for reassurance.

I gave him a nod. "She'll be fine, Aldhard, you have my word."

Aldhard reluctantly let go of Elvara's hand and watched as she was led up the main staircase of the Elderwood.

"She'll be well," Sabrina clarified again, this time with a soft smile.

Aldhard let out a shaky breath, and I watched as he unclenched his balled-up fists.

Rowen waited silently before gesturing for us to follow him deeper into the Elderwood. "Come," he said. "As usual, we have much to discuss."

It wasn't long before we reached the Hollow.

Rowen moved to the center of the room and gestured for us to sit. Sabrina plopped down immediately, her arms resting on her knees, as she grinned up at me. I sat beside her, rolling my eyes.

Aldhard, however, stood for a moment, his eyes sweeping over the Hollow. His gaze lingered on the maps, towering roots, and the intricate carvings etched into the bark of the room. Finally, after a while, he lowered himself into a chair, sitting stiffly across from Rowen.

Rowen cleared his throat and opened his mouth to speak, but Aldhard was faster. "Before you begin," Aldhard started, "I have questions."

Rowen raised an eyebrow but nodded, gesturing for him to continue.

"Who are you?" Aldhard asked. Given his background, it wasn't surprising that he already would have formulated many questions about his predicament.

"I am Rowen Pellehan," Rowen answered evenly. "The

leader of the Lupine here in Sylphreach."

Aldhard's eyes narrowed. "The leader?" he echoed, the skepticism in his voice evident. "Forgive me, but you don't exactly look like *them*."

Rowen's lips twitched, though I couldn't tell why. "You are correct," he replied. "Unlike the others here, I am human—as you are. I hail from Moonveil, though that was many years ago."

"And how does a human like yourself go on to lead this town of... I'm sorry, what are these peculiar people?" Aldhard questioned, shooting a look at Sabrina.

Sabrina raised her hand but began speaking before she could be called on. "We, sir," she began, "are Lupine. An ancient and—might I add—superior race, far beyond the comprehension of mere—"

"Sabrina," Rowen interrupted, cutting her off before she could take it any further. "This is not the time."

Sabrina smirked as her red eyes gleamed with amusement. "Of course, Your Highness."

Rowen sighed, the barest hint of exasperation flickering across his face before he turned his attention back to Aldhard. "As she said, they are Lupine—a race tied to the Elderwood and the lands of Velora. Their gifts, such as the transformation you've undoubtedly heard of, are innate to them."

Aldhard scratched his head, presumably trying to come to terms with everything he was being told. After a short while, he leaned forward.

"Okay, I understand." he finally spoke up.

Wait, that's it? I questioned in my head. Why was he acting as if it were that easy to accept the existence of a race of ancient wolf-life beings tied to a sentient forest?

Aldhard must have caught the look on my face because he added, "I didn't say I understood the whole situation, only that I understand what you've told me so far." He leaned back far in his chair, staring up at the ceiling. "It's... a lot to take in, but I'm willing to listen."

Rowen gave a small nod, acknowledging his response. "That is all I ask," he said. "And in time, I believe you will come to understand much more."

Sabrina leaned toward me, whispering. "He's taking this better than you did," she teased, poking a finger at my cheek.

"Oh, quiet, Sabrina," I muttered under my breath, though I couldn't help but feel a little defensive. She wasn't wrong—but still.

Rowen ignored our exchange and spoke to Aldhard once more. "The reason you are here today," he began, his tone steady and deliberate, "is because we believe you may be able to help us."

Aldhard's brow furrowed slightly. "Help you?" he repeated, his voice laced with curiosity. "How exactly?"

Rowen glanced at me briefly before continuing. "According to Isaac, you possess a rather unique ability: the skill to train fiends, specifically Dreadbeaks."

Aldhard shot me a look, his eyes narrowing. "And you've been talking about me, have you?" he asked, his voice dry but not entirely unkind.

I shrugged, trying not to look too guilty. "It came up," I said. "I figured it might be useful."

Aldhard sighed, pinching the bridge of his nose before answering. "Yes," he admitted, "it's true. I've studied and worked with fiends extensively, including Dreadbeaks. But I'm not sure I understand why you'd need such a skill."

Rowen folded his hands in front of him, his gaze steady. "There is someone here," he began, "Someone very dear to me—my daughter, Celine. She is... unique among the Lupine, and there are aspects of this uniqueness that remain a mystery to us."

Aldhard raised an eyebrow as Rowen continued speaking. "I have reason to believe that information about her— knowledge that could be crucial to her future and ours— exists in enemy territory."

Aldhard frowned, clearly processing this new information. "You're suggesting I train these creatures to aid you in retrieving this information?" he asked, more a statement than a question.

Rowen inclined his head. "Precisely. Your knowledge and abilities could help us retrieve this information far quicker than we could alone. With the Dreadbeaks, we would be able to slip in undetected."

Aldhard leaned back, his expression contemplative. "And if I were to say no?" he asked.

"That is your choice," Rowen replied, his tone steady but carrying an undercurrent of gravity. "But this is not only about my daughter. What we seek could hold the key to protecting all of us in the future, especially Isaac. What you choose to do with that knowledge is entirely up to you."

Aldhard looked at me and then back at Rowen. "Explain."

"Isaac's presence here is no mere coincidence," Rowen started. "It is clear there is a greater plan at play that involves him, though I am not sure what it is."

There was a long pause as Aldhard processed this. His fingers tapped lightly on his knee. Finally, his gaze softened slightly, though the edge in his voice remained. "And you're telling me this because you think it will sway me?"

Rowen tilted his head. "I tell you this because it is the truth."

I couldn't stay silent any longer. "Please, Aldhard," I said, practically pleading. "If this could help, Celine—if it could give us answers we don't have—I'll do whatever it takes to help you. Just... please, for my sake."

Aldhard's eyes locked on mine, analyzing my expression. For a moment, I thought he might brush me off, but then something softened in his expression. He exhaled and glanced back at Rowen.

"Then I'll need to know everything," he said, his tone firmer now. "No half-truths, no omissions."

Rowen nodded. "You have my word. In time, you will know everything you need to."

Aldhard leaned back slightly, exhaling as though to steady himself. "Well then, I suppose it's time I check on my mother," he said, standing and brushing imaginary dust from his cloak. "Where is she?"

Rowen nodded. "Of course. Sabrina can take you to her quarters."

Aldhard shook his head, a small, polite smile touching his lips. "That won't be necessary. I'll be more than fine if Isaac accompanies me. We have much to catch up on."

Sabrina gasped theatrically, pressing a hand to her chest. "Oh, is it the way that I smell?" she asked. "Is it the wolfishness that drives you away? I assure you that I bathed in the finest spring... last month."

I rolled my eyes, fighting back the smile creeping onto my face. "I'd love to catch up, Aldhard, but Sabrina knows this place far better than I do. Maybe it'd be best if she—"

Sabrina waved me off, a pout growing on her lips. "No, no, Drifted. Let the man have his preferences. I suppose I shall survive the slight."

Aldhard gave a faint chuckle, shaking his head. "It's nothing personal," he said dryly. "Isaac and I simply need to speak."

Rowen gestured toward the path. "Very well. Isaac, see to it that he finds her safely."

I nodded, standing to follow Aldhard as he started toward the exit of the Hollow. Just as we were leaving, I caught Sabrina speaking to Rowen.

"Be honest with me. Do I truly smell that bad?"

Aldhard glanced over his shoulder briefly, while I stifled a chuckle. Rowen's response was too quiet to hear clearly, but I didn't need to catch his words to imagine the annoyance likely etched across his face.

We walked in relative silence for a while, the quiet shuffle of Lupine surrounding us. Aldhard eventually broke the silence with a question. "That Celine Rowen mentioned earlier... is it the same, Celine? The one you were looking for when you came to Eclipsia those months ago?"

I nodded, glancing at him. "Yeah, that's her."

Aldhard chuckled softly. "She tends to get herself into trouble quite a bit, doesn't she? Seems like you've made it your job to be her knight in shining armor."

I laughed, shaking my head. "Hardly. If anything, she's far more capable than I am. At the end of it all, it's usually her who does the saving."

Aldhard let out a chuckle. "Capable or not, she's fortunate to have someone who cares for her as much as you do."

His words caught me off guard, and I felt heat rising to my face. "It's not like that," I muttered, looking down at the floor. "I... she's important to all of this, you know?"

Aldhard didn't press the matter, though the small smile on his face told me he wasn't convinced. After a moment, his expression changed, growing more serious. "What about Brute? He was with you when you came to Eclipsia. Is he here as well? Can we visit him?"

My shoulder sagged instantly. "Brute wasn't who we thought he was," I whispered, my voice tightening. "He... tried to kill me. There was some plan—something I still don't understand—that I got tangled up in, Aldhard. He was an enemy pretending to be an ally."

Aldhard's brow furrowed deeply, his steps slowing as he processed my words. "That's... hard to believe," he said, his voice tinged with disbelief. "I've known Brute since he was a child. He was loyal, dependable... How could someone like that—"

He paused mid-sentence as his eyes landed on my face. Whatever he saw there—maybe the tension in my jaw or the way I was staring hard at the path ahead—made him stop himself. He let out a small sigh and straightened his posture.

"I see," he said quietly. "I can tell you've been through a lot, Isaac. You've grown in a short amount of time."

I nodded, grateful that we chose to change the subject. "You think so? I still feel the same." I replied.

Aldhard gave a faint chuckle, shaking his head. "You may feel the same, but trust me—you've changed. It's evident in the way you carry yourself. You look stronger, more confident. Even the way you speak is different."

I hadn't known Aldhard for a long time, but even in that short amount of time, he was able to analyze me so deeply.

"I'm just doing what I'm told—what feels right," I said, scratching the back of my neck.

"Whatever you're doing, it's pushing you forward. That alone is making a difference." Aldhard replied.

I wasn't sure how to respond to that, so I settled for a quiet "Thanks," letting his words linger in the air between us as we continued down the path.

After a while, I spotted a Lupine standing near the edge of a large, moss-covered root. She looked to be on guard duty, scanning the surroundings. I approached her, hoping she wouldn't mind a quick interruption.

"Excuse me," I said, stepping forward. "Could you tell us

where Elvara's quarters are?"

She tilted her head slightly before answering. "Yes... the new human woman." She tapped a finger on her chin. "Take the main staircase up to the third floor. Her quarters are on the left at the end of the hall. You shall know it by the woven crest on the door."

"Thank you," I said with a nod. She dipped her head slightly in return before returning to her duties.

I turned to Aldhard. "Looks like we're headed up."

We ascended the staircase, the wood beneath our feet creaking with each step. By the time we reached the third floor, the air felt lighter, and the hum of the Elderwood was quieter but no less present.

At the end of the hall, just like the guard had said, a door carved with an intricate woven crest stood slightly ajar. Aldhard stepped forward, hesitating for a moment before glancing back at me. "Alright, Isaac, this is my stop," he said quietly.

He lingered for a moment, his hand resting on the edge of the doorframe. "I get the feeling I'm going to be very busy in the coming days," he said, glancing over his shoulder at me. "It... helps to have someone familiar around. Someone I can trust."

I nodded, unsure of what to say. There was a weight in his words I hadn't expected. "You can always count on me," I finally replied.

Aldhard gave me a small smile—a subtle curve of his lips, but it felt genuine. "I know," he said simply. Then, with a deep breath, he pushed the door open and stepped inside.

As the door closed behind him, I lingered in the hallway, staring at the woven crest on the door.

Aldhard's words stuck with me. *Someone he can trust.* It was strange to hear him say that, almost as though he needed the reassurance as much as I did. This place—these people—it was all so different from anything either of us had known. And yet, here we were, trying to find our place in it all.

With a sigh, I turned and made my way back down the creaking staircase. I didn't know what the coming days would bring, but for the first time since Celine's absence, I felt like I wasn't facing it alone.

CHAPTER 18

A couple more months passed since Aldhard's arrival in Sylphreach. The days grew a fraction lengthier as time went on and the sun hung in the sky longer. The chill in the air faded slightly, giving way to the faintest promise that the long winter might finally be winding down.

During that time, I kept up with my training with Lood. I remembered how earlier sessions had left me battered and bruised, struggling to keep up in the slightest. But now, things clicked. My footing grew more confident—enough that on rare occasions, I was able to land a couple of punches on Lood. Each minor victory sparked a sense of pride in me that kept me going day after day.

Celine's absence still irked me. I still hadn't caught so much as a glimpse of her. I tried to ask around to any Lupine I met in the halls, but no one ever had any information to spare. It was almost as if the entire town was made aware that we were meant to be separated.

Sabrina and Rowen also stayed fairly absent. Preoccupied with their own responsibilities. Sabrina took up helping out Aldhard with his studies on the fiends, so we only shared quick nods whenever our paths crossed. She was so busy that she forgot to tease me whenever we did see each other. It felt like an unspoken distance had grown between us, one that neither of us seemed quite sure how to bridge.

On the days when the loneliness felt too deep, I found my way to Aldhard's workshop. He never seemed to mind my visits, even if they consisted mostly of me hovering near his benches, watching him fuss over training Dreadbeaks or scribbling in notebooks. There was comfort in his work, and just being there made me feel a bit better.

As I was in thought over the past months, I made my way down the bridges and toward the arena. Lood made it clear to me yesterday that I wasn't to be late under any circumstances.

As I reached the vine-covered opening, I rolled my shoulders and cracked my knuckles, preparing myself for whatever Lood planned to throw at me for the day. I didn't know exactly what he had planned, and admittedly it made me nervous, but there was no way I was going to let that scare me off.

Slipping past the thick, intertwining vines, I entered the arena. My thoughts were already drifting, half-focused on greeting Lood and half on the exercises to come. "Hey," I said absentmindedly, my eyes looking down at the shoelace untied on one of my boots.

But as I looked up, I came to a dead stop. My heart fluttered, and I felt the blood drain from my face. There, standing right in front of me, was Celine—conversing with Lood as if no time had passed at all. I blinked and rubbed my eyes, certain I must have imagined her there, but no, there was no denying it. Celine was here.

For a moment, it felt like the whole world had narrowed to the three of us. I stood frozen, trying to convince myself that this wasn't some dream. Yet it was real enough—her voice, her posture, the familiar tilt of her head as she listened intently. Celine, the person I had worried about endlessly, the one whose absence had gnawed at my thoughts every night, was suddenly in front of me—and I had no idea what to do next.

Celine turned her head in my direction, and for a second, I could have sworn the entire town had fallen silent. She looked at me, and a smile slowly curved on her lips.

"Good morning, Drifted," she said.

My throat felt tight. I tried to speak, but all that came out was a stuttering breath. I wanted to ask her a thousand questions, but they all collided in my mind, getting stuck in my throat as they tried to stampede out.

Before I fully realized what I was doing, I rushed forward. My hands found hers as if drawn by some magnetic pull, and I gripped them tightly. "Celine—where have you been? I mean, I know where you've been, kind of. But why, I mean, are you okay? I—I thought... I mean, I looked everywhere for you. How did they keep you so hidden in this place, anyway? Are you hurt? What did they put you through?"

The words just came tumbling out. I barely gave myself any time to breathe. Even as I heard myself rambling, I couldn't seem to stop. It was like every question, every worry, every ounce of fear I had needed to be expelled from my lungs.

"Drif—" Celine tried to get a word in, but I couldn't stop my own.

"I can't believe I'm actually seeing you here. I thought maybe—well, I didn't know what to think. I asked everyone, even Sabrina, but nobody would tell me where you were or what happened. I was afraid something terrible might have—"

"Drifted..." Still, I didn't respond to her.

"I mean, I guess it's okay now—you're here and safe—wait, you are safe, right? Oh, by the moon, what am I thinking? I didn't even check if you were safe. I'm sorry, I—"

"Drifted!" Celine yelled this time, the smile still on her face.

I froze, feeling my mouth snap shut.

"S-sorry," I whispered, swallowing hard.

Celine kept her eyes on mine. "I am unharmed, truly," she

said. "Do forgive me, Drifted. I would have revealed myself sooner, yet the circumstances needed me to remain out of sight. I am sorry for the worry my absence has caused you."

The relief of seeing her, hearing her, nearly overwhelmed me, and I took a steady breath.

Celine glanced over at Lood, who stood nearby with his arms folded across his chest. I might have been mistaken, but there was a subtle hint of amusement on his face. Celine returned her attention to me. "I am safe, and it appears so are you. Worry not—I shall explain everything in time."

As I studied Celine more closely, I noticed something different about her. Something I couldn't immediately put a finger on. Then it struck me. Her hair. Where it had once tumbled past her shoulders, it was now cut into a sleek, straight bob that framed her face.

"Hey, you cut your hair," I commented, staring at her new do.

Celine tilted her head and then nodded. "Indeed," she replied. "It was Father's suggestion. He maintained that my former style placed me in needless harm—that it could be easily seized in the midst of battle." She hesitated, taking a moment to continue. "Does it displease you, Drifted?"

I noticed how rude I must have sounded, blurting it out like that.

"No... I mean, no, not at all," I said, fumbling over my words. "It looks good on you. Different, but... in a good way."

A bit of relief passed over her face, and the tension in my shoulders eased up a bit.

Lood cleared his throat behind us, and rather loudly at that. I turned my head and found him watching with a straight face. I glanced down and realized I was still clutching both of Celine's hands in mine. Flustered, I let them go and stepped back clumsily.

"Sorry," I muttered to Celine, then looking at Lood.

Lood stepped up. "If you both are finished exchanging pleasantries, might we proceed? I believe we had a lesson awaiting us, and I do not favor delays."

"Right," I said. "Yes, training."

Celine dipped her head toward Lood. "Yes, Sir Lood. Let the training commence."

I started stretching, expecting Lood to lead us through the usual drills, but he gave me a long look. "Today," he began, "shall be somewhat of a special lesson, Drifted. Rather than face me, you will spar against one another."

I froze. "Wait... with Celine?" I looked at her, confused. Sparring with her was the last thing I anticipated—especially with her being gone for so long.

Lood raised an eyebrow. "Yes, Drifted. Did you imagine she spent her time idly while she was away? She was honing her skills as well, out of sight." His gaze moved to Celine. "I expect you both to make good use of what you have learned these past few months."

My heart started hammering. There was no way I could spar against Celine. Not because I thought I could hurt her—in fact—quite the opposite. Celine could read my every move. It was how she had always been so good at advising me on dodges and counters, anticipating the way fiends would strike long before I could see any telltale sign.

I stood there nervously grinding the arena's dirt beneath my boots. Lood watched me closely, ready for me to protest. I knew that any display of doubt would only earn his displeasure. I studied Celine's features. She was calm, arms rested at her sides. She looked entirely at ease with the notion of us fighting.

"Drifted, are you ready?" she asked. "Let us see how far we have come."

"Oh, erm, yeah... of course," I replied to her. Though I was sure my stance said otherwise.

I swallowed hard, looking over at Lood, who was now tapping a foot on the ground. "We do not have the entire day," he said. "Proceed."

Without another word, I dropped into the stance Lood had drilled into me—knees slightly bent, weight balanced, hands raised to protect my face and torso. Across from me, Celine did the same, but she kept her palms open. I couldn't help but marvel at how much stronger she appeared than before.

A part of me wanted to back away, to claim I wasn't ready or some other excuse. But I pushed the thoughts down, believing in how far I'd come, how many times Lood had knocked me flat only for me to stand up again. If nothing else, I wasn't that same untrained, unsure person I had been on the day I arrived in Sylphreach.

"Drifted," Celine called out to me.

I looked at her, and she gave me a nod with a subtle smile on her lips.

I returned the nod and gave her a smile of my own.

Then, without further warning, she rushed forward.

She was on me in an instant. It was obvious she had gotten faster since I'd last seen her. I had only a split second to prepare myself before she sent a palm hurtling toward my head. I moved my head to the side, narrowly avoiding the blow, but I could still feel the air around my ear quiver with the force of her strike—it was enough to jar me slightly.

I could practically feel the weeks—months—of training emanating off her, the steadiness in her stance and the speed behind each move. I sucked in a sharp breath, trying to settle my nerves. If I wanted to stand a chance, I would need to stay focused and trust in my movements.

Celine followed up, preparing herself for another attack. I could hear Lood's voice ringing in my head, barking at me from our previous sessions. *"Keep the guard up. Watch the shoulders. That is where the attack begins."*

I tried to do exactly that, focusing on the subtle changes in Celine's posture. Her shoulders dropped a bit, signaling that a strike was aimed at my ribs. I moved to deflect it with my forearm, tightening my fist to tense my muscles. The impact came quickly, vibrating through my bones, and I had to dig my feet in to avoid giving her any ground.

She immediately pivoted, sending a kick at my midsection. I stepped and moved my arms to block the other side of my body. The force of her leg against my arm felt like a plank of wood being slammed into me. I cursed under my breath and instead planted my foot again for stabilization.

I couldn't keep this up. If I were to stay on the defensive, she would wear me down in no time. Determined not to let her push me back and further, I decided then and there to switch tactics. On her next attack, I would look for an opening.

I watched as Celine's movement changed again. She switched on one leg and sent a sweeping kick toward my thigh. I was prepared and lifted my leg, meeting her shin with mine. The collision sent her slightly off balance. *There it is*, I told myself.

I sent a punch toward her midsection with all the speed I could muster. It came close—close enough that I felt my knuckles brush the fabric of her tunic—but before it could connect, her hands latched onto my arm. She dropped backward onto the arena floor, dragging me off my feet with her. She lifted her feet, and using my momentum against me, she dug them into my stomach. An instant later, she rolled onto her back and propelled me up and over her, sending me flying into the air.

I twisted midair as I tried to calm my nerves. Desperate to avoid crashing face first into the ground, I tucked in my limbs and landed upright roughly. I took a quick breath, thankful that I could avoid a total wipeout

But that small moment was all I was given. Celine was already on me again. I saw her palm moving toward my side, way too fast for me to dodge. Realizing I wouldn't have enough time to move, I clenched my abs and braced myself. Her strike connected, and a flare of pain went through my ribs. I staggered back, biting down as the burning radiated across my torso.

I barely had time to recover from the blow before Celine pressed again, driving her palm against my forehead. My head snapped back, and for a brief moment I saw stars across my vision.

Even as I fought through the haze, I caught the movement of her next strike coming toward my side. With a burst of adrenaline, I twisted my torso and trapped her arm between my side and elbow, pinning it firmly against me.

I threw a punch with my free arm, ready to drive it straight at her face. But as my fist got close, I saw the slightest flinch in her eyes—enough to stop me in my tracks. My knuckles hovered in the air just in front of her face. I couldn't do it. I couldn't follow through with the blow.

Celine, sensing my hesitation, moved instantly to break free. She raised her leg and kicked it heavily against my hip, forcing me to stagger back. Her pinned arm slipped from my side, and I fell to one knee, clutching my burning hip.

My pulse thudded loudly in my ears as Celine approached. I looked up to see her standing over me, hand raised and ready to deliver the final blow. I tensed my body and closed my eyes, preparing myself for the hit.

"Enough!" Lood's voice boomed through the arena.

Celine dropped her hand immediately and took a few steps back, her breath ragged, while I also fought to steady my own breathing. Before I could stand, Lood was in front of me, grabbing a fistful of my tunic and pulling me into the air.

His eyes were burning with anger—an intensity I'd rarely seen from him. "Drifted," he growled. "What foolishness caused you to withhold your strike?"

I wanted to speak, but I knew whatever excuse I would come up with would only anger him further.

He started shaking me roughly, as if trying to force the words out of me. "In battle, there is no room for hesitation. Every moment you pause could be your last," he continued. "Or worse, it might cost the life of one you hoped to protect. Whether it is friend, foe, or someone dear to you, an enemy will not spare you because you show some cowardly mercy."

I frowned, unable to defend myself.

"Or do you imply that Lady Celine is beneath you, too weak to handle a strike by your hand?" Lood questioned again, squeezing my tunic even tighter.

My cheeks got hot with a mix of shame and anger. "No, it isn't that. I... I just couldn't--"

Lood's eyes got even narrower, silencing me with a burning glare. "You did not," he said bluntly. "And if I had not stopped her, you would be lying flat on the dirt beneath you."

He turned his head toward Celine and then dropped me to the ground. "We are done for today," he declared. "I expect you to learn from this, Drifted. The path ahead will not tolerate your weakness."

With that, he turned and strode away, leaving me to swallow the sting of his words. I felt Celine's eyes on me— concerned, perhaps even remorseful—but I couldn't bring myself to look at her.

I saw her hand appear in front of me, palm open in a quiet invitation. At first, I hesitated, but finally I let out an inaudible sigh and reached up. She pulled me to my feet, and I brushed the dirt from my clothes.

She tilted her head slightly and gave me a smile. "Come, let us get some food and recover our strength after such a bout."

I gave her a small nod, still a little uneasy but grateful for the offer. Together, we left the arena, and I realized for the first time in months we were walking side by side again. Despite the lecture from Lood, a part of me felt relieved.

As we walked out into the cooler air, we made our way up the bridge. Celine kept a gentle pace, giving me a moment to catch my breath.

We neared the Elderwood, and I noticed a cluster of Lupine gathered outside, whispering in hushed voices. At first, I paid little attention, assuming they were gossiping about the day's events. But then I caught a word—*Moonveil*.

I stopped and tried to listen closer. That's when I caught another word—*attacked*.

My heart dropped. The name alone shocked me, but I willed myself to keep my composure. I glanced at Celine, and the concern in her eyes told me she had heard what I did, as well.

Without waiting, we slipped through the crowd, gently pushing past the Lupine who were at the Elderwood's entrance. I caught more bits and pieces as we moved. "devastation," "ambush," "casualties," none of which helped the knot that was forming in my chest.

"Please allow us through," Celine called out, firm enough that the cluster of onlookers parted. I heard the whispers intensify as we hurried by, making my thoughts spin with fear for what might have happened.

Once we were clear of the throng of people, we ducked into the Elderwood. My heart was pounding, half from being exhausted and half from panic.

We made for Rowen's throne immediately. Celine and I expected to find him seated there—calming the Lupine, or at least giving information about what was going on. But the throne was empty, its wooden seat unoccupied.

Celine's brows furrowed. "Perhaps the Hollow," she said quietly.

I nodded, swallowing back the worst of my rising dread, and we set off through the hallway to the Hollow. As soon as we stepped inside, I noticed the heavy atmosphere, like the air brimmed with tension.

There, in the center of the room, sat Rowen, Sabrina, and Aldhard—each of them sitting in silence. As we entered, they each turned their heads toward us. No one spoke at first, and I could practically feel the weight of bad news hanging between them.

"Why isn't anyone speaking?" I snapped. "Someone tell me what's going on. Is it true? Was Moonveil attacked?"

Sabrina looked down at the table and then back up at me. "Drifted," she said softly. "You may want to take a seat."

I shook my head. "No, I don't want to sit—I want to know what's happening!" I yelled.

Rowen inhaled slowly and then let out a breath. "Isaac, the reports are true," he said. "Scouts have confirmed that King Cassius orchestrated an ambush on Moonveil using the fiends."

I felt my stomach sink.

But then, Rowen's next words hit me hard. "They specifically targeted Lunaria..."

Lunaria—my birthplace, my home.

Before I could force out a single word, Rowen locked his

eyes onto mine. He raised his hands from the table, as if trying to prepare me for his next words. "Isaac... your uncle Alfarr has been taken."

And there, as if suspended in time, the chapters of my life changed once again.

CHAPTER 19

I clenched my fist, struggling to control my short, uneven breaths. I turned on my heel, prepared to storm out of the Hollow. My ears felt stuffed, and my mind was a storm. I had heard enough. I wasn't going to sit here—I needed to do something.

Before I could take another step, something quickly moved in front of me. Sabrina stood, her eyes trained on me. In the moment I wasn't sure, but it almost looked as if there was pleading in her expression.

"Drifted, what exactly do you plan on doing?" she asked.

My blood boiled at her question. "Get out of my way, Sabrina!" I snapped back at her.

She didn't move. If anything, she planted herself more firmly in the exit, holding her arms out to block any possibility of me passing.

"Is that truly what you wish?" she mused. "To storm out filled with rage, falling right into Cassius' trap."

I took a long deep breath, willing myself to not do something I would regret. "I don't have to explain anything to you," I turned, now facing everyone who sat silent in the Hollow. "To *any* of you."

Silence took over the room. No one spoke. Not even Celine, who remained beside me. They all watched me, waiting.

Then Rowen exhaled slowly. "I understand that you are upset, Isaac, but—"

"You promised," I cut him off. "You promised you would watch over them, take care of my family." My throat tightened as I took a step closer to the table. "What happened to that?"

Rowen held his eyes on mine. I couldn't read his expression, but I could feel the sorrow in it. Again, he fell silent, not answering right away. That silence only made my chest burn hotter.

"Answer me!" I yelled, staring up at the ceiling.

Suddenly, I felt a large hand on my shoulder, turning me around.

It was Lood. Distracted, I hadn't heard him come up behind me.

"You forget yourself, Drifted," Lood said. "That is no way to speak to one regarded so highly as His Highness, Prince Rowen."

Lood's hand was heavy, almost holding me in place. It felt like he was daring me to shake it off. I clenched my jaw tighter. Every fiber in me wanted to push back.

"Get your hands off me, Lood, this doesn't concern you!" I snapped.

Lood's eyes darkened over. His hand lifted from my shoulder, only to ball into a large fist. The sheer size of it made my stomach tighten, but I kept my gaze glued to his.

"Watch your tongue, Drifted. Have you no sense of shame?"

Before he could bring his fist down, Rowen's voice shot out.

"Lood!" he said with a firm tone. "Lower your hand."

"But. Your Highness..." Lood questioned, dropping his fist slowly.

Rowen's eyes returned to me, looking me over, studying me. "Tell me, Isaac—what is your plan?"

Without hesitation, I growled. "I'm going to protect my family, something *you* should have been doing."

Rowen said nothing, waiting.

I took a step forward, placing a hand on my chest. "I'm taking one of Dreadbeaks Aldhard has been training," I declared. "And I'm heading to Thornwallow, my damn self."

The room fell silent once again. Then, Lood scoffed. "Preposterous."

Rowen, however, lifted a hand, signaling for Lood to quiet. He kept his eyes on mine and began stroking his beard. "I will not stop you," he said at last. "When you first arrived here, I told you that you were free to leave at any moment you saw fit. I will not go back on that word."

Lood took a large and heavy step further into the room. "Your Highness, with all due respect, I must reject. If something were to happen to him, then—"

"Lood!" Rowen yelled out this time, slamming a fist on the table.

Lood went silent.

"Do you disagree with my judgment?" Rowen questioned.

For a moment, Lood looked as if he might have fought back. But then he slowly lowered his head. "I do not."

Rowen let the words hang for a bit before turning to me again. "Then, it is as I have said. You are free to leave, Isaac. The decision is yours to make."

I didn't hesitate. I turned on my heel, heading straight for the exit.

Lood was still in my way, his broad figure blocking the path. He held his ground for a moment, and then, with a slow exhale, he stepped aside. Begrudgingly.

I didn't give him a second glance.

As I was leaving, I caught Celine give Rowen a small bow from the corner of my eye.

Then, I heard soft footsteps behind me. I didn't need to turn to know that she had followed me out.

"You don't have to come with," I muttered to Celine, not

turning around or slowing down my pace.

"That would be quite impossible," she said. "Allowing you to go alone would be nothing short of foolish."

I exhaled. "Celine, I don't need you getting tied up in whatever disaster this is going to become. Stay here with your family."

Celine moved in front of me, and I barely had time to stop before nearly colliding with her.

"Such words from you are ridiculous," she said, her violet eyes piercing my own. "Do you truly believe I would allow you to walk headfirst into this storm alone?"

I frowned, but before I could respond, she continued.

"The moon has long since cast its light upon our shared path, Drifted. You may try to step into the shadows, but I will not be so easily left behind." She tilted her head slightly. "So, unless you intend to waste even more time arguing beneath its gaze, I suggest you accept what has already been set in motion."

I stood there dumbfounded. I didn't know exactly how to respond to her. Hell, I was sure nothing I would say would l matter. Though, I was thankful for her choice to be there with me every step of the way, no matter the issue.

A small smile tugged at my lips as I opened my mouth. But then, I was cut off.

"Wait for me!"

I sighed and ruffled my hair as I turned toward the voice.

Of course, it was Sabrina.

She was striding toward us, head held high in the air, chest puffed out. And beside her, walking with far less enthusiasm, was Aldhard.

"I cannot believe you two were truly going to leave me behind!" Sabrina declared, placing a hand on her hip. "To wallow in the dull monotony of Sylphreach, while you rush off toward a grand adventure? How utterly cruel."

I could already feel a headache forming. "Sabrina, you're not coming."

She gasped dramatically, clutching her chest. "Not coming? Do my ears deceive me, or has Drifted taken to spouting nonsense?" She stepped closer, grinning. "No, no, no, that simply will not do. You would be lost without me. Do you not agree, Lady Celine?"

I ran a hand through my hair, shaking my head. "Sabrina, this isn't some game. I mean it. You're not coming."

She tilted her head. "And yet, here I am. Will you be stopping me? Besides, I am the only one of us who has unfortunately stepped foot in that accursed town."

I looked at Celine for some kind of backup, but she merely shrugged.

I then turned my attention to Aldhard. He stood there as if waiting to say something.

"What? You want to join as well, Aldhard?" I asked, surprised by the thought.

His expression didn't change. "No."

I raised an eyebrow. "Then why are you here?"

He let out a slow breath. "I came to warn you."

I frowned, half turning back toward the hallway. "I don't need you to tell me how dangerous of a decision this is. I already know that."

Aldhard grabbed my shoulder, turning me around. "Listen, Isaac. The Dreadbeaks I have been training here in Sylphreach aren't exactly ready. I've only had two months' time at best. That is barely enough time to ensure they will follow commands, let alone to trust that they won't turn on you." He gave my shoulder a slight shake. "The ones I trained in Eclipsia? I worked with them for years. I knew how they would react, knew their limits. But these?" He shook his head.

"I cannot guarantee your safety once you are in the air."

I felt a heavy weight on my chest. I wasn't sure what it was—fear? It didn't matter.

"You still intend to take one," he said, more statement than question.

I exhaled. "Yes."

Aldhard looked at me for a long moment before nodding. "Then at least keep in mind my warning."

I returned his nod with my own. Then I turned to head toward his lab, Celine and Sabrina following close behind.

We climbed a high staircase, the air thinning out the higher we went. Aldhard's lab was situated at one of the highest points in the Elderwood, nestled on a stretched out flat, sprawling branch. I still remember the day I watched the massive branch grow from the tree, all because it sensed that it was needed.

The lab itself was pretty spacious. An open, vast platform built into the trunk, with wooden railings encircling the edges to prevent anyone from falling. Lanterns hung from vines along the railing, lighting up the various tools, feeding stations, and tables scattered across the area.

On one side, a cluster of massive perches jutted out over the open air, each reinforced with thick rope and metal bindings. On them sat Dreadbeaks, their beaks wrapped shut with thick binds.

As we approached the center of the lab, one of the Dreadbeaks shuffled uncomfortably. Then it expanded its wings and tried to take flight. The thick rope and metal forbade it from doing so, keeping it grounded, but the beast thrashed violently against the restraints, letting out a muffled screech through it's closed beak.

I paused, holding up my hands, trying to calm the beast. "Woah there, I won't harm you," I said in a hushed tone.

The Dreadbeak's beady eyes zeroed in on mine, wild and distrustful. Its dark feathers ruffled, and I could feel the untamed energy rolling off of it.

I swallowed, a bead of sweat forming on my forehead. Was this really a good idea?

I tightened my fists.

I had already made up my mind, hadn't I? I was going to do this. I had no other choice.

Could I really fly straight into Thornwallow on an untamed beast with no guarantee it would even obey me? Aldhard himself couldn't vouch for them.

Sure, I had some previous experience with flying them, but I was far from mastering the act. If something went wrong in the air, I'd have no way to stop it.

I clenched my jaw, inhaling through my nose.

It didn't matter. It couldn't matter.

I had already wasted enough time.

Just as I had finished building up the courage, Sabrina let out a low whistle from behind me.

"Well, are they not a lively bunch," she mused, crossing her arms behind her back as she strolled around the lab. "I never liked these things—overgrown chickens with an attitude."

Before I could respond, she took a step closer to another Dreadbeak perched nearby. The moment she got close, the fiend let out a deep hiss and yanked against its restraints, its talons scraping against the wood.

Sabrina clapped her hands harshly. "Oh, hush you," she said, waving a hand, like she were scolding a pet.

"Hey, Sabrina, cut that o—" I took a step towards her to stop her from bothering the fiends, but Celine stepped in front of me with a curious look in her eyes.

"Drifted," she said softly, "do you truly believe this is a

wise decision?"

I hesitated. No doubt she could read the reservation on my face.

Despite all my determination, doubt hung over me. There was a very real possibility that I was making a reckless choice. If even Celine was questioning the journey, maybe I really was making a grave mistake.

Celine watched me closely, as if she could read every thought I struggled with in my mind.

She spoke again.

"Because if you do, then I will not question your decision."

She took one of my hands in hers. "I trust your judgment fully, Drifted. Please do as you see necessary."

I looked down at our hands, feeling her grip anchor me. Slowly, the warmth of her touch took over any doubts I had.

I nodded slowly. "Thank you, Celine," I said.

This was it.

My decision was made.

I turned back to the Dreadbeaks still being chastised by Sabrina.

"We're going to Thornwallow."

Sabrina, who was now making faces at one of the Dreadbeaks, turned to me and let out an exaggerated sigh. "Oh, finally! Please do make haste Drifted, we have not all day."

I ignored her as I took a step toward the perches.

There were three Dreadbeaks before me, each one larger than the ones I saw in Moonveil many months ago.

I scanned them carefully, trying to assess which of the three would give me the least amount of headache.

The first Dreadbeak that was positioned closest to me was the largest. The longer I looked at it, the more its muscles tensed. Its body grew stiff as it glared at me, and its beak twitched against the bindings as if it were ready to snap at anything that got too close. That one was out of the question.

The second was slightly smaller, but no less intimidating. It was restless, shifting from one leg to the other. Although not outright aggressive, it was agitated.

Then my eyes landed on the third.

This one was the smallest. It didn't thrash or struggle like the others. Instead, it watched me with cautious black eyes. It flexed its talons against the perch but did not move to fight.

This is the one, I thought to myself as I took a step toward it.

Sabrina hummed behind me. "Bold choice, Drifted. Though if it flings you from the sky, I would like to request ownership of your blade."

I shot her a look, and she grinned, raising her hands.

I took another step forward, keeping my eyes locked on the Dreadbeak. Sure, it was the smallest of the three, but it was still a fiend at the end of the day.

As I got closer, the creature let out a muffled grunt and shifted back. Its wings twitched and for a brief second, I thought it might try to pull away entirely.

I slowly raised a hand. "Easy now," I whispered, trying to keep my voice low.

The Dreadbeak's eyes flicked to my outstretched hand, then back to my face, as if trying to decide whether to attack me.

I moved carefully, wrapping my fingers around the thick leather reins fastened around its beak. The fiend flinched at the contact, but it didn't thrash or snap. That was a good sign.

I took a deep breath. "Let's hope I don't regret this," I muttered under my breath.

Then, without another second of hesitation, I reached down and undid the bindings keeping the Dreadbeak secured to the perch.

The moment the last restraint came undone, the Dreadbeak let out a loud cry, shaking out its wings. For a moment, I wasn't sure if it was about to take off or try to throw me from the platform entirely.

Slowly, I eased the Dreadbeak down from the perch.

Its head twitched in quick motions. The way its eyes looked at me, unblinking, sent a chill through my spine. It tilted its head once, then again, each motion more abrupt than the last.

I tightened my grip on the reins, resisting the urge to flinch as its beak clicked under the bindings. If this was going to work, I couldn't show it any weakness

Celine took a step behind me and placed a hand on my shoulder. "Be careful, Drifted," she cautioned, her eyes watching the fiend's erratic movements.

I didn't respond, too focused on trying to keep my calm under the Dreadbeak's gaze.

"Yes, yes, do be careful," Sabrina said, folding her arms. "If it takes your hand, I would hate to have to explain why the great Drifted is suddenly one sword hand short."

"You're not helping, Sabrina." I said, scowling at her.

"Ah, yes. My apologies," she replied, making a motion of locking her mouth with a key.

I took a breath and began lowering the Dreadbeak.

When its body got low enough, I lifted myself onto its back. Making sure to keep the reins tight in my hands.

Then, almost instantly, the Dreadbeak let out another muffled screech. Its wings flared as its body trembled under me. It started pacing around the lab, nervously scraping its talons against the wooden floor.

I tightened my legs around its sides, trying to hold the reins as steadily as I could while my mind scrambled to recall Aldhard's training back in Eclipsia.

Confidence.

That was the most important part of riding these creatures: Making the Dreadbeak believe that I was in control.

I inhaled deeply and sat up straighter, forcing the tension from my body.

I wasn't going to let it throw me.

"Stop!" I commanded.

The fiend let out a muffled screech and juddered, its wings flaring as it jerked its body in an attempt to throw me off. My grip on the reins tightened, and I hunkered down against its back as I fought to stay grounded.

Confidence. Stay firm.

"Stop," I said again, this time with more authority.

The Dreadbeak quaked and scraped its talons against the platform. Then it reluctantly stood still. Its breathing was heavy, and it was stomping as if it wanted to move, but it remained in place.

"Well done, Drifted," Celine said.

"Hah! And here I was, certain that would be the end of you." Sabrina laughed, placing a hand over her chest. "Such a shame. I was already planning my heartfelt farewell."

I shook my head in annoyance and began petting the Dreadbeak, trying to soothe it. The creature flinched at first, but after a moment, it relaxed.

"Well, it's your turn," I said, flicking my head toward Sabrina. "Pick a Dreadbeak."

Sabrina scoffed. "Oh, no, no, no. There is no chance that I will be lowering myself to *that,*" she said, pointing at the bird. "Learning to fly one of these things is far beneath me."

I smirked. "You're scared, aren't you?"

Sabrina gasped. "Scared? Me, the bravest Lupine in all of Sylphreach, scared? Please. I simply have no interest in participating in such a barbaric act. A Lupine of such high stature as myself should not be caught learning such things."

Celine let out a soft sigh. "Sabrina, if you do not wish to learn to fly a Dreadbeak, how exactly do you plan on accompanying us?"

Sabrina grinned, flashing her fangs. "Simple, I will ride behind Drifted. He has already allowed himself to be sullied, so it should be no problem."

I shook my head immediately. "Absolutely not."

Sabrina blinked, feigning innocence. "Oh? And why not? Surely you do not plan on making me fly on my own?"

"There is no way I'm putting up with you midair with nowhere to run once I inevitably get tired of your yapping," I shot back.

Sabrina gasped, pressing a hand to her chest as if I had just insulted her honor. "How cruel, Drifted! You wound me!"

"You'll live," I replied. "Plus, Celine's going to ride on her own. What makes you think that I'll be your personal reinsman?"

Sabrina scoffed, a mischievous glint in her red eyes. "Well, obviously, Lady Celine is far more capable than I." She placed a hand on her hip. "And besides, who better to keep you entertained mid-flight than me?"

Before I could argue further, she effortlessly leapt onto the Dreadbeak and wrapped her arms around my waist.

The fiend reacted instantly, squawking through the bindings around its beak. I tightened my grip on the reins, barely keeping the fiend still as it shifted uncomfortably beneath our combined weight.

"Sabrina, get off," I growled, twisting slightly to look at her.

Instead of listening, she tightened her arms and rested her chin against my shoulder with an infuriating grin. "Stop wasting time, Drifted. It shall be dark soon."

I clenched my jaw. "Sabrina."

"Yes?"

Before I could snap at her again, Celine stopped me.

"Drifted, allow her to ride with you," she said. "We are wasting time."

"But—" I started to protest, but she continued.

"Sabrina is right," she added. "We have wasted far too much time, and I would rather not have my first flight be in the dead of night."

I stared at her. There was no use in arguing. Why couldn't it have been Celine who rode with me instead?

I let out a long; slow exhale and pinched the bridge of my nose. "Fine," I muttered.

Sabrina suddenly nuzzled her head against my shoulder. "Ah, I knew you could not resist me, Drifted."

"Don't push your luck," I warned.

"A spoilsport as usual," she replied, pulling at my cheeks.

I jerked my head away. "Would you stop that?"

Ignoring me, she hummed to herself, clearly pleased, while Celine stepped forward toward the remaining Dreadbeaks. I watched as she made her way to the largest of the three—the one I had immediately dismissed for being too temperamental.

I stiffened. "Celine, that one's more difficult than the others," I warned. "It's way larger and—"

She didn't reply and reached for the bindings.

My hands instinctively tightened on my reins as she undid the first strap, then the next. The moment the final binding came loose, the Dreadbeak jerked against the perch, its body thrumming with pent-up energy. Its wings snapped outward, and the wooden platform creaked beneath the weight of its talons as it thrashed around.

I cursed under my breath, already preparing to jump off

my mount to assist her.

But before I could, Celine lifted a hand.

"Stay where you are, Drifted."

I hesitated, still ready to move, but something in her tone stopped me.

Then, to my shock, she stepped closer to the creature.

With a slow motion, she placed a hand against its dark feathers.

"Hush, little one," she whispered.

The Dreadbeak stopped almost instantly. It still breathed heavily, but it wasn't as erratic anymore. The wildness in its black eyes slowly faded away, and before long, it settled down.

My jaw dropped.

Sabrina let out a low whistle. "Well, well, well. Lady Celine, you continue to surprise."

I sat there staring, trying to understand what I witnessed. How could she have settled down an enraged fiend so easily?

Celine looked at me, her face straight, as if she didn't realize the impressive feat she had accomplished.

"What do I do next, Drifted?" she asked me.

I cleared my throat, trying to force my brain to catch up.

"Right. Uh... next, you need to secure the reins and mount it confidently." I eyed the Dreadbeak again, watching for any sign of resistance. "It may not be fighting now, but don't let your guard down."

Celine gave me a small nod before turning back to the fiend. Without hesitation, she took one strap of the reins in her hand and then jumped onto the Dreadbeak's back.

I braced myself, expecting it to start bucking.

But it didn't. In fact, it barely moved. There was next to no resistance from it at all.

I was utterly stunned.

"What..." I muttered.

Celine sat tall in the saddle, her posture poised. Her hands rested lightly on the reins, as if she had done this a thousand times before. The Dreadbeak, the same one that had been wild and restless only moments ago, remained perfectly still beneath her.

Sabrina chuckled from behind me, clearly enjoying my disbelief. "Oh, dear. Drifted, do be careful. If you gape any harder, your jaw may unhinge."

"How...?" I finally managed, still staring at Celine like she had just performed magic.

She turned her gaze to me, as composed as ever. "Is something the matter?"

"Erm... no, it's nothing," I lied. I didn't want Celine to know how much of a struggle it was for me to mount the Dreadbeak, even though she already witnessed it. Still, it felt embarrassing.

Celine watched me for a short moment, and then she turned her attention back to the Dreadbeak. "And what now, Drifted?"

I exhaled, pushing away the embarrassment. "Command it to fly. Give it a clear, firm order."

Celine nodded, and then gently tugged at the reins. "Fly," she said in a low and calm voice.

I smiled smugly. I was sure the Dreadbeak wouldn't listen to her now. There was no way she had been strong enough in her command. "Ah, no, Celine, actually you have to—"

The Dreadbeak responded.

With a powerful push, it launched off the platform, wings flaring out and flapping as they caught air beneath them.

The gust of wind from its takeoff swept across the platform, rustling my cloak as I watched, dumbfounded, while Celine hovered effortlessly into the sky.

No resistance. No struggle.

Sabrina clapped her hands together. "Well, would you look at that? Lady Celine must be a natural, eh, Drifted?"

I swallowed, gripping my own reins tighter. "Yeah, must be..."

"Drifted!" Celine shouted down to me. "Hurry, we must move."

I gulped.

I could practically feel Sabrina's grin burning a hole in my back, waiting for the moment when my Dreadbeak would refuse to listen. I didn't care much about what Sabrina thought, but I sure as hell didn't want to humiliate myself in front of Celine.

Though there was no time to waste. This was it. The moment of truth.

I took a deep breath. I had done this before. Back in Eclipsia. Sure, it's a different Dreadbeak, but they can't be that different, right?

You can do this, I told myself.

"Fly!" I commanded.

For a single, agonizing second, my Dreadbeak didn't respond.

Then, right as I heard Sabrina open her mouth, the creature flapped its wings hard and launched itself into the air.

The force of the takeoff nearly threw me backward, and Sabrina's grip around my waist tightened as we shot skyward. My stomach dropped as the platform below became smaller and smaller.

But... it worked.

I let out a shaky breath of relief, adjusting my posture to stabilize myself.

Sabrina, of course, was laughing behind me. "Oh, thank the moon. I was so sure we were about to crash straight into the Hollow."

"Shut up, Sabrina," I muttered, but even I couldn't help the small smirk tugging at the corner of my lips.

We were airborne.

Celine, hovering beside us, turned her eyes to me.

"To Thornwallow then?" she asked.

"Right," I said, nodding. "To Thornwallow."

With that, we angled our Dreadbeaks forward and made our way north.

CHAPTER 20

We flew on the Dreadbeaks, high in the sky. So high, in fact, that we were now above the clouds, making it impossible to see the forest below. Celine suggested we fly so high as to not draw any attention to ourselves from any Lupine who may be wandering the forest.

The shock of discovering my uncle's kidnapping still haunted me. I had been furious, but now that fury had hardened into resolve.

I glanced behind me as Sabrina clutched my waist tighter.

"Doing alright back there?" I asked her, an eyebrow raised.

She hesitated, her voice catching as she replied. "This is a ridiculous mode of travel," she said with a pale face. I could see the barely contained queasiness in her eyes. "I much prefer to be on the ground."

I let out a chuckle. "You look like you're about to hurl, Sabrina," I teased, trying to distract her. "If you hold on to me any tighter, you might just lose all your dignity."

"How far is Thornwallow anyway?" I asked her, trying to focus her on something other than barfing on my back.

Sabrina took a deep breath before letting out a dramatic sigh. "By foot, it would have taken us about five days to a week," she explained. "But at the rate these overfed pigeons are moving, I would wager we should be there in a day's time."

A smile grew on my lips. I was ready to get my uncle and return him safely to Lunaria.

Celine, soaring next to us, interjected. "Let us not let our haste cloud the dangers that await."

My smile dropped; she was right. If King Cassius was

anything like his late wife, then this mission would be far from easy. I gave Celine a small nod in acknowledgement as my thoughts slowly returned to the unease swirling in my gut.

"Fear not, Drifted," Celine added, possibly noting the worry on my face. "With your courage, we shall face whatever awaits us together."

I nodded absent-mindedly. There was a balancing act being fought in my head. The hope of success and the fear of the conflict we were walking into whirled around. For now, the path was clear, and with Celine and Sabrina by my side, I could almost convince myself that maybe—just maybe—things would go as planned.

"Try to think of this flight as the calm before the storm, Drifted," Celine added with a grin.

"If by storm you mean a land full of enemies who shall be waiting for us with open claws and sharp teeth, then yes, perhaps, Lady Celine." Sabrina, still clutching onto me, added with a hiccup.

Celine shot Sabrina a look, shaking her head. "Sabrina..."

"Yes, Lady Celine?" Sabrina replied.

"Let us not give Drifted more to worry about," Celine remarked dryly. "He is already carrying enough weight on his back," she said smugly.

"I suppose you are right, Lad—," Sabrina postured up on my back, and I could practically hear her brain deciphering Celine's jab. "Wait a moment. Lady Celine, was that a joke at my expense?"

"I don't know what it is you are referring to," Celine replied, raising her nose in the air.

Sabrina huffed and shook her head as she leaned into me. "Lady Celine," she snapped playfully, "do not presume that a little queasiness makes me dead weight! I may be riding this dreadful beast with a churning belly, but I assure you, I have got plenty of fight in me!"

I grinned, rubbing my neck. "Alright, alright, we get it, Sabrina."

We fell into a brief silence as the steady flap of the Dreadbeaks' wings filled the air. Then, as if summoned by our unspoken fears, far on the horizon, I noticed a darkened area beneath the parted clouds.

I pointed to the area. It was still too far to make out, but the spot was such a stark contrast with the greenery that surrounded it.

"Is that it?" I asked Sabrina.

Sabrina shifted her grip on my back to peek over my shoulder. "Aye, Drifted," she replied. "That miserable patch is Thornwallow—colder than an empty wolf's den. I hate it more than I care to admit; honestly, I would sooner tumble headfirst into a briar patch than set paw there!"

"Looks umm... inviting," I joked.

"Do not worry, Drifted, we are here with you." Celine yelled over from her Dreadbeak.

"Besides, with the one and only Sabrina by your side, your fears are misplaced." Sabrina added.

Then, without warning, a violent shudder came from my left. I looked over to see Celine's Dreadbeak bucking, its wings flailing erratically as if spooked by something.

Celine leaned forward, petting the Dreadbeak, trying to calm it. "Steady, little one, do not lose your nerve."

It seemed to work for a moment, but as quickly as it calmed down, the Dreadbeak grew erratic again.

"Celine!" I yelled out, but there wasn't much I could do while guiding my own Dreadbeak.

I wasn't sure what was going on. It was as if the beast had suddenly lost all sense of control.

It was then that Aldhard's previous warnings came into

my mind. *I cannot guarantee your safety once you are in the air.*

Before I could process any further, the Dreadbeak began a rapid barrel roll. Its huge body twisting in a dizzying spiral, and I could see Celine clinging desperately to its back as the creature tried to shake her loose. As the air spun around Sabrina and me, the beast's wild eyes locked onto mine. This wasn't going to end well.

I could see Celine, her eyes wide, but focused with alarm. And then, in a heartbeat, her grip faltered.

Sabrina let out a loud gasp behind me.

I watched in frozen horror as the beast flung Celine off. She tumbled into the air as her body grew smaller in the sky.

"Celine!" I shouted.

"Sabrina, take the reins!" I yelled at her, posturing up on the Dreadbeak.

"Me?!" she questioned. "I do not know how to even begin controlling this beast!"

"You'll figure it out!" I yelled back.

Without waiting for a reply, I leapt off the Dreadbeak, my heart pounding in my ears.

The wind rushed past me—deafening—as I plummeted toward Celine, my arms stretching desperately as we fell through the sky.

The world blurred around me as my focus narrowed to the one thing that mattered: catching her. I pulled my arms close to my body, streamlining myself to slice through the air faster. My eyes watered against the harsh wind, clouding my vision, but I refused to close them.

"Celine, hold on!" I yelled. But I was sure that the wind's roar drowned out my shouting.

Slowly, I closed the gap between us, and as I reached out my trembling hands, I managed to grab her arm and pull her toward me. Our bodies collided midair, and I wrapped my arms around her, trying to stabilize us in the middle of our tumble.

In the deafening wind, I yelled out, "Are you okay?" But before I could hear her answer, I saw her eyes widen. In that instant, she kicked me away, the force sending us both spinning wildly through the sky.

From the corner of my eye, I saw what scared her. A black figure darted through the gap Celine had just made. I steadied myself in the air as I realized what was happening. The Dreadbeak that had thrown Celine off was circling back around, coming to finish the job.

Damnit! I cursed to myself, already changing my trajectory to try to make it back toward Celine. She was far in front of me, and I knew there was no way I would reach her in time before the Dreadbeak caught back up to us.

"Behind you, Celine!" I yelled, seeing the Dreadbeak grow larger behind her.

Celine, having stabilized herself, quickly arched her body around the Dreadbeak, barely dodging out of harm's way. Then, with a quick motion, she extended a hand and caught one of the fiend's wings, attempting to throw it off course as it headed toward me. "Drifted, incoming!"

The Dreadbeak came in at an alarming speed, but thanks to Celine, I was able to swing my body out of the way, kicking off of the fiend to give myself the right amount of distance needed.

I could tell the kick jarred it slightly, but the creature was far from subdued—it squawked through its bound beak and veered away.

The fiend circled once more, its talons raised as it closed in directly behind Celine. "It's coming in again, Celine!" I yelled, pointing behind her.

Celine looked behind her and turned her attention back to

me. "Drifted! I will send it back to you once again!" She yelled.

I gave her a nod, understanding what I had to do to end this chaotic ballet that we were locked in. I braced myself as the beast swooped in with renewed fury. This time, Celine bent low as the Dreadbeak barreled toward her. From under it, she gripped a massive wing again, forcing it to change course.

"Drifted! Prepare yourself!" She yelled as she hung on, forcing the creature's wing to send it straight into me.

Without hesitation, I leaned forward, sending myself over the fiend and closing my hand around one of the reins, clinging for dear life.

The wind tore at my face as the beast bucked and thrashed, barely giving me enough time to fumble for my sword at my belt.

My hand found the hilt, and I drew the blade in one swift motion. As the Dreadbeak struggled beneath me, I plunged the sword deep into its side. The steel sank in with a squelch. and the creature let out a guttural squawk, its eyes flashing in pain.

The creature flapped its wings erratically for a moment before failing to support its weight. With a struggle, it succumbed to gravity and began to freefall from the sky.

I pulled my sword from the Dreadbeak's body and let go of the reins, Celine and I kicking off the beast.

Celine's hand grabbed onto mine. We were plummeting, with nothing to catch us. I pulled Celine in close as we began freefalling. I could feel her heart pounding against mine.

As the world around us continued to blur, I stole a glance downward, and my stomach dropped—below, the ground surged up to us. Jagged rocks, trees, and tangled underbrush marked the terrain, providing us with barely any cushioning for our fall.

Not good! My mind screamed.

One look at Celine, and I could tell that she was thinking the same thing. There was no possible way that we would be able to survive a fall like this.

I tightened my grip on her hand, preparing myself for the impact as I clung to Celine like our lives depended on it—because, in that moment, it did.

"Celine, I—" I started, but was quickly cut off.

A sharp whistle pierced through the turmoil in my mind. My eyes snapped upward, and I saw Sabrina—flying in fast. The Dreadbeak she was coming in on was flapping its wings frantically.

Sabrina's eyes were beaming with a glint of mischief, and possibly even enjoyment despite the high-stakes situation we were in. "Seems like I am quite the natural at flying after all, Drifted!" she yelled, cupping her hands over her mouth.

She clapped as she pulled her mount into a tight dive straight for us.

Relief surged through me, but the danger wasn't over yet. Sabrina quickly positioned her Dreadbeak beneath us and caught us with a sweep. Celine and I both landed on the Dreadbeak's back with a thud, and for a brief moment I thought we might just escape this aerial nightmare.

However, as Celine and I began steadying ourselves, the Dreadbeak let out a strained squawk. I looked down to see that it was frantically flapping its wings, desperately trying to support the combined weight of the three of us. It gave one last strained flap and almost immediately began plummeting towards the floor below.

"Sabrina! Do something!" I yelled.

"What do you suppose I do, you simpleton!?" She yelled back at me.

I felt sick as our shared panic grew. We were going in for

a crash landing.

"Everyone, prepare yourselves!" I heard Celine yell through the clamor.

In that moment, time seemed to slow—the wind, the fear, and the weight of our impending impact combined into a single, breathless moment. As the ground surged up to meet us, a tight knot formed in my stomach. Closing my eyes, I braced myself for the crash landing.

CHAPTER 21

My eyes fluttered open slowly.

The world that came into view was a mess of muted light and blurry shadows. My thoughts were in a fog, struggling to piece together how I had come to be here.

The scent of damp earth and crushed foliage filled my lungs. But there was also something rancid—feathers, sweat, and the faint trace of blood.

I groaned, the sound barely escaping my lips as I tried to move. Pain shot up my ribs with each turn, making me wince as I looked around. My fingers curled into the dirt as I tried to force myself to focus. Where was I?

The crash. The Dreadbeaks.

It came back in fragments—the wind against my face, the look on Celine and Sabrina's faces as we fought to keep control. Then, the sudden, violent descent. The world rushing toward us. The chaos of impact.

I forced my gaze upward. It was fairly light out, with the sky peeking through twisted branches overhead. Somewhere nearby, I could hear the faint rustle of movement, but my head was still too heavy to turn.

Were they alive?

I parted my lips to call out, but my throat was dry. Instead, I listened, hoping that I was not alone in the aftermath of the crash.

Suddenly, something wet splashed against my cheek. I thought it was rain, but the scent that followed told me otherwise.

My fingers instinctively lifted, brushing against the wet

streak running down my face. My stomach tightened as I pulled my hand back. It was exactly what I feared it to be: blood.

Slowly, I forced myself to look up.

The sight sent an unsteady exhale through my lips—half relief, half unease. Suspended above me, tangled in the wreckage of shattered branches, was the Dreadbeak we landed on. Its massive body was limp, and its wings were draped lifelessly over branches. Its dark feathers were ruffled and soaked with blood, and a thick branch protruded through its chest, holding it in place.

I swallowed. The sight was gruesome, but at least it wasn't Celine or Sabrina.

I turned my head, ignoring the fresh ache in my skull, scanning the ground for any sign of them. They had to be here. They had to be alive.

Using the tree behind me as support, I pushed myself up from the forest floor. The world swayed for a moment, but I steadied myself.

"Celine? Sabrina?" My voice was hoarse, and I could barely get out more than a whisper.

Silence.

I took in a deep breath and tried again. "Celine!"

Nothing.

My stomach curled tightly.

I pushed myself off of the tree, ignoring the way my ribs burned with the effort.

As I stood, I heard a faint voice come through, it was so low I almost missed it.

"Drifted…"

It was Sabrina.

The moment I heard her, my body began moving. My head still reeled, my vision swam, but none of it mattered. She was well, and possibly with Celine.

I staggered to my feet as my legs threatened to buckle, but I forced them to move. Before long, I was running, driven by sheer desperation.

"Sabrina!" I called out.

Though I got no response back this time.

Branches smacked at my face as I pushed forward, crashing through the undergrowth. My boots slipped against the uneven ground, each step threatening to trip me, but I didn't stop.

Then, through some broken trees not far off in the distance, I saw someone. Though, it wasn't the voice I heard call out to me. Instead of finding Sabrina, I only saw Celine.

She was half buried beneath a mess of shattered wood, her dark blue cloak tangled around her limbs. Her hood had fallen back, revealing strands of her hair matted with dirt and blood.

I dropped to my knees beside her, hands trembling as I reached out to grab her face. "Celine! Celine, can you hear me?"

Her eyelids fluttered, her deep violet eyes barely visible beneath them. She tried to move, but winced, and slumped back against the ground.

I swallowed hard as panic set in. "Don't move—I'll get you out of this."

Quickly, I began pushing away the debris, my hands shaking as I worked to free her.

She was alive—but how badly was she hurt?

"It was I who called out to you, you know?" I heard a voice coming from above me.

I froze, holding my breath as I slowly lifted my gaze.

There, suspended above me, caught in a mess of thick vines and branches, was Sabrina.

She hung awkwardly, her arms pinned at her sides, her legs

LUPINE

tangled like a puppet caught in its own strings. A deep frown formed on her lips as she squirmed, trying—and failing—to free herself.

"A most undignified position," she muttered, twisting in an attempt to loosen the vines. "I wish you had looked up sooner. My pride has suffered greatly."

Despite the pounding in my skull and the gnawing worry for Celine, I sighed. "Sabrina."

She perked up at my tone. "Yes, dear Drifted?"

I dragged a hand down my face. "By the moon, how did you manage that?"

She scoffed. "Oh, as if this was my intention. I would not so willingly place myself at the mercy of foliage." She wiggled again, but the vines only tightened around her limbs. "Let us focus on what truly matters: getting me down!"

I glanced at Celine, still half-buried, her eyes opening and closing slowly.

"Assist... her... Drifted," Celine rasped. "She can help you free my body."

I nodded, pushing myself to my feet. "Hold on, Sabrina. Try not to—"

She jerked her body in another attempt to break free. The vines pulled tighter briefly, and with a sudden violent *snap*, she dropped like a stone.

Straight toward me.

I barely had time to react before she crashed into me, knocking the breath from my lungs as we both hit the ground in a heap.

Sabrina groaned against my shoulder. "Ah. Freedom at last."

I let out a strained grunt, shoving her off. "Get off of me."

She grinned as she sat up, brushing leaves from her hair. "Really, Drifted, your heroism knows no bounds."

I ignored her as I rubbed my already battered ribs. My body truly wasn't in any condition to take a hit like that.

Celine coughed, bringing my focus back.

"Sabrina," I said, my tone tense. "Help me get her out."

The teasing glint in her eyes faded. She nodded as she scrambled to assist me.

Together, Sabrina and I worked quickly, pulling away the debris that had pinned Celine. My hands were still unsteady, and my muscles ached with every pull, but I pushed through. Celine barely made a sound as we worked, and I had to keep checking to see if her eyes were still open out of fear she had passed out.

Finally, after what felt like an eternity, we moved the last heavy branch.

I knelt beside Celine, scanning her face and body. "Can you stand?"

Sabrina let out a short scoff. "A foolish question, Drifted. Look at her."

Celine attempted to push herself upright, but the moment she tried to move, an agonized cry tore from her throat. Her body trembled violently, and she immediately collapsed.

I caught her before she could hit the ground fully.

She was in bad shape. Really bad shape.

I wiped the sweat from my forehead, begging myself to remain calm, but I was scared. I had no way of knowing the extent of her injuries. With the way she screamed in pain at the slightest movement, I feared something was broken—or worse.

Sabrina knelt on Celine's other side, eyes looking her over with a rare seriousness. "We cannot remain here. The scent of blood will draw unwanted company before long."

I knew she was right, but moving Celine was going to be dangerous. If her injuries were severe, forcing her to walk—

if she even could—would make things worse.

Celine exhaled slowly, eyes fluttering. "I… I need but only a moment." Her voice was breathless, tight with pain.

I frowned, shifting to better support her. "We need to get out of here before something finds us first."

Her fingers dug weakly into my arm as if bracing herself. "Then help me… to my feet."

I hesitated. As much as she wanted to stand, it was clear she wasn't going to. If shifting her weight had caused her that much pain, walking was out of the question.

I sighed, adjusting my grip on her. *She's not going to like this.*

"There's no other way, Celine," I muttered, already moving. Before she could protest, I turned around, hooked my hands beneath her legs, and lifted her onto my back.

She let out a strained breath, her fingers clenching at my shirt, but she didn't fight me. That alone told me just how badly off she really was.

"Only… because… it is necessary," Celine said as she let out a quiet, strained breath against my shoulder.

"Only because it's necessary." I repeated as I stood.

Sabrina tilted her head, watching with mild amusement. "It is rather endearing, you know. A noble knight carrying his wounded princess."

I sighed. "Can we not?"

Sabrina grinned. "Oh, but why not? This is a rare moment of tenderness. I must savor it."

Ignoring her, I fixed my grip on Celine's legs and glanced at the forest ahead. "Now what? Where do we go from here? Should we head back to Sylphreach?"

I felt Celine's grip tighten on my shoulders.

"No, we have yet to complete our original mission." She said weakly.

I frowned. With her being this injured, there was no way

that we could continue to Thornwallow. We may as well be marching right to our deaths.

"Celine, you can barely move. We can find another way—" I started, but she cut me off.

"No." Her voice, though weak, held an unwavering edge to it. "I refuse to return to Sylphreach unless it is with your uncle accompanying us."

My throat tightened at her words.

The stubbornness in her tone was nothing new, but something felt different.

"If you hesitate because of me," she continued, her breathing labored. "Then put me down. I shall find a way to get there myself."

I turned my head slightly, trying to catch even a glimpse of her expression. "That's not going to happen."

She exhaled harshly, a mixture of frustration and exhaustion. "Then do not waste time considering what is not an option. We press forward, Drifted."

I sighed, rolling my shoulders slightly to settle her more comfortably on my back. "You really don't give me much choice, do you?"

A faint hum was her only response.

Sabrina, who started pacing back and forth, finally stopped in her tracks. "That is exactly the response I expected from our fearless princess!"

I sighed through my nose. I still didn't think it was a good idea. Celine was hurt—badly—and continuing forward in this state would only make things worse. If it were up to me, we'd be turning back, finding another way to rescue Uncle Alfarr.

Celine had made her own decision. And as much as I hated it, I had to let her.

I knew she wasn't reckless. If she believed we could still press forward, then I had to trust that she knew her own limits.

I had to make sure that if she was going to continue, she wouldn't be doing it alone.

I adjusted my grip again, bracing my nerves. "Alright, we keep moving."

Sabrina clapped her hands together, grinning. "Ah, there it is! That determination, that resolve—I daresay it is inspiring." She glanced at me, eyes glinting with mischief. "Do you think you shall carry me as well, Drifted? I am quite weary."

I rolled my eyes at her. "You're walking."

She sighed dramatically and then gave me a bow. "How cruel! After you, oh gallant steed."

I started walking ahead of her, trying to move as steadily as possible to not agitate Celine's injuries. She remained silent, her breathing slow and heavy against my shoulder, as if she was conserving what little energy she had left.

Sabrina walked alongside me, hands folded behind her head, moving with an ease that made me question if she had ever really been in that crash at all.

I exhaled, keeping my focus ahead as the trees stretched in front of us. The air here felt heavier than it did in Sylphreach, dirtier. It held the kind of weight that settled deep in your chest. The sooner we were out of these unfamiliar woods, the better.

"How far do you think we are?" I asked Sabrina, breaking the quiet.

She hummed and tilted her head. "Difficult to say," she tapped her chin before glancing up at the sky. "I estimate three, maybe four days. Though with your limp and the princess' injuries, I am not too sure."

"Three to four days!" I repeated in disbelief. "We were only about a day out before!"

Sabrina grinned. "Maybe you have yet to notice, Drifted.

but we are no longer airborne. Were you not present to the same crash Lady Celine and I were?"

I sighed, "Well... yeah..."

Sabrina clicked her tongue, probably in annoyance. "Had we remained airborne, we would likely have arrived by now. Alas, those wretched buzzards had other plans."

I stayed silent. I mean, it was my fault that we rode the Dreadbeaks at all.

Sabrina, always observant, picked up on my silence. "I warned you not to trust them. Birds are flighty creatures."

"Yeah, very funny," I said with an eye-roll.

"Did you appreciate that one?" Sabrina asked with an enormous smile on her face.

"It was alright." I replied, not wanting to inflate her already swollen ego any further.

She immediately puffed her chest out and pointed her nose in the air. "As I expected."

Well, that didn't work. I thought to myself.

"How can you even be telling jokes at a time like this?" I questioned.

Sabrina gave a lazy, audible shrug. "I do not know."

I was worried about the new time estimate. I wasn't sure if Celine would be able to make it three to four days in the condition she was in. Though there was no choice. We were already closer to Thornwallow than we were to Sylphreach, and turning back now would only waste precious time—time that Celine didn't have.

The problem was, our destination wasn't a place we could simply walk into. The Lupine there wouldn't hesitate to kill me the moment they laid eyes on me. Thanks to their indoctrination by Cassius, to them, I was nothing more than a pest.

Still, if we could get in unseen, I could at least steal

296

something. Medicine, bandages, anything that would help Celine.

I wasn't sure how, but I'd figure it out.

As we walked further and the sun dipped beneath the horizon, the hardly covered trees took on eerier shapes. Their pointed branches stretched, and the cool night air crept in, bringing with it an unsettling quiet.

Then, from behind me, I heard a soft, strained sound— followed by a sudden, violent fit of coughing.

I stiffened immediately, turning my head to glance back at Celine. "Celine, are you—"

Before I could finish, something wet and warm brushed against my cheek.

I froze.

Sabrina, coming up beside me, stopped as well, her eyes widening as she looked at me.

"I do not think she is," she said, her voice quieter than usual. "Drifted, there is blood on your cheek."

My heart kicked against my ribs.

I shifted my grip and carefully lowered Celine to the ground so that I could see her face. Even in the dimming light, I could make out the dark stream of blood trailing from the corner of her lips. Her eyes were closed, and her face was pale.

"Celine!" I yelled, quickly placing my ear on her chest, closing my eyes to focus better.

Thankfully, she was still breathing, though it was shallow.

"Sabrina," I said, my voice edged with worry, "I don't know what to do. What do we do?"

She was already scanning the area, taking in the thickening darkness around us. "We stop here. It is already late. She needs rest."

I gulped. I didn't like the idea of stopping, not here, so far away from home. But we didn't have a choice.

Celine needed time to recover, and I needed time to figure out our next plan.

"Alright, yeah," I replied, looking around the forest to find a clearing off the path. "We'll set up camp."

Picking up Celine, I carried her a little further off the path, my eyes looking for a suitable place to settle. In that small amount of time, the forest had grown even darker, the tall trees blocking out the last traces of daylight. Eventually, I spotted a small clearing—sheltered enough to keep us hidden. But open enough that a fire wouldn't be a risk.

"This should do," I muttered.

Carefully, I knelt and eased Celine down against the base of a tree. I stayed crouched beside her for a moment, watching the faint rise and fall of her chest. As I put the back of my hand against her cheek, I recoiled slightly. She was ice cold. Worried, I stood up quickly, facing Sabrina.

"She's not doing too well," I said to Sabrina. "We'll need a fire to keep her warm. I'll go grab some wood."

Sabrina nodded. "And I shall find us some water. There should be a small stream somewhere nearby."

"Will you be alright on your own?" I asked her. Almost immediately, regretting the words as they left my lips.

"Worried for my safety, Drifted?" she smirked.

Before I could respond, she turned on her heels, already walking off, humming to herself as she disappeared into the trees. "Worry not. I am capable, you know."

I ran my hand through my hair before looking back at Celine's unconscious body.

Okay, one thing at a time, Isaac. Let's get some firewood. I told myself.

I turned toward the thicker treeline, looking over the ground for anything dry enough to burn. The forest had a damp chill to it, and with the ground still wet, the options were slim.

I took one look back at Celine before taking a step away from our makeshift camp.

As I took a large step over an overgrown root, a painful shock shot through my left calf, forcing me to suck in a breath through my teeth. I shifted my weight onto my other leg, gritting my teeth as a pulsing ache settled in my leg.

Right. I had been so focused on everyone else—one making sure Celine and Sabrina were alright, on figuring out what to do next—I had completely forgotten about my own wellbeing.

It was clear I wasn't unscathed from the crash. Not even close.

The pain in my ribs, which I had been ignoring up until now, throbbed dully with every breath. My arms were sore, and my lungs burned as I tried to take deeper breaths.

I exhaled through my nose and pressed my hand against my side, wincing as I poked at the tender spot below my ribs. They were bruised, possibly worse. But there was no point in thinking about it now.

Celine was in far worse condition than I was. I didn't have the luxury of relaxing just yet.

Shaking off the pain as best I could, I bent down and grabbed a branch, adding it to the growing pile in my arms. Celine needed warmth. We needed a fire. I could deal with everything else later.

After I gathered a sizable bundle of burning material in my arms, I turned back toward camp.

As I stepped back into the clearing, I caught sight of Sabrina emerging from the opposite side with a small leather waterskin sling over her shoulder. She arched her brow as she saw me limping—but said nothing.

I moved to Celine, carefully setting the firewood down before crouching beside her. She was exactly as I had left her, her body unnervingly still against the tree. My chest tightened as I leaned in, watching for any movement.

She was still breathing, *thank the moon.*

I let out a sigh, wiping a hand down my face.

"Has she not stirred?" Sabrina asked, stepping closer.

"No, not yet." I shook my head, moving a strand of hair from Celine's face. "But she's breathing."

Sabrina crossed her arms. "Lady Celine is strong. She shall be fine after a well-deserved rest."

I could hear the concern in her voice, no matter how hard she was trying to hide it.

"She needs more than rest," I muttered. "We need to get her real help."

Sabrina leaned against a nearby tree. "Which is conveniently located in a town full of Lupine that would sooner rip us apart than look at you."

I exhaled. "Yeah. I haven't forgotten."

There was a brief silence, save for the chirp of crickets beginning their nightly routine.

Sabrina crouched down, pulling the pouch of water from her shoulder. "Well, Drifted. Get that fire started." She smirked. "Unless you wish to add gut-wrenching illness to our growing list of problems?"

I gave her a tired look. "I think I'll pass."

She grinned and set the pouch down.

For now, all we could do was wait.

And hope Celine would wake up soon.

CHAPTER 22

The fire I built crackled softly and painted a golden glow on the surrounding trees. Beyond it, darkness swallowed the entire forest. The sky above us stretched endlessly in a deep shade of black with a large half-moon—stars speckled around it.

There wasn't much noise in the forest now, save for the chirp of crickets and the occasional hoot of a distant owl. I should've been more alert, more cautious of my surroundings, seeing as how we were in a land I wasn't used to. But all I could focus on was making sure her breathing didn't stop.

She lay beside me, her face pale, her body's struggle still clinging to her face. Still, even in rest, there was strength in her features that never wavered.

I fixed the cloak draped over her, making sure she kept warm.

Sabrina sat across from me, leaning against a tree, legs pulled up to her chest. She looked toward the fire and then up at me, letting out a big yawn. "You know, Drifted, if you gaze at her any harder, you might wake her with sheer willpower alone."

I exhaled. "I'm making sure she's alright."

She smirked, tilting her head. "Ah, keeping watch, is all?" Her smile grew wider. "And here I thought you were planning to nuzzle into her side like a pup missing its mother."

I sighed, knowing that she was going to start her usual antics.

"What? I feel as though it is sweet." She stood up now,

making dramatic movements and hand gestures as she tried to mock me. "You are all broody over there, playing doting guardian while she slumbers. It is like you are some tragic hero from one of those awful human performances."

I ran a hand down my face. "You know, Celine's the princess of Sylphreach. You should be thanking me for keeping watch over someone so important to your people."

Sabrina gasped, clutching her chest as if I had struck her with the gravest of insults. "Drifted, do you imply that I do not care about our princess?" she took a step closer, eyes wide. "Oh, the audacity! The sheer gall of you!"

I gave her a flat look. "That's not what I said."

She ignored me entirely, walking circles around the campfire, her ears twitching. "If Lady Celine had known you would perch beside her like some grief-stricken crow, watching over her with all the sorrow of a poet at his own funeral, she would not stand for it! It is a disgrace to Lupine pride."

I shook my head slightly, pinching the bridge of my nose. "What are you even talking about anymore?"

"I am simply stating that the honor of our princess can obviously not be safeguarded by one who looks as though he might compose a mournful ballad at any moment."

I scoffed, not entirely sure what she was implying, but I knew enough that she was trying to call me 'sappy'. "I'm not composing anything, *Sabrina.*"

"Ah, but it is all in the eyes, Drifted." She tapped her temple. "And yours weep tragedy."

I threw my hands up. "Well, if you're so concerned about pride, why don't you take over?" I gestured towards Celine. "Go on, show me how a true Lupine would watch over someone unconscious."

Sabrina grinned. "Were I not already far too comfortable,

I might have considered it." She plopped back down onto the ground, stretching her legs out.

I rolled my eyes and turned my attention back to Celine. I'm sure Sabrina was partly correct. Celine was good at taking care of me whenever I got injured, but she wasn't so good at relying on others when the roles were reversed. Still, I didn't care if this was going to damage her pride. All I cared about was her getting better.

Sabrina tossed a twig into the fire, the sounds snapping me out of my thoughts. "Lady Celine will be quite alright, Drifted. She is a Lupine after all."

I nodded, but I still had doubts.

"Just like you, the moon also favors us, Lupine. Even greater so." She continued.

I looked toward her now, my interest piqued. "What do you mean?"

Sabrina leaned back on her hands, her red eyes catching the firelight. "Your wounds may mend quickly, but ours mend quicker. It is in our nature."

I took a quick glance at Celine. "Even her?"

Sabrina smirked. "Aye, even with but half our blood, she is still far beyond you in that regard. Worry not, Drifted. Hopefully, she will stir soon, and when she does, I wager she will scold you for fussing over her so."

A steady breath escaped my lips. It reassured me a bit, but only slightly.

"In truth, I understand why you are troubled. It is difficult to watch another suffer, least of all one you care deeply for." She shrugged. "But Lady Celine is strong, stronger than even she knows. It will take more than this to break her."

I nodded again, letting out another sigh of relief.

Sabrina huffed, resting her head back against the tree. "Mayhaps I should start keeping count of all the times you have sighed this night."

I chuckled. "You'd run out of numbers."

She laughed. "Ah, then I should simply count the times you have stared at the princess with that longing gaze of yours." She tapped her chin. "Or better yet, the number of times you have professed your undying attraction in your head, though I fear I would lose track before the hour is through."

Heat rushed to my face, and I picked up a twig to toss at her. "You don't know what you're talking about!"

She grinned, all sharp teeth and mischief. "Oh, but I do. I see it as clear as the moon above. The way your eyes soften, the way you hover over her like a doting mate," she tsked, shaking her head. "You humans are ever so lovesick. Had I known, I would have brought an extra satchel to get sick in."

I shook my head hard. My face red-hot now. "Would you shut up already!? You're misunderstanding everything."

"Then explain why you are as red as the embers before us, Drifted."

I clenched my jaw, looking anywhere but her. "I'm worried about her. That's all."

Sabrina hummed, unconvinced. "Of course, of course. Don't worry, it shall be our secret, Drifted"

"There's no secret to keep!" I yelled back.

Sabrina threw up her hands, a wide grin still stretched on her face. "Very well, very well! No need to shout, Drifted. I shall take your word for it." She leaned back against the tree, her smirk lingering. "But if I ever hear a heartfelt confession escape those lips, know that I will demand compensation for my silence."

I exhaled, shaking my head. "You're impossible."

Just as she was about to deliver another remark, something in her expression shifted. The playfulness drained from her face, and her eyes widened. Her ears twitched, then swiveled, her entire posture stiffening in an instant.

I sat up, immediately on edge. "What is it?"

Sabrina didn't answer right away. Instead, she rose to her feet, her body fluid yet tense. Her hands curled slightly, and she extended her claws. "Get up."

I was already moving before she finished speaking, pushing myself to my feet. "What is it? What do you hear?"

Her eyes were darting from side to side, and her ears were now twitching frantically. "Something is near," she said in a low, cautious voice. "But I cannot yet tell what."

I reached for my sword, a bead of sweat slowly making its way down my forehead. I noticed the insects and owls had also gone silent.

Swoosh.

A flash of movement that I could barely catch shot between us. A gust of wind followed in its wake, hitting us hard enough to snuff out the fire.

Darkness swallowed everything, but not before I saw the glowing eyes of our enemy as it passed. A Grimroot.

"Sabrina!" I yelled out. "I know what's surrounding us."

Sabrina's ears still twitched as she tried to track the unseen threat. "Oh? Then please out with it, Drifted, for I seem to be lacking your keen insight!"

"Grimroots," I said. "We're surrounded by Grimroots."

Sabrina scoffed, though there was an edge to it. "That is preposterous. There are no fiends in Velora, they have no reason to be here."

No reason to be here? I thought to myself. But before I could question it, a symphony of noises flooded through the air.

A low, creaking noise echoed from the trees, deep and unnatural, like the groan of bending wood under immense strain.

Sabrina and I locked eyes as we stood still.

The moment stretched thick with silence. Then—Sabrina's ears twitched and swiveled behind her. A small movement, but enough to set my instincts on edge.

Before I could react, she was already in motion. She twisted to the side and ducked low, narrowly avoiding something that lunged past her—a flash of wood, metal, and flesh.

I could see the Grimroot clearly now.

Its appearance was as grotesque as I remember, a twisted coagulation of tree and fleshy material. Its bark-like skin cracked and split in places. Revealing pulsing veins of something sickly and dark beneath. Large, bulbous spores clung to its body, their surfaces shifting, pulsing as if breathing. A sickly-sweet scent followed, filling the air with a somewhat floral scent.

It was like any other Grimroot I remembered, but something was different about this one.

This Grimroot was larger than I've ever seen. Noticeably so. The ones Celine and I had encountered before had been monstrous, yes, but this one stood taller, its limbs stretched in unnatural ways and its body was swollen like something that had been left to fester. Thorns protruded from spots on its body, with a sticky dark substance leaking from the protrusions.

My thoughts shattered into chaos as the Grimroot lunged forward.

It moved quicker than any Grimroot I had ever seen. I barely had enough time to react before it was on me, its bladed arm arcing toward where Celine lay vulnerable behind me.

I stepped in front of her, sword raised, bracing myself as the creature's arm came down. The impact sent a shock through my arms, and the sheer force rattled my bones as the metals collided.

"Drifted!" I heard Sabrina yell.

But she couldn't help. As I looked over the shoulder of the Grimroot attacking me, I saw that another had already emerged from the tree line and intercepted her.

The Grimroot in front of me pulled back and spun. Its blade came whipping around toward my head.

I dropped low, ducking as the edge whizzed past, close enough that I felt the wind of its passing. A dull crack followed as the blade buried itself deep into the thick trunk of the tree behind me.

I snapped my head up, gripping my sword tighter as I sucked in a deep breath. That had been too close.

The Grimroot writhed, jerking and pulling as it struggled to free its blade from the tree. The trunk groaned, bark fragments coming down on my head as it struggled.

I swung upward with my sword, bringing it across in an arc. My blade met the rotted flesh and bark, slicing clean through the joint where the creature's bladed limb connected to its body.

The Grimroot recoiled as its severed arm squirmed, still stuck in the tree. A groan rattled from deep within its sappy chest, and its spores pulsed wildly, as if in distress.

As if barely inconvenienced, the fiend lunged again, sending its remaining blade snapping down. I stepped into the strike, tilting my sword to catch its blade. I rolled my sword along the creature's blade, deflecting the force past me. The Grimroot's momentum carried it forward, throwing its balance off for the briefest of moments.

Then, with an inhale, I drove my sword straight into its chest.

The steel sank deep, sliding into the flesh-like tissue.

With a screech, the Grimroot's body seized around my sword. The fungi around its body slowed, and soon their pulsing came to a stop.

I planted my foot against the fiend's shoulder and wrenched my sword free. Panting heavily as my eyes darted to check on Sabrina.

She dipped low beneath a sweeping strike of the Grimroot before launching herself into a tight spin, sending herself up and over the fiend.

The Grimroot tried to turn, but it was too slow. Sabrina was already behind it.

Her hand shot forward. Clawed fingers plunged through the back of the Grimroot, driving through bark and flesh with ease. A squelch filled the air as her hand burst through the other side, emerging from its chest in a spray of dark liquid. The creature spasmed violently before its body locked up and went limp.

Sabrina's eyes gleamed in the moonlight as she leaned in, her voice a teasing whisper. "Poor thing. You hardly put up a fight."

With a hard jerk, she ripped her hand free. Then she sighed, shaking the dark fluid from her claws as she stepped back from the corpse. She turned to me, flashing a grin.

"You know, Drifted," she called, her voice light despite the battle we just went through, "I believe these creatures take great offense to you."

I exhaled. "Yeah? Well, the feeling's mutual."

Sabrina stretched her arms over her head, rolling her shoulders as if she had finished a chore rather than tearing through a monster with her bare hands. "I did expect more of a struggle."

I adjusted my sword in my hand again. My focus wasn't on Sabrina's words. Something felt... off.

My gaze drifted to her ears.

They weren't swiveling, not twitching, not angling toward

the forest in search of movement. They were completely still.

Too still.

A heavy feeling settled in my gut.

Sabrina's ears were always moving, always reacting to the slightest shifts in sound. Even when she wasn't paying attention, her body did. It was instinct. A Lupine's senses were too sharp to allow them to be caught off guard.

So why weren't hers? Why weren't her ears detecting the movement of the several Grimroots that should have been nearby?

I ran my tongue over my teeth, scanning the area again. Everything I had ever been taught—everything that I had ever seen—told me that Grimroots never attacked alone. They moved in packs, attacking together when the opportunity presented itself. Relying on their speed and numbers to overwhelm their targets.

But only two had attacked us. That was hardly enough.

I forced myself to listen, to focus. My own instincts screamed at me, but there was nothing. No movement in the trees. No rustling of unseen fiends shifting in the underbrush. Not even the usual distant hum of nocturnal life.

Sabrina was still talking.

Her voice, light and unconcerned, pulled me back. She was brushing off the fight as if it had been nothing, likely preparing another teasing remark at my expense.

"—truly, if this is all those fiends have to offer—"

"Sabrina." I cut her off.

She paused, one ear finally twitching toward me.

I swallowed. "Doesn't anything seem... weird to you?"

She blinked, tilting her head. "Weird?"

I gestured a hand towards the dark tree line, shaking my head. "Grimroots, don't attack like this—at least, not with only two. They move in numbers. They don't pick fights like

309

this unless they have the advantage."

Sabrina waited for a moment, letting the quiet forest wash over us. Then she let out a short laugh, crossing her arms. "Oh, Drifted, you give these wretched things far too much credit." She pointed lazily toward one of the fallen Grimroots. "They are simply fools. Dumb creatures acting on base instinct, nothing more."

She smirked, tilting her head. "Do you truly believe such rotten creatures have the capacity for strategy? What next, shall they start setting traps for us as well? Whispering to one another in secret tongues?" She tapped her clawed finger against her chin, mockingly in thought.

"No, Sabrina. I'm telling you. Something isn't right." I replied, my eyes darting around the forest.

"If something was amiss, my ears and nose would not have warned us of the danger already?" She gestured to herself, pulling on the ears atop her head. "Come now, Drifted, I am not so dull as to let danger creep upon us unnoticed."

I swallowed, glancing at her ears again. They were still, barely twitching. Her nose hadn't wrinkled, hadn't picked up on anything unusual.

She sighed, shaking her head. "You must relax. The battle has ended, yet here you stand like a frightened hare, expecting another fight." She smirked, rolling her shoulders. "If there were something lurking in those woods, I would have sensed it long before you."

That should have been reassuring, but in all honesty, it wasn't.

Sabrina, however, seemed content to put the matter to rest. With an exaggerated sigh, she plopped herself back onto the forest floor, stretching her legs and arms out with a yawn.

"Honestly, Drifted," she mused, reclining back on her hands. "You spend far too much time worrying over nothing.

It is exhausting to watch."

But then the ground trembled.

It started faintly at first, an almost imperceptible shudder beneath my boots. But before long it grew stronger. A deep, low vibration that thrummed through the land, rattling the fallen leaves and sending tiny ripples through the dirt.

Sabrina stiffened and shot up immediately.

Her ears flicked up, her nose wrinkling slightly as her body tensed. I could tell that even she couldn't pinpoint exactly where the trembling was starting.

My attention quickly shifted to Celine.

I stumbled toward her in the darkness, barely keeping my balance as the ground shook beneath me. She was still lying there, wrapped in her cloak. But as I knelt beside her, my stomach churned slightly.

Her face was twisted in discomfort, brows furrowed, her breathing shallow.

"Celine..." I murmured, reaching out, pressing my palm against her forehead. She was warm now—too warm. A thin sheen of sweat clung to her face, and her fingers twitched, as if they were trying to grasp something I couldn't see.

She let out a soft, strained breath.

Her lips parted, barely moving.

"Run..."

The word was faint, little more than a whisper, but it sent a cold wave through my chest.

"Run? Run from what?" I questioned, holding her shoulders tight.

But she didn't answer, only soft breathing followed.

"Sabrina!" I shouted over the deep, shuddering vibrations. "What the hell is going on?"

Sabrina's ears flattened. I could tell she didn't know the answer immediately. Her red eyes darted from shadow to shadow, her nostrils flaring as if catching a scent carried through the trembling air. Then, slowly, her eyes widened.

"We are surrounded, but this time from below," she said, her voice tense.

CHAPTER 23

The ground was moving.

I stumbled back as a patch of dirt near my foot buckled inward, pulling dead leaves and soil into a slow, spiraling motion. All around us, the forest floor churned, not merely shaking from underneath—but like something was coming up.

"What in the—" I started, but the words quickly faltered

Sabrina had gone still. Her eyes darted to and from different patches of moving dirt with a caution I hadn't seen in her before.

That's when I saw it—thin, blackened stalks rising slowly from the earth, each one twisting unnaturally as it reached toward the sky. One. Two. Then a dozen. Thick bramble-like roots followed, snapping out of the ground like limbs breaking free from shallow graves.

Grimroots. Lots of them.

I quickly knelt in front of Celine's unconscious body and hoisted her carefully onto my back, tightening my arm beneath her legs as I rose to my feet, my heart pounding in my chest.

The Grimroots were rising faster now, every second bringing more of those twisted creatures clawing their way up through the floor.

How had we missed this?

A chill settled in my chest as the realization struck. The first two... they weren't just wanderers. They must've been scouts—testing us all the while, revealing our location.

And we'd failed to notice it.

I turned in place slowly. The clearing was no clearing at all—it was a nest. Grimroots rose in a wide circle around us, their bark-covered forms cracking and stretching as they broke free of the dirt we had been standing on. We'd been walking over them the entire time.

"Drifted, we must move!" I heard Sabrina yell.

Her command was clear as day. But my legs didn't react. Something kept me there, feet locked to the floor as if the very roots in the ground had taken hold of me.

My body refused to answer. My muscles tensed, breath held tight in my chest, but no matter how loudly my mind screamed to run—I couldn't.

All I could do was watch as more Grimroots clawed their way up through the soil in droves. Each unfurling like a nightmare blooming into the world.

As my eyes frantically scanned the surrounding chaos, one of them looked at me. Eyes locking on with a burning intent.

Its body was only half-emerged, shoulders still tangled in roots, but its head turned with a slow motion.

And in that moment, it felt like it *knew* me. I couldn't explain the feeling, but it almost felt as if it were looking for *me*.

The sounds of the forest dulled into a distant, muffled hum. My heart thudded in my chest, but even that felt far away.

Sabrina appeared in front of me, red eyes wide with distress. Her mouth was moving quickly, urgently—but I couldn't hear her. I could only make out the shape of her lips, the intensity in her gaze, and the way her hands gripped my arms like she was trying to shake me free from whatever I'd fallen into.

Then, Sabrina took my hand firmly, and the next thing I knew, we were sprinting through the forest.

In an instant, the fog shattered, and sound came crashing back into the world—the crackling of roots, the shriek of bark tearing apart, the pounding in my ears.

Branches smacked my arms and face as we ran. The air stank of rot and damp wood. Roots continued bursting from the soil behind us, slamming into trees and gouging the earth like claws desperate to drag us back.

I didn't dare look back. Hell, I didn't need to—the sounds told me enough. The Grimroots were chasing us now, the loud clicking of their joints flooding through the forest.

Every step I took was a gamble. One bad move would prove fatal. Sabrina was ahead of me, moving seamlessly through the thicket. I did my best to keep up as my lungs and legs burned.

For a split second, I thought about stopping. Maybe turning to confront our pursuers head on.

Stupid, I thought. There was no way we would be able to fight off the sheer number of them.

My legs continued to burn, and soon my throat was dry. And even as light as Celine was, I couldn't deny that her weight pressed harder on my back with every stride. We couldn't outrun them forever. And part of me, a dark, desperate part, wondered if we were meant to.

Sabrina didn't slow down, though almost as if she sensed my desperation she yelled out.

"Drifted, do not give up on me yet. I possess a plan!"

I didn't know if she was trying to keep my hopes high—not that I had the energy to question it. My ribs ached with each push and there was a shooting pain in my side.

Suddenly, something flashed to my right.

A Grimroot, faster than the others, broke out from the treeline. I barely had enough time to turn my head before it lunged, its blades glistening in the moonlight. Reactively, I tried to crouch down, but recognized this would place Celine in harm's way. Having no other option, I decided I'd take the hit head-on.

"Drifted, your side!" I heard Sabrina's voice cut through a split second before the impact.

Her foot shot out in a brutal kick. The impact made a loud crack as it sent the Grimroot flying off course, its body twisting before slamming into a tree. A wet and garbled shriek rang out as it crumbled into the dirt. I didn't slow down. Knowing that the remaining Grimroots were mere steps behind us.

Sabrina caught up to me easily, her breathing steady despite the chaos unfolding around us. "I could have sworn that Lood and you worked extensively on awareness. Seems it all but went to waste, eh?"

"I didn't exactly have a ton of time to react, you know?" I replied, my breathing getting more labored in-between words.

She huffed a short laugh before easily running ahead of me again. "Excuses."

Up ahead, the trees broke abruptly, and a good distance in front of us was a ravine. A natural trench, narrow and winding, with walls of packed dirt rising on either side.

"Keep up, Drifted!" Sabrina yelled from in front of me.

"There's a ravine in front of us!" I yelled at her.

"Aye, that is the point!" She replied, picking up her pace.

This was her plan? To trap us in a corridor of dirt and stone? To block us in on either side and funnel us into a tight space, limiting our escape routes? There'd be nowhere to run in there, no high ground.

"Sabrina..." I started, trying to catch my breath. "What—what exactly is your plan here?"

She didn't slow, didn't even glance back. Her cloak fluttered behind her as she kept her pace.

"To vanish," she called, her voice echoing between the walls. "Or to mislead them. Whichever the moon wills."

I continued to follow, but I still didn't understand. My eyes darted from wall to wall, from root to root, as the ravine twisted ahead like a serpent's spine.

"Mislead them how?" I yelled ahead.

"This path forks not far ahead," she answered. "You will take the left."

"Okay... what about you?" I replied.

"Do not worry for me," she said without hesitation. "You keep moving. Do not look back."

Split us up? I thought. It sounded risky.

"I don't think separating is a good idea, Sabrina. Even you can't outrun them forever." I replied.

She turned her head slightly, and I saw the glint of one of her fangs as she smiled. "Outrun? Who spoke of running?"

What? She was planning to hold them off alone? Impossible.

"No," I said, breath ragged. "Absolutely not. I'm not leaving you with them."

"Drifted—"

"I said no!"

There was a brief pause—long enough for her next words to sting.

"Spare me the dramatics," she said flatly.

She glanced over her shoulder again. Her red eyes caught mine as the flicker of a smirk to appeared at the corner of her mouth.

"It is not because I care for you," she added. "You simply happen to be carrying the future of Sylphreach on your back. That is all."

I tripped, caught somewhere between insulted and... weirdly reassured.

"Listen, Drifted," She continued. "There is not much time now."

She slowed down to make sure I was listening to her.

"Remember—take the left fork. Find somewhere to hide, preferably on higher ground. Cover your tracks if you can, and do your best to remain silent. Do not come out of hiding unless you hear the sound of my whistle."

She turned to me now, making sure our eyes met fully.

"If after a day you have not heard from me... carry on to Thornwallow."

I stared at her as my chest tightened. She was planning for the case that she didn't make it out.

Up ahead, the path started to split. Two narrow trails veered in different directions; each swallowed quickly by the ravine's walls.

I went quiet.

I couldn't argue with Sabrina. She'd already made up her mind. And deep down, I knew she was right—we couldn't lose them together. Not like this. Not with Celine unconscious on my back.

The only thing I could do now was trust her, even if every part of me hated it.

The fork was closing in fast, the dirt walls pressing tighter around us as the path divided. My pulse pounded in my ears, drowning out everything but the sound of our own breaths and the distant shrieks of the Grimroots behind.

"Get ready," Sabrina said, voice firm. "And do well to remember what I told you."

Her tone left no room for doubt—no room for hesitation.

"Left path. Find shelter. Do not make a sound unless you hear my whistle," she repeated. Then, quieter, "And if a day passes without me..."

I clenched my jaw. Knowing that no words would change

anything, I nodded.

She gave one last look before her head swiveled to look behind us.

"Now! Go on, Drifted!" she ordered.

And then she stopped.

I kept my eyes forward as I ran ahead of her. Not daring to look back as the sound of Grimroots grew ever closer.

From behind me, I heard Sabrina yell out.

"Do not die before we meet again, Drifted. It would be embarrassing."

A lump formed in my throat, but I swallowed it down and forced my legs to move faster. The left path was ahead, narrowing into a shadow. The dirt walls here pressed even tighter, funneling the sounds from behind me straight through.

The last things I heard were the crack of splintering wood, a heavy thud, a strained grunt—and then a breathless chuckle.

Sabrina had already made contact and was quite literally fighting for her life back there. And I just left her.

I lowered my head and sprinted harder, forcing Celine and me deeper into the ravine, letting the sound of battle fade behind us.

CHAPTER 24

The forest swallowed every noise behind me.

I couldn't hear Sabrina anymore—not her voice, not the clashing of Grimroot blades, or the sounds of their screeching. Just the crunch of my boots against the damp ground and the faint sound of Celine's breath against my neck. I had no idea how far I'd gone or how long I'd been running. It could've been minutes. It could've been hours. Time didn't seem to matter anymore.

The night air was thick and hazy. Everything was still as moonlight barely filtered through from above, covering everything in a silver film. Every breath I took obscured my vision briefly. Every shadow looked like it could move if I stared for too long. But I kept going, because stopping meant thinking. And I wasn't quite ready for that yet.

The path I was walking on wasn't actually a path at all—just roots and mud and the occasional glint of moss. Every so often, I had to shift Celine's weight, her arms limp around my shoulders, her head resting against mine. She was warm at least. That was something.

The night blurred all together. My legs moved on their own now, guided only by the echo of Sabrina's voice in my head.

'Find cover, hide yourself well, do not make a sound until you hear my whistle.'

I could still see her face when she said it—a fang ridden smile on her face, as if she were telling me about all the meat she consumed at the mess hall.

I stopped in my tracks briefly, forcing myself to breathe

quieter so I could listen. There were no footsteps behind me, no voices. Only the gentle rustling of the forest and the occasional creak of old limbs swaying in the wind.

I kept walking, but every step felt more aimless than the last.

Every tree looked the same. Every shadow, the same. I couldn't tell if I was getting further away from where I split off from Sabrina, or if I had been circling in some cursed loop. I needed to stop and get my bearings, but stopping without a plan could get both Celine and me killed.

I scanned the immediate area surrounding me, looking for anything that felt safe.

An old thicket? *Nope.*

A hollowed trunk? *Not large enough.*

A dip in the ground? *Not deep enough.*

Nothing felt secure enough. I considered staying down low, maybe tucking us beneath a root system or curling into a divot, but the thought didn't sound good enough.

With Celine on my back, I wouldn't be able to run if were cornered. If Grimroots surrounded us down there, it'd be a grave.

I stood still for a moment, catching my breath, heart pounding. That's when a thought came to me.

Grimroots, their arms were built like blades—bony, and rigid—not built for climbing. I remembered that from a lesson back in Lunaria. Professor Rennard had drawn one on the chalkboard, all sharp elbows and serrated limbs.

"Grimroots are poor climbers," he had said, tapping the drawing with his stick. "They can slash, they can skewer, but they cannot grasp. Too stiff. Keep to higher ground if you're ever caught in a bind with one."

I looked up.

The tree beside me was large and with a wide trunk. Its

bark was split and rough—perfect for gripping. Thick branches stretched out above me, their leaves already beginning to grow back from the passing winter. It was high enough that it would give me a clear vantage point, and covered enough that Celine and I wouldn't stick out.

It wasn't perfect, but it was the best option we had at the moment.

Still, one slip could prove disastrous for us, especially in our current condition. Climbing with Celine hanging lifelessly to me would be too risky.

I glanced around, searching nearby trees for anything that could help. That's when I spotted a tree a few paces off, wound thick with curling green vines. They coiled up the bark like snakes, and knotted thick in some areas.

Without thinking twice, I made my way toward it carefully, as to not jostle Celine too much.

Pulling out my sword, I wedged the blade under a vine and tugged, sawing through it until it snapped free with a crack. I gave it a few testing tugs to make sure of its strength—it held.

I wrapped the vine around us both, making sure it was snug and tight. Looping it over my shoulders and under Celine's legs, across her back and around my chest. I tied it off best I could with a rough knot near my ribs, then tested the weight with a few light jumps.

Celine was secure and wouldn't fall unless I did.

I looked back up the tree.

Alright, Isaac. Let's do this! I thought to myself. "Let's hope you're still as good at climbing trees as you were when you were younger," I muttered under my breath.

I took my first hold, bracing my hand against the rough bark, feeling the grooves bite into my palm. One step, then another. I pressed my boot into a notch in the trunk and pulled myself upward.

The first few feet were slow. I kept close to the tree, hugging it with all my might. My arms strained under the added weight, and the vine dug into my chest with every shift.

I found a thick knot in the wood and used it to push myself higher, grabbing at a low branch and hauling myself up.

Despite my better judgment, I paused halfway up and threw a glance over my shoulder.

I had expected the ground to be much closer, and its distance instantly tightened my stomach. A strange weight pressed against my ribs.

An audible gulp came from my throat as I swallowed.

I used to be good at this kind of thing, climbing trees and all. Back when I was younger. Back before I knew what it meant to fall.

I tore my eyes away from the ground, gluing them to the tree. No good would come from me staring down there all longer.

My fingers trembled slightly as I flexed my hand. I shook my head hard, trying to clear the haze settling in. *Get it together, Isaac.* I forced a breath through my nose, then another. We were already so close to the top.

I pressed on, climbing higher up the tree, branch by branch. My muscles were already tired and aching from what had transpired earlier in the day, and my shoulders had an intense pain in them with every pull, but I couldn't stop.

Finally, I reached a thick, large branch wide enough to straddle easily. Leaves grew densely around it, forming a curtain that would shield us from sight.

Carefully, I swung a leg over and settled in, one arm braced around Celine's back as I leaned us into the trunk.

I reached down and began undoing the vine, fingers fumbling slightly as I worked the knot loose. Bit by bit, the tension around my chest released until the last loop slipped free. I held onto Celine carefully the whole time, making sure she didn't tilt too far.

Once we were unbound, I gently positioned her against the tree trunk, using one hand to control her shoulder while I shifted my legs.

Then, slowly, I slid myself behind her, wedging my back against the tree. I pulled her close so that her back rested against my chest, with her head beneath my chin.

It wasn't the most comfortable position, but it would have to do.

I glanced at the vine still coiled in my other hand.

It was long enough that it could serve another purpose other than just getting us up here.

I took the length of it and wrapped it around us both, securing us together. I made sure it was snug but not too tight, enough to keep her from slipping if I happened to nod off.

Then, I swung one end of the vine under the branch we were resting on, grabbing the end as it fell onto Celine's lap. I pulled it tight, tying it off with a firm knot against the rest of the binding at my side.

It wasn't perfect, but it would keep us from falling too far if we slipped.

I leaned my head back against the tree, letting the bark press into my skull. I was exhausted, and the fatigue of the day was finally catching up to me.

My eyes grew heavy, and I was soon fighting to stay awake. I tried to listen for ever twig snap or rustle—but it was hard... and only getting more difficult as time passed.

Being up here, relatively safe, calmed me down and allowed me to drop my guard. Celine was warm against me— extremely warm, despite how cold the night had grown. I watched with cloudy eyes as her body rose and fell with every quiet breath she took.

Her hair was soft beneath my chin, the strands gently tickling my neck with every breeze. And her ears twitched now and then, the furry tips brushing against my cheek. It was strange how something that once confused me now brought me so much calm.

I shifted slightly, adjusting my grip around her waist, and let out a slow, tired breath.

Just for a little, I told myself. *Just for a small moment*, I would allow my eyes a break. I wouldn't sleep, not fully. Just... rest.

Though everything melted together into something too comfortable to fight. My limbs got heavier, the ache in my back dulled, and my head leaned slightly to the side.

And before I knew it... sleep took me.

A sudden noise snapped me awake.

I shot upright with a quiet gasp, my arms tightening around Celine. A quick glance showed she was still sound asleep. I blinked, trying to get my eyes to tune to the darkness still surrounding us. I couldn't tell how much time had passed. The moon had moved in the sky slightly, but everything else looked the same.

Another sound came—the snap of a twig. Something was below us.

For a second, my heart stopped. Sabrina? Had she finally caught up with us?

I opened my mouth to call out to her.

But then, her voice echoed in my head. *Stay silent until you hear my whistle.*

I froze and closed my mouth immediately. If it were her, she'd be able to smell us out and know to give the signal.

Which meant... it wasn't.

I pressed my back tighter to the trunk, keeping Celine

close and my body still as stone. My ears strained for another sound. A breath. A step. Anything.

I didn't move, didn't speak. I just listened.

A few seconds later, I heard footsteps. Slow, far too heavy to be an animal. Each one came with a faint crunch of the forest floor and the scuff of something dragging.

I tightened my grip around Celine's waist and then slowly leaned my head over the branch.

Through the trees, figures—two—no, three, too dark to make out, searched the area beneath us.

I slowed my breathing, hoping to quiet any noise that could've given away our position. My heart thudded so hard I swore they'd hear it from below. I didn't dare pull back from the edge. I watched and waited. Praying to the moon that the leaves held strong, and the wind didn't blow too hard.

And then—

"...nnn..."

It was barely a sound. A soft murmur against my chest.

Celine.

She moved slightly in her sleep, her head brushing my collarbone, a quiet breath escaping her lips—no louder than a whisper, but loud enough.

Worried, I cupped a hand over her mouth, hoping to silence any further sound that might have wanted to escape her lips.

But it was too late. Directly beneath us, the figures stopped right in their tracks.

Like watchdogs, their heads snapped up in unison.

One crouched down and let out a low, deep sound.

Another stepped forward slowly... directly toward the base of the tree.

It was clear they noticed the sound had come from our general direction, but thankfully, they hadn't yet seen us in the canopy. The thick leaves, the height, and the shadows from the tree all worked in our favor. But that could change in an instant.

I held my breath as one figure circled around the trunk. Its head tilted upward for a moment—not looking at us, not quite—but scanning the sky as if it sensed something out of place.

A second figure took a step closer too, its body half-lit by a sliver of moonlight. I could make out the arm of it, something long, bent, humanoid. But that is all I could see before it was back in the darkness again.

The third figure moved last, crouching at the base of the tree. It stood still for a long moment. Listening.

Then it pressed a hand against the bark. And I heard it— soft at first, barely audible—but unmistakable. Sniffing.

I thought maybe it was the wind or brush moving. But the longer it went on, the clearer it became. Heavy inhalations, dragging along the length of the tree bark.

The figure moved around the base of the tree in a slow circle, its breathing growing louder and more focused. Sniffing up and down the trunk as if it were following an invisible trail.

Another figure joined it, mimicking the motion. Then the third. They fanned out, surrounding the tree, their bodies moving around the roots with purpose.

I didn't move. Couldn't. My entire body had gone still.

Celine remained motionless against me. Her warmth was the only thing grounding me—reminding me I was still alive. But for how long… I wasn't sure.

Whoever—or whatever—the figures were, they were too close for comfort.

I tightened my arm around Celine, pulling her in a little closer.

Slowly—extremely slowly—I eased my free hand

downward, inching it toward the hilt of my sword.

I didn't draw it. Not yet. But I held it just in case.

If they climbed—if they saw us.

I was ready to fight.

Even though I knew it wouldn't be enough.

Below, they continued circling. One of them paused and scraped something against the bark. Another let out a low exhale—almost a growl, but too soft to be certain. Another sniffed again, louder this time, its head tilting as it began angling its head upwards. Right below where we were.

I could feel my heartbeat in my teeth.

And then—*crack*.

The sound of splintering wood echoed through the forest, distant but sudden. A tree limb, maybe. Broken under weight. Far enough that I could tell it wasn't in our immediate vicinity... but close enough to catch attention.

The effect was immediate.

All three figures froze. Their heads snapped toward the sound. One let out a short huff and took a step back from the tree. Another turned fully, peering into the dark beyond the foliage.

Then—without a sound—they moved.

One by one, they slipped into the shadows, melting into the undergrowth toward the noise.

I kept my hand on the hilt of my sword, eyes fixed on the spot where they had vanished. The underbrush still shifted faintly, branches swaying from where they had passed. I followed the motion with my eyes, tracking them as far as I could.

The sounds of their movement grew fainter—brush crackling, leaves rustling, then... silence.

Still, I waited. Just to be sure.

Only when the forest stilled completely—when the wind

settled and even the trees seemed to breathe easier—did I finally loosen my grip on the sword.

I let out a quiet breath and leaned my head back against the trunk. My fingers still hovered near the sword, tense with the memory.

What were they?

Grimroots—that's what I thought at first. The humanoid limbs, the way they moved, the sniffing. It all kind of fit. But... Something felt off.

It was too dark to see clearly, and I hadn't dared move enough to get a better look. But their presence... it didn't quite match up fully. Their movements were too precise and too focused.

I swallowed, eyes scanning the dark below again, even though I knew there was nothing left to see.

Whatever they were, they had come too close. And they had been looking for something.

No... not something. Someone.

But I forced the thought away before it could root itself too deep.

There was no point in spiraling. I didn't know what those things were. And right now, I didn't have the luxury of figuring it out. All I could do was stay alert... and keep us hidden.

We got extremely lucky. Who knew if next time would be the same?

I turned my gaze toward the forest again, scanning the shadows between the trees.

Sabrina. I thought to myself.

Where was she?

She still hadn't appeared. No whistle. No signal. Nothing.

Had she gotten lost trying to find us? No, it should've been easy for her to find us with our scent.

The thought tightened in my chest. I didn't want to believe anything had happened to her... but I couldn't shake the unease crawling up my spine.

She was supposed to lead the Grimroots away and find us. But now... nothing.

The night felt colder all of a sudden.

CHAPTER 25

The first rays of daybreak spilled through the leaves above us, striking me directly in the face. I barely registered it at first, my mind somewhere between exhaustion and focus. It was the persistent, rhythmic chirping of birds that finally broke through my absentmindedness, pulling me back into myself.

I blinked up at the light above, the shapes of leaves and branches blurring together as my eyes struggled to focus. My body felt heavy, weighed down by the night's unrest. Every muscle and bone in my body ached with a tiredness that the little sleep I got couldn't chase away.

After the encounter with the figures beneath the tree, any thought of rest had been torn from me. I hadn't slept a single hour after that.

With a heavy breath, I pushed myself upright. Even though my limbs were protesting, another day had come, whether they were ready or not.

I tightened my arms around Celine's waist. She was still unconscious. As I brought my head around to look at her face, my heart sank. Her face was pale—too pale, with a thick layer of sweat clinging to her skin.

I quickly placed the back of my hand on her forehead, making my heart sink even further. Her skin felt like it was on fire.

"No, no, no..." I muttered under my breath, brushing the damp hair away from her face. She didn't stir. Not even a twitch.

I placed my head closer to her face, trying to check her breathing. It was shallow, even more than before. It was painfully clear her injuries were eating away at her.

If we were by a stream or on the forest floor, maybe I could find some cool water to help fight against her fever. Or if we were on the forest floor, I could gather some medicinal herbs to help heal her injuries. Something, anything.

But the thought barely finished before reality caught up with me. I couldn't.

In an area so foreign to me, I wasn't willing to tempt fate by ignoring her warning. Sabrina knew this land and the dangers that lurked in ways I didn't. If she told me to stay put, it was more than caution.

But where the hell was she? The night had passed. Morning had come. And still... no sign of her.

I was stuck. Forced to wait and watch as Celine's strength withered away before my eyes, powerless to do anything about it.

What could I even do?

Even If I wanted to go searching for Sabrina, leaving Celine alone in her condition was out of the question. Not out here. And carrying her through the forest again, while I was already so low on energy, was a death wish.

Where would I even go from here?

It wasn't like I knew where to find her in the first place.

All I could do was stay and wait. Pray that she would return before it was too late.

I sat back against the tree, my mind spiraling with every terrible possibility that I couldn't stop from creeping in.

Time slipped by unnoticed, lost in an endless loop of worry. Between tending to Celine and keeping watch for any sign of Sabrina, my thoughts spiraled. I couldn't say how long I'd been sitting there—minutes, hours—it all blurred together.

When Celine's breathing hitched briefly, I snapped upright,

panic rushing through me all over again.

Without thinking, I awkwardly turned my weight, nearly slipping from the branch beneath us. With barely enough room to move, I tore off my cloak, bunching it up in my hands to use as a fan as best I could.

It was pathetic.

The branches poked at my arms, the angle made my shoulders ache, and the little air I managed to create barely reached her flushed skin.

But I kept at it anyway, desperate for any sign that it was helping.

"Come on, Celine," I whispered to her hoarsely, my voice cracking. "Stay with me..."

She didn't respond. Obviously.

The only things I could hear were the frantic beating of my own heart and the pathetic rustle of fabric as I fanned her.

I continued clumsily fanning until a sound cut through the forest.

Snap

Rustle.

I froze.

The cloak slipped from my hands, landing on a branch below us.

Damnit, I cursed at myself. Hopefully, whatever was near didn't hear it.

Every muscle in my body locked up as I strained to listen, barely daring to breathe.

Something was moving out there, and it was close.

I moved my hand to the hilt of my sword, doing my best not to make a sound. The tree creaked faintly under me as every sound felt ten times louder in the silence.

I stayed as still as possible, a bead of sweat forming on my brow as I listened and waited for whatever had found its way into our little corner of the woods.

Another dry crack split the air, followed by the low rustle of branches being disturbed—closer this time. I pressed myself even tighter against the tree's trunk.

Through the weave of branches and morning mist, I caught a glimpse of movement—a dark shape snaking between the trees. Too quick to make out clearly.

I couldn't tell what it was. But what I could tell was that it was only one person—or thing.

The figure moved again, and then it was gone. Swallowed by the forest once more.

Was it Sabrina?

I swallowed hard, my brain screaming at me to stay hidden. To wait. To be sure.

As I was about to move to get a better look, a low whistle cut through the trees.

My heart practically leapt into my throat.

Relief surged through me so quickly it nearly made me dizzy. It had to be her. It had to be Sabrina.

I opened my mouth, ready to call out—then stopped.

What if it wasn't?

I forced my jaw shut, not making a sound.

How could I be sure it was actually Sabrina's call? What if someone had overheard our discussion that night and knew that would be the signal I was waiting for?

I nestled Celine and me further up against the tree, my excitement warring against my doubts.

If I called out to the wrong thing, I wouldn't just be putting myself in danger — I'd be putting Celine at risk too. I had to be sure.

Another whistle came. Slightly louder this time.

The figure was moving toward us. I could hear the faint crunch of leaves beneath careful steps and the subtle shift of foliage being pushed aside.

Fear of being caught and desperate hope that Sabrina was finally coming for us kept every muscle in my body coiled tight.

I ground my teeth, forcing myself to wait a little longer.

One wrong move could cost us everything.

The figure pushed through the last line of trees, and for a moment, the branches still masked them.

Then a break in the leaves gave me a clear look—

It was Sabrina.

She let out another low whistle and looked to either side of the forest as her nose caught our scent.

All the air nearly left my lungs when I saw her.

"Sabrina!" I called out, my voice cracking.

She stiffened, and her head snapped up toward the sound of my voice, eyes trying to scan the tangled branches above her.

"Drifted, I cannot locate you!" she called back, her voice a low whisper.

She stepped closer, moving carefully between the thick roots at the base of the tree. A moment later, she stood almost directly beneath us, craning her neck as her red eyes scanned the canopy until she found us through the mess of leaves.

When her eyes finally locked with mine, she let out a short breath, half scoff, half a sigh.

"How in the moon did you even manage to haul the princess up there?" she asked.

She shook her head before I could even try to answer.

"Nevermind that. No time for such riddles. Work your way down here, Drifted. We must take our leave."

I gave her a quick nod and prepared myself for the descent.

I reached for the vines and began working at the knots I'd tied the night before. As they loosened, Celine sagged against me, her weight pressing in for a moment. I gently steadied her, stepped over her to position her behind me, and looped the vine back around us, fastening it snugly across our chests and shoulders.

Once I was sure the knots were secure, I tightened my hold on Celine and carefully began working us down the tree.

As I made my way down, I stopped at the branch Celine's cloak landed on. There was no point in losing supplies when we already came out here so light.

I snagged the cloak as I passed, securing it between Celine and me as I made my way lower down the tree.

After what felt like an eternity, my boots hit the last branch.

Sabrina was already moving beneath us, her arms raised to help ease us down.

"Slow and steady, Drifted."

I tripped down from the tree, and once on flat land, my legs nearly gave out. I staggered forward a step, breathing heavily as each inhale felt like it scraped against my bruised ribs.

Sabrina caught my arm, helping me with a firm grip.

"Come now, Drifted," she smirked. "Do not tell me you are tired."

I gave a shaky nod, but I could barely find the strength to answer.

Every inch of me ached — my arms, my back, my legs — all of it worn raw from the climb, from the carrying, from the past two days of hell with barely a moment's rest between.

It took everything I had just to stay standing.

Sabrina guided me carefully to sit against the tree. Then she undid the vines and lowered Celine carefully onto a softer patch of moss and leaves. She brushed aside the sweat-slick hair from Celine's pale face and let out a quiet sigh.

"She is running a high fever," Sabrina muttered, a frown

forming on her face. She carefully pulled Celine's cloak around her, most likely trying to keep her warm. "Rest for a moment, Drifted. I shall tend to her for the time being."

I didn't have the strength to argue. Every muscle in my body agreed. My limbs felt like lead, and exhaustion clawed relentlessly at my senses. Yet my mind wouldn't let me rest—not yet, at least. I raised my head, voice hoarse but urgent.

"What happened to you? Why did it take so long?"

Sabrina stood up, clearing her throat. I knew immediately that she was getting ready to brag.

She tilted her head, a smug look flashing across her face. "You should have witnessed me, Drifted," she began. "Surrounded by fiends on all sides—there must have been thousands. I fear I lost count somewhere around the third hundred."

I shook my head slowly and rolled my eyes. "Thousands? And you made it out alive?"

Sabrina gave a wide, toothy smile.

"Such feats are nothing extraordinary," she said lightly, turning her attention back to Celine. "At least not for a Lupine of my exceptional skill."

Even as worn down as I felt, I couldn't help the faint, relieved laugh that escaped my lips.

Sabrina got closer to Celine, carefully peeling back layers of clothing to examine her wounds.

I watched as she worked, trying to hold my head up to stay alert. But now that she was there, I felt that my mind could actually relax and take a break from thinking of every possible danger. My body suddenly felt unbearably heavy, and even my breathing sounded distant in my head.

Sabrina glanced at me briefly and gave a slight nod. "Rest now, Drifted," she murmured quietly. "You have done enough. Allow yourself a moment's peace."

My body, and my mind—they were done. A reply wouldn't even form in my head. Everything blurred, my head dipped forward, and before I knew it. I was asleep.

An insistent shaking pulled me abruptly from rest. I sat upright, blinking as my vision slowly adjusted. Sabrina knelt beside me, rattling my shoulders.

"Awaken, Drifted!" she shouted. "I did not tell you to sleep the day away."

I rubbed at my eyes and took in the orange haze that now covered the forest. It was evening. My entire body still felt battered, but Sabrina's yelling snapped me fully awake.

"It would be unwise to remain here after nightfall," Sabrina added.

I took a glance toward Celine, who lay quietly nearby. She was still unconscious, with her forehead wrapped in some long leaf, most likely a medicinal herb that Sabrina had foraged.

"How is she doing?" I asked, gesturing my head towards Celine.

"She lives yet," Sabrina assured me quickly. "I have done what I can, given the circumstances. However, without adequate treatment, I am not sure how long I can keep her stabilized."

I pushed myself upright, biting back a groan as the stiffness in my body flared painfully. Sabrina was right. With night approaching and Celine's health on the decline, we needed to make it to Thornwallow, and fast.

"We'd better get moving then," I said, forcing myself to my feet. My legs wobbled a bit, but I caught myself.

Sabrina gave a firm nod. "Indeed. The sooner we depart, the better."

I knelt beside Celine and eased her gently onto my back again, feeling the strain instantly settle across my shoulders. My neck screamed and my back stung, but I clenched my jaw shut.

Sabrina made sure Celine's cloak was secure and then stepped forward towards the tree line.

We moved quietly through the forest, our footsteps muffled by layers of fallen leaves and moss.

After a long stretch of silence, I finally spoke up, voice hushed but carrying clearly in the stillness. "How far are we now?"

Sabrina slowed her pace slightly, glancing back at me. "Not far. By my reckoning, we shall reach Thornwallow by tomorrow evening."

A moment passed, then she turned more fully toward me, her gaze intense and serious. "But heed me well, Drifted. Keep your eyes and ears open. Remember clearly where it is we are headed—we walk straight into the heart of enemy territory."

Instinctively, I gulped. Scared or not, we had no choice. Celine needed help, and Thornwallow was our only hope.

We continued onward, the shadows lengthening around us as the daylight slipped away.

"Do you think we'll really find help in Thornwallow?"

Sabrina glanced back at me, her expression thoughtful but resolute. "Of a certainty, Drifted. Thornwallow is well-stocked with the supplies we require. Acquiring those supplies, however..." She gave a small shrug, the faintest hint of a smile playing at her lips. "That, I confess, I have not yet thought through."

I smirked as she turned to start walking again. As I took my first step, I stopped, a sinking thought coming into my mind.

My chest tightened, a sudden dread creeping back into the edges of my mind. With everything that had happened—Celine's injuries, Sabrina's disappearance, our near-death encounters—I hadn't even had time to consider the real reason we'd ventured out here in the first place.

My uncle, Alfarr.

A cold shudder ran down my spine as images of the horrors they might be inflicting upon him flashed through my mind. I clenched my jaw tightly, forcing myself to shake away those dark thoughts.

I exhaled slowly, gripping Celine tighter, steeling myself for whatever lay ahead. *One step at a time*, I reminded myself silently.

Ahead of me, Sabrina abruptly halted. She stood perfectly still, tilting her head back slightly, her nose lifted toward the sky as she sniffed.

I stared at her, brow raised. "What's the matter?"

She didn't respond immediately as she took another sniff. Then she lowered her head and turned toward me with a look I couldn't discern from worry or amusement. "A storm approaches," she said simply.

I glanced upward through the branches. The sky that peeked through was clear, covered with only the colors of sunset.

"You sure?" I questioned. "I don't see any clouds."

Sabrina fixed me with a smug look, her red eyes low. "Quite certain."

Something in the way she answered told me not to press her further. I'd learned well enough by now to trust her instincts, even if they were beyond my understanding. Readjusting Celine on my back, I followed as Sabrina turned and continued through the forest.

As we pressed forward, there was a strange change in the

forest ahead. The trees we were moving towards seemed unnaturally dark—blackened, even. It almost seemed as if someone had drained the life from them. Their branches twisted upwards like desperate hands, completely bare of any leaves.

It wasn't only the appearance of the trees that disturbed me; it was how abruptly the healthy forest ended and the desolation began. There was no gradual transition, no slow decay. Instead, it was almost as if there was an invisible boundary that separated this section from the rest of the world.

"Sabrina," I murmured uneasily, slowing my steps as we neared the stark line dividing the trees. "What is this place?"

Sabrina paused beside me, her eyes tracing the boundary. "This marks the edge of the forest surrounding Thornwallow," she said in a low voice. "Once we cross this partition, we shall officially be within Cassius' domain."

As if summoned by her words, the sky suddenly darkened above us. A fierce gust of wind tore through the branches, followed swiftly by heavy sheets of rain that crashed down with substantial force. Lightning flashed overhead, illuminating the bleak forest momentarily, before plunging it back into darkness.

I tilted my head upward only to be pelted by rain.

How fitting. I thought to myself.

Sabrina stepped closer to me, silently reaching up to pull the hood of my cloak over my head.

Without a word, she moved around behind me, and did the same to Celine's

Finally, she stepped back and drew up her own hood. For a brief moment, our eyes met through the veil of rainfall. Her expression was calm and determined despite everything that loomed before us.

"Are you ready, Drifted?" she asked softly, her voice barely audible above the rumble of distant thunder.

I reluctantly nodded, barely able to see her clearly through the heavy rain.

"As ready as I can be," I replied loudly.

"Stay close," Sabrina said. Then, without waiting for a reply, she turned and stepped across the threshold.

I adjusted Celine on my back one more time and crossed the stark divide between the two worlds.

The moment I stepped into the treeline, everything changed. The air grew colder, heavier. Visibility dropped to near nothing—fog and shadow thickened around us, and the only things I could make out were the jagged silhouettes of trees.

Thorns covered nearly every surface—wrapping around trunks, stretching across branches like a creeping disease. Thick, dark vines laced with barbed thorns, some as long as my fingers, twisted through the forest like veins.

This was the final stretch before Thornwallow, I thought with a shudder.

I kept as close to Sabrina as I could manage, never letting her silhouette drift more than a few steps ahead of me. In a place like this, it would be far too easy to get separated.

The heavy rain pounded against the floor and trees so loudly that it drowned out nearly any other sound there could be. I couldn't hear footsteps, couldn't hear branches swaying, and couldn't hear wildlife. Though it didn't seem any would want to be here, anyway.

All I could do was keep my eyes on Sabrina's hood, following her deeper into the thorns and shadows. Each step forward felt like plunging further into a world that didn't want us there. I admittedly felt nervous. But I knew turning back wasn't an option.

Up ahead, Sabrina suddenly lost her footing, stumbling forward. She caught herself just in time to avoid falling face-first into a bundle of thorns. One knee hit the ground, and she stayed there for a moment.

I hurried closer, careful not to trip over anything myself. "Sabrina!" I called out, raising my voice. "Are you alright?"

She looked up quickly, brushing wet strands of hair from her face as she pushed herself upright. "Aye, Drifted. I am fine." She replied, her voice hoarse. "Merely slipped on the wet ground is all."

But as she rose, I caught her hand lingering at her right side, pressing into her waist. She held it there for only a second before her eyes flicked toward me. The moment she recognized I had noticed, she dropped her hand and straightened fully, keeping her eyes hidden beneath the hem of her hood.

"Sabrina, what's wrong?" I asked, frowning.

"It is nothing," she replied quickly. "I must have pulled a muscle when I caught myself. Now let us move."

Before I could press her further, she started walking again, her pace faster than before.

I knew she was hiding something.

For Sabrina to lose her footing—on ground this relatively flat—was strange. The Lupine moved fluidly through the forest, even when the terrain was rugged and wild. There was grace in everything they did.

But just now... she'd slipped and caught herself at the last possible second, like someone whose body wasn't responding the way it should.

I kept my eyes on her back as she moved ahead. Questioning her would be fruitless. She'd never show an injury so easily. I had to see it with my own eyes.

So I followed her deeper into the darkened woods, silent

and watchful as the storm crashed and howled even more violently around us.

Then, suddenly, Sabrina turned to me, her eyes intense beneath her dripping hood. She was mouthing something. I could see her mouth moving, and the urgency in her eyes, but the rain drowned out the message.

"What?" I called out, getting closer to hear her better. "What did you say?"

But she didn't repeat herself.

Instead, she grabbed my hand and pulled until we were both running.

Branches snapped beside us. Roots and thorns tangled under my boots, but Sabrina didn't slow down. Celine's weight pressed hard into my back with every stride, and my mind spun with confusion.

What were we running from?

"What's going on?" I called out again, throat dry as we pushed through the wet underbrush.

"They are following us," Sabrina shouted back, her voice brimming with urgency. "Cassius' goons. I believe they have found us."

My heart skipped a beat.

Sabrina cursed under her breath. "The rain—it drowned out their steps... covered their scent. I did not notice until they were nearly upon us."

I glanced over my shoulder as we ran, trying to catch any sign of movement through the blackened trees. But there was nothing—no shapes darting between trunks, no flicker of motion in the shadows.

If we were being followed, I sure couldn't see them.

But Sabrina could feel them. Her instincts were keener than anything I could hope to match. If she said they were close, then they were

We kept running, feet slamming into the slick ground, ducking under low branches and weaving through vines. The icy rain stung my eyes, blurred my vision—but I didn't stop.

Then I noticed something strange.

I was now in front of Sabrina.

At first I thought it was adrenaline—maybe I'd caught a second wind—but as the trees blurred past us. I got further away from her.

I turned my head back as I ran, blinking through the downpour. It wasn't possible that I was running faster than she was. What was going on?

I noticed a limp as she ran. Subtle, but growing worse with every stride.

She was trying to keep the weight off her right side, the same side she'd held after her stumble earlier.

I slowed down to stay beside her.

"Sabrina," I said, breathless, "you're hurt."

She didn't look at me. Didn't answer.

But I could see it in the way her jaw clenched.

She was in pain, and she'd been hiding it from me the whole time.

"Sabrina," I said between breaths, glancing around the rain-soaked forest, "we need to stop. Find cover. Something. We can't outrun them like this—you're limping."

She shook her head sharply. "Pointless."

"What? Why?" I asked.

"They will smell the blood," she said, voice low and bitter. "Mine. Even through this storm, they will catch the scent. Hiding would not even buy us seconds."

Before I could respond, she moved.

She slammed into me, shoulder-first. I staggered, losing my grip on Celine as the three of us crashed to the muddy ground. The fall knocked the air from my lungs, bark and thorns scraping my side as I hit hard.

"What the hell—!" I started, but Sabrina was already upright, crouched like a beast ready to strike.

I followed her gaze—and froze.

Not ten paces ahead, just barely visible through the wall of rain, a large wolf stood in the path, its dark coat soaked and clinging to its body. Its red eyes cut through the rain like crimson embers, fixed on us with unnatural stillness. No snarl, no movement.

And then, as if the storm itself summoned them, others appeared—slipping soundlessly from the trees. Shapes moving beyond the reach of the dying light, fur slick with rain, eyes aglow. One. Two. Then more. Closing in.

We were surrounded.

I scrambled up to crouch beside Celine, shielding her with my body as I drew my sword. My fingers were trembling, but I wasn't sure if it was from exhaustion or fear.

The wolf in front of us didn't move. Neither did the others flanking it.

A new figure emerged from the darkness. It stepped between the trees with ease, the rainfall parting slightly around its bulky body.

Tall, broad-shouldered. Cloaked in a deep, soaked hood that masked most of its face. The only thing I could clearly make out was the way the rain gleamed against the scars along their bare arms and the silent power in the way they walked.

Sabrina shuffled beside me, rising slowly to her feet despite her injury. Her posture was tense, and her voice was dry with disdain.

"I knew I could smell your stink," she said, lips curling into a half-snarl. Then, with venom dripping from her words, she added, "Agnes."

The hooded figure stopped a few strides from the wolves

flanking us, then slowly raised her head. I couldn't see her face clearly beneath the hood, but I didn't need to. Her voice gave everything away—crude, mocking, and thick with cruel amusement.

"Well, if it is not little Sabrina," she said, dragging the name out like a curse. "So nice of you to join us once more."

Her tone rose with sarcasm, each word steeped in smug satisfaction. She took a step closer, boots squelching against the wet ground, the other Lupine parting slightly to let her through.

"I must admit, I did not expect you to return so soon. Especially not after the beating I gave you last time." Her head tilted, a smile in her voice. "Or are you simply a glutton for punishment?"

Beside me, I felt Sabrina's posture shift as she tried to settle her weight evenly across her body.

She's trying to hide her injuries, I thought to myself.

Sabrina lifted her chin slightly, rain trailing down her cheek as she let out a faint scoff.

"Aye, well," she said, her tone dry as flint, "I figured if I was going to walk into a nest of pups, I might as well bring the loudest one to heel first."

Agnes didn't laugh, but the wolves behind her stirred slightly.

Sabrina's hand, still hanging at her side, twitched once—two fingers brushing against her thigh. Then she pointed behind her cloak further down the darkened path. The movement was subtle, but I understood it immediately.

She wanted me to run, to take Celine and escape.

I hesitated, eyes darting around the area. The task seemed impossible. Wolves surrounded us—in front, on the sides, and in the rear. Their glowing red eyes piercing the night through the rain. Even if I stood up and bolted right now, I doubted I'd make it ten steps before they would take me down.

Suddenly, a loud whistle cut through the downpour.

Without waiting, Sabrina's hand reached for her pouch and in one fluid motion, she pulled out a small, capped flask. Without pause, she threw it toward the base of a nearby tree.

The moment it struck the trunk, the contents ignited with a bright flash—an alchemical flare. The tree erupted in light and smoke, the sudden burst casting long, warped shadows across the clearing and sending several of the wolves back on their haunches.

The fire hissed and cracked through the wet bark, not strong enough to burn long—but enough to disorient. Enough to buy seconds.

"Go!" Sabrina snapped as she made a beeline straight toward Agnes, ready to attack.

I bent low and grabbed Celine, heart pounding as the heat of the flare licked at my heels. I was about to run when a voice cut through the storm.

"Do not leave so soon, boy," Agnes called out. "You will not want to miss this."

I froze.

And despite everything inside me screaming to move, I turned.

In the flickering light of the fire, I saw them meet. Two silhouettes colliding in the rain, one all speed and the other strength.

Sabrina struck first. She leapt into the air with a wide overhead kick. But just before her foot connected, her body faltered. She winced, her arm briefly clutching her side to keep herself composed.

Agnes raised an arm and caught the kick effortlessly. She pivoted and threw a heavy punch straight toward Sabrina's chest.

Sabrina brought her arms up to block, but the impact echoed through the clearing. The sheer force of it sent her skidding backward across the slick ground, boots dragging through the mud as she fought to keep her balance.

Then she planted her feet and immediately charged again. I watched as the mud splashed beneath her boots as she lunged straight at Agnes. She threw a punch right at Agnes' jaw, but Agnes saw it coming. Easily.

She caught Sabrina's wrist mid-swing and twisted her body, driving a fist into her exposed side—right where she'd been hiding the injury.

Sabrina screamed, a raw, involuntary sound torn from her throat before she quickly bit it back, trying to stifle it behind clenched teeth.

"Oh, what is this?" Agnes asked, her tone mockingly sweet. She leaned in as if she were savoring the moment. "Something... tender?"

Without waiting for a reply, she drove another blow into the same spot. Sabrina buckled slightly, her body shuddering as she fought back another scream.

Agnes kept hold of Sabrina's wrist, yanking her forward, and drove another punch into her side. Then another. And another. Each blow striking the same spot.

Sabrina's composure finally cracked, and she let out a bloodcurdling scream. It was raw, agonized, and full of pain, cutting through the storm, through the thunder, and through the rain. It was the kind of sound that lodged itself in your chest and refused to let go.

I flinched with every hit, my legs frozen in place, my throat tight. Watching her cry out, watching her body bend and jerk with every hit—it was too much.

I rose almost without realizing, Celine still barely conscious in my arms. I eased her to the ground and brought up my sword with shaking hands.

"Let her go!" I shouted, storming forward, my blade pointed at Agnes. "Now!"

Agnes turned slowly, still holding Sabrina by the arm. Her lips curled into a smile.

"If you would like the beating to stop, boy," she said coolly, "drop your weapon and approach me quietly."

I hesitated. Coming to a stop.

Sabrina's head snapped up. Her eyes met mine through the rain, wide with pain and fury.

"Do not!" she screamed, her voice hoarse. "Drifted, go! Retreat!"

Agnes tightened her grip on Sabrina's arm and lifted her straight up, dangling her in the air. Then, she drove her fist into her side again. The sound of the punch was dull and wet, making my stomach churn as Sabrina let out another scream.

"Quiet," Agnes muttered.

I stood frozen, my knuckles white around the hilt of my sword, heart pounding so hard I could hardly hear the thunder anymore. My feet refused to move, torn between trying to retreat, and the sight of Sabrina getting torn apart right in front of me.

Then, Agnes slowly raised her fist again.

"You can end this, boy," she said, staring straight at me.

I gritted my teeth, the pressure building in my chest like something about to snap. Her fist drew back higher.

"Alright!" I shouted, the word tearing from my throat. "Alright! I'll do what you want!"

I let my sword fall. The steel hit the mud with a heavy thud.

My boots squelched through the wet earth as I stepped forward slowly, hands raised, rain sliding down my arms. I glanced back to where Celine lay motionless, curled in on herself beneath the cloak.

As I drew closer, the wolves around the clearing growled in unison from the shadows.

Agnes held up her hand without turning. "Settle, everyone," she said with mock sweetness. "All in due time."

I kept walking, heart pounding against my ribs. My breaths came short and shallow, and even though the rain covered most of them, I could feel the eyes of every beast in the clearing on me.

Right as I got within reach, I saw Sabrina lift her head. Her face was streaked with blood and rain, her body limp in Agnes' grip, but her eyes still burning.

"You fool," she croaked, barely more than a breath.

Agnes chuckled. "He is being a good boy," she cooed.

Then her fist came forward—fast, brutal. I barely saw it before it connected.

Pain exploded across my face.

And then—nothing.

CHAPTER 26

Cold water slapped against my face, shocking me awake, pulling me from a foggy darkness into a glossy, disorienting reality. I coughed, gasping as droplets ran down my cheek and neck. The world around me swayed unevenly, and for a moment, all I could see were vague splotches swimming through my vision.

"Wake the hell up, human!" snarled a voice.

Blinking, I tried to clear my sight, allowing the room to gradually come into view. The first thing I noticed was a brain-splitting headache that made the back of my eyes pound. The second, a Lupine, hovering in front of me. His features were stern, and his eyes burned with contempt. He had markings on his face, the same style that I noticed in Lostsummit—deep scarlet symbols that went from his chin to his forehead.

I tried to move my arms, but only just realized that coarse rope bound my wrists above me, digging into my skin.

"Where—where am I?" I croaked, throat raw.

The Lupine sneered, his lip curling in disgust as he grabbed my chin roughly, forcing my eyes upward.

"You are exactly where humans like you deserve to be," he hissed. "And you would do well to remember your place here."

He shoved my head back, banging it against the wall behind me. It was hard enough to blur my vision again.

I felt my heart drop as the scuffle from the forest replayed in my mind. I was in enemy hands, and mercy wasn't something they had planned for me.

"Oh my, how brave," came a voice from my left, weakly. "Picking on a human who clearly cannot fight back. Your courage is inspiring."

I turned my head, only now noticing that Sabrina sat restrained against a far wall, a tired smirk on her lips.

I turned my head to the right to see Celine slumped against the other far wall, her eyes closed, still unconscious. I wasn't sure whether to feel dread or relief that they were here with me.

The guard whipped around, his attention moving to Sabrina. His eyes burned as he crossed the room.

"You would do well to keep quiet, human-sympathizer," he growled, practically spitting as he spoke. He raised his boot, pressing it hard against Sabrina's cheek as he forced her head to the side. "You are a disgrace, a waste of Lupine blood."

Sabrina coughed slightly beneath the pressure of his boot, yet I could still see the smirk on her face. She tilted her head enough to glance defiantly up at him with one eye.

"Tell me, does it require great effort to be this much of a simpleton, or does it come naturally to you?" she replied.

The guard's jaw tightened visibly as his fist clenched at his sides. Sabrina had struck a nerve.

He drew his boot back and slammed it into her chest. Sabrina jerked from the impact, her breath escaping in a strangled gasp.

The guard raised his boot and brought it down again. And again. And again.

My stomach twisted. Helplessness and rage boiled in my chest as the guard continued his assault. He stomped viciously into her arms, legs, anywhere he could reach, his eyes alight with cruel satisfaction. Sabrina curled defensively, unable to shield herself, each blow echoing throughout the cold stone chamber.

"You think yourself clever, traitor?" he snarled, stomping into her shoulder. "Allow me to teach you some respect!"

His boot landed squarely on Sabrina's injured side. Sabrina's entire body tensed violently, her jaw locking shut as she desperately fought to silence her agony. Tears shimmered at the corners of her eyes, but I could tell she was refusing him the satisfaction of hearing her scream.

"You are weak," he hissed, landing another kick to her ribs. "A blight upon our blood. Filth!"

"Enough!" I shouted, straining desperately against the ropes that held me. "Stop! Leave her alone!"

The guard turned slowly, glaring down at me with dark eyes.

"Silence, human," he spat coldly. "Or you shall suffer double her fate."

He lowered his foot from Sabrina's trembling body, panting as if struggling to regain his composure. Slowly, he stepped toward me, leaning down so his face was mere inches from mine. His breath was hot and foul as he spoke to me.

"Consider yourself fortunate, Drifted," he growled bitterly. "Had King Cassius not wished to deliver your death personally, we would have ended your miserable existence back in that forest. You would not have seen the walls of this place."

His words hit me like a slap to the face, though I wasn't sure why I was surprised.

I stared blankly into his cold, merciless eyes. Unable to think of a response that wouldn't anger him further.

The guard straightened with a disgusted scoff, clearly satisfied that his words had an effect on me. He cast one last disdainful glance around the cell, his eyes lingering coldly on

Sabrina, before turning toward the exit.

Without another word, he marched through the doorway, slamming a heavy iron gate closed behind him.

Silence filled the room, broken only by Sabrina's shallow, labored breathing and my pounding heartbeat.

"Are you okay?" I asked, my voice low but tight with concern. I could see the bruises already forming beneath her collar.

Sabrina gave a weak chuckle and leaned her head back against the wall behind her. "Aye, never been better," she muttered, voice laced with biting sarcasm. "This is exactly how I imagined spending my day."

I let out a frustrated breath. "Your mouth will get you killed one day."

She opened one eye, still smiling. "Perhaps," she whispered. "But at least I shall die entertained."

Despite everything, I couldn't help the flicker of a smile that tugged at the corner of my mouth—quickly swallowed by the grim reality around us.

I glanced toward the iron bars the guard had disappeared behind, then turned back to Sabrina.

"This probably isn't the best time for questions, but do you know where we are?" I asked quietly.

She tilted her head slightly, gaze drifting toward the darkened ceiling as if listening for something I couldn't hear.

"Not exactly," she said weakly. "But judging by the stench of mold and the charming hospitality, I would wager they took us to one of the outposts near Thornwallow."

Great, I thought to myself. It didn't feel too good, being taken prisoner again in an area where everyone hated me.

"Why'd they bring us here, anyway? They easily could have killed us while we were unconscious." I questioned.

She gave a small nod. "Did you not hear? It seems they

plan on making a spectacle out of you."

I swallowed hard. "Make a spectacle out of me..." I repeated, thinking to myself. "You mean Cassius wants me alive?" My eyes widened at the realization.

Sabrina looked up at me with darkened eyes. "Appears that way. Unfortunately, I do not think it is for your benefit, Drifted."

The thought frightened me. Cassius wanted me alive—not because I mattered, but because of the grudge he held against my family. And he would make sure I never forgot it.

I shook my head, willing myself to focus on anything other than my impending doom. I turned my sights to the room we were in. Maybe I could devise a plan to get us out of here alive.

The space was small and claustrophobic, but not so small that they'd leave us close together.

I was bound to the middle wall; cold stone pressed into my back, and dampness seeped through the tattered edges of my shirt.

To my left, near the far wall, sat Sabrina. She slouched against the stone, pulling her legs up to ease the weight from her sides. She looked like hell—bruised, bloodied.

Celine lay against the right wall, her head resting against her shoulder, eyes still shut. Her breathing was faint, but at least it was present.

We were all in the same cell, yet they'd made sure we couldn't reach each other. Like animals in a cage, strung up and waiting. I couldn't move. I couldn't protect them. And if the looks we'd been getting meant anything... they had no plans to let us rest for long.

Suddenly, the distant sound of footsteps broke my train of thought.

I sat up straight as best I could, the ropes around my wrist chafing with the motion. Sabrina's head lifted as well, her expression turning into something more alert.

A figure stepped into view outside the cell—a different guard this time. He was broad-shouldered beneath a fur-lined cloak, and his presence filled the corridor with cold wind.

"Up," he barked. "You are not here to rot. On your feet."

Another guard appeared behind him, leaner but watchful. His arms were folded, and his gaze was stern—clearly the insurance should any of us think of resisting.

The first guard stepped forward and unlocked the gate with a dull clank. The door groaned open, and before I could even speak, he undid the ropes that held my wrists and hauled me up by the collar.

"Move," he growled, yanking Sabrina up next and moving us toward the center of the room. Then, he pulled out more thick rope. He linked us together with a short length of it around our waists. Then he wrapped another length tightly around our ankles, allowing enough slack to walk but not to run. Last, he bound our wrists again, though there was more slack this time.

Sabrina groaned under her breath. "Well," she muttered, "this is cozy."

The guard didn't even acknowledge her.

He turned his attention to Celine, who still hadn't stirred. Her head lolled slightly, and her hands twitched feebly in the ropes that bound her.

"You," the guard snapped. "Did I not give you a command?"

He stepped forward, raising his boot like he might kick her awake.

"Wait!" I shouted, taking a stumbling step forward that yanked Sabrina along beside me. "She's injured. She's been unconscious for days—she needs medical attention."

The guard looked at me with disgust, as if the very act of speaking had offended him. His gaze drifted back to Celine, and without a word, he raised his fist.

"Stop!" I barked, stepping in front of him without thinking. The rope binding me to Sabrina pulled taut, dragging her forward with me again. I planted myself between him and Celine, heart pounding, fists clenched in front of me.

"Hitting her won't do anything," I said, breathing heavily. "She's unconscious—I already told you that."

For a moment, the guard stared at me, his expression unreadable. Then, a bitter smile played on his mouth.

"Then you shall not mind taking her punishment for her."

Before I could brace myself, his fist slammed into my stomach like a hammer. The air exploded from my lungs as I dropped to my knees with a choking gasp. The rope dug painfully into my side as I doubled over, struggling to breathe.

Above me, I heard the guard scoff. "Get them moving," he said to the one outside the gate. "They have wasted enough time. Leave the withering one here."

Rough hands grabbed my collar, jerking me upright before I had a chance to recover. My legs barely held beneath me, and every breath burned in my chest—but at least they left Celine alone.

As painful as it was having my stomach nearly caved in, I'd take it a thousand times over if it meant she stayed out of their reach. At least for now.

"Move it!" the guard barked, yanking Sabrina and me forward by the rope at our waists.

"Easy," she muttered through clenched teeth, staggering to keep her balance. "I am not exactly light on my feet right now... given the circumstances."

Together, bound and battered, we were shuffled out of the cell, the cold air of the corridor greeting us like a slap to the face. The second guard followed close behind, eyes never leaving us. We were nothing to them—bodies to be moved and beaten.

The hallway they led us down was barely lit, narrow, and cold. The stone we walked on was slick in places where water had pooled in shallow dips. Unevenly spaced torches mounted along the walls created light that barely pushed back the shadows. The air stank of mildew, old sweat, and a stench that would stick to your clothing if you stuck around too long.

Iron bars lined the cells on either side of the corridor; most of the cells were empty—dark, silent voids seemingly untouched for weeks. But every so often, I caught movement in the corners of my vision. A body curled against the far wall of a cell or a shape huddled beneath what might have once been a blanket.

I heard the soft murmur of voices—repeating the same phrases over and over again in tones that sounded too detached to be prayers.

"They're watching."

"The truth."

"Don't trust the eyes unseen..."

Hysteria. There was no doubt in my mind about that. My stomach twisted. That meant that these people were human. Humans who no longer remembered who they were.

I barely had time to process it before the guards shoved us forward again toward a thick wooden door, braced with iron.

It creaked open with a groan, and a blinding light poured in.

I flinched instinctively, eyes clamping shut as the daylight pierced them. I heard Sabrina grunt beside me, muttering something under her breath about preferring the cell.

Slowly, I forced my eyes open, blinking against the brightness until the world came into focus.

High walls of dark stone and timber, the wood charred in places as if reclaimed from fire, ringed the outpost sprawling before us. Watchtowers topped the walls, manned by silent Lupine with watchful eyes.

Smoke curled from a bonfire near the far end of the outpost, and I could hear the rhythmic pounding of hammer on stone. Elsewhere, workers hauled and stacked crates, and Lupine soldiers marched in tight formations between the paths, each shooting glances toward us as we passed through.

"Well," I heard Sabrina mutter behind me, "at least the decor is consistent—filthy and miserable."

"Quiet," one guard snapped immediately, his voice cracking through the air like a whip. "No talking."

Up ahead, the path opened onto a wide clearing. Dozens of bodies moved in grim patterns—picks swinging, backs hunched, hands blistered and blackened with dust.

They were mining. Rough walls of grey stone surrounded the pit, with carts piled high with rocks being dragged across uneven tracks. The workers—most of them—were human. I could tell from their eyes. They wore torn tunics, frayed trousers, skin burnt and scraped from days in the sun.

But what made me pause wasn't the humans.

It was the Lupine among them.

There weren't many, only a handful—but they were there. Working right beside them. Their movements were as exhausted and worn.

I blinked, confused. That didn't make sense. Why would they be among the laborers?

But before I could dwell on it, I felt the ropes tug again. We were being dragged straight toward the quarry.

As we passed the first group of workers, the atmosphere changed.

The humans didn't speak to us—at least, not directly. But

I heard their Hysteria fueled whispers.

Guards stalked the perimeter, shouting over the noise.

"Faster!"

"Pick up the pace!"

"Again, or I shall have your hands off your wrists!"

The sound of punches followed—some workers flinching under the noise, others not even reacting.

But as we passed, I noticed something strange.

Some of the Lupine looked up, just briefly. A few gave a small nod—some to me, most past me.

I turned confused... then realized it was Sabrina they were mostly acknowledging.

She held her head a little higher now. She didn't return the nods, probably out of fear for their safety, but I saw the way she held her nose slightly higher in the air.

These Lupine must've been from Sylphreach, prisoners of the ongoing conflict, perhaps. They were greeting one of their own.

We came to a stop near the edge of the quarry floor, where a massive chunk of uncut stone jutted from the earth. Its surface was uneven, split in places from previous strikes, but still solid enough to make the task ahead miserable.

One guard stepped forward, tossing two worn pickaxes to the ground in front of us. The wooden handles showed splintering, while the iron heads were chipped and rust-streaked.

"Get to work," he said flatly.

I stared at the tools, then at the wall of stone, then back at him. "What exactly do you want us to do?"

The guard's eyes narrowed. He took a slow step forward until his face was inches from mine.

"I did not think I would have to spell it out," he said, voice laced with venom. "But I suppose I should not be surprised.

Stupid human."

He jabbed a finger toward the stone.

"Take the picks. Break the rocks. Load the rocks. And if I see you slow down…" He let the threat hang in the air, then turned to Sabrina. "I shall find something else for her to break."

I clenched my jaw, every muscle in my body tightening at the threat. Sabrina didn't say anything, but I could feel the tension in the rope between us—like she was holding back a thousand insults she wanted to spit in his face.

With a scoff, I bent down, picked up the rusted tool, and turned toward the stone. There was no use arguing here. We simply had to bide our time and wait for the perfect moment to escape.

I lifted the pick and brought it down hard against the stone in front of me.

The blow barely chipped the surface, but I didn't have the energy to put any more strength into it.

Splinters from the cracked handle dug into my palms while the impact sent a rattle up my arms. I grit my teeth and struck it again—harder this time. I could already feel new bruises forming under my skin, old wounds protesting every movement.

Beside me, Sabrina stayed silent.

She moved stiffly, every swing of her pick short, like her body was doing its best not to fall apart entirely. Her breathing was shallow, but thankfully, she was still standing.

All around us, the sound of labor echoed off stone and timber. Picks cracked against rock, and boots scraped through the dirt. The guards circled slowly, eyes and hands tense, as if they were hoping for someone to mess up.

A loud cry rang out ahead of us—one human had dropped their cart, the wheel splintering under its weight. Before the man could even scramble to lift it, a guard drove a boot into his back, shouting something I couldn't make out.

The man coughed, curled tighter on the ground, and tried to push himself upright.

Suddenly, I felt something hard strike me, right above the brow. A thin, dull throb spread across my forehead, followed by the wet feeling of something running down my face.

I staggered back a step, blinking as the liquid slid into my eye. I wiped my forehead, looked at my hand, and was surprised. Blood.

I looked up to see that at the top of the quarry ridge, two tiny figures stood beyond a low fence. A pair of Lupine children, no older than seven, maybe younger, sat pointing. One of them grinned wide, while the other stuck out her tongue, laughing as if she'd just played a harmless game.

"Smelly human!" one child yelled.

Their faces were smudged with dirt, eyes wide with mischief, and in their small hands they each held another rock, ready to throw again. As I opened my mouth, they took off running, giggling in delight.

"Get back to work!" A guard yelled at me from the side.

Beside me, Sabrina spoke—quiet, breathless, but clear.

"Don't let it fester," she said. "They know no better. Only mimicking what they have been witness to."

The sting above my brow was nothing compared to the pain behind her words. This hatred had already been fed to them at such a young age.

"I know," I muttered, lifting the pick again. "That's what makes it worse."

I lowered my head and turned back to the stones, jaw clenched as another droplet of blood slid down my temple.

I didn't know how long we'd been mining. But it had been at least four hours, maybe more. My arms burned, my back ached, and my hands were raw and bleeding where the splinters had torn through the skin. And every time I shifted my hands, fresh pain spread across my palms.

Sabrina hadn't spoken for a long while. She moved slower now, shoulders tight with pain. I could see her legs trembling with each swing of the pick, her breathing short and uneven. But she didn't stop. No one did. We knew better.

I turned back to the stone and lifted the pick again with a shaky breath.

But before the pick could fall, a loud voice cut through the air.

"Enough!"

Other voices followed—more guards shouting, barking orders across the quarry. Tools dropped all around us, clattering against stone and dirt. The endless rhythm of labor finally broke, leaving only the sound of breathing and the distant churn of carts being wheeled away.

I let the pickaxe fall from my hands. Sabrina did the same.

Thank the moon, I thought as my hands trembled.

I stood for a moment, swaying, too spent to even wipe the blood and sweat from my face.

My legs were jelly beneath me. My arms hung useless at my sides. I wanted to collapse right there in the dirt. But I couldn't. Not with the guards still watching.

The moment of stillness didn't last long.

Through the haze of exhaustion, I heard the crunch of boots approaching. I didn't even need to look to know who it was. The same two guards from before.

"Move," the louder one snapped, stepping up beside us. "You have had enough rest."

I barely had the strength to nod, let alone argue. My legs stumbled forward on instinct alone, dragging the frayed rope between me and Sabrina taut as we shuffled back across the quarry floor.

I glanced at Sabrina. Her face was pale, streaked with grime, and her steps uneven—but she walked. Somehow, she still walked.

We passed the other prisoners again, all of them slumping, too tired to even lift their heads. The sun was lower now, and dark shadows danced across the outpost as we were herded back through the crooked rows of buildings. We passed the rubble and the empty carts, until the dark stone of the holding cells came into view.

After another painful walk back, the iron gate of our prison groaned open once more, and we were shoved inside, back into the filth.

As I staggered toward the wall and sank down, I caught of glimpse of Celine.

Still slumped against the right wall, right where we'd left her. She hadn't moved. Her chest barely rose and fell, her eyes were still closed and her lips parted slightly. She seemed untouched—no fresh bruises, no blood. Thankfully.

But that didn't mean she was fine.

My gaze lingered on her face, her arms, the way her body leaned awkwardly against the wall like she hadn't moved in hours. She was fading. Holding on, maybe, but barely.

She'd already been in need of medical attention before we were captured. And now? In a cell like this, without food, water, or even the chance to rest properly? These conditions were only making her health worse.

I looked down at my hands—blistered, torn, streaked with blood and stone dust—and clenched them weakly into fists.

If something didn't change soon... I wasn't sure how much more any of us could take.

A guard stepped inside, but this time he was carrying a plate—if you could even call it that. Molded wooden planks, each with a hunk of stale bread and a moldy cup of brown water to match.

He tossed one tray toward me. It hit the ground with a loud clatter, the bread rolling off into a damp patch of dirt. Another landed near Sabrina, who didn't bother reaching for it.

"Well," the guard said, smirking as he glanced toward Celine, "it appears we will not need a third plate."

Another guard chuckled from behind the first. "She is not eating anything in that state. May as well save it for the rats."

I stared at them as the turned to leave the cell, anger simmering beneath the exhaustion in my bones. But I kept quiet. I looked down at the tray—at the crusted edge of the bread, the murky water sloshing in the cup.

I reached down, picked it up, and pulled the bread into my lap.

For now, surviving meant choking down whatever they gave us. Even if it tasted like crap.

I chewed slowly, each bite turning to dust in my mouth. It tasted foul, but I ate it anyway, letting it sit in my empty stomach like a stone.

The Lupine were smarter than I'd given them credit for.

They didn't need to beat us bloody to keep us obedient— not when they could just work us into the ground. They'd starve us, drain us, break us down so thoroughly that by the time we thought about how to fight back… we wouldn't have the strength left to do it.

Across from me, Sabrina let out a short breath, her head resting back against the wall.

"They must be saving the proper meals for the better-performing servants," she muttered, voice dry and cracked. "Wouldn't want to waste fine cuisine on us lowly underachievers."

She gave a short, brittle chuckle, but it faded as quickly as it came.

I didn't have the energy to respond.

Turning my head, I looked once more at Celine, still slumped against the wall.

She needed care. Rest. Anything but this.

I leaned my head back against the stone, closed my eyes, and let the silence take over as the guards returned to redo our binds.

We were running out of time.

CHAPTER 27

Morning came, or at least I assumed it had. The cell hadn't changed. Still damp, still cold, and still stinking of blood, mildew, and worn-out hope.

My back ached from the hard stone wall, and my hands still throbbed, torn and raw from yesterday's labor.

I turned my head slowly, my eyes landing on Celine.

She was slouched over. Her back was hunched, head hanging low, barely held up by her own neck. Her hair draped forward, hiding most of her face, and her body was still. Way too still.

I moved without thinking. The ropes around my wrists jerked taut instantly, dragging me back with a pull that slammed my spine against the wall. Pain shot through my shoulders as the tension cinched tight.

"Celine," I called. "Hey—Celine!"

No response.

From where I was, I couldn't tell if she was breathing. I couldn't hear anything over the sound of my panic growing louder by the second.

"Celine!" I called again, louder this time. Desperate.

Nothing.

A sick feeling bloomed in my gut. Something was wrong. More wrong than before. She looked like she was fading. Like she was slipping past the point of return.

Behind me, I heard a groggy voice stir in the corner of the cell.

"What is with all the shouting?" Sabrina mumbled, her words thick with sleep. "Do not tell me they brought another round of gourmet bread…"

"She's not moving," I said, barely able to keep the tremble out of my voice. "Celine—she's not responding. I don't… I don't think she's breathing."

That shook her awake fast.

I heard the scrape of her boots on the floor as she shifted up against her restraints.

"Guards!" she shouted. "Someone get in here, we need assistance!"

Her voice bounced off the stone, loud enough to make my ears ring.

"Get in here, damn it!" she yelled again.

Heavy footsteps echoed down the corridor.

The gate creaked open a moment later, and the familiar, broad figure of the same guard who had beaten Sabrina yesterday stepped into view. His expression soured the moment his eyes landed on us.

"Shut your mouths," he barked, voice echoing through the stone like a slap.

Sabrina didn't flinch. "She requires aid," she snapped, nodding toward Celine. "Look at her! She is not moving. Do something!"

The guard looked at Celine. Barely a glance, like she was a stain on the floor.

"I am not here to make sure your little companion stays alive," he said with a shrug.

My body moved before I could think.

I yanked against the ropes with everything I had. The cords dug deep into my wrists, scraping raw skin as I twisted and pulled.

"What the hell did you just say?" I growled, the heat in my chest burning. "Didn't you hear what she said? She's dying!"

The guard's smirk faded.

He stepped forward without hesitation, raised his boot—and pressed it against my cheek. Slowly, forcefully, he pushed my face back until my other cheek was crushed against the cold stone wall behind me.

He leaned in, his voice low.

"Lower your tone, boy," he muttered, his voice dripping with contempt. "If you think a dirty human like you gets to speak to me in such a way… you are widely mistaken."

The pressure of the boot stayed, grinding into my cheek, until it felt like the bone might give way.

"Remove your boot from him!" Sabrina shouted, voice cutting through the cell like a blade. "The girl is dying, damn it! Do you want a corpse on your hands?"

The guard didn't move at first. Then, with an annoyed grunt, he stepped back. The boot lifted and left a pulsing ache in its place. I stayed still, breathing hard through clenched teeth, blood wetting the side of my mouth.

"She is not my concern," he muttered, glancing lazily over his shoulder at Celine. "If she dies, that is one less burden for the outpost to carry."

I wanted to scream. To lunge. To beat him against the same stone he'd pinned me to. But the ropes held firm, and my body—already worn thin from the day before—barely had the strength to tremble with anger.

I couldn't do anything.

Not for her.

Not for anyone.

The guard turned back toward us. There was something smug in the way he tilted his head.

"Well," he said, "since the two of you are up bright and early… it must be time to get to work."

He whistled lightly, and another guard soon came in behind him. Thick ropes ready in hand like a leash.

I could hardly move.

My body was too tired, too sore, but more than that... my mind couldn't catch up. I couldn't understand how they could be this ruthless. They were completely careless of the lives of others.

Celine was barely breathing. And they just walked past her like she were nothing. Like her life didn't matter in the slightest.

I knew they hated humans. That part I'd accepted. But Celine... she had Lupine blood. That should have meant something. Should've counted for more than this.

But maybe it didn't.

Maybe to them, the fact that she'd fought beside me—helped me—made her worse than human. A traitor to her own kind. Someone worth less than a corpse on the floor.

The thought gnawed at me. We truly were less than nothing here.

The thinner guard stepped forward, undid my binds, and without a word yanked me upright. I staggered. The motion jarring my sore limbs.

Sabrina was pulled to her feet next, wincing as the motion tugged at whatever bruises still hadn't settled from the day before. Neither of us resisted.

The coarse rope was secured around our waists, then down around our legs again, binding us together like yesterday. Tighter, maybe. No slack. No chance of falling without dragging the other down.

I took another glance at Celine as we were marched out of the cell.

Please, hold out until I make it back, I thought to myself, my heart aching.

I felt dull listening to our boots echoing down the corridor as the torchlight flickered against the walls. Back through the same damp hallway and past the cells.

I squinted as the large wooden door opened, blinking rapidly as the sky spread wide above us. The quarry lay ahead exactly as we'd left it—grey, cracked, and crawling with bodies bent to the ground.

We descended into the quarry, dust filling my lungs with every step. The same sour smell of sweat, stone, and iron hung in the air—thick enough to taste. Dozens of workers were already scattered across the pit, back broken under the weight of their tasks.

We were led to a pile of jagged slabs—chunks that had been smashed loose from the quarry walls but left behind for sorting and moving.

"Lift them," a guard snapped, pointing to the rocks. "Stack them by the wall."

Then he turned and walked off like they had better things to do.

I looked at the stones, then at Sabrina.

Bound as tightly as we were—waist to waist, barely any room to move without tugging the other—we'd have to lift in tandem. Step together. Haul together. If one of us stumbled, we'd both hit the ground.

Sabrina let out a breath that might've been a laugh if it weren't so thin. "Well," she muttered, "maybe this shall prove fun?"

I didn't answer. I just bent down slowly, hands trembling as I reached for the nearest slab. It was heavier than it looked—rough, awkward to grip, and still damp from the morning dew. Sabrina moved with me, her hands sliding beneath the opposite end.

"One, two—lift," I grunted.

We staggered upright, grunting under the weight of the rock as we both focused on not dropping it on our toes.

We shuffled toward a far wall, the weight of the slab heavy on our arms.

Sabrina and I shot a look at each other. We both knew we were only one bad lift from our bodies giving out entirely. But we didn't stop. Because stopping meant worse.

We reached the wall and lowered the stone with as much control as our shaking bodies could manage. It hit the ground with a dull thud, sending dust curling around our legs. I stayed bent for a second, catching my breath, feeling the sweat trickle down my back beneath the ropes.

"Where is he?" I questioned.

Sabrina looked at me, brows furrowed slightly beneath the sweat on her face.

"Cassius," I clarified. "Why hasn't he come? Why keep us here like this? Why drag this all out?"

She was quiet for a moment as we turned to fetch another slab.

"I do not know," she said finally. "If I had to guess... he probably has yet to return from Moonveil."

We crouched again, fingers finding another heavy rock.

"When he shows, trust me... we shall be aware." she added, her voice strained while we lifted.

I sighed deeply. I didn't know how long this was going to last, but we didn't have much left in us.

Sure, I healed faster than most. Scrapes, cuts, even bruises—my body usually pulled itself back together quicker than it should've. But lately? Every day brought new wounds. New bruises. New damage to struggle through. And with no food, no rest, and barely enough water to keep us standing... even that edge dulled. I could feel it.

I glanced at Sabrina long enough to see her grimace as she fixed her grip on the stone.

And her—by the moon, I didn't know how she was still

moving.

The wound on her side hadn't closed. Not really. It bled constantly, soaking into the fabric at her hip, staining her shirt a deeper red with every step we took. The ropes didn't help— pulling at her waist, digging into torn skin. On top of that, the labor only made it worse. This was grinding her down.

And then there was Celine.

My steps slowed at the thought.

The image of her slumped against the wall, completely still hadn't left my head since we were dragged out of that cell.

I'd left her there. And if something happened to her while I was gone, I'd never forgive myself.

My steps faltered. The stone dipped in my hands, nearly slipping from my grip.

Sabrina grunted, shifting her weight to keep it still. "Drifted," she hissed. "Focus."

"Sorry," I muttered, tightening my hands as we staggered toward the wall again.

We lowered the slab onto the growing stack with a loud thud.

I barely had time to catch my breath when a shout cracked through the air.

"You two!" a voice barked. "Get back to work!"

I turned my head to see a guard storming toward us, his eyes locked on me like I'd insulted him. His expression was already twisted into something between fury and anticipation.

"We're getting to it," I said, breathless, the words slipping out firmer than I wanted. "Lost my balance."

"Why, you!" the guard muttered, raising his fist.

I braced myself for the impact, staring him down. But then, something stopped him in his tracks.

A subtle tremor rolled beneath my boots—enough to rattle the rocks in the pile behind us.

The guard hesitated mid-step, his fist still in the air.

All around the quarry, movement slowed. Heads lifted. Picks paused. The air felt so heavy I could feel it weighing everyone down.

The guard's fist was still hovering mid-air when the ground lurched again—harder this time.

A deep tremor rolled beneath our feet, like something massive had moved far beneath the surface.

"What was that...?" Sabrina muttered beside me.

Before I could answer, a voice rang out from a tower along the outpost wall.

"Fiend sighted!" a guard shouted. "South wall! It is—"

Another quake struck—strong enough to send stones tumbling from the quarry edge. The guard in front of us stumbled, nearly knocking me over as he tried to regain his footing.

Screams followed.

Distant at first, then closer—shouts of confusion, orders being barked, bodies scrambling across the yard. Even the Lupine guards weren't prepared.

Something was coming.

And judging by the way the land groaned beneath us, it was massive.

A guard ran into the camp, panting heavily as he fumbled for words.

"An Ursaroot! It is an Ursaroot!"

Suddenly, a deafening, bone-shaking bang that echoed through the quarry like thunder tearing through the sky.

My head snapped toward the sound just in time to see stone and timber erupt into the air. Dust and debris poured outward like a wave, and everyone dropped, protecting themselves from shrapnel.

I looked up, and my heart sank.

The colossal form of an Ursaroot came crashing through the breach.

Chapter 28

Dust and debris sprayed the courtyard as the Ursaroot trampled through the remains of the wall. Its paws were like boulders, every step caving the ground. The stench hit next—pungent and hot, like spoiled meat wrapped in pine sap. Its fur, if it could still be called that, was matted with streaks of blackened bark and tangled thorns. Spores that pulsed jutted out from its body haphazardly, flaring as the beast lifted its head to let out a roar.

"Move!" I heard someone shout—maybe a guard, I wasn't sure. The whole outpost had erupted into panic. Screams overlapped any sense of control the guards tried to maintain.

The remaining guards who weren't barking orders scrambled—some rushing toward the breach, others turning tail as their discipline crumbled under the weight of what stood before us. I watched as one tripped in the frenzy, crawling back on hands and knees as the shadow of the beast grew over him.

The ones who confronted the beast tore their cloaks from their bodies and began contorting into their Lunar forms. Limbs lengthening into lean muscle and fur.

They rushed toward the Ursaroot like a wave, leaping high and low. A group lunged for its neck while another darted beneath, clawing at the joints in its hind legs.

But the gigantic creature barely flinched. A tree trunk of a forearm came crashing down, flattening one wolf beneath it with a sound that turned my stomach. Another got sent flying, colliding with a far wall.

The Ursaroot roared again, its voice somewhere between

a howl and an earthquake, and the pressure of it alone knocked some of the remaining guards back to the ground.

I froze.

I had read about them. Sketched diagrams, memorized notes in those dry, cramped schoolhouses. Ursaroots—classified as Greater Fiends. They were rare, dangerous, and extremely unpredictable. Though no one knew what it was that attracted them.

But none of those old notes prepared me for this.

The creature that stood before us dwarfed every record. It stood like a walking siege tower, shoulders nearly scraping the tops of the outer watch posts. Thick, rotting moss clung to its back in shaggy tufts, and jagged thorns jutted from its shoulders like natural armor. Its mouth hung unnaturally wide, teeth yellowed and cracked, covered in sap-stained strands of shredded bark. It shouldn't have been this big. No lesson had ever hinted at this scale.

But somewhere deep beneath the noise and dust, I remembered what Celine had told me.

The fiends would keep changing. Growing larger. More feral. More vile. Until the source of their anger was dealt with.

But what that source was, I still had no clue.

"Off your ass, Drifted!"

A voice brought me back to reality.

"Can you not recognize a golden opportunity?"

I turned, startled, to see Sabrina already kneeling beside me. The rope connecting us together was taut in her hands as she sawed it against a jagged shard of stone jutting from the rubble.

The rope frayed as she worked quickly, her face deadly focused. It was almost as if there wasn't a raging beast destroying the outpost.

"How are you so calm right now?" I whispered.

Sabrina didn't even glance at me. "I am not," she said plainly. "I simply hide it better than you do."

The Ursaroot let out another roar behind us that sent a vibration running up my spine. A tower groaned, then collapsed into itself with a violent crack, sending dust and shattered wood everywhere.

Sabrina clicked her tongue. "Come now. I have no interest in dying beside you today."

The rope snapped, and Sabrina tossed the frayed end aside, rising to a crouch.

"Down," she urged. "Your legs, Drifted. Cut them free. I shall not be doing it for you."

I blinked at her, still crouched low as the Ursaroot let out another roar, this one closer than the last. The sound sent a tremble through the stone beneath us. My ears rang, and my thoughts felt tangled, sluggish.

"Now, Drifted!" Sabrina snapped.

I shook my head, trying to clear the fog. "Right," I muttered, eyes darting until I spotted a jagged stone near my feet.

Twisting awkwardly, I dragged the thick rope binding my ankles against it. Each scrape tore at the fibers, and each second that passed pushed my pulse higher into my throat. The rope bit into my skin, but I kept pulling, harder, faster.

"Hurry, Drifted!" Sabrina said, glancing toward the fiend. "That thing will not take its time to eat us whole."

"I'm trying!" I replied.

A few more strokes. One last tug.

The rope snapped, and my legs sprang free.

Before I could catch my breath, Sabrina reached down and grabbed my arm, yanking me to my feet with startling ease.

"On your feet. Follow me and stay low."

I ducked my head and fell in behind her as we slipped into

motion.

The courtyard was a war-zone.

We wove through the wreckage, dodging twisted beams and shattered stone. Fallen bodies lay sprawled across the mud—some guards, some wolves. I tried not to look too long at them. The scent of blood hung heavy in the air, thick and metallic, mixing with the stink of decomposition pouring off the Ursaroot.

A soldier stumbled in front of us, clutching a wound at his side. He didn't even see us. His eyes were glassy, distant, and fixed on something far away. We slipped past him and kept running.

The ground shook again as the Ursaroot let out another enraged howl. Its massive frame shifted in the corner of my vision, swatting away another attacker with ease. A flash of red fur vanished beneath its paw.

Sabrina maneuvered like she could see the whole battlefield at once, ducking and turning at the perfect moments, never stopping, never hesitating. I stayed close, matching her pace as best I could.

"We need to get Celine," I said, breath still short. "She's still in the cell."

Sabrina didn't slow. "Do you truly think I require you to tell me that?"

I narrowed my eyes.

She glanced back, that ever-present smirk tugging at the corner of her mouth. "Worry not, Drifted. I am quite capable of keeping track of my unconscious princess."

The same door they had marched us through that morning came into view.

Sabrina reached it first, quickly pressing her hand to the iron handle and slamming her shoulder into it.

We ran, our boots echoing through the corridor. One

empty cell passed, then another. The silence here was thicker than outside—like the stone was holding its breath.

Suddenly, the path ahead was cut off by rubble and fallen timber.

A collapsed beam had split the floor. One of the Lupine guards lay beneath it, crushed at the waist. His upper half was barely visible, arms stretched out toward the opposite wall with fingers curled.

Sabrina hopped over the rubble easily, but I slowed down, seeing something at his side.

A key ring, still hooked to his belt.

I reached for it.

"What are you doing?" Sabrina asked in a sharp whisper.

I stood, the keys cold in my palm. "Everyone in here deserves a fighting chance."

Then I turned and ran down the corridor. Straight toward the cells we'd passed without thought. I didn't know who was inside. Didn't care.

They were still locked up. Still trapped while everything outside these walls burned.

I slammed the first key into the lock I saw, heart hammering. Metal scraped, clicked, and then the door swung open.

A face blinked back at me from the shadows. Dirty, wide-eyed, and confused.

"Get up. Now," I said. Already sprinting to the next cell.

I jammed the key in the next lock and turned it.

Another door swung open, then another.

I kept moving, unlocking each cell door. I couldn't wait to see if the person inside had gotten themselves out, there wasn't enough time. But at least this way they had a chance. If they could move, they would.

Behind me, I heard Sabrina tapping her foot. The sound

echoed in frustration, but she said nothing.

Another cell.

Another lock.

Another chance.

"Go," I shouted over my shoulder, hoping someone—anyone—would hear me. "If you can walk, run. If you can't, crawl. Just don't stay here."

I didn't know how many cells I opened. My lungs burned and my legs ached. But I didn't stop until I saw the end of the corridor ahead.

Finally, I reached the end of the corridor and started my way back to Sabrina.

Most of the cell doors now hung open, some swinging gently in the breeze that crept through the cracks in the walls. Some prisoners slowly stepped their way out of the cells. Many ran, while others stared in confusion.

When I got to Sabrina, her arms were crossed as she leaned back against a wall. She didn't say a word. She smirked at me as I staggered to a stop.

I exhaled, trying to catch my breath. "Okay... let's go," I managed.

She nodded before running toward the last cell. Where we were once held captive.

I fell in behind her, my breathing still uneven.

We moved as quickly as we could while the building shook, trembling with each distant crash the Ursaroot caused. Somewhere above, part of the structure groaned under its own weight—splintered wood and cracked mortar falling down to the floor. We needed to be quick; I wasn't sure just how long this building would hold.

Ahead of us, the cell was slightly ajar.

Sabrina reached it first, pushing it open quickly and stepping inside.

I came in slightly after, and thankfully, Celine was still there. Exactly where we had left her.

She sat slumped against the wall, hands still bound above her, head tilted heavily to the side. Her hood had slipped down, revealing the soft fall of her hair, and her cloak had gathered dust and flecks of rubble. One boot was twisted awkwardly beneath her while the other stretched forward like she'd tried to move at some point and hadn't finished the motion.

Sabrina knelt beside Celine and placed two fingers gently against her neck.

I stepped in behind her, foot tapping quickly as I waited in anticipation.

"She is alive," Sabrina said, voice low. "but only just."

I crouched beside her, my hand hovering inches from Celine's shoulder. Her skin glistened with sweat, and even in the cold air, she felt too warm.

"We have not much time," Sabrina started, removing a rock from her pocket.

She slid the stone beneath the rope that bound Celine's wrists and began sawing through the fibers.

The rope fell loose, and I wasted no time. I picked up Celine, lifting her carefully. She was light, but limp at the same time.

Her shallow breath was warm against the side of my neck.

"I've got her." I said, rising to my feet.

Sabrina nodded once, already turning toward the door.

"Then let us move," she replied. "I have grown repulsed by the stench of this place."

We stepped back into the corridor, the faint echo of distant collapse vibrating through the stone. The small quiet we'd found down here was beginning to crack. The outpost wasn't going to last much longer.

I looked to the right of the corridor. We were already at the end. That meant, unfortunately, the only way out was the same way we'd come in.

Right back through the courtyard.

Sabrina led the way without hesitation, her steps quick and soundless. I followed, Celine's weight pressing on my already weary bones.

As we neared the door, Sabrina glanced back at me. Trying to ensure I was prepared.

"Now what?" I asked her, my breath heavy.

"There is an armory across the east end. I saw it while they dragged us through earlier." She replied.

I nodded. "Think it's still standing?"

Sabrina offered a half-smile. "If it is not, we shall improvise. But I am fairly positive there should be something in there to help Lady Celine."

I nodded again. "Alright then, let's do it."

Sabrina turned and threw the door open, and we were immediately met with chaos.

Dust hung thick in the air, turning the late-day light into a haze of gold and gray. The ground was a scar of shattered stone and torn soil, littered with bodies. Some still stirred. Most didn't.

Sabrina pressed forward, maneuvering between broken beams and toppled carts. I followed close behind, Celine's weight growing heavier with every step, though I knew it was only my arms weakening.

The Ursaroot was still thrashing, its massive body destroying walls and buildings with every movement. Countless guards circled it. Some still fought. Some didn't move.

We ducked low beneath a collapsed archway, where blood had pooled thickly around a mangled body. I forced my eyes forward as we continued running.

Ahead of us, a slab of stone had fallen across the path, forcing us to scramble over it. I climbed carefully, shielding Celine as best I could.

Suddenly, my boot struck something soft, and before I could even get the chance to look down, I felt it move.

Something shot up and clamped my ankle, nearly making me lose my balance.

"Sabrina—!" I called out.

She spun, already lowering into a crouch, claws drawn.

A Lupine guard, the same one that had kicked Sabrina senseless, lay half-buried beneath some rubble. His lower body was pinned under stone, and blood soaked through the torn leather across his ribs. One eye had swollen shut while the other fixed on me with a fading glow.

He tried to speak, but all that came out was a rasp of air and a twitch of his fingers against my boot.

He tried pulling himself out from under the rubble, using my leg as a crutch. But suddenly, he let out one last raspy breath before his grip loosened and then slipped entirely.

He was gone.

I swallowed hard, suddenly stuck staring at the scene before me.

"We must move, Drifted," Sabrina said in a low breath.

I tore my eyes away from the body and kept following her.

We were on the last stretch of open ground before the armory before I heard a noise rip through the air.

"Move!" Sabrina shouted, turning and tackling Celine and me to the ground.

Right as we hit the floor, a boulder the size of a wagon wheel came hurtling past us. It smashed into the dirt a few paces ahead, sending up a geyser of dirt and wood.

"Close one," I said shakily, hardly registering what had

happened.

"We are almost there..." Sabrina let out with a puff of air, blowing a stray hair that covered her face to the side. "Try not to die before we get there, yes?"

We got up and ran again. The armory was up ahead. Its doors were crooked, and there was a large hole in the side of the building, but at least it was still standing.

Sabrina veered toward the break in the wall, motioning me forward without a word.

As we slipped through the hole, I ducked low, shielding Celine's head as we passed into the dark.

Inside, the noise from the carnage fell away, but barely.

The air was dry and still, carrying only the faint scent of dust, leather, and long-cooled ash. The space was wide, but barren. Shadows clung to the corners, and racks lined the walls, most of them empty. A few scattered daggers littered a table near the back, their metal rusted.

I glanced around, frowning.

This was supposed to be an armory?

Sabrina moved ahead, her gaze sweeping over the bare walls without interest.

I shifted Celine's weight on my back, then carefully knelt and eased her down against a low bench.

"She's burning up," I muttered, brushing a hand across her cheek.

"Aha! I knew these would be here," Sabrina said.

I looked up as she strode toward me, something clutched in her hands. Three small glass vials, each filled with a thick golden liquid that shimmered even in this dark room. The color caught my eye immediately, and my stomach tightened.

That glow. I'd seen it before

"Is that..." I started, my voice quiet. "Is that what I think it is?"

Sabrina grinned and nodded. "Mhm, Lupthera. And enough to rattle our souls back into place."

I stared at the vials in her hands, a memory coming back:

Trapped in a cell beneath Lostsummit, my body wracked from the beatings Brute and the guards gave to me. I had been too weak to stand, too tired to care. Every breath hurt, and my ribs were definitely cracked. My vision swam in and out, and the cold stone beneath me felt like it was trying to drag me under.

That was the first time I met Sabrina—though I didn't know her name then. She was merely another Lupine guard to me—mean, crass, and scary.

I remember waking when she knelt outside the bars. I'd been sure she was there to drag me off somewhere worse. Maybe finish what the others started.

Instead, she offered me a vial of Lupthera—with a warning, of course. This elixir shortened your life each time it was consumed. By how much? No one knows. It could be days... it could be years.

I drank the strange liquid then, not that there was much of a choice.

The moment the glass touched my lips, warmth bloomed in my chest. Not just heat—life. I could feel it moving through me, pulsing down my limbs. My breath deepened. My heartbeat steadied. And then, right before my eyes, I saw the bruises across my arms fade. The cuts on my knuckles and arms closed like someone had pulled a thread through them.

The pain didn't disappear completely, but it became manageable. Bearable.

And now, sitting here watching her hold that same vial, brought that unforgettable warm feeling back into my chest.

Sabrina knelt beside me without a word, uncorking the vial with a twist.

"Prop the lady," she said. "Hold her head still."

I nodded, sliding an arm behind Celine's back and gently raising her against my chest. Her head lolled limply to the side, hair falling across her face.

Don't worry, Celine, you're going to feel better in no time.

"Hold her still," Sabrina said again. "She will not be able to drink it on her own."

Sabrina reached out and gently pressed her fingers to Celine's cheeks, guiding her jaw open. Then, slowly, she brought the vial to her lips and poured.

The golden liquid slipped into Celine's mouth, vanishing down her throat one warm breath at a time.

For a moment, nothing happened. But after a short while, I saw the effects take hold.

Color returned to Celine's skin—not all at once but surely. That pale, lifeless hue faded, replaced by the soft flush of life. Her brow twitched, and a slight breath escaped her lips.

I held her tighter, eyes fixed on her, watching—hoping.

I could feel the warmth pulsing from her skin, like a heartbeat. Her breathing was steadier now, and her cheeks reddened. She wasn't waking yet, but she was no longer fading.

The door of the armory slammed open.

A voice barked through the dimly lit room. "You two, you are not supposed to be in here!"

Sabrina was on her feet in an instant, though she staggered slightly. I rose as well, slower, leaving Celine on the bench as I used my body to block her. I raised my fist, intending to defend myself, but I knew I had no energy to do so.

The guard stormed in, blood spattered across his clothing, eyes wild with panic and rage.

"What do you wastes think you are doing in here?" he shouted, eyes drifting toward the empty vial in Sabrina's hands. "Stealing our rations?"

"We're just trying to survive—same as you." I replied to him as calmly as I could.

"You think you would have more important matters to attend to," Sabrina added, gesturing a finger toward the gaping hole in the wall behind us.

But the guard wasn't listening. His attention was locked on us, and his fists clenched tighter with each step he took.

"This is all your fault!" he growled, pointing a finger at me. "You and your half-dead girl should have been left to die out in that forest."

Sabrina straightened, but I could tell she was swaying on her feet. I wasn't doing much better. Neither of us could take him in the shape we were in.

The guard swung wide, aiming a fist straight for my head. I raised an arm, catching worst of it on my forearm—though I was too weak for the block to matter.

The punch sent me crashing against a nearby table, knocking a pile of dull daggers across the floor.

As I tried to rise, I saw Sabrina lung from the corner of my eye.

The guard turned fast and caught her mid-step, one hand gripping her neck, the other her shoulder. With a loud grunt, he threw her backward into a shelf lining the wall. The wooden frame cracked under the impact, and a cloud of dust and splinters rained down around her as she slumped to the floor.

I forced myself up, barely breathing, and raised my fist.

I threw a punch, slow as all hell, and the guard ducked it easily. He drove his knee into my stomach, and I folded over.

Before I could hit the ground, he grabbed a fistful of my hair and yanked me back up.

Then his fist came crashing into my face with enough force

to cloud my vision.

I couldn't block. I couldn't think. Hell, I could barely breathe. My head snapped with each blow, pain cracking across my jaw and temple. Each hit felt heavier than the last, like he mean to bury me right then and there.

The room spun, and my vision went hazy. There was hardly any strength left in me.

And then—it stopped.

The fists, the yelling, my vision darkening.

My body sagged as I blinked through the haze, blood dripping from my nose, my breath wheezing out in short gasps.

Slowly, I raised my head to see the guard's eyes wide as he stood still.

And then he dropped to his knees.

Behind him, Celine stood, her arm raised, her hand in a chopping position.

She was swaying slightly, her eyes were barely open, but she was standing.

Awake and alive.

CHAPTER 29

"Ce... Celine..." the name escaped my mouth in a whisper. Even though she was standing right in front of me, I felt uncertain. As if saying it any louder would break whatever spell had brought her back.

Her eyes slowly found mine, just as deep and violet as I remembered. While they were unfocused and confused, she was undeniably awake.

"Drifted...?" Her voice was faint, barely more than a breath, but it resonated through my chest all the same.

"I—I'm here," I stammered, my heart pounding so loudly that there was no way she couldn't hear it. I straightened my posture as much as my body allowed, unsure what to do with my hands hanging awkwardly at my sides. "You... you were out for so long. We thought... I thought—"

"Easy now, Drifted," Sabrina croaked from the corner, pulling herself up from the rubble. "Allow the princess to breathe first."

Celine managed a weak smile, struggling to hold herself upright. Without thinking, I reached out, my hand hesitating near her elbow. She noticed my hesitation, and her smile widened ever so slightly.

"Thank you, Drifted," she murmured, her voice clearer now. "I can manage, but your concern is warming."

Warmth rose swiftly into my cheeks, and I glanced away. Sabrina chuckled softly, shaking her head beside me, clearly amused by my awkwardness.

"It is good to see you awake, my princess," Sabrina said warmly. "You have worried our poor Drifted nearly to death."

My face burned hotter, but I didn't deny it. Instead, I nodded, eyes on Celine's face as she took a deep, steadying breath. For the first time in days, the tension in my chest eased.

Suddenly, the ground beneath us shuddered violently, knocking loose dust and rubble from the ceiling. A loud crack split through the building as planks creaked and groaned, threatening collapse.

"Perhaps we might save our touching reunion for a later hour," Sabrina said dryly, already reaching across the floor. She tossed something toward me, and my hand shot up instinctively, catching the small vial out of the air.

I stared down at the glowing liquid inside. Lupthera.

Immediately I felt my stomach twist, and my gaze snapped back up toward Sabrina, the anxiety probably as clear as day.

"This again...?" I questioned Sabrina, my voice weak.

Sabrina's expression softened, though her eyes still held their familiar teasing glint. "Do not look so stricken, Drifted. You are young, and strong enough. A few less years at the end shall hardly matter." She paused, raising a similar vial in her own hand. "Besides, trust me, you shall require it shortly."

Without hesitation, she uncorked her own vial and swallowed the contents down. She shook her head slightly as a shiver ran through her body.

"Come now," she teased gently, "do you wish for me to hold your hand as you drink?"

My eyes narrowed at her, but I could feel Celine's gaze resting softly upon me, and I knew Sabrina was right.

I sighed. Whatever awaited us, I'd need all the strength I could muster. With a shaky breath, I pulled the cork from the vial and lifted it to my lips.

The liquid burned gently as it slipped down my throat, immediately spreading warmth through my chest. That same familiar, prickling sensation washed across my skin, causing goosebumps to ripple over my arms and neck. I shivered slightly, waiting for what I knew came next.

And then, slowly at first, I felt it—the dull aches and throbbing bruises, the swollen, stuffed sensation lingering from days of dried blood—all melted away, fading into nothingness beneath the Lupthera's warmth. It felt strangely soothing, despite the eerie awareness of the cost that came with it.

I flexed my fingers, marveling at how quickly strength returned to my limbs. Sabrina's eyes met mine, and the corners of her mouth curled upward with amusement.

"See?" she said, her voice softly teasing. "Hardly worth all your fretting."

The room shook again, harder this time, nearly knocking me off my feet. The wooden beams above us cracked loudly, sending another cloud of dust cascading down.

"It is time to leave." Sabrina urged, already moving toward the jagged hole in the far wall. "Now!"

Celine stepped toward me, extending a slender hand. Without hesitation, I took it, feeling warmth spread through me again, this time entirely unrelated to Lupthera. Her fingers squeezed mine, and I gave her a wide smile.

We hurried toward the crumbling gap in the wall, Sabrina waiting impatiently ahead. But as we reached it, a thought jolted in my brain.

My sword.

I froze abruptly, tugging gently on Celine's hand to get her to stop. She and Sabrina both turned to look at me, their ears flattening against their heads.

"What now, Drifted!" Sabrina snapped, an irritated, questioning look on her face.

"I—I can't leave yet," I fumbled, feeling self-conscious

under both of their gazes. "My sword—I can't leave without it."

Sabrina's face coiled as she stared me down with crimson eyes. "Drifted, we can get you another sword fashioned in Moonve—"

"No," I cut her off, shaking my head. "That sword was the last thing my father left me. I'm not leaving without it."

For a moment, silence stretched between us, save for the distant rumbling and screaming. Sabrina exhaled, preparing to shake her head again.

"We shall go and retrieve his sword." Celine spoke up quickly.

"But your—" Sabrina started to protest before being swiftly cut off again.

"You are free to go ahead, Sabrina." Celine began, a delicate smile growing on her lips. "Though, know that Drifted and I shall be retrieving his sword before following."

Sabrina stared at her, mouth agape as she struggled to think of a response. Then, she sighed with a smirk.

"Very well," she conceded. "It seems the two of have conspired to leave me little choice."

She threw her hands up in defeat and turned toward the hallway, gesturing for us to follow.

"Come," she called back over her shoulder, urgency returning to her voice. "Let us make haste before you two decide to chase after any other lost trinkets."

Sabrina led the way again, heading deeper into the outpost. The halls that were definitely once orderly were now a mess of cracked stone and shaky beams. Lanterns swung violently from the ceiling above, filling the room with smoke and dust.

We moved fast, dodging debris and stepping over fallen furniture. I stayed close to Celine, our hands only separating when the path narrowed too tightly for us to walk side by side.

"Wait," I called out to Sabrina as we rounded a corner. "How do you know where it is? My sword—I mean."

Sabrina didn't break her pace, answering calmly back. "I do not."

I nearly stumbled at her response.

"What I do know is Agnes' scent," she added. "If she kept your sword, it will be near her. If she does not have it... we will make her tell us who does."

I glanced at Celine, who nodded in agreement. Newly healed from the Lupthera and Sabrina was already looking for another fight.

Still, I didn't argue. My father's sword was all I had left. And if Agnes had it, then I wanted her to see me take it back.

The corridor ahead of us was more intact. Thankfully— the worst of the destruction missed this part of the outpost. As we passed beneath an archway, the flickering light caught the edge of something hanging on the far wall: a massive pelt, stretched and framed. Beneath it, the hallway opened into a large room.

Sabrina paused, sniffing the air like a wolf catching the scent of prey.

"She is close," she said. "This way."

As we entered the area, Sabrina held up a hand, signaling for us to stop. She turned her nose towards the air again, sniffing as her ears swiveled.

Suddenly, I heard heavy footsteps coming up from a staircase that descended into shadow. It was Agnes. Her red eyes gleamed in the low torchlight, and a smirk tugged at her lips as if she'd been waiting for us all along.

"Well, well," Agnes said, her voice low and taunting. "You have returned. Like lambs straight to the slaughter." Her grin widened. "I was beginning to think you had found some sense and fled."

She was standing in front of the staircase, blocking it with her bulky figure.

Sabrina stepped forward without hesitation, her arms loose at her sides. "Charming as ever," she said flatly. "I shall spare us all the posturing—where is Drifted's sword, Agnes? We would like to be out of your fur as soon as possible."

Agnes chuckled, the sound deep and mocking. "Oh, it is down there," she said, cocking her head and motioning lazily over her shoulder toward the stairs. "Why not go and fetch it?"

She stepped aside—not enough to let anyone through, but enough to tempt us. She rolled her shoulders slowly, and they cracked with tension.

Celine's hand drifted toward mine, her fingers grazing lightly against my wrist. I didn't need to look at her to know she was ready.

"Just give us the sword, Agnes," I said, trying to hide the fear in my voice. But I heard the way it trembled. I hated that she probably did too.

Agnes tilted her head slowly, a smirk curling deeper across her lips.

"Oh. The human can actually speak," she said, mock surprise coating every word. She turned her eyes toward Sabrina. "How did you manage that trick? Was it treats? Praise? You always did have a soft spot for helpless things."

Suddenly, Celine placed a hand on my shoulder and stepped forward, her own shoulders squared.

"You can either choose to move," she said calmly, "or remain and prove what I already suspect—that your strength lies only in intimidation."

Agnes' smile dropped, and a scowl was now on her face.

"You posture like a Lupine," Celine continued, her violet

eyes fixed on Agnes without even a flicker of hesitation, "but you bar our path with words. To me, it seems as if you are afraid."

Agnes took a large step forward. Her eyes burning. "Afraid?" She scoffed, her jaw tightening. "You are greatly mistaken!"

Then she charged.

With startling speed for someone her size, Agnes lunged forward, teeth bared, aiming straight for Celine. Celine held her ground, shifting into a defensive stance, hands poised and ready.

But before Agnes could reach her, a blur of motion cut between them—Sabrina.

Her boot caught Agnes square on the jaw, the impact spinning Agnes mid-step and sending her crashing hard across the stone floor, skidding in a heap.

Sabrina landed low, balanced and wild-eyed, already stepping toward where Agnes lay groaning.

"Go!" she shouted, without looking back. "You two, retrieve the sword—I shall handle her alone."

I stood frozen for a second, fists clenched at my sides, my feet refusing to move. I didn't want to leave her—not again.

"Sabrina—"

"I said go!" she snapped, her voice fierce, echoing off the walls.

Then I felt Celine's hand slide into mine, pulling me toward the stairwell.

Begrudgingly, I let my feet fall into motion with Celine's, and as we descended into the stairwell, all I could hear was the sound of claws and fists clashing behind us.

CHAPTER 30

The deeper we descended into the stairwell, the thinner the air got. The sounds of fighting above were more muted now, muffled echoes that made my stomach uneasy.

As we reached the bottom of the steps, the stone beneath our feet was slick and damp, and the walls gave off a strange warmth.

There were thick, knotted roots that jutted out from the walls in every direction—some twisting in loops, others sunk deep into the stone like veins. They chimed with a strange hum, something like a quiet twinkle

I stepped forward slowly, staring at one of the roots in confusion. "What are these? I didn't see any trees large enough around here to grow roots this deep."

Celine didn't answer right away. She moved past me and placed her palm gently against one root, closing her eyes like she was listening to something I couldn't.

"They are roots from the Elderwood," she whispered.

I blinked. "You mean... like all the way from Sylphreach?"

She nodded once. "Aye, the heart of Sylphreach breathes even here."

I stared at the roots.

"How is that even possible?" I asked. "I mean, we're so far."

Celine pulled her hand away, turning to me as the roots creaked.

"The Elderwood stretches beneath the entirety of Velora," she replied. "Its roots were here long before this outpost was ever raised, before Sylphreach was even known by name."

I looked closer, noticing now that some roots were darkened, parts of them turned brittle and black. "Something's wrong with some of them," I muttered.

"An illness," she replied, her voice low. "Slow. But spreading."

"The same sickness that you told me was spreading throughout the land almost a year ago?" I asked.

Celine's eyes lingered on the blackened root. "Aye. Though even I still do not know what is causing this plague."

I watched her closely. It was clear she wasn't being cryptic for the sake of it. She was being honest. And that somehow made it worse.

"It's like something is rotting from the inside out." I replied.

She nodded, dropping her hand away from the root. "There is naught we can do for it now. Come, we cannot afford to linger."

I followed her deeper into the corridor as the stone passage sloped down into the ground the further we ventured. The air steadily thickened—wet, heavy, clinging to my skin. Everything was damp. The walls. The floor. Even the roots had taken on a glistening sheen.

A strange scent tickled my nose. It was faint at first, but grew stronger with every step until I had to breathe through my mouth to keep from gagging.

We passed a row of barred cells, carved from the stone and half-swallowed by the walls. Much like the ones we'd been held in up above.

"Overflow?" I asked quietly.

Celine glanced toward one of the doors. "Likely. For when the upper chambers were filled."

Thankfully, none of them were occupied now.

We ignored them, and the corridor curved, turned left, and

then left again. And that was when the smell hit us full force—like something had died and never stopped dying.

I gagged, stumbling a step as I pressed my sleeve to my nose. "By the moon..."

Celine slowed down as well, cupping her nose with her hand.

We rounded the last bend and entered a wide space. The next thing I saw froze me in place.

Piled in the center of the room like discarded rags were bodies. Dozens of them.

Some were animal—foxes, birds, even what looked like a stag with half its skull caved in. Others... weren't. Arms, legs, and human torsos, mangled and twisted; stacked like firewood.

I staggered back a step, bile rising in my throat.

"What... what is this?" I choked.

Celine's eyes narrowed, but she didn't speak. She took a single step forward, her eyes sweeping across the room like she were trying to piece something together.

To the left of the pile was a wide, roughly dug hole. The surrounding dirt was dark and wet, and the edges opened like something had been buried and then pulled back out.

"What is this place?" I questioned again, still staring at the pile of bodies. "Some kind of mass grave?"

"I am not sure, though something is gravely wrong." Celine replied.

The longer I stared at the pile, the stronger the unease in my gut grew. These bodies didn't just look discarded—they looked as if they had been collected. Chosen. Thrown together in a single heap for a reason. But what that reason was, I couldn't even begin to understand.

I looked at Celine. She wasn't staring at the bodies anymore. She was now standing at the edge of the hole, staring down into it. Her face was pale, eyes wide.

"Celine?" I said, taking a step toward her. "What is it?"

"We should leave," she said.

Her sudden shift in demeanor unsettled me. "Huh, what's wrong?"

I crossed the room and stopped beside her, peering over the edge of the hole.

At first, I couldn't tell what I was seeing. There was a shape curled in the dirt, still and sunken. But as my eyes adjusted to the darkness, the shape began to take form.

Lying on its back was a large person—no, a creature. Some kind of fiend. But it wasn't like any fiend I'd ever seen before.

Its chest jerked, like something that hadn't quite decided whether it should still be breathing. Its limbs were all wrong— too many of them, and none of them matched. One arm was thin and furred, like it belonged to a wolf. Another arm had scales and bent backward. A leg was human, half-charred. A second was avian, talons stiff and curled.

It looked like a Fungoid, only much larger and more malformed. Its skin was stretched taut in some places and saggy in others. A human face was half-formed on one side of its head—eyes shut, mouth slack. But beside it, twisted into the same skull, was the snout of a deer.

My eyes widened, and I staggered back.

"What... what the hell is that!" I screamed.

Celine didn't answer. She stared at it, her ears perked completely upright.

Her face had gone pale, lips slightly parted, attention fixed on the thing in the pit as if trying to convince herself it was real. I'd seen her stand unfazed in the face of countless things—but now?

She looked afraid.

I shuffled back toward the hole, struggling to bring myself

over the edge once more.

The creature's chest still rose and fell in that sick, uncertain rhythm… but now, its eyes were open.

Wide. Glassy. Staring straight up at the ceiling.

Not twitching. Not blinking. Just… watching.

I took a large step back, and my foot caught on something soft. I tripped, falling hard against the floor, my hand landing on a matted tuft of fur that had once been part of something living.

I scrambled back, gasping as my eyes darted to Celine.

She still hadn't moved, not a twitch. Her body was perfectly still, locked in place as she stared down into the hole.

"Celine!" I shouted.

No response.

Two large hands—if they could be called that—rose up from the edge of the pit. Massive, bloated things, fingers too long in some places, too short in others and riddled with open sores. They gripped the stone lip of the grave, right beside where Celine stood.

My heart seized.

"Celine, move!" I called out to her, scrambling to my feet.

As I got closer, I saw the creature's face.

Warty, swollen, and contorted in ways no living thing should ever be. Patches of skin peeled back to reveal raw muscle. And from one cheek, two jagged beaks jutted sideways like bone. A long tongue slithered past its cracked lips as it flicked the air.

"Celine!" I grabbed her arm hard. Her body jolted under my grip, but her eyes were still fixed on the beast.

I gripped her arm tighter, wrapping my other around her waist and yanking her back.

The fiend was pulling itself up and would be upon us shortly. "We need to get out of here. Now!"

Her legs dragged as I pulled her away from the edge, boots scraping the floor. "Snap out of it, Celine!"

I turned us back toward the corridor we came from, trying to get us as far away from the creature as possible.

Celine still didn't speak, but her legs started moving—stiffly, like she was waking from a nightmare she hadn't left behind yet.

We were almost at the corridor before everything went dark.

A massive shadow swallowed the light above us, blotting out the walls and ceiling. I looked up to see that the creature had launched itself straight over us.

A writhing tangle of body parts, flesh, feathers, scales, and fur soared over us. It twisted in the air clumsily. Its mouth—or one of them—hung open mid-flight, as it let out a hollow rasp from its throat.

It landed in front of us, hard. The floor trembled beneath its weight as it crashed down between us and the exit, blocking the exit entirely. Dust and splinters of rock burst outward in every direction, and I had to shield Celine as the ground buckled beneath our feet.

The creature stood there now, heaving. Its back was hunched, but even still it towered over us. That horrible face twitched as it dropped its head toward us.

I desperately scanned the area; there was only one other opening I could see. With barely a thought, I grabbed Celine again and spun us toward the only other corridor. It was half collapsed with rubble, but it was open.

"This way!" I shouted, dragging Celine toward it.

Behind us, the creature shifted, and I heard its bones cracking. A shiver shot up my spine as we ran, but I refused to look back.

We bolted through the narrow opening, squeezing

ourselves tight against a wall and snaking around roots that twisted throughout.

As we got through the corridor, it opened up into a small, cluttered room.

I took a quick glance back to see the beast's large body at the other end of the corridor, blocking out most of what little light was left. It stood there, bouncing from foot to foot, making the ground shake as it landed.

I took a deep breath. We were as safe as we could be, for now.

Glancing around the room, I noticed old crates and trinkets lined the walls, most of them broken. Tools and shackles hung not too far. Tattered Lupine cloaks and weapons sat in a pile in the corner of the room.

Wait, weapons. The thought jumped into my mind.

I spotted it immediately, half-buried beneath a pile of rusted metal and discarded scabbards. The worn leather of the grip, the faint notch on the crossguard—I knew it like I knew my own heartbeat. My sword.

They must have brought it here when they took us. Stored with the other belongings of those who never made it out.

I practically dove to grab the hilt and pulled it free.

I turned the sword in my hand briefly. Having it back comforted me, but I couldn't focus on that for too long.

Celine stood inside the doorway. Her eyes were still wide, fixed on something that wasn't even there anymore.

"Celine," I said, stepping toward her. "Hey—look at me."
She didn't respond.

The roots around the room creaked, and down the hallway I could hear the creature breathing heavily.

"Celine!" I said louder, grabbing her shoulders. "You need to snap out of it!"

Her lips moved, barely.

"I... I saw its face," she breathed, voice thin and distant. "It should not be."

Her eyes finally met mine. There was still fear in them, but something else too. A deep sorrow.

"It does not belong to this world," she whispered. "Not to the trees, nor stone, nor sky. It is a wound. A mistake the forest cannot heal."

I stared at her, unsure of what to say.

"Yeah," I mumbled. "I don't know what that thing is... but we can't stay here."

I gripped the hilt of my sword tighter, forcing down the tremble in my fingers.

"We need to get back to Sabrina. And I can't get us there without you."

Celine held my gaze for a moment longer. Then she gave a slow nod.

"I will manage," she replied. Her voice was steadier now, and her breath more even. She blinked once—twice—and then rolled her shoulders back as she lifted her chin.

I could tell she wasn't exactly whole, but at least she was present.

I turned toward the corridor, sword still in hand, and crept toward the edge of the wall. The sight that awaited me as I leaned to peek over the wall made my hair stand on end

Staring down the other end, half covered in shadow were the multiple eyes of the creature. Big, small, swollen, bulging. Human and animal, watching and waiting.

I pulled back quickly, pressing my back to the wall as my chest heaved.

"It's... it's blocking the entrance," I whispered to Celine. "I don't know how we're going to get past that."

Celine turned toward the nearest wall where the crates and discarded gear were scattered.

She sifted through the wreckage and, after a moment, pulled something free.

A simple bow, worn, but the string still intact. And a loose arrow she found to go along with it.

She turned to me, holding them out. "Perhaps you can use this?"

I blinked. "I mean... sort of?"

"I used one when I was younger," I said, taking the bow carefully. "Just for fun. We used to shoot at hay bales back behind the fields in Lunaria. I was never any good with it—never stuck with it either."

I examined the string. It wasn't in the best condition, but it was something.

I was never a good shot. There was no chance that I would be one now. But at this distance, maybe—just maybe—I could land a hit.

"I'll give it a try," I muttered, squeezing the bow. "We don't really have a ton of options."

Celine stepped beside me, quiet as ever, her gaze fixed on the corridor.

"When you fire," she said, voice low but firm, "I shall move first."

I turned to her. "What?"

"I am quicker than you are," she continued, already pulling her cloak tighter around her shoulders. "If your shot draws it away from the opening, I shall dart out and attract its attention. That should give you enough room to follow."

I nodded. "Okay, sounds like a plan."

I pressed my back against the cold stone, the bow trembling in my hands.

Breathe steadily. Don't jerk the shot. My mind flashed back to the muddy fields behind the house, hay bales falling apart, my father's voice laughing as I missed again and again.

Focus, Isaac, you can do this.

I took a breath, then another. Stepped from cover and turned hard into the corridor, bringing the bow up with the motion.

The creature was still there—still watching with its dozen eyes.

I picked one and let the arrow loose.

It flew faster than I expected, hissing through the air as it weaved through the rubble. It sank with a squelching sound, right into one of the larger eyes near the front of the creature's misshapen head.

The beast shrieked—a roar that shook the corridor walls and sent dust cascading from the ceiling. It reeled back, arms flailing and claws scraping at the floor.

Celine shot forward in a flash, already moving before I could fully process the shot.

Her cloak whipped behind her as she slipped past the threshold, feet barely touching the ground.

Before the creature could react, Celine was past it, running toward the center of the open space.

I stayed back, watching a limb slam into a wall and another scrape across the floor as it turned to follow Celine. That was my moment.

I weaved my way out quickly, sword drawn now, and yelled at the top of my lungs. "Hey! Over here!"

The thing halted mid-step.

Its spine arched unnaturally, and its limbs froze. Its head twisted around forward with a grinding sound. Then, it grinned. That's what I think it was trying to do, at least.

Its many mouths stretched and split, then curled upwards. And then... it laughed.

A low, raspy sound at first, like air being dragged through rotted leaves. Then it changed and became something too close to human. A phlegmy, broken giggle echoing off the walls—high, gurgling, and utterly wrong.

I froze. Not entirely from fear, but more from confusion. What the hell was this thing?

I glanced toward Celine as she had made it to the far side of the room. Her expression was as dumbfounded as mine, lips parted, eyebrows furrowed.

The creature's heads twitched, and then the laughter sputtered before stopping all at once.

The air went still. And then, it moved—fast.

The creature dropped forward and launched itself toward me, claws tearing across stone, legs hammering the ground, causing the room to shake.

I dove out of the way as the creature went bouldering past me.

It skidded as it turned, letting out a roar that rattled through my chest.

As I got ready to stand, the ground vanished beneath me.

I barely had time to register the pressure around my ankle before a force yanked me upward.

My body whipped through the air like a rag doll, the ceiling spinning past my eyes. The breath punched out of my lungs as I dangled upside down.

The creature's tail had me. It coiled tight around my leg, holding me aloft like I weighed nothing.

It turned one of its heads toward me, eyes blinking out of sync. Mouths twitching, grinning, and drooling.

"Drifted!" Celine called out, running toward me.

The beast snarled and then snapped its tail. In an instant, I was thrown sideways.

I collided with something solid. Celine.

The two of us went crashing to the floor, sliding across it in a tangle of limbs until we hit a wall. My sword skittered off, hitting the wall a few feet away.

My ribs screamed. My head throbbed. And I could feel Celine's breath shallow against my shoulder.

I pushed up slowly, blinking through foggy vision, hand searching blindly for my weapon.

Celine stirred beside me, groaning softly as she sat up.

"You alright?" I asked, breathing unevenly.

She nodded once, tight and curt. "Aye, I shall manage."

We both rose unsteadily.

The creature let out a low growl, and then dropped to all fours.

It ran toward us, chipping the floor as it charged.

"Wait," Celine whispered beside me, her voice stern. "Wait for my word."

I looked at her, tightening my stance and nodding. The beast snarled, drew back a massive arm, and leapt—fist raised high above its heads, every mouth open in rage.

"Now!" Celine yelled.

We split—her veering right, me to the left, both of us just in time to dodge the blow.

The creature's fist slammed into the wall behind us, tearing through the stone with a thunderous crack.

Its arm wedged deep into the shattered rock, and it struggled to free itself. It was trapped.

I dropped into a roll toward my sword. My hand closed around the hilt and immediately slashed the blade down into the beast's arm.

The blade cut deep and then came to a stop in the mess of flesh and muscle. I hacked at the limb once, twice, and then with a last swing, I severed it completely.

The arm went limp in the wall and twitched as the creature howled in pain. It grabbed at its injured arm with one of its others.

Then, its roaring turned into something else. Something... human.

"Help me!" it cried, voice warping in and out. "Please— help—"

I stood there frozen. My sword felt heavier all of a sudden.

"It's... crying..." I muttered to myself. My mouth wide open.

Before I could process it, Celine's hand took mine firmly, and she yanked me toward the passage behind us.

"We must leave Drifted, now!"

I didn't argue. I couldn't even formulate the words if I wanted to.

We ran, retracing our steps through the hall, but I couldn't stop myself from looking back. Just once, long enough to see the creature fall to its knees beside its arm.

Its cries echoed behind us—slipping back and forth between agony and pleading. Between beast and man.

The sound dug into my skull. I couldn't wrap my head around what we had encountered. Part of me thought I was making it up. The other part of me hoped that's exactly what was happening.

Finally, we reached the stairwell, and neither of us hesitated up the stairs. We climbed fast, boots slamming against the stone as the light from above trickled down.

At the top of the stairs, we burst through the opening. I leaned over, panting as I held my knees.

I looked up slowly, taking a deep breath

The room was ruined—furniture tossed about haphazardly, stone broken in some places, and debris scattered in every direction. Sitting in the middle of it all was Sabrina, sat on top of Agnes' unconscious body.

Sabrina lazily lifted a brow as we stumbled toward her.

"Well, there you two are," she said. "I was starting to

believe something down there decided you looked tasty."

Neither of us answered.

Sabrina's smirk faded, and she tilted her head, her eyes narrowing as she looked us over.

"By the moon," she muttered, sliding off of Agnes and walking toward us. "You two look like prey that wandered too close to something even the wolves would not give chase," she said in a low voice.

I let out a breath I hadn't realized I'd been holding.

"You have no idea," I muttered, staring at the ground.

Sabrina didn't press. She just gave me a long look, then turned away.

"Whatever it was, we shall have plenty of time to dwell on it once we leave," she said. "Come, we have lingered here long enough. Lostsummit awaits."

Celine looked at me and then moved ahead. I followed after taking a breath. My legs felt heavier than I expected as the image of the creature replayed in my mind.

We slowly walked further into the open stretch of the ruined hall, stepping over the debris and shattered wood.

As we got to the far end, I felt the ground tremble. Something was running toward the building, and fast.

Sabrina's head snapped toward the far wall.

"Lady Celine!" she shouted.

Before I could even wonder what was happening, Celine slammed into me from the side—shoulder first, tackling me hard.

We hit the ground together as the wall beside us exploded like it were made out of paper.

I looked up to see the burning eyes of the Ursaroot staring us down.

I'd almost forgotten it was even out there.

CHAPTER 31

"On your feet!" Celine yelled, holding her hand out to me.

I grabbed it quickly, locking my fingers with hers as she pulled me up.

The air was dense with dust, stinging my eyes and burning my throat as I tried to gather my bearings. The hall shuddered again as the Ursaroot tried to force its massive body through the gaping hole it busted in the wall. Stones buckled under its weight, and a beam overhead threatened to collapse.

It was halfway in now—shoulders hunched, one clawed paw dragging across the floor as it tore up the ground beneath it.

The fiend threw out a large swing, swiping at Sabrina. She jumped back into the air, barely dodging out of its way, landing next to us.

"It will not stop," she started. "Every step it takes brings the whole place closer to collapse."

The ceiling groaned again, a fracture spreading across the stone. The wall buckled further as the beast continued to wedge itself into the hall.

"We cannot fight it here," Celine said. "If we remain, it will bury us."

"Then we best not wait to be entombed," Sabrina replied.

"Follow me," Celine commanded, turning on her heel.

We ran, boots pounding as we flew down the corridor, navigating our way over the wreckage left in the hallways.

Behind us, a low rumble and then a loud thumping sound came following us as the building continued to crumble.

I glanced over my shoulder and saw the far end of the

corridor get blown outward as the Ursaroot shoved a large arm through from the outside.

It was tracking our path, forcing us forward like cattle. Every few steps, another crash erupted from somewhere behind or beside us.

"Left!" Celine shouted, and we banked into a wider corridor. I recognized the space—barely. The armory room was up ahead.

A portion of the wall behind Sabrina exploded as thick claws punched through, dragging vines and rubble in their path. We all ducked as stones went flying dangerously close over our heads.

We turned the corner, and the broken entrance to the armory came into view—that breach was our only shot.

I didn't dare look back—mostly because I didn't need to. The tremor beneath my boots, the splintering of wood behind us, and that gurgling roar echoing through the corridor like thunder in a canyon... it was all the confirmation I needed to know we were still being chased.

Celine said nothing as she ran. Sabrina was right behind her. I pushed my legs harder, teeth clenched, lungs burning. The exit was close.

Closer.

Almost—

"Down!" Celine shouted.

We all dove the instant we cleared the gap. As we flew through the space, a roar split the air behind me.

Jaws snapped just past the hole we had emerged from as the Ursaroot missed us by a hair. It was close enough for me to feel its breath, hot and moist across my back like a flame.

The force of its movement sent my cloak flailing around me as I hit the ground.

We tumbled through the dirt, the three of us scrambling

to turn into a kneeling position, readying ourselves.

I looked back, breath burning as it left my lungs.

The Ursaroot skidded to a halt several paces behind us. It turned, eyes low and brooding as its claws raked deep into the land.

"This isn't going to be easy, is it?" I asked rhetorically. My fingers found and then tightened around the hilt of my sword.

Sabrina let out a slow, exasperated breath. "I could be back at Sylphreach right now. Sitting by the hearth. Eating one of Caldryn's decadent meals."

"Focus!" Celine snapped.

"You must excuse me, princess," Sabrina muttered. "It is hard to maintain mental fortitude when you have been on a moldy bread diet."

"It will charge us soon," Celine replied, ignoring Sabrina's remark. "We must break its rhythm. Drifted, stay light on your feet. Wait until you see an opening."

I swallowed hard. "What kind of opening?"

Celine replied, her eyes never leaving the beast. "The kind that will shift the battle in our favor."

The Ursaroot shuffled, and vines tensed along its back like a bowstring being pulled taut.

Then it ran.

The ground trembled as it charged forward, crashing through the courtyard.

"Sabrina!" Celine shouted as she ran toward the fiend.

"Aye, right behind you!" Sabrina replied, hot on Celine's tail.

Celine got in close and leapt, twisting her body mid-air. When she got close to the Ursaroot's foreleg, she slammed her heel into it. The blow landed clean, forcing the beast to stagger—but only slightly.

Sabrina was up next. She launched herself up and grabbed

a thick vine along the Ursaroot's shoulder. With a shout, she tried to sink her claws into the side of its neck—once, then again.

The Ursaroot roared and shook its head violently, throwing Sabrina from its side and sending her straight into a far wall. Her body collided with it with a thud.

"Sabrina!" I shouted, but she was already dragging herself upright.

"Do not worry about me, assist Lady Celine!" she hissed.

I nodded and charged toward the Ursaroot with my sword drawn.

As I approached, Celine was darting beneath the creature as it raised one of its limbs. She slammed her palm into the back of its knee joint, and the impact rippled up through its wood-rotted leg. The beast staggered forward, stumbling as fell off balance.

There. That was it. My moment.

I rushed forward with a yell, aiming my sword at the same knee Celine had struck. I thrust the blade forward, giving everything I had to drive the sword right into the fiend's knee.

It should have gone deep. But it didn't.

The sword barely sank in more than a few inches before stopping hard—caught in the dense, bark-plated hide of the fiend. I clenched my jaw as I tried to plunge it deeper, twist it, anything.

The Ursaroot let out a slow snarl. Then its massive head turned toward me. Its gaze locked with mine—dark, shining with rage.

It opened its jaws to reveal teeth jagged like cracked stones. It was going to swallow me whole.

I froze as its gaping mouth drew closer to my body.

But something cracked the side of its skull.

Sabrina.

She came flying in from the side, spinning mid-air before delivering a ferocious kick straight to the fiend's temple.

The Ursaroot reeled back with a loud howl, and its head snapped sideways. The force of the movement jerked the leg I was stabbing upward, lifting me off the ground.

I flew backward, crashing across the courtyard as the Ursaroot reared fully upright.

I slammed onto the ground hard, skidding across the stone until I hit a pile of debris. My body stopped hard, and the breath was knocked out of my chest.

A loud clang echoed beside me as my sword clattered to a stop within arm's reach. Sap coated it, and it was scratched, but thankfully, it was still intact.

I reached for it with shaking fingers as I forced myself off the ground.

Across the courtyard, Celine landed hard and rolled to her feet. My eyes darted to Sabrina, who was crouched beside a broken pillar, blood on her lip, chest heaving.

We were all still standing. But for how long?

The Ursaroot roared again. It hadn't slowed down any. If anything, it was angrier.

I stood up shakily. My fingers clenched around my sword's hilt.

Nothing we were doing mattered. I mean, hell. Even my sword couldn't cut through its hide.

Celine dodged beneath another claw swipe, barely slipping past the beast's massive arm as it smashed the ground where she'd been.

"This thing refuses to tire!" Sabrina called out, running toward the fight again. "What is it made of!?"

"Malice," Celine replied as she twisted away from another attack. "And far too much of it."

"It is like striking a mountain!" Sabrina growled, leaping

forward to land a fist against the fiend's. The beast barely budged from the attack.

I gritted my teeth, eyes scanning its body—its bark-plated legs, the tangled vines, the bramble that wrapped it like armor. Nothing gave.

Every part of it was protected. How were we even supposed to deal any significant damage to this thing?

The memory of standing face to face with the Ursaroot moments ago flashed in my mind.

The way it lowered its massive head toward me. Staring me down with those rage filled eyes.

Burning.

Angry

… Exposed.

The eyes, they had no armor. They were black, uncovered, and furious.

I sucked in a breath and took off running. That was it. That was our opening.

"I have an idea!" I shouted.

"What!?" Sabrina yelled as she dodged beneath another swing of the Ursaroot's arm.

"I'm going for the eyes!" I yelled back in response. "Just get it into position for me!"

"Easier said than done!" she replied, already moving into position.

My boots slammed against the ground as I charged forward, sword raised, vision tunneled in on the pulsing eyes.

The Ursaroot looked at me, and then I felt a shift in the air. It started lifting its head, almost as if it knew what my plan was.

Its eye twitched, its neck lifting higher, too high—too fast. My angle was gone. I wouldn't make it in time.

But Celine moved before I could even curse.

She ran straight toward it and leapt—her body turning in the air fluidly. She caught hold of a thick vine dangling from the side of its neck and yanked with everything she had, digging her heels and dragging the creature's head lower.

It roared in response and thrashed in an attempt to free itself.

Sabrina shot forward next, grabbing another coil of vine on the other side and adding her weight to it.

Together, they pulled.

The fiend's head lowered—inch by inch—its massive body resisting, but not fast enough.

Celine's voice rang out over the roar.

"Do it, Drifted!"

The world narrowed to a single point—me, the sword in my hands, and the creature's face now feet from the ground.

Its head was twisted slightly, pulled to the side by the force of both Celine and Sabrina. One huge eye—bloody, swollen, and wide with rage—turned to meet mine.

I let out a roar of my own and drove the blade forward with everything I had.

There was a nasty crunch, a wet snap of pressure giving way as the steel pierced through the soft tissue and into whatever lay behind it.

The creature let out a howl unlike anything I'd ever heard—deep, broken, and full of pain. Its limbs convulsed, and its entire body started recoiling violently.

The vines snapped upward, throwing Celine and Sabrina back as the beast panicked.

My sword was yanked from my hand, lodged in the fiend's large skull as it reared on its hind legs.

Then, with a shriek, the Ursaroot turned and took off—crashing through the far edge of the courtyard.

Celine shot past me in a flash.

"Wait—where are you going?!" I shouted, stumbling after her.

She didn't answer, leaping and catching one of the trailing vines of the Ursaroot. She swung herself up and planted her heels into the creature's back as it barreled through the hole it left in outpost's wall.

Only then did she look back, her voice slightly drowned out by the wind. "I am retrieving your sword!"

I stood there for a half-second, stunned. My sword?

What? Is she crazy?!

I took after her. Sabrina was at my side in a heartbeat.

"Celine!" I shouted, panting. "Let it go. I'll get another one!"

She didn't even look back. Just hunkered down tighter against the beast.

The thing was massive, but it moved like it weighed nothing. Each of its strides covered ten of ours. The treeline came on ahead, and with every passing second, we were falling further behind.

"We're not going to catch up like this," I muttered, breath burning in my chest. "We're losing her."

Sabrina didn't respond, her eyes fixed on the retreating beast.

"Transform," I said, glancing at her. "Your Lunar form—you should take it."

She scoffed without looking at me. "That is pointless, Drifted. I could not stop that thing even if I wanted to."

"I'm not asking you to stop it." I looked at her, serious. "You'll be faster. I can ride you."

She nearly tripped at my words.

"What—no!" she blurted, her face instantly flushing red. "Absolutely not."

I blinked, utterly confused. "Why not?"

She avoided my eyes, visibly flustered. "Because—just—no! I refuse!"

"This isn't the time to be prideful!" I snapped. "We'll lose her if you don't."

Sabrina groaned, her ears flattening against her head. Her face was now practically the same color as her eyes, but I could tell she knew I was right.

After a moment of hesitation, she pulled a small leather satchel from her side, unclasped her cloak, and shoved them into my hands.

"Fine," she muttered. "But do not lose these. No matter what. Got it?"

I eyed the bag in confusion, but took it regardless, throwing the cloak over myself and wearing the satchel. There wasn't enough time to question why she was being so weird.

I nodded. "Got it."

She turned away from me, already preparing to shift.

"Also," she added, her voice lower, "if you tell anyone about this. I swear by the moon I shall skin you like a hare."

Before I could respond, the air around her churned. Her body shifted—fur, muscle, and bone stretching and reshaping as she took her Lunar form.

In seconds, she stood in her wolfish body—sleek, powerful, and taut with energy. Her red eyes caught the light as her claws dug into the ground.

She looked at me and dipped her head before running out slightly in front of me.

I sprinted after her and leapt—landing on her back mid-stride, barely finding my balance as she flew forward. I wrapped one arm tightly around her neck and hunkered down, pressing low to avoid the wind whipping against my face.

The ground blurred beneath us, trees became streaks of

black, and wind howled past my ears. My stomach dropped with each sudden turn as she weaved through the forest. I could hardly catch my breath.

So this was their speed. Fighting one was intense enough, but riding a Lupine in this form? It was breathtaking—literally.

We closed in on the Ursaroot quickly, even with it tearing through the trees like they were nothing.

I narrowed my eyes—and there, clinging to its back, was Celine. Her body was pressed low, and her claws were dug deep into the matted fur and bark along the fiend's spine. She crawled forward, inch by inch, toward its head.

"Celine!" I yelled, slightly raising my posture on Sabrina's back. "Get off! Leave it!"

She ignored me again.

I cursed under my breath, then tapped Sabrina's side, motioning with one hand. "Closer—get me closer!"

She let out a huff and then veered hard toward the Ursaroot's flank, kicking up leaves and dirt as she pushed forward.

We came up alongside the beast—close enough now to feel the ground quake with every step it took.

I reached out—grabbed a thick vine dragging off the creature's side and then jumped.

My body jerked forward as I caught hold, using my free hand to grab at the coarse fur along its side. The momentum threatened to tear my shoulder from its socket, but I held on, swinging inward and slamming against the fiend.

I clenched my jaw and began scaling the Ursaroot, one fist over the other, dragging myself up through the bramble and prickly fur.

As I reached the top of its back, Celine was already ahead at its head.

She crouched right above its eye, fighting to stay upright as the beast jostled. She held on tightly to a tuft of fur with one hand and reached for the sword buried in its skull with the other.

With a grunt, she gripped the hilt and pulled.

The blade came free, and the beast roared in pain, throwing its head back.

The momentum sent Celine tumbling backward along the Ursaroot's back. She bounced along it, coming dangerously close to flying off the side.

As she flew next to me, I reached out and caught her, one arm locking around her waist.

The two of us slid slightly before I could dig my knees in and pull her close.

"You're insane," I muttered, breathless.

She looked up at me, wind whipping strands of hair across her face. A small smile played at the corner of her mouth.

"Aye, but I retrieved your weapon."

I shook my head and let out a dry laugh before taking the blade from her, sliding it back into its sheath with trembling hands.

The sound of barking broke through the air.

I turned my head and looked down the side of the Ursaroot—Sabrina was racing below us, her eyes wide as she stared at me.

She nodded her head forward, motioning again and again.

I followed her gaze, straightening to see past the bobbing rise and fall of the Ursaroot's massive skull.

Just ahead—beyond the thinning trees and broken trail— was a cliff. And we were headed straight for it.

I grabbed Celine by the arm. "We've got to go. Now!"

The Ursaroot didn't slow down. If anything, it felt like it sped up.

We scrambled to our feet, stumbling as the creature's back shook beneath us.

"Come on!" I shouted.

We sprinted across its spine, barely staying upright. The edge of the cliff was mere seconds away.

The Ursaroot let out one final, broken roar—

And went over the edge.

Celine's hand found mine, and we jumped.

The fiend fell out beneath us as we floated in the air trying to claw our way through the sky toward the ledge.

The only thought in my mind as we fell was one I'd had far too often lately:

Man, I am so sick of falling.

CHAPTER 32

The ledge was right there. A little farther. Just—

I fell short, my fingertips grazing the ledge before slipping away. Gravity took hold fast, pressing down on our bodies.

"Damnit!" I shouted as the wind howled past us.

We were going to fall straight to our deaths.

A sudden jerk snapped through my body, halting our descent so violently it felt like I got punched in the chest. My back slammed hard against the rock wall, the impact forcing the breath from my lungs.

I groaned, blinking the dizziness away as I looked up to see what stopped our fall.

Clamped tight around the back of my cloak were a pair of gleaming white fangs. Sabrina. Her claws dug into the floor above, muscles tense, every limb shaking from the strain of holding us up.

Slowly, she began pulling us up, inch by inch. I swallowed as I looked down at the forest floor past Celine. The sheer distance of the drop we almost took made my skin prickle.

I glanced at Celine, still gripping my hand. "You alright?" I rasped.

She nodded, her face pale. "Aye."

The moment I was close enough to the ledge, Sabrina yanked me back, pulling me up the rest of the way onto solid ground. I crouched down, a hoisted Celine the rest of the way up right after.

I coughed, then cleaned off my clothing with a few pats. "Thanks, Sabrina. You really saved our hides there."

Sabrina snorted and then rolled her eyes. Even with the fur and fangs, you could still read her sass.

Celine pushed herself to her feet slowly, brushing down her cloak as she made her way to the ledge. She said nothing at first, staring down into the rocky basin below.

"It is still," she murmured. "But I believe it yet breathes… if only barely."

I staggered, walking to her side to peer over the cliff carefully.

The Ursaroot was there—its massive body sprawled out. One of its limbs twitched faintly, and blood pooled beneath its head, seeping from the wound where my sword had struck its eye.

Its back was twisted at an unnatural angle, and I couldn't tell what they were from this distance, but I saw thick black tendrils spreading through the open wound. It looked… like it was losing shape, almost as if the pieces that held it together were unraveling.

"Still alive after that?" I muttered. "How?"

"I am unsure," Celine replied. "Though, whatever it is. It is not strength."

A sudden bark made me jump.

I turned to see Sabrina standing beside me. She nosed at the small satchel hanging at my side. Her eyes flicked up to mine, expectant.

I looked down. "Oh… you want this?"

She gave another huff, this time far more impatient, and I unclipped the strap, holding the bag out to her. She took it in her teeth, then rolled her eyes—again—before stalking off into the woods without another sound.

I watched her go, blinking. "What's her deal?"

Celine was quiet for a moment. Then, she stepped to the edge of the trees and folded her arms behind her.

"I observed you rode Sabrina to catch up with me, Drifted," Celine started.

I looked at her confused. "Yeah? There was no way I would've been able to catch up to the Ursaroot on my own."

"To mount a Lupine is a serious gesture, Drifted," Celine continued.

I furrowed my brow. "What are you talking about?"

"It is not merely a means of transport," she said at last. "To allow another to ride in such a way is a mark of deep trust. Intimacy. Among our kind… it is an act reserved for those bound together. As mates."

My mouth opened. Then closed. Then opened again.

"What—no. No, no, that's not—I didn't know! I wasn't trying to—"

I raised my hands as if to fend off some invisible accusation. "You were stuck on a giant bear barreling through the trees! I wasn't thinking about—" I groaned.

"I was not stuck," Celine interjected.

"You did! You would've gone off the cliff if I wasn't there!" my arms were flailing now.

"I required no aid." She replied again.

My jaw dropped as my mind raced to come up with a reply.

"So," Celine said evenly, "you hold such fondness for Sabrina, then?"

I blinked. "Wait—what?"

She turned to face me, her expression blank.

"It is good to know," she went on, "that your heart lies with her. I shall endeavor to not be a bother."

Be a bother? I questioned in my head.

"What? No—Celine, that's not—!" I felt my soul about to leave my body. "I don't—lie with anyone's heart—I mean, not Sabrina's at least!"

Celine said nothing, turning her back to me again.

My face was burning up. Was she upset? Why was she even pressing me about this?

426

"Celine..." I called to her, holding a hand out.

As I took a step forward, I saw her shoulders move slightly. The tiniest motion followed by a quiet chuckle. Then, her shoulders bounced lightly.

I narrowed my eyes. "Are you... laughing?"

Celine turned around, her lips pressed together as she tried to stifle her laugh. "Forgive me," she breathed. "I could not resist."

She walked a few steps closer, folding her hands neatly in front of her. "I am not upset, Drifted. You had no other choice—and I am grateful you acted without hesitation." Her voice regained its usual calm, composed flow. "But what I said remains true. Among our kind, such an act is rarely shared."

I groaned and ran a hand through my hair. "Well, now I've apparently proposed to Sabrina in Lupine tradition. That's... fantastic."

"She will not hold it against you," Celine replied. "Truth be told, I am sure she would sooner rather wipe it from memory."

I dropped my head into my hands. "That sounds about right."

I heard twigs snapping as Sabrina emerged from the trees. She was now back in human form.

I raised a hand. "Hey, so about that whole back-riding—"

"The sooner that we forget about it," she started waving a hand dismissively, "the less gross I shall feel."

I blinked. "Hey—what's that supposed to mean?"

As she ignored and walked past me, I noticed she was wearing a new set of clothes. Some loose forest-green tunic over dark leggings.

"Wait—you changed clothes?" I asked.

"Yes, Drifted," she said over her shoulder. "I am sure you

have noticed by now that when a Lupine takes their Lunar form, we return rather ... indecent."

"Oh, yeah... right." I looked at the floor, blushing slightly.

Sabrina sighed and shook her head. "That is why I carry extra clothing whenever I travel. You never know when you shall have to shift and save someone dangling off a cliff."

"It really wasn't up to me," I muttered.

"I recall it differently." She replied.

Before we could start our usual arguing, Celine stepped forward. "You do recall that I, too, was dangling from that cliff, do you not, Sabrina?"

Sabrina's eyes sparkled. "Ah, but you, Lady Celine, are hardly the same as Drifted. You at least had the decency not to flail like a startled squirrel."

"I wasn't flailing," I blurted. "I was calculating momentum."

"Of course you were," Sabrina said with a grin.

Celine gave a slow blink. "Indeed. His limbs did appear... active."

Sabrina laughed, and I groaned.

"Wonderful," I muttered. "Glad you two are enjoying yourselves."

I turned toward Sabrina, cracking my knuckles and stretching my arms above my head. "Alright, so... where do we go now?"

She gestured with a tilt of her chin. "Look over there."

I looked far past the edge of the cliff, squinting through the mist in the air.

There was a tree that was much larger than the ones surrounding it. It was black and twisted, like the rest of the trees in this area, but thicker, with large thorny vines wrapped around its branches. Even from this distance, I could see the way it dominated the land beneath it. And at its base—half-hidden in the gloom—were structures. Low buildings shaped into the earth, almost grown from it.

"It looks like Sylphreach. If it had been starved and devoid of any life." I said, narrowing my eyes.

Sabrina clicked her tongue. "Cassius always did like to play copycat. He built himself a little kingdom in the mud and pretended it was worth something."

"It certainly does not look welcoming," Celine chimed in.

"You've got that right," I replied. "How long until we get there, Sabrina?"

Sabrina held a finger up to her chin and held up her hand. As if trying to measure the distance.

"I figure we can reach there by nightfall if we are hasty!" She replied with a clap.

"Then let's get moving," I said, pulling up my cloak.

We began our descent down the cliff. As we reached the bottom, I noticed the ground here was more solid, but equally devoid of any nature. The soil was dark and damp, like the ground had seen no sunlight in weeks.

The further we walked along an already beaten path, the taller the trees got. Closer together. More sinister.

Their black thorny vines grew thicker, and their branches hung dangerously low. You could easily get an eye poked out if you weren't paying attention.

None of us spoke for a while. Even Sabrina, who never seemed to run out of clever things to say.

At one point, I could've sworn I saw a vine twitch ahead of us. I paused, squinting my eyes.

"Is anything the matter?" Celine asked from beside me.

"No... I think this place is playing tricks on me." I replied. "Everything about this forest feels wrong."

"Mhm," she hummed. "Thornwallow was born from the rotten core of many Lupine. It is wrong."

I looked at Sabrina, expecting her to add some quip, but she didn't. Her eyes were focused forward, and her lips were pressed tight.

I didn't feel like bothering her. Truthfully, I was happy to get some peace and quiet. Besides, maybe she was listening for danger, focusing on navigating us the rest of the way safely. I'm sure this area of land demanded all of her attention.

As we pressed on, the light in the sky dropped slowly, struggling to find its way through the haze that clung to the air.

A strong smell crept in with it—something rotten and sour.

I lifted the edge of my cloak to cover my nose. "What is that?"

"The smell has been growing for quite some time." Celine answered. "I take it you smelled it some distance back, had you not, Sabrina?"

Sabrina wrinkled her nose, grimacing. "Unfortunately, yes. Drifted is lucky—his dull nose probably spared him the worst of it."

I wasn't sure if that was supposed to be taken as a compliment or not.

"We should be coming up on whatever it is now." Sabrina continued.

As we walked, the sound of loud buzzing came from ahead. The source seemed to be somewhere behind the next line of trees. The sound vibrated in my ears, making my skin itch.

"You hear that?" I asked, balancing looks between them.

Celine gave a nod. "Aye."

The sound grew louder as we stepped into a small clearing.

A large and moving mass buzzed on the ground, shifting and churning like something trapped in a net.

It wasn't until we stepped closer that I realized what I was looking at.

Dozens of insects were swarming over a single shape. Their bloated dark bodies twitched as they crawled over one another. Each one was nearly the size of my fist with veined, glossy wings equally as large.

"Festerlings..." I muttered under my breath.

A type of fiend that thankfully wouldn't harm the living. Though that was only because they preferred their meals dead.

I'd seen a few here and there in Moonveil. But never in such large amounts.

We got closer, and they scattered.

Instinctively, I raised my arms as the swarm lifted into the air with a sudden, synchronized buzz. They peeled away from what held their attention, vanishing into the trees.

As the last of the Festerlings dispersed, I could finally see what had them so preoccupied. The figure beneath them was a deer—or had been. Its body was curled unnaturally, and its limbs were bent at odd angles. Though, it was what constricted the deer that made my stomach churn.

Thick, bark-covered tendrils wrapped around the deer's legs and torso—some wrapped so tightly they'd split the skin. They were coming from beneath the carcass, twisting around it as if the land reached up and grabbed it.

I took a cautious step forward, my heart racing at the sight.

"What... what the hell is this?" I whispered.

No one answered.

I turned, expecting some explanation—anything. But Celine stood silent, her violet eyes weary as she stared at the body. Sabrina, too, said nothing. Her mouth was pressed into a firm line, arms crossed as her gaze swept over the surrounding ground.

"I've never seen anything like this," I added. "This isn't... this isn't normal, right?"

"I do not believe it is," Celine said softly.

She stepped forward, kneeling down to the ground beside the creature. "It is not the first time I have seen this... though I hoped it would have been the last."

That only confused me further. "So, what is it?"

Celine reached a hand out toward the body, and the roots almost seemed to bristle at her presence. Curling tighter around the deer's limbs as if giving her a warning.

Did those roots just move?!

My eyes widened, but Celine reacted as if nothing happened. Maybe I was seeing things.

"I do not know," she admitted. "Not fully. The forest does not behave as such. Not naturally."

She knelt down, interlocked her fingers backwards and made her thumb tips touch at the top. Then, she whispered something, and gave a nod to the remains before standing back up. "But it has been happening more frequently. In plain, the land has given up."

"Given up?" I repeated, unsure if I'd heard her right.

"Would you not have, Drifted?" Sabrina chimed in, giving the same gesture to the corpse Celine had. "Would you not be upset had you been made to hold so much carnage?"

I blinked. "Wait, what does that even mean? Angry? The land is angry?"

Sabrina turned to me, and for a moment there was no sarcasm in her voice.

"You are not yet ready to understand," she said.

I frowned. "Why not?"

She tilted her head slightly. "Because you do not yet know where you stand. And it is not my place to decide when you will."

432

I stared at her, lips parted. Yet again, Sabrina was withholding information from me.

"Then who gets to decide, Sabrina?!" I yelled. "Who gets to decide when I am ready?"

"The moon," she said simply.

I blinked. "The moon?"

I looked at Celine, but she said nothing. Her expression had grown distant again.

The moon? I thought. How the hell does the moon decide anything? It's a rock?

I stepped forward. "Sabrina, what does that even—?"

She turned briskly and walked away.

"We must move," she said over her shoulder. "If we do not hurry, we shall not get the chance to set up camp before nightfall."

Celine turned to me with sorrow in her eyes. I knew that she too didn't have all the answers and that my confusion conflicted her. With a nod, she turned to follow Sabrina.

I stood there for a moment, gripping the strap of my cloak.

So that was it. Another question left hanging in the air.

I let out a heavy breath and then followed after them.

Eventually, Sabrina led us to a rocky overlook with narrow, uneven terrain.

I stepped past her and looked out across the ridge.

There it was, Thornwallow.

It rose in the distance, some miles away, a broken shadow at the edge of the dying forest. The large, blackened tree I'd seen earlier was even more disfigured up close, its limbs gnarled as they slouched. Beneath it, the homes—if they could even be called that—seemed to bleed into the earth, low and sunken, wrapped in thorns at the base and flickering with dim light.

Sabrina crouched in an area of empty land, sweeping it

with her hand before setting her gear down.

I turned to her. "Why are we stopping here? Why not head in now? It'll be dark soon. Wouldn't that make it easier to sneak around?"

She looked up at me.

"Sure. Easier for us." She pulled a roll of cloth from her satchel and unfurled it. "But all it will do for you is make it harder to see the ones attempting to kill you."

I opened my mouth, but she shut me up.

"We see well in daylight and darkness, Drifted. You do not. Best we not stumble into some guards because your eyes can not keep up."

I turned away, jaw tight. Even as forward as she was, she had a point.

Still, I needed to move. Sitting still with my thoughts twisting like the roots around us wasn't helping. I stepped toward the edge of the camp, into the treeline.

"Where are you going?" Sabrina called out, without looking up from the gear she was unpacking.

"To get firewood," I muttered.

She straightened quickly, her red eyes locking onto me. "You shall give away our position."

I paused mid-step.

"This close to the town," she continued, her voice suddenly dead serious, "one wrong sound, one miscalculated move, and you shall be dragging enemies straight to us."

I clenched my fists. "Then what do you expect me to do? Sit here and be useless?"

Neither of them answered.

I looked between them, my voice rising enough to let the edge slip out. "He's close, Sabrina. My uncle—he's down there somewhere. That's why we came out here. Have you forgotten?"

Sabrina rose to her feet slowly, dusting her hands as she fixed on me with a look that burned.

"If you want to get your uncle and yourself slaughtered, then by all means," she said coldly. "Attempt to gather your sticks. But I swear by the moon, Drifted, I shall beat you senseless before I allow you to jeopardize Lady Celine and me as well."

My blood rose, and I took a step toward her, fist clenched. "What did you just say?"

"Enough," Celine said, stepping between us.

She turned between the two of us. "Arguing among ourselves will not change our situation. Nor will it bring us any closer to our goal."

Her eyes lingered on me. "We must be still now. Quiet. Focused."

I took a breath and took a large step back.

Sabrina said nothing more. But she didn't look away either.

I dropped to the ground with a heavy sigh, crossing my arms tightly across my chest.

"Whatever," I muttered. "I'm leaving at the first sign of daybreak."

Celine turned her gaze to me. "Yes," she said softly. "That plan is desirable."

I didn't answer—too upset. I kept my eyes low.

The night dragged in, thick and strange.

Without a fire, it felt colder than it should have. I couldn't see more than a few feet ahead of me. Even the moon, which had followed us faithfully across so many nights, seemed dimmer here.

Out of the corner of my eye, something moved.

Sabrina extended her hand, holding out a small bundle of nuts and dried roots in her palm.

I glanced at her; then turned my face away briskly.

"Still upset with me, Drifted?"

I didn't answer.

She sighed dramatically. "Hmm… I know what might fix it."

I frowned.

"Perhaps another kiss," she mused. "Like the one I gave you when you first woke in Sylphreach. That seemed to work wonders last time."

My face flushed instantly as I whipped my head around. "Shut up."

"A kiss?" Celine asked.

My heart stopped.

"Huh? No—I mean, what? I—I have no idea what she's talking about," I stammered, waving my hands vaguely in front of me like that would help.

Sabrina let out a breathy laugh. "Oh, how could you forget, Drifted? It was our very first interaction."

"Sabrina, shut up," I muttered again, louder this time.

Celine tilted her head. "What is… a kiss?"

Both Sabrina and I went completely silent.

I slowly turned my head toward Celine. Sabrina did the same.

"Oh, Lady Celine," Sabrina said, her voice full of surprise, "surely you know what a kiss is."

Celine shook her head.

My jaw dropped. There was no way she was being serious.

Sabrina chuckled softly. "Well… you see, it is the way humans show affection toward one another," she explained. "Albeit a strange way to show it, if you ask me."

Celine nodded slowly. "I see."

"It's more than that," I added. "It's usually meant for someone you're… close to. Someone special to you."

Sabrina gasped, pressing a hand to her chest. "Oh? So I

was special to you, then?"

I glared. "That's not what I—"

She cut in, grinning. "It cannot be that special if you have already forgotten the one we shared."

I sighed and pinched the bridge of my nose, wishing I could disappear from existence.

"Why have we not shared one?" Celine asked, looking straight at me.

I froze. And in that moment the forest fell completely silent.

"...What?" I managed to croak, lowering my hand.

Celine turned her body to me, staring me down with her a look that made my chest hurt. "I have known you longer than Sabrina," she said plainly. "I have fought beside you. Trusted you with my life. If such gestures are reserved for those who are special to you, then I find myself wondering... why have we not shared one?"

My brain short-circuited. There was no right answer to that question.

I opened my mouth, but nothing came out.

"Well," Sabrina said, letting out a low whistle. "I am sure Drifted would just love that."

I turned to glare at her, but she ignored me and placed a hand on Celine's shoulder. "Though I wouldn't want you to catch anything, Lady Celine."

I groaned and dropped onto my back as I covered my face with both hands. I wanted to disappear. To sink into the dirt and vanish. I didn't know how to answer Celine. I didn't even know if I could.

But I could feel her eyes on me—calm, curious, patient. "Drifted?"

I rolled over, turning my back to her. This wasn't a problem I was equipped to solve.

Behind me, I heard Sabrina's voice again—low, almost gentle.

"In due time, I am sure, my Lady. I think we have broken the poor boy," she said. "Now... do try to get some rest."

I closed my eyes, trying to force myself asleep. But between the silence of the woods, the awkwardness of Celine's question, and the ever-present danger of Thornwallow ahead... sleep would not come easy.

CHAPTER 33

A strong gust of wind slipped through the trees, waking me from sleep.

The sky above started to brighten as the last of the stars vanished into the light of the morning. My back ached from the root I had rolled on in my sleep, and the air was cold enough to make my throat hurt.

Celine was already awake, sitting cross-legged with her back against a tree. Her hood was drawn, and her eyes were focused on something only she could see.

A soft rustle from my left drew my attention. Sabrina emerged from the brush and crouched beside us, brushing dirt from her knees.

"The sun is nearly up," she said. "We move as soon as it breaks."

I nodded, though I couldn't keep the nervousness from curling in my stomach.

Sabrina let the silence linger before speaking again—this time quieter. More serious.

"Thornwallow is not like Sylphreach," she said. "There are no gentle paths, no hidden kindness. If they so much as catch your scent, Drifted... there will be blood."

She unclasped the fastener at her throat and slipped off her cloak, tossing it toward me. "Wear this."

I caught it awkwardly; it was still warm. It smelled like pine, sweat, wet stone.

"You're kidding," I muttered, wrinkling my nose.

"Worked up quite a sweat these past few days," she said, her tone far too casual for my comfort. "That should help mask you—at least for a little while."

I looked down at the moist cloak in my hands, then back up at her. *Gross.*

"If you refuse to wear that, we shall be caught before we even get started."

I sighed, removed my cloak, and then pulled her fur one over my shoulders, trying not to breathe in too deep. It was heavier than mine, and a little damp near the collar.

Sabrina cleared her throat before speaking again.

"Our plan is simple. We move unseen and unheard. Through the outer sprawl, past the broken terraces, and into the central heart—where the tree stands. No detours. Fight only if we must. Anything else puts us in danger."

She looked between Celine and me.

"As you both have experienced firsthand, the Lupine here are not like those back home. They were born into hatred. As such, that is all they know."

"If anyone sees us, if even one of them notices us moving through their streets, we risk losing everything."

Her voice dropped a few decibels. "There is a substantial chance that we do not make it out of there alive."

I looked down at the ground as a strong sense of guilt started building in my stomach.

Every step that these two were making toward Thornwallow was for someone they didn't even know. A cause they agreed to with no personal ties to my uncle. And yet, they were here, following me into a den of wolves ready to tear us apart in an instant. What made it worse—it was all for me.

I trembled as I stared at the ground, my hands balling up against the forest floor. What was I doing? How could I have been so selfish?

"Hey...you two..." I started with a weak voice. "Maybe you

guys should sit this one out."

I looked up slowly as they stared at me in silence.

I heard soft footsteps approach, and a moment later, felt the weight of a hand settle on my shoulder. Celine's voice followed.

"We shall not fail here," she said. "We have come too far for doubt, too far for regrets. Do not carry burdens that are not yours alone to bear."

I glanced over my shoulder, and she met my gaze.

"There is purpose in what we do," she continued. "And I have chosen to see it through. Not only for the one we seek… but for you, Drifted."

Sabrina scoffed. "And besides, Drifted. There is no possible way I am letting you have all that fun on your own."

She stretched her arms above her head and rolled her shoulders. "Not to mention… If we let you go in alone, who would be there to drag your remains back out?"

A slight smile tugged at the corners of my lips. Even with her teasing, I could feel the warmth in her words. They had my back. Not because they had to... but because they wanted to.

And in that moment, even with danger so close by, all I could feel was gratitude.

I gave them both a strong nod. "Right, then let's do this!"

An hour passed as we moved in silence toward Thornwallow.

Sabrina stayed a few paces ahead of Celine and me, weaving us through the more tangled branches that covered this area. She opted for a wide approach—one that kept us far from the beaten trails, far from any patrols that might wander too close to the outer section of the town.

Every so often Sabrina raised a hand—halting us to stop. Her ears would flick and swivel toward some distant sound. I never heard what she did. But I could tell, just from the way her posture changed, that something out there had caught her attention.

We waited during those moments. Deathly still, breaths held. Then, with a slight nod or twitch of her hand, she'd move again, and we'd follow.

It felt like hours passed that way. Moving when she moved. Stopping when she stopped. Until finally, the forest thinned out.

Ahead, through the last line of trees, I saw our destination.

Sabrina waved her hand quickly, and we each split to cover. I pressed my back against the rough bark of an old trunk, its surface damp and cold beneath my fingers. Carefully, I leaned forward enough to see past the edge.

Thornwallow.

The surrounding forest had already been bleak, but the city itself was worse—like the land had been drained of life entirely. There was no green here. No vines curling around stone, no patches of grass between the paths.

The haze hung over everything. It was low and thick, covering the shapes of the buildings ahead. Much like Sylphreach, the structures here seemed to grow straight from the large tree toward the back. Though they were rougher here, less symmetrical.

The people I noticed moved slowly. Some alone, others in tight-knit pairs, wrapped in thick dark cloaks or leathers the color of dried blood. Their faces were stern and grim, like the town had fed on their joy. They fit the scenery all too well.

I swallowed hard, shrinking back behind the tree.

Sabrina crouched low, and peeked over her shoulder, scanning the town.

"That is the first patrol ring," she said. "They walk in overlapping patterns. Three pairs, one loop every fifteen minutes. We move when the second pair vanishes behind that far building."

"We shall cut through that lower grove—see that slope by the hollowed trunk?" She pointed with two fingers, just barely above the tree bark. "That shall lead us behind the older dwellings. We take that path. Quietly."

I looked at Celine, and we both gave Sabrina a nod.

Sabrina took a deep breath and then turned to face the town.

"Alright," she whispered. "Prepare yourselves."

She slipped out from behind the trunk, crouching low as she darted toward the slope. As quickly as she moved, she still managed to do it quietly, even as her boots brushed over the ground.

We waited until she raised her hand from across the way— two fingers, a quick flick.

The three of us moved from tree to tree, closing the distance between us and the town. Several beads of sweat rolled down my forehead as we broke free from the forest completely and crossed into the border of Thornwallow itself. There was no transition, no thresholds. The same dark soil and unnatural mist curled at our feet.

Sabrina led us toward a small, slumped building that looked half-swallowed by the base of a twisted root. Its wooden frame was dark, warped, and partially overgrown with thorns. She crouched beneath a low overhang on its side, peering around the far corner.

We caught up behind her and waited while she peeked over the next corner.

She glanced back, nodded, and then moved again, slipping around the edge. Her hand shot up, signaling for us to stay put. Then a slow wave, calling us over.

We crept behind her, staying as low as possible and trying to make as little noise as we could. It was much easier for Celine, given her Lupine blood. But I had to try extra hard with my clumsy human limbs.

We moved with the natural curve of the buildings, wrapping wide to remain unseen.

As we got to the next building, Sabrina's head twitched toward the left, and her ears perked up.

I froze in place, and Celine beside me did the same, already still before I'd even processed the sound.

There was a faint scraping sound that paused and resumed periodically. Someone was close.

Sabrina knelt down beside a broken beam. Then, right as the mist parted, we saw the source of the sound. Two figures further up the path, walking shoulder to shoulder. Both wearing dark leathers, one of them carrying what looked like a lantern on their hip.

A patrol.

Sabrina didn't move, her back tight and arched with tension. We watched as they turned the corner a few paces ahead.

I held my breath as best as I could, slowing pulling the cloak Sabrina gave me up to my mouth to cover even the slightest scent of my breath.

When the faint clinking of their steps finally faded, I eased the tension in my shoulders a bit.

If they had just looked behind them, or turned their heads over so slightly before they hit the corner. We would've been done for.

Sabrina looked back, motioning us forward. We moved to her position one at a time.

"We are headed for the tree now," she whispered. "If

Cassius is anywhere, it shall be there."

"The closer we get to the center, the thicker the patrols will most likely be. From this point on, the path will be more crowded. I shall do what I can to guide us through it, but you both need to be ready."

She tapped two fingers against her temple. "Eyes up. Every corner. Every rooftop. Every open window. Assume we are being watched. Assume someone is listening."

She scratched her chin before continuing. "If we are lucky, we shall not have to fight at all."

She paused, and added dryly, "But luck has not exactly been our closest ally lately."

We moved deeper into the city. The path narrowed as the buildings pressed in around us. The homes were a bit different from the ones on the outskirts. They were more hunched, crooked things, stacked close together like they were hiding from something.

Sabrina led us into a tight and damp alley. The passage curved beneath a windowsill at the base of a home lifted by thick wooden stilts.

We moved under it, but as we reached the middle, a subtle creak came from above.

All three of us froze instantly.

The sound of boards groaning inside came out. A soft thud followed. Then another.

Then, voices came from inside the house.

"What is it?" a voice said—muffled.

"I hear scurrying behind the house," came the reply. Male. Low and suspicious.

A pause. Then, "Ah, do not bother. It is probably just vermin running about."

"No, I do not think so," the voice replied. "It is probably those children again. I warned them not to play back there."

I pressed my back hard against the wooden frame, holding my breath. Beside me, Celine's ears turned as she listened to the footsteps within the structure.

The boards shifted again as footsteps began moving further away from the window.

Straight toward the front door.

My stomach knotted, but I didn't have time to dwell on that. The sound of a wooden door being pushed open floated through the air and then footsteps approaching—fast.

I turned my head slowly, glancing back down the alley we had come through. The footsteps were already right around the corner.

Damn it.

I turned back, ready to ask what we should do. But there was no one beside me. Celine and Sabrina were both gone.

I looked around frantically. Where could they have gone so quickly?

I felt a tap on my head.

I looked up to see Celine peering down at me from the rooftop above. She didn't say anything, holding her hand out.

They scaled the building that fast?

I took her hand and quietly scrambled my way up after her, trying not to think about how much noise I made as I avoided thorns on the way up.

I rolled onto the roof, laying as flat as possible, like Celine and Sabrina were doing.

As I huddled beside them, I heard the footsteps circling below. I desperately tried to control my breathing to keep us concealed.

Then the voices came through again.

"You see? I told you it was nothing," said the first voice.

"No." The second replied. "I heard it without any doubt. Someone was here."

"Oh, do give it up, dear." The first voice spoke again. "As we both see, you are being paranoid."

Some silence stretched before the male spoke again.

"I am going to check the roof."

My blood turned cold.

I slowly turned my head toward Celine. She was already looking at me, holding a finger up to her lips.

I took a low breath, trying to calm myself, though I'm not sure it was working.

As I looked past my boots, I saw tan fingers curled over the edge of the roof's ledge. Gripping it tightly.

They were seconds away from cresting. We were trapped and had no escape. Were going to have to fight our way out of Thornwallow.

A loud whistle rang through the air, echoing through the alleyway.

A voice, distant and commanding, came after:

"Inhabitants of Thornwallow, gather near the inner terrace. The King has returned. Your Majesty approaches the Root."

The hand on the ledge hesitated.

"Dear, get down, The King returns!" The woman yelled.

"But—" The man started before being cut off.

"No buts. I am not risking a flogging for you. Now let us go!"

The hand released with a frustrated huff.

I stayed still, listening as the footsteps quickly faded down the alley.

Only when the last echo disappeared did I let out a slow, trembling breath.

"That was close," I whispered.

Sabrina crawled on her elbows, slinking across the other end of the rooftop. She reached the edge and peered over with only the smallest portion of her head visible.

She motioned us forward.

Celine and I followed, keeping low, careful not to disturb even a loose splinter of wood. We pressed up beside Sabrina and slowly peered over as well.

Below, a decently sized crowd had gathered. Their heads bowed low, and their shoulders hunched as they raised their arms up, palms facing the sky.

Through the center of the crowd walked a man draped in heavy robes. A large pelt that looked to be made of bear fur with black jewels hanging from it. A cloak hung from the man's shoulders, clasped with a metallic crest I couldn't make out from this angle. The way the people reacted, and the way he moved—there was no mistaking who he was.

"Cassius?" I whispered.

"Mhm," Sabrina replied.

My eyes drifted behind him. Another figure followed, much slower, shuffling their feet.

They wore a thick and tattered cloak that nearly dragged on the ground. Their hood was pulled low over their heads. I couldn't see their face—but the way the figure walked, limping, shoulders sagging, made my stomach twist.

The figure turned slightly to be berated by a guard. The hood slipped, just for a slight moment.

The edge of it fluttered back enough for me to see the side of the face—sunken, pale, and bruised, was the unmistakable profile of my uncle.

My body moved before I could think straight, and I started to rise instinctively.

Celine's hand was on my shoulder in an instant. I turned to her, and she shook her head slowly.

"He's right there," I whispered desperately. "That's him. That's my uncle!"

"You rushing in will be a death sentence for the both of you." Sabrina's voice cut in.

I froze, but my hands wouldn't stop shaking.

"We do this quietly," she continued. "Or we have no chance of getting out of here with our lives."

I opened my mouth to protest, but Sabrina cut me off.

"We know where he is now, Drifted." She said. "We should be able to reach him soon."

I swallowed the fire that was burning in my chest and forced myself to nod. Every fiber of my being knew she was right, and I hated it.

Reluctantly, I lowered myself back against the rooftop, just in time to see my uncle disappear beneath the shadow of the large black tree—following Cassius and the guards into its hollow entrance.

He was right there. So close, he probably would've heard if I yelled his name.

But this wasn't the time to be reckless. Not yet.

CHAPTER 34

We kept to the edges of the town, slipping between the shadows of buildings and overgrown roots. The streets were busier with Cassius' arrival, but they still felt hushed in a way that made each step louder than it should've.

The sight of my uncle hadn't stopped playing in my head since we left the rooftop. Uncle Alfarr, alive... and being corralled like cattle made my blood boil.

Sabrina moved ahead of Celine and me. She hadn't spoken since we dropped down from the roof, focused on navigating us quietly. But every so often, she'd glance back to make sure we were still close.

"Are you alright?" Celine whispered beside me.

"No," I replied.

"It would have worried me if you replied otherwise." She added.

We turned another corner and descended a wooden flight of stairs that led toward the main courtyard that sat right at the base of the massive tree. We were close.

We stopped at the bottom of the stairs, and Sabrina motioned us forward to look past the edge of the wall her back rested on.

The courtyard was more open than the alleys and areas at higher elevation. Cracked wooden paths curved around dark root beds and crooked lampposts, most of them long since burned out.

Thankfully, the crowd that had gathered earlier to greet Cassius had dispersed, probably going back to their mundane lives. This left a clear path to the main tree.

The tree wasn't alive, not in the same way the Elderwood was. It was massive, yes—but it looked sickly. The bark curled back in various places, flaking and bruised, oozing dark sap from deep splits in the wood. Its roots had swallowed half of the surrounding buildings, and what was left of the town clung to its base like dead moss.

A jagged doorway sat at the front of the tree. Two guards stood on either side of it; tattoos adorned their faces. One leaned back against the tree, yawning, while the other kept glancing behind him as though he feared being reprimanded.

Sabrina slowed her steps, then stopped. She turned her head enough to whisper over her shoulder.

"We make no sound, understood?"

"Wait," I whispered back, my brows drawing together. "We're going in straight through the front?"

She glanced at me, eyes half-lidded, like I'd asked her the dumbest question in the world.

"Aye, luckily for us, Drifted," she murmured, "Thornwallow is not exactly known for its hospitality. Next to no one ever wishes to come here... save for those already twisted enough to belong."

She nodded toward the guards. "Even then, their numbers are few. No one expects intruders in a place like this."

Celine's voice came next in a hushed whisper. "Which means we do not get a second chance if we fail."

I swallowed and breathed out. The thought kind of made my chest hurt.

"Right," I muttered. "But how are we going to deal with the guards out front?"

Sabrina turned a bit and flashed a smile at me. "One of us shall cause a distraction. The other two shall take them down before they can so much as blink."

I raised an eyebrow. "And by 'one of us,' you mean me,

don't you?"

She smirked faintly. "Well, you do look the most... out of place. Should not be too hard to draw their attention."

I frowned. "Great..."

"Listen, Drifted," she said. "The plan is fairly simple. You step out far enough to catch their eye. Trip over a rock. Do a silly little jig. I do not care how—just capture their interest."

"And then?"

"You lead them back here. Lady Celine and I will handle the rest."

I turned to Celine, hoping she would propose another idea that didn't involve me as bait. But she stood there, giving me a nod with an awkwardly held thumbs up. At least she was ready, I guess.

Sabrina gave me a pat on the shoulder. "Do try not to die," She said as she pushed me out into the open courtyard.

I stumbled forward, barely catching my balance as my boots hit the slick floor. The fog here was thinner—no more shadows to hide in. Only me, standing out in the open like an idiot.

The guards noticed me immediately. The one that was leaning straightened and squinted in my direction. His accomplice leaned forward and took a step forward.

"Oi," he called out. "Should you not be indoors at this time?"

I pulled my hood lower to conceal my face. If they figured out I was human, they'd surely raise the alarm.

I turned my back to them and kept quiet. I'm sure they would've been able to hear in my voice that I wasn't a Lupine.

"Hey!" the same one barked again. "Hard of hearing?"

Footsteps approached from behind me. Fast.

I stood my ground; eyes fixed on the staircase until I could feel their presence close enough. Once they were within a few feet, I started moving. Not too fast. But enough to bait them in.

"Halt!" One of the guards yelled behind me.

I didn't look back as I got to the staircase. To my surprise, when I reached it ... no one was there.

What the hell?! I thought to myself.

Where in the world could they have gone so quickly?

I froze as I reached halfway up the steps. There was nowhere left for me to run.

Behind me, boots slammed against the floor.

"Have you got a death wish, brother?!" one of the guards shouted.

I turned around slowly with my heart banging against my insides.

They stood at the base of the staircase now. One had his arms folded and the other tilted his head, narrowing his eyes to get a better look at me.

"Wait a moment..." he muttered. "Is that—? He is human!"

They started climbing the staircase.

My foot slid back instinctively as my brain screamed at me to run.

A slight shuffle came from above, and I looked just in time to see two blurs dropped down from the roofs above

The guards barely had enough time to look up before Celine and Sabrina landed on either one. In sync, they delivered quick blows to the backs of the guard's heads, immediately knocking them out.

Both bodies fell limp on the steps beneath me, folding awkwardly.

I let out a breath and then a loud huff.

"You guys could've warned me that was the plan, you know?" I said as I tried to calm my racing heart.

Sabrina stood up and dusted her hands off, glancing at me with a smile. "You were doing such a fine job panicking. I almost did not want to interrupt."

Celine stepped up quietly, shaking her head to clear the dust from her hair. "Come. The entrance will not remain unguarded for long."

The three of us moved quickly. I crouched beside one of the unconscious guards and hooked my arms beneath his shoulders. He was heavier than I expected—muscle wrapped in layers of damp furs that smelled like mildew.

Sabrina grabbed the other one by the ankles, dragging him with a bit less care. "You would think they would bother bathing," she muttered.

We hauled them around the side of a half-collapsed building, and into a narrow alley covered in shadows. I eased my guard down beside a mound of old crates while Sabrina plopped hers next to mine.

Celine stayed at the edge of the corner, watching the path.

When we were done, I stepped back and wiped my hands on my cloak.

"Let's hope no one comes looking for them."

"Hopefully by the time that occurs," Celine replied, already moving, "We shall be long gone."

We slipped out of the alley and crossed the courtyard in silence. I kept close to the others, eyes fixed on the massive tree ahead. The closer we got, the more unnatural it looked. The bark was somehow darker up close, with streaks of deep crimson running like dried veins across its surface.

Sabrina was the first to approach the entrance. She raised a hand as she neared it.

"Wait here," she whispered. "Allow me to check first."

Celine and I waited behind a thick outcropping of roots as Sabrina crept forward.

I watched as she got near the entrance, paused, and then disappeared into the black.

After a few seconds, her voice floated back through the air from inside. "Clear."

Celine moved, and I followed right after her.

As I got inside, the air that hit me was cold and stale. It almost felt like the walls were exhaling around us. The light was sparse, nearly nonexistent. Only thin slivers of red bled through the cracks in the walls, accompanied by the occasional flicker of a dim, half-spent torch.

The space was wider than it looked from the outside— much like the Elderwood. The interior stretched out in every direction, and the walls were lined with roots and overgrown shelves. And there, in the very center of the chamber, was a staircase.

It rose and wound upward through the center of the tree. Looking up, I couldn't even see the top.

"He's all the way up there, isn't he?" I whispered.

Sabrina turned her head to the air and sniffed before covering her nose. "Aye. He is there indeed."

Celine took the first step toward the staircase, testing it with one foot. It groaned slightly beneath her weight.

I went next, following behind Celine as Sabrina took up the rear. Each step of ours echoed faintly into the vast hollow above us. The air grew even colder as we climbed, and some low-hanging roots brushed our heads.

As we climbed higher, I caught glimpses of carvings in the bark—symbols that I couldn't decipher, warped and half-consumed by rotting wood.

"This place..." I whispered, eyes scanning the walls. "It gives me the creeps... I feel like it's listening."

Celine replied from in front of me. "It is."

She ran her fingers along the inner curve of the staircase's wall as she walked. "Even here... this tree is an extension of the Elderwood," she said quietly. "Twisted—yes, but still bound by root and breath to the same ancient body."

I scowled at the unsightly wood. "It doesn't feel anything like the Elderwood back in Sylphreach."

Sabrina chimed in from behind. "That is to be expected. Not after all the malice that has seeped into this place. The land remembers what its people carry. And Thornwallow has carried nothing but hatred for a very long time."

I frowned and kept walking, brushing aside a hanging root with thorns that caught on my cloak. "Then why doesn't the Elderwood stop feeding it? If this part is so rotted, why keep giving it anything at all?"

Sabrina let out a slow breath behind me—half sigh, half something like a laugh.

"Because the Elderwood is a home," she said. "A place meant for all Lupine to live, regardless of how far we think they have strayed."

She trailed her hand along the bark, her fingers dragging through a line of dark, sticky sap.

"In a sense, it serves the will of the Lupine people," she continued. "Whatever that will may be. Even if it turns wicked... the Elderwood only answers."

I looked around again. "So this," I muttered, "this is what answering looks like?"

"No," Celine replied quietly. "This is what happens when the answer is never questioned."

A few turns higher, we came to a narrow landing—just wide enough for two people to stand side by side. There was an opening to a corridor made of the tree wall, almost hidden by hanging thorns. Light flickered dimly from within, and with it, came voices.

Celine raised a hand, prompting us to stop.

"... Still no word," one voice muttered. "I would not be surprised if something has gone wrong. That thing was unsightly."

"Aye," another spoke. "I have seen grotesque before. But that one is sure to keep even the strongest willed up at night."

Celine turned to me, put two fingers up, and pointed toward the corridor.

Two guards.

She moved first—darting to the other side of the opening to position herself out of view on the far side of the archway.

I moved after, tiptoeing to the closest wall and pressing my back against it.

Celine looked at me and gave me nod. Then, she cupped her hands over her mouth and let out a quick whistle.

"...Did you hear that?" one guard muttered.

"Check it," the other responded. "I shall cover from here."

Footsteps followed, light and cautious. They drew closer— just one pair. Celine didn't move a muscle; she stayed so still I could barely make out the side of her cloak through the shadows.

A figure stepped around the bend, a tall male Lupine

As he got ready to turn his head in my direction, Celine snapped her fingers to distract him.

That was all I needed.

As he leaned forward to crane his head toward her—I lunged from the other side.

My arm wrapped around his throat, and I drove my weight into him, pulling him back toward my side of the wall. He struggled as I tightened my grip, brought him down to the floor, and with one swift strike to the temple—he went still.

The other guard's footsteps started quickly coming down the corridor.

Before I could look up, I saw Celine move. She slipped

into the opening, and after a short, muffled scuffle everything fell silent.

When I peered around the bend, I saw her standing over the second guard—a female—now slumped to the floor, unconscious.

Celine glanced up and gave me a quiet nod. "We must move. Their absence will not go unnoticed for long."

Footsteps approached from behind, and Sabrina stepped into the corridor with a soft clap of her hands.

"We need not worry about that," she said, her voice low. "We are already here."

Her eyes flicked to the guards on the ground. "Good work. Both of you."

Celine gave a quick nod and turned toward the far end of the corridor.

I stood, wiping my palms against my tunic as I followed them.

"Wait," I whispered. "You mean we're... we're already at Cassius' quarters?"

Sabrina responded with a serious look on her face. "There is no need to whisper anymore, Drifted."

She tilted her head, gesturing forward.

At the end of the hallway stood a large wooden door, darker than the rest of the tree around it—old, bowed with age and moisture. Twisting thorns wrapped along the frame like a natural barricade, some curling into jagged points as if warning anyone who dared to pass through.

"He already knows we are here," she breathed.

I stared at the door as my stomach felt queasy. It wasn't fear exactly—but something close to it.

Celine stepped ahead of us. Her movements tense as she reached the door.

She placed a hand on the knob, and her ears immediately

snapped upright, and she froze. Her body went rigid, and she held her breath.

"Celine?" I called out, taking a step forward.

She didn't answer.

I rushed to her side, Sabrina close behind. I placed a hand on her shoulder, feeling how tense she was beneath my fingers.

"Are you okay?"

Celine dropped the handle and let out a trembling breath. She stepped back, her breathing quick and unstable as she bent over, bracing herself with hands on her knees.

She lifted her head slightly, eyes fixed on the door, voice shaky.

"Ready yourselves," she said. "This shall be nothing like we have ever faced before."

CHAPTER 35

My hand hovered on the knob.

The wood was rough and cold as it pressed against my palm. Though I couldn't force myself to turn it. My pulse thudded somewhere between my ears, chest, and throat, drowning out any noise around me temporarily.

From the other side of the door came a dark energy. I couldn't quite explain what I felt, but it was unbearably heavy on my limbs.

It pressed against my thoughts and body with a thick presence that hung to my very bones. It was foul.

My body wanted to run, to escape the uncomfortableness of it all. But Cassius was in there, and with him, most likely my uncle.

I drew in a slow breath, then another. My foot tapped against the floor as I tried to settle the trembling in my arm.

Open the door, I told myself. *That's all you have to do. One turn. That's it.*

But I knew there was no turning back the moment I crossed this threshold. Hell, I could turn around here. Escape with Sabrina and Celine back to Sylphreach; try to devise a smarter plan to rescue my uncle.

If we came back with an army, then we would be able to save him easily. But would Rowen risk the lives of so many to save one person? That, I wasn't so sure of.

A hand slid over mine. Extremely warm.

I turned my head to see Celine standing beside me, her violet eyes connecting with mine without a word.

She gave me a nod, gripping my hand slightly tighter.

Sabrina approached my other side, placed a hand on my shoulder, and gave a nod of her own as well.

I returned their nods with one of my own and turned the knob.

The door groaned as it swung inward, its creak breaking through the silence.

Thick, stale air that carried a foul scent came tumbling out. It smelled of aged wood, old blood, and something else I couldn't pinpoint. I took one last breath before stepping in, letting the air fill my chest.

The chamber was enormous. Surprisingly so.

The first thing I noticed was how clean it was. The floor was smooth and looked like it had been polished to a dull sheen. Every object in sight looked like it was placed with obsessive care. A narrow desk rested on the right, empty save for a single quill and a closed book at its center. A row of shelves lined the left wall, and even the maps and trinkets within them looked untouched. Everything was positioned so precisely it made me feel as if my presence was ruining the aesthetic. Nothing in this room was left to chance. Even the silence felt arranged.

Toward the back, the tree's body opened into a vast hollow. Faint light from outside spilled in through it, but it was weak.

And there, right beneath the hollow, in the very center of it all, sat a man.

He sat in a tall, thorn-ridden chair made of the same twisted blackwood as the tree. The roots coiled tightly beneath him. His posture was regal—too still, too purposeful, as if he himself were carved from stone. One leg was neatly crossed over the other, and his fingers tapped on his lips as if in thought.

Jet black hair fell to his shoulder in smooth, deliberate

strands, clashing against his pale skin. His jaw was sharp, his nose well-formed, and in the darkness he sat in, I could see his eyes—a burning crimson that pierced with a cold judgment.

He didn't move. Didn't blink. He simply stared, like a man observing a game he'd already won. To top it all off, there was a smirk playing on his lips, as if we had arrived exactly when he expected us to.

Cassius. It had to be.

"Ah... the boy arrives," he said smoothly. "I had begun to wonder if you had lost your way here."

He leaned forward slightly.

"It is good to see you. I had feared you might have turned tail and ran."

"Well, this is disappointing," Sabrina spoke up, stepping up beside me. "No red carpet? No speech? And here I thought we were important guests."

Cassius' eye slid toward her—slowly, like he was glancing at a bug he hadn't decided if it were worth stepping on.

"And I see you have brought pests," he said. "Had I known you would arrive with such... company, I might have prepared someone to... entertain them."

His gaze shifted to Celine.

"You... have we met?"

The corner of his mouth curled. And he raised an eyebrow.

Before Celine could answer, Cassius looked up toward the ceiling and tapped a finger to his chin.

"Ah... no, that would be quite impossible." He said mockingly. "This one's leash seems a bit tighter. You lack the spine for a proper retort, girl?"

"Is this how you pretend to maintain control, Cassius?" Celine asked, tilting her head ever so slightly.

Cassius lowered his gaze slowly, and for a moment the

amusement in his eyes disappeared.

"A question?" he mused. "And from a stray, no less."

He uncrossed his legs and leaned forward more in his chair.

"I should not lower myself to such trivialities, but alas, every pup requires proper rearing."

"Girl, control is not something one feigns. Nor is it something that needs displayed. It requires no flaunting. True control is quiet—unshaken. There is no obligation for it to be announced."

"Those who must show their control are those who have a fear of losing it... and it simply remains that there are no threats to my control before me."

I hated how smug he was while facing three enemies before him. There was something in the way he spoke—in every measured word, every breath he took—that reeked of authority.

He didn't need to shout. I could tell the power he carried was woven into who he was. It was the way he sat, the way he moved, the way the air appeared to bend around him.

There was an energy feeding off of him—subtle, but smothering. The room felt chilly, yet I was sweating. My nerves spiraled, and it felt harder to breathe.

But through it all, one thought kept me composed.

My uncle.

The one who knew where he was sat in front of me, behind a mask of arrogance.

I clenched my fist and took a step forward.

"That's enough, Cassius," I said, trying to keep my voice as firm as possible. "You know why we're here."

Cassius' eyes snapped back toward me, and his smirk vanished. I felt myself shrink under his gaze. The resolve that had carried my voice forward wilted away. My lungs tightened, and my hands ran cold.

His voice was smooth, almost amused as he continued speaking.

"I beg your pardon?" he said. "You talk as though I should know what you speak of."

Before I could answer, Sabrina stepped forward, folding her arms.

"Perhaps your age is finally catching up with you," she said dryly. "Memory is a delicate thing, after all."

Cassius didn't even look at her.

"Oh, yes," he said, his tone laced with cruel satisfaction. "Perhaps you refer to that silly man I plucked right from that poor excuse of a town... what was it called again?"

He flashed a sharp canine right at me.

"Lunaria."

I felt my stomach drop and my jaw clench before I realized it. "Where is he?!" I yelled.

Cassius didn't answer.

He looked past me, as though I hadn't spoken at all.

"We were not even going for him, you know," he went on. "One of the children was supposed to be taken. A clean sweep. But your uncle—ah, so noble. So loud. He just had to try to make himself useful."

He waved a hand dismissively, as if swatting away an insect.

"He offered himself up in their place. How idiotic."

Lunaria. My uncle. The kids. The words twisted inside me. My hand moved before I could think, gripping the hilt at my side. The sound of the steel rang briefly as I pulled.

But by the time I could get the sword halfway out of the sheath, Cassius was already right in front of me.

His breath was cool against my ear, and I hadn't even seen him move.

"*Tsk. Tsk,*" he clicked his tongue. "There is no need to be so hasty... Drifted."

Time slowed to a crawl as the edges of my vision stretched out in front of me. I could hear my own heartbeat and the sweat trailing down my neck.

How?

How did he cross the room so fast? I hadn't blinked, hadn't looked away.

I only had enough time to tense my body before the world around me snapped sideways.

In a flash of movement, Cassius' fist hit me like a bolt. The impact sank into my stomach and tore the breath out of my lungs as I flew through the air.

"Drifted!"

Celine and Sabrina's voices overlapped each other as I crashed through the open space.

I barely saw them as I went flying—just two obscure shapes rushing forward—but I felt them. Two bodies slammed into mine, breaking my fall before I could hit the far wall.

Celine's arm wrapped around my back, and Sabrina sunk her shoulder beneath mine as their boots skidded across the wood, slowing the force of the blow.

The momentum carried us, and we slid until we hit the far end of the chamber with a thud. I didn't want to imagine what would've happened if they hadn't been there to absorb the impact.

I was on the ground—half curled, with both of them kneeling beside me. Celine held me upright, and Sabrina's hand gripped my shoulder.

Celine leaned in. "Drifted, are you harmed?"

I coughed, blinking through the taste of copper on the edge of my tongue.

"No, I'm alright. Thanks to you two."

I looked past them toward the center of the chamber, where Cassius stood still—arms behind his back. "How the hell is he so fast?"

"I told you," Sabrina said with her voice low. "He is unlike any other Lupine you have faced before."

Celine and Sabrina helped me to my feet before Sabrina continued speaking.

"It shall take the three of us in order to stand a chance," she continued. "And even then I am not certain it shall be enough."

Cassius turned and began walking back toward his throne, his boots echoing against the polished wood.

"Now," he said. "Is that enough to deter you pests?"

I looked at Celine, then at Sabrina.

My breath was still shaky, but my voice came through steadily. "Then we'll do it together."

Both of them nodded, almost in perfect unison.

"Right!" they replied.

Celine helped pull me the rest of the way to my feet.

I stepped forward, drew my blade, and pointed it right at Cassius.

Celine moved to my right and took a low pose. Sabrina took my left, already cracking her knuckles.

Cassius tilted his head slightly as he turned back to face us. He tapped a finger on his chin as if mildly curious.

"Hmm... how... peculiar," he murmured. "Even after witnessing how fruitless this battle shall be for you... you still persist."

He let out a slight chuckle and looked between Celine and Sabrina. "I thought you two were Lupine, no?"

"You both should recognize just how fruitless a battle this shall be... how very human of you," he continued. "Even when faced with certain death, your minds cannot comprehend when to capitulate."

His eyes fixed back on me again—burning with amusement.

"As if willpower alone could shift the outcome."

I held my sword in two hands, bringing it close to my body. My ribs throbbed, and my head still hurt. But I wasn't going to back down.

Not while these two were standing beside me. And not with my uncle here.

"You will give me back my uncle, Cassius."

A slow, mocking smile spread across his face.

"Are we truly still fixated on that?"

He clicked his tongue.

"No matter," he said. "Some things are easier to bury when the grief is still fresh."

With a shout, I rushed him, blade raised high in both hands. I could hear Celine and Sabrina closing in from either side, slightly behind me.

I reached Cassius first and brought the sword down quickly, aiming straight for his head.

He dodged. One step to the right—fluid and quick—and my blade swiped through nothing but air.

Before I could recover, Sabrina was already there, darting in from his right with a jab aimed for his ribs.

Cassius moved again with a slight twist of his torso to send her punch past him. Then, with a snap, he trapped her fist between his body and forearm, locking her in place.

Celine came in from the left now, her leg swinging high in a kick to drive him back. But Cassius was already turning—using Sabrina's momentum against her. He spun and shoved her into Celine. The two collided mid-stride and stumbled back.

I brought my sword up again, slashing as I tried to break

his defenses.

Cassius flicked his hand, clawed fingers deflecting the edge of my blade effortlessly.

"Come now, Drifted," he said, his breathing perfectly in rhythm. "You must be quicker than that if you intend to strike me."

I raised my sword again, and he twisted his arm up beneath mine, forcing my blade upward.

Before I could react, his palm drove straight into my chest. I got pushed back, feet skidding across the floor as I tried to catch my breath.

Celine and Sabrina were rushing back in now after recovering.

Celine struck from the right this time, a wide kick aimed at his midsection. Sabrina darted in from the left, with a pointed claw jab aimed at Cassius' throat.

Cassius didn't move from his spot. He blocked both attacks at once—one hand catching Celine's leg, the other maneuvering around Sabrina's claws and catching her wrist.

Then, in the same breath, he swung his body and threw them, one after the other, toward me.

They hit the floor hard, tumbling in a mess as they fought to recover. As the two of them reached me, they turned their bodies, skidding to a stop—each placing one hand on the floor, kneeling.

All three of us were panting, struggling to hold our formation.

I dragged in a breath. "We haven't landed a single hit on him yet."

Celine pushed herself up, brushing strands of hair from her face. "He has not even broken a sweat."

Sabrina groaned, flopping on her back for a moment. "Perhaps he will let us go train for a few years and then come back to try again?"

Cassius stood exactly where we'd left him—arms crossed over his chest, one foot lightly tapping the ground.

He looked... bored. Like we were wasting his time.

I forced myself up. There was no way I was going to allow him to mock us like this.

"We're not done," I said. "Sabrina. Get up."

She blinked, still flat on her back. "Oh—yes. Right."

She scrambled to her feet and shook out her arms like she hadn't gotten hurled across the room a moment ago.

This wasn't over. We were only getting started.

"Sabrina, you'll take charge. Celine, you take up the rear," I instructed.

They both looked at me with mild confusion on their faces before nodding in agreement.

"Ready?" I asked.

"Ready!" They replied in unison.

Sabrina darted forward first, closing the distance between her and Cassius in seconds. I followed close behind, taking up second.

As soon as she reached him, Cassius shifted his weight, pivoting on his heel.

He caught her strike and sent her flying sideways again, her body crashing to the floor.

I didn't slow down. I slashed hard at his center as I got to him.

Cassius turned, deflecting the blow again—but this time, I let the blade leave my hands, releasing it upward into the air.

A small shadow grew above me as Celine soared upwards, leaping up and catching the hilt of the blade.

She flipped the sword in her grip and angled it downward, the point of the blade aimed straight for Cassius.

She let gravity carry her down, her cloak billowing wildly

behind her.

Perfect, I thought to myself. Celine recognized my plan without any discussion.

Cassius moved, his arms rising to intercept the strike. But I was already prepared for that.

I lunged forward and grabbed his right arm, dragging it off course with all the strength I had.

I looked to my side to see Sabrina already there, grabbing his other arm.

Together we wrenched them apart, shattering open Cassius' guard, while Celine came crashing down.

We had him.

Time held its breath as I used every ounce of strength I had. Cassius' body tensed beneath my grip... and then went limp with the sound of blade meeting flesh.

My heart was pounding. Had we done it?

A few drops of blood hit the floor near my boot. Dark and heavy red.

I lifted my gaze slowly, panting in anticipation.

But what I saw made my stomach turn.

A wide, bleeding gash was carved across Cassius' cheek.

Instead of hitting its mark, my sword was buried in his upper shoulder instead. It was lodged, but far from fatal.

He must've turned his head at the very last second to avoid the full blade.

And there stood Celine.

Between him and us, hand still on the sword, panting heavily.

It wasn't enough.

Cassius tilted his head, and a shadow cast over the top half of his face.

Then he smiled. Wide and feral. Fangs glinting beneath his lips, teeth bared in a grin that stretched from ear to ear.

He started laughing. A low chuckle at first. Then it grew louder—rising into a full, unhinged cackle that echoed through the chamber.

His eyes were wide now, and he threw his head back.

"Oh... yes," he breathed, laughing still. "How long has it been since I have felt this? Real pain. True pain!"

His voice was almost ecstatic.

"This is what it means to be alive, is it not?" he snarled through laughter. "Exhilarating!"

He looked down at me now, eyes locked straight with mine as he hissed the words. "And no less... at the hands of Malikai's son."

I felt my throat tighten.

"We must retreat!" Sabrina shouted. "Fall back!"

Celine tried to wrench the sword free, but her footing stumbled. Her grip slipped, and the blade stayed buried.

We scrambled, all of us moving at once as Cassius stood there cackling.

"This is bad. Really bad," Sabrina whispered under her breath as we sprinted toward the exit.

I didn't know what was to come, but there was no way I was going to argue with Sabrina's intuition.

My brain screamed at me to keep moving—to run faster, to get out before whatever came next hit us. But then I heard from behind—

"Leaving so soon?"

Cassius' voice echoed through the chamber, deeper now. Somehow even more sinister.

A moment later, I heard the sound of something heavy hitting the floor with a clatter. Without turning, I knew it must've been my sword.

I felt the air stir—pressure, like the atmosphere had suddenly thickened. Cold and wrong, making my skin prickle.

A blur obscured the corner of my vision—too fast to register.

Something struck Sabrina. Hard.

She let out a loud yelp as something flung her body like a doll to the side. The crack of the impact thundered behind us.

"Sabrina!" I yelled, skidding to a stop.

I turned, but I didn't have time to see if she was okay.

In the next instant, something hurled Celine across the chamber, ripping her from my side. Her body hit the floor ahead of me, and she bounced across it before stopping in a heap.

"Celine!" I yelled out this time.

Another blur cut in front of my face.

I turned my head to see a wolf standing before the door we were running to.

It was large and black as pitch, its eyes bitter. It was sleek, controlled, and aware. Its coat seemed to drink the little light that was left in the chamber.

Cassius had taken his Lunar form. He was done holding back.

CHAPTER 36

I took a step back as Cassius slowly approached me. Each step he took was padded and quiet, but they still made my heart race. His black fur shimmered under the pale glow of the chamber as the light reflected off of him like some blade.

I reached for my sword, only to find my sheath empty, forgetting that Celine had dropped it behind me earlier.

I brought my hands up out of discipline. My stance was shaky, but I clenched my fist, just as I had been taught.

I'd trained for this. Weeks of being slammed into dirt, tossed through the air and lectured by Lood made it so I wasn't completely helpless.

But I doubted any of that would matter. Not against a foe like this.

In this form, Cassius would be even faster, and his instincts would be that much more heightened.

I dropped slightly, lowering my center. My breath came out unevenly as I forced it through my clenched teeth. I knew I wouldn't be able to take two steps before he was on me. I had to make a stand and defend myself.

Cassius began to circle left slowly.

I kept my eyes fixed on him, but his footsteps were barely audible—hell, my heartbeat was louder than each footfall. He might as well have been floating across the floor.

I turned as he circled me at a tighter angle, desperately trying to not lose sight of him. I didn't blink despite how much my eyes burned. My legs were braced and ready to spring the moment he made a move.

Then he was gone.

One second he was there, and the next there was nothing.

I hadn't looked away, hadn't gotten distracted for even a second. But he wasn't there anymore.

A chill ran through me as a gust of wind swept across my neck. I turned, spinning hard and swinging my fist wide.

My punch cut through the air. The space behind me was empty, and there was no sign of anyone having ever been there.

Then another gust—this one brushing against my back.

I spun faster this time, throwing a kick to the side.

Still nothing.

I steadied my footing, trying to think, but then—

Another shift of air, this time from the left.

I whipped around again, my body tensing for impact. A punch, a grab, anything.

The same damned nothing.

He was playing with me. Toying with me like this were some sick game. To him... maybe it was.

I spun again with my fists clenched so tight they ached. My back was slick with sweat. It was all pointless.

I blinked, and a shape materialized in front of me, and I froze. Cassius was directly in front of me.

His large body rested on his haunches like an oversized hound, posture relaxed, tail curled loosely around his side. He barely moved as he stared at me with those deep red eyes. I wanted nothing more than to wipe that unbothered look off his face.

I swallowed hard, but my throat was dry.

"Quit fooling with me!" I yelled as I ran at him, fist raised.

I didn't know what I planned to do. Land a hit? Scream in his face? I didn't know. Anything to take that smugness away.

The air shifted on my left, and pain exploded in my ribs as something struck me clean across the side—I got sent flying, but I twisted my body mid-air, catching myself. My feet slammed against the ground, and I planted my boots to keep from falling.

Before I could lift my head, another hit came. This one from behind.

I was sent forward, stumbling before hitting the ground with my hands and knees as the next blow came. This one was straight on, knocking my head backward.

Another hit from the right.

Then another.

And another.

I couldn't see him, couldn't follow his movements. He moved faster than I could think, faster than my eyes could track. All I could do was sit here and take it.

A strike to the back. A cuff to the side of the head. A slam to the ribs. Another to the spine.

I didn't know where the next one would come from.

I couldn't fight it.

I could barely brace for it.

Another strike cracked against my shoulder, sending me sprawling again. I groaned, coughing as I pushed myself up on shaking arms.

I can't see him. I thought to myself.

The torches started to smear, and my hands slipped on the sweat beneath them. My ears rang. My ribs burned, and panic threatened to consume me. I was immediately bracing for his next hit, and even that was too slow.

If I couldn't see his movements, then maybe my eyes were useless.

I stayed low, bowed my head, and shut my eyes.

I strained myself to focus. There was no point trying to track Cassius visually. My eyes were only slowing me down.

Pain pulsed through my ribs, my shoulder, my legs. My

whole body throbbed with every breath—but I shoved it aside.

If I can't see him… then maybe I can hear him. Feel him. Heighten every other sense—by cutting off the weakest one.

"Sight is a crutch. Instinct is far faster than thoughts." Lood's voice echoed in my ears.

The Lupine weren't so quick to react because of their natural speed. It was that they fully trusted their instincts, regardless if they could see what was coming or not.

Another shift in the air—too close—came from my right. I started to turn but was too slow.

A crack slammed into my side, beneath my arm. I bit back a cry, teeth grinding as I willed my body to stay straight.

Stay focused. I told myself.

I focused on my other senses and allowed everything to go still.

My mind—which was loud and frantic only seconds ago— quieted.

No thoughts. Only empty space.

The ache in my ribs dulled as my mind pushed the pain far away. My muscles loosened just enough to breathe again.

And in that stillness, I listened.

I could hear the air move. How it curled and slipped through the chamber. How it pressed against the floor, dragged along the bark and roots and shifted past my shoulders. I felt it as it brushed my skin—threading through the tiny hairs, stirring them one by one.

I could visualize it in my mind—the way it swirled when something moved through it. The shape of Cassius as it swirled around him.

I followed those patterns in the wind. Tracked the subtle changes in pressure. The slightest changes in sound.

And for the first time, I could tell where he was.

476

I visualized the wind as he ran circles around me in a weak tornado.

Then, it curved and funneled toward me, pushing a burst of air on my body.

He was coming straight toward me. Coming in for another attack.

I let out a slow breath as the air thickened.

Now!

I twisted my body and pivoted hard to the side.

Cassius tore past me, the gust of his momentum trailing behind him. His claws scraped against the bark as he slid.

I opened my eyes just long enough to see him whipping around, shaking his head in confusion.

I dodged him—barely—but it was enough to prove it was possible.

I was grinning now—shaking and bleeding, but smiling nonetheless. I could do this.

I closed my eyes again as the air shifted once more. He was coming in.

I locked my stance and grounded my feet.

This one, I told myself, *I'll counter head-on.*

The wind curled toward me. I felt it dance along my skin. The same funneling as before.

I followed it and waited, allowing it to get closer with a steady gust.

A few feet in front of me, the pressure suddenly spiked, and the wind howled.

A rush of air shot toward me, ten times faster than before. I barely had time to register it before Cassius crashed into my stomach like a battering ram.

I went flying as I was lifted off my feet. I crashed against the ground and rolled straight between Celine and Sabrina.

A low groan tore from my throat as I forced myself

upright. My arms shook under my own weight, and everything on my body hurt.

The difference in our battle histories was clear. Cassius hadn't been toying with me for amusement... he'd been watching me. Learning.

While I was scrambling to keep up, he was already three steps ahead.

He allowed me to think I could track his speed. Made me think I was adapting. But the truth was he'd never been moving at full speed to begin with.

He let me think I had a chance. Simply so he could rip it away.

Celine stirred beside me, her eyes fluttering open with a soft gasp. She winced as she moved, curling one arm around her side.

Sabrina pushed herself up slowly, breathing shallow and fast.

I looked at them both in disbelief as pain throbbed throughout every inch of my body.

"I tried," I said, my voice hoarse. "I thought... I really thought I could keep up with him."

I shook my head, jaw tightening.

"I don't know what to do anymore. I'm out of ideas."

Celine's eyes met mine, but she didn't speak. There was nothing to say. We were all out of ideas. Cassius truly was unbeatable.

I looked at them—Celine, trying to sit upright despite the pain etched across her face. Sabrina, resting on her hands, blood drying along her jaw.

I brought them here.

I brought them into this fight. Dragged them into a war that wasn't theirs, all because I thought maybe—maybe—we could save my uncle.

I clenched my fist against the ground as my eyes stung.

"Damnit!" I yelled out. "If only we were faster. Stronger. If there were some way to fight on his level. Why didn't I listen? How the hell did I think we could—"

My voice cracked, and I hung my head in defeat.

"I was stupid to think we could even stand a chance."

I heard Cassius whimper mockingly. Further pressing the weight of failure down on all of us like a boulder.

"Lady Celine—the necklace!"

Sabrina's voice suddenly snapped. She pushed herself upright, eyes wide now, focused on Celine.

Celine's head turned slowly, her expression tightening as if she already knew what Sabrina meant. Her hand shot to her chest.

Her fingers closed around a rope necklace just beneath her collarbone.

And from beneath the folds of her cloak she pulled into view a glass vial in the shape of a curved fang. Inside, was a dark and thick liquid, deep red.

I watched in confusion as she held the necklace up with both hands, bringing it to her lips. Her fingers moved toward the small cork at the top—

Then, in a flash, she was gone.

A violent crack split the air as Celine was launched backward from Cassius slamming into her from the side.

"Celine!" I shouted, scrambling up. Sabrina was right beside me as we ran to where she had landed at the base of Cassius' chair.

She groaned as we reached her, one hand braced on the ground, the other pressed to her ribs.

"Are you alright?" I asked, dropping beside her, trying to help her sit upright.

She didn't answer. Instead, she lifted her hand and pointed.

I followed her gaze to Cassius. He sat silently several paces away. Dangling from his mouth between long curved fangs was the necklace.

The vial swayed slightly with every breath he took.

"What... what was that?" I asked, turning to Sabrina.

Her wide eyes stayed fixed on the vial.

"That was our only chance of getting out of here alive." She replied, her voice shaky.

Cassius gave a slow exhale through his nose, something like a laugh, and took a step back.

Celine coughed, steadying herself with one hand against the floor. Her voice was strained, but clear.

"We must get that vial."

I looked at her, then at Sabrina, then back to Cassius.

I didn't fully understand what was happening. I didn't know what was in that vial, or why it mattered.

But if that was our only hope of surviving, then I wasn't about to let that go. Not without a fight.

I forced myself onto my feet.

"Alright," I said, fixing my eyes on the black-furred beast before us.

"Let's get it back."

Sabrina and Celine stood, and we slowly spread out.

Celine moved to the left with a limp, her palms open and ready to strike. Sabrina broke right; her eyes locked onto Cassius like a hawk.

I moved straight down the center, clutching my battered ribs.

Cassius barely stirred from his spot. He sat there, shaking the vial left and right while wagging his tail.

Celine lunged first—a jab to draw his attention. Cassius turned his body away from her, but that gave Sabrina the opening she needed.

She dashed in from the right, swiping for the vial.

Cassius pulled back quick, letting the strike pass through the air. But I was already moving.

I came in from the middle, trying to throw him off-balance. He turned away from me, retreating two steps back.

That's when it dawned on me: for the first time since this battle started, we had him on the back foot.

Behind him was a wall. And in that moment I'm sure we all understood what the plan was with no need to say anything.

Our only hope was to get him pressed up against it.

I looked between Celine and Sabrina. Both of them gave me a nod, solidifying our unspoken plan.

We pressed in again, tighter this time.

Strike.

Feint.

Circle.

Bit by bit, we pushed him across the chamber floor.

His paws slid across the wood beneath him, claws digging in, and I could tell that even he couldn't ignore the pressure building.

We moved again.

Celine darted in, forcing Cassius to turn away.

Sabrina followed tightly half a breath later, cutting off his escape to the right.

And I was there in the center, covering his only option left.

Cassius glanced over his shoulder once. His space was running out, and he knew it.

We had him right where we wanted him. There wasn't enough room for him to keep retreating. He was officially cornered.

I looked between Celine and Sabrina. They were both ready.

I ran forward, setting my target right on the vial in Cassius' mouth.

He tensed, and then leapt into the air, clearing me slightly. I went barreling past him, skidding hard across the floor with my boots to stop myself from hitting the wall.

Oh, no you don't!

I planted my foot, twisting hard to spin on my heel. My arms shot back as I pivoted, eyes locked onto him as he descended.

With me coming up from behind and him midair, there was nowhere else for him to escape.

I had him just where I wanted.

"Now!" I shouted.

Celine dashed in from the left, while Sabrina ran in from the other side.

All three of us converging at once—an ambush from every angle. The necklace swung wildly as he sank, a gleam of red catching the light.

We had him. We actually—

Cassius' form changed. Fur vanished, and his human limbs returned in an instant.

He placed a single hand on the top of my head as I came in from behind. His fingers gripped tight, using me as leverage.

Then, his legs split outward.

One heel cracked square into Sabrina's face, and the other slammed into Celine's jaw.

Both of them recoiled as their heads snapped back, falling to the floor hard.

The force of the push on my head knocked me to my knees as I struggled to catch myself.

By the time I turned and looked up, Cassius had already landed. Silent and unbothered.

He stood there, swinging the necklace from his fingers,

laughing.

A low, raspy sound escaped his lungs. Like it had been buried in his chest for years.

"You ought to see your expressions," he said. "The anticipation. The hope. And now... the bitter truth."

His eyes swept over us, full of venomous delight.

"You have failed—yet again. And I must admit..." He breathed in deeply, lips parting into a slow grin. "It is glorious."

He raised the vial to his face, turning it slightly as it caught the light.

Then he drew it to his nose and sniffed.

His brow furrowed as he sniffed again, slower now.

"...Blood?" he murmured. "Human blood?"

His nose crinkled. Confusion flickered behind his eyes.

Human blood? I thought to myself.

My eyes widened as the realization struck me.

The blood must've been mine. Had Sabrina collected it back in Sylphreach? Maybe she had Celine keep it with her in case of emergency, for cases like this?

If Celine had drunk my blood, she could've taken her Lunar form. The great wolf that she couldn't access on her own. The form that only my blood could unlock.

That form might have ended this.

Cassius looked at the vial once more, turning it slowly between his thumb and forefinger. His eyes drifted from the vial to me.

"I do not know what it is you three had planned," he said with a tilt of the head. "But the look upon your face suggests this was... important."

His lips curled into a creepy smile.

"Very well."

Without another word, he tilted his head back and

swallowed the vial.

Silence wrapped around the chamber like a noose. None of us moved. Not a breath. Not a sound. Celine was frozen beside me, and Sabrina was still half-curled on her side.

We had no plan now.

Cassius turned his back on us as if we weren't even worth watching anymore, strolling across the chamber floor. He moved toward his throne, where a thick wooden chest sat between thick trunks of the tree.

The sound of the latch clicking open was the only thing that broke the stillness.

He reached inside and pulled out a long, dark cloak. Slowly, he draped it over his shoulders and fastened it at the neck, covering his body.

"Why so quiet?" he asked, voice low and amused. "We were all having such a grand time just moments ago."

He glanced over his shoulder, smiling.

"But now? Now it seems you are taking this loss a touch too seriously."

He smoothed out the cloak with a slow brush of his hand, then cleared his throat.

"Guards."

The door behind us burst open almost immediately, the heavy creak of bark parting as a half-dozen figures rushed in.

"Keep the two girls company," Cassius said coolly, not even sparing them a glance. "The boy and I shall continue our little game… somewhere more private."

Before I could even react, he was beside me.

"Shall we keep the fun alive, son of Malikai?" he whispered into my ear.

His hand grabbed the collar of my tunic, and I was ripped from the ground.

I felt a strong rush of air slamming against my back as I

was launched sideways through the chamber.

Thrown like a rag doll through the wide opening in the chamber wall, out into the open air beyond the Elderwood.

"Drifted!"

I heard Sabrina and Celine's voices cry out as I flew past the edge.

I crashed downward, snapping through branches and thorn-covered limbs. Each hit sliced and tore as I fell helplessly.

A loud thud shot through the air as I hit the hard ground.

I groaned, rolling onto my side, as I tried to lift myself from the ground.

My vision swam in and out of focus as my head spun.

When my sight cleared, I could make out an open area of sorts—a large ring covered by wooden pillars, their tops etched with Lupine markings.

As I looked around, I heard slow, heavy chains dragging across the floor.

The hairs on the back of my neck stood up as I flopped on my back, still unable to right myself.

There at the far edge of the ring was a towering, hulking figure.

Gray-skinned, broad-shouldered. A mountain of muscle and rot.

A Fungoid.

It drooled as it strained against the iron chains that bound it to a pillar. It struggled and thrashed, desperately trying to reach me.

"What is the matter, Drifted?" I heard the cold voice of Cassius float down to me.

My head snapped toward it.

He stood atop one of the wooden pillars high above the ring, his cloak billowing slightly in the breeze, arms held out like he was presenting a show.

He tilted his head down and smiled.

"Were you not requesting to see your uncle?"

CHAPTER 37

I pushed my chest off the ground, the pain in my back still present from the fall.

"What? What do you mean?" I answered back to Cassius.

I looked around the ring. There was no one here. Beside the Fungoid and the rattle of chains behind me.

I stared back at him. "Where is he!?" I shouted, my voice cracking more from confusion than anger. "Let me see him!"

Cassius chuckled.

A low, throaty thing that echoed in the still air, far too calm for the madness swirling behind those red eyes.

"You already have," he said, his gaze never once leaving mine. "Though I wonder... do you not recognize him?"

My blood ran cold as Cassius slowly raised a hand and pointed to the thing behind me.

The chains rattled again, and I turned, almost too afraid to look. The Fungoid thrashed again. Patches of matted hair clung to the grey sinewed muscle beneath its head. Its jaws hung open uselessly, and thick dark ropes of drool fell from its mouth.

He's lying. He had to be lying.

I whipped back toward him.

"That's impossible!" I shouted. "My uncle isn't a fiend— what the hell are you talking about?!"

Cassius let out a cruel, hearty laugh. It echoed in the space like thunder, full of malice and delight.

"Well..." he said, resting his head on his knuckle, "it sure seems like he is to me."

Cassius stepped forward, slowly descending the pillar.

"Has no one told you, Drifted?" he said. "No wise scholar, no little wolf-girl at your side, not even your own father has thought to reveal it?"

He tilted his head, the smile on his face widening.

"Where do you think they come from?" he asked, voice calm but cutting. "These fiends you humans fear so dearly. Did you believe they simply manifested from thin air?"

My lips parted, but nothing came out.

My legs carried me backward before I realized it, my boots scraping the wood as I turned to look at the thing behind me again.

The Fungoid growled, and my head whipped around, staring at its features more closely.

I stared through the decay. Past the rot.

Those eyes.

The shape of the jaw. The old scar across the brow— barely visible beneath the filth and growth.

No.

No, no, no, no, no.

My stomach felt like there was a war raging inside. I slapped my hand over my mouth, choking back the vomit that surged up from my gut.

It couldn't be. How could this even be possible?

"Uncle..." The word slipped out. But it felt wrong.

Cassius clapped his hands slowly as he stepped behind the Fungoid.

"Ah, now you are finally catching on, boy."

He paced slowly behind the creature, fingers trailing along the thick chains binding it to the pillar.

"Indeed. This monstrosity here is your beloved uncle."

A roar filled my ears. It was so deafening that I thought I'd gone deaf.

I ran forward, rage pouring into my chest like a fire.

"What have you done?!" I screamed, voice cracking. "Cassius—what the hell did you do?!"

As I neared, he turned his head slightly to look at me from the corner of his eye. His voice was quiet.

"Do not blame me, human," he said.

Then he yanked the chain.

"Blame the very land you sullied."

With a snap, the iron links shattered, and the Fungoid came charging.

I threw myself sideways, rolling across the ground as the creature came crashing past where I'd stood.

By the time I got back to my feet, Cassius was no longer in the same spot. He had leapt back onto the pillar, now seated cross-legged on its edge. One arm rested lazily on his knee, propping his head up; the other was draped across his lap.

"I shall watch from above," he called down. "A family reunion deserves space."

He leaned forward slightly.

"Though do be careful, Drifted. Your uncle seems rather upset with you."

"Damn you..." I cursed under my breath, turning back toward the creature.

It stood hunched with its shoulders heaving, dark breath spilling from between rows of cracked, uneven teeth. Its arms twitched like it were itching to deliver its next strike.

I held up my hands in front of me, taking a few steps back.

"Easy," I said to the creature. "Please, calm down."

It was foolish. I knew that. It couldn't be reasoned with, but the odds of me defeating this thing on my own were next to impossible.

The Fungoid shrieked, prompting me to cover my ears. And then it charged again.

I dove to the side once more, rolling on my shoulder and

recovering quickly.

"Speaking to it? How precious," Cassius said with a laugh. "Is that what they teach you humans back home? That you can just reason your problems away?"

I spat the dust in my mouth onto the ground, staring at him in contempt.

"Do you believe that if you converse enough, it will remember you? Recognize you?" Cassius clicked his tongue. "Admirable. Naive, but admirable."

The fiend was already recovering, rising again with a snarl. Its arms swung wide, dragging claws across the ground, tearing shallow trenches in the wood.

I stepped back, readying myself to dodge, but this time it came faster.

At the last second, as I moved to dive aside, the Fungoid threw out one massive arm.

My eyes widened as I crossed my arms in front of my face. It barely helped. The clothesline caught me, sending my body airborne before I slammed back first into a nearby pillar. The force pushed the air from my chest, and I crumpled to the floor in a heap, wheezing for breath.

Somewhere above, Cassius gave an exaggerated wince.

"Oh dear," he called down. "You may want to focus, boy. That looked like it hurt."

I could barely hear him over the ringing in my ears. I managed to lift my head, though my vision was blurred.

The Fungoid was already towering over me, its fist raised high.

Move, Isaac. Move! My mind screamed.

I rolled to the side with everything I had as the fist came down like a hammer. It slammed into the pillar, splintering the wood and sending massive chunks flying in all directions. Shards flew across the floor. One struck my leg, glancing off my shin, but I kept rolling against the pain.

Dust filled the air as the pillar groaned, then collapsed fully behind me in a loud heap.

I scrambled away, heart pounding, chest burning from the particles in the air.

"Drifted!" the name came from higher above.

My head snapped up to see Celine. She and Sabrina stood at the edge of the opening. The guards had them held at the ledge, arms pinned behind their backs. One of the Lupine guards shoved Celine forward slightly, and she barely caught her balance.

"I figured your friends would enjoy watching the demise of the great Drifted," Cassius spoke with a yawn.

"You must fight back!" Celine shouted, her voice cutting clean through the chaos. "That thing is no longer your uncle!"

I felt sick to my stomach.

"He will not—he cannot stop," she said. "He will kill you, Drifted!"

I looked up at her, and then back at the creature, which was turning again, snarling.

I had no sword. No real plan. Only a truth that I wasn't ready to face yet. But I didn't have any choice.

The Fungoid was barging again, barreling forward with the weight of a collapsing mountain.

I darted to the side, feet stumbling as I pushed off a loose stone, barely staying ahead of its reach. My lungs burned, muscles screaming with every step.

There—up ahead—were the broken chains Cassius had snapped.

An idea struck. It was reckless and desperate, but it was all I had at the moment.

I bolted toward them, weaving between rubble, leading the fiend closer and closer. Its heavy steps shook the ground, making me stumble as I fought to keep balance.

I reached the shattered links and spun as the creature reared back.

It swung wide—I ducked low—and then bolted behind it.

I threw myself onto its back, arms wrapping around its neck as I dragged one of the chains with me. The iron scraped against my forearm as I looped it around the creature's thick neck, locking it in place and pulling with every ounce of strength I had left.

The beast thrashed and roared. Jerking and throwing its body side to side as it tried to throw me off. I tightened my grip and planted my feet against its back, using them as leverage to pull harder.

"Come on... go down," I muttered through clenched teeth.

It roared again and, in a wild panic, slammed its head against the pillar in front of us.

A loud crack filled the air as the pillar split. The fiend stumbled, then collapsed backward. I jumped off its back as it went down to the ground and rolled across the rubble.

The Fungoid groaned, its limbs twitching weakly as it lay sprawled out on the floor.

Cassius' voice floated down from above like a smug breeze. "Ooh," he said with a low chuckle, "Smart move."

"Drifted! End it now!" Celine yelled down. "You must end it before it can recover!"

I looked around frantically.

My eyes caught a long shard of splintered wood. Its edge was jagged and crooked. It would be strong enough to do the job.

I rushed toward it and gripped the large shard with both hands.

I turned back to the fiend. It was shaking as it tried to clear the confusion from the hit it took.

I stepped forward, my breath heavy as I raised the splinter high above my head.

"Now is your chance, Drifted!" Sabrina's voice joined Celine's from above. "Do it!"

I stood over the creature, arms raised, the fragment ready to fall. All I had to do was bring it down.

I looked at the Fungoid again. Its head turned slightly, dazed and weak.

Just. Bring. It. Down. I thought to myself.

The Fungoid looked up at me, and our eyes met.

They were sunken, dulled by whatever horror had taken hold of it—but they were his.

They were my uncle's eyes.

My grip loosened as my throat tightened, choking back spit.

Suddenly, the weight of what I was about to do felt heavier than anything I'd ever carried.

My arms trembled, and the wood felt like lead in my hands. I stared into my uncle's eyes, and my legs buckled. My arms lowered, and the shard slipped from my hands.

"I can't..." I said, my voice choked back. "I... can't do it"

The room fell silent momentarily.

Then Cassius' voice echoed down, steeped with mocking disappointment.

"Oh, such a shame," he sighed. "We were just getting to the best part."

The Fungoid moved, and before I could react, a rough hand latched around my ankle.

My eyes widened in disbelief as it stood up fully.

"Drifted, no!" Celine screamed.

But it was too late.

The next thing I knew, I was upside down with the landscape spinning violently.

My uncle hoisted me into the air and then slammed me down with all his strength, sending me straight toward the ground.

I twisted at the last second, tucking my head into my arms and shifting my weight sideways to soften the blow.

I hit the ground hard.

A searing pain exploded in my right arm, and I screamed in agony, immediately knowing that it was broken.

I clutched my arm against my chest. Every movement sent a fresh wave of pain throughout my body.

The world spun in a haze of pain and dust—but even through the blur, I could see my uncle's face.

He loomed over me now, a large broken shadow who snarled and drooled. Pieces of the shattered pillar clung to his back, and blood—mine or his—dripped from his hands.

He raised one massive foot, hovering it above my head.

I stared up with a mixture of disbelief and resignation, my good arm pushing helplessly against the ground behind me.

I turned my head to the side. There was nothing I could do.

His foot began to descend, and I watched as the shadow closed in on me.

But it stopped abruptly before it could end me.

A pale hand clutched the creature's ankle, halting it mid-motion with ease.

Cassius stood there beside me now, his head tilted slightly as he smiled up at my uncle.

"Tsk, tsk, tsk," he clicked his tongue. "This reward is mine alone."

And without another word, he twisted.

The sound of bone breaking snapped through the ring, and Uncle Alfarr let out a roar of pain, collapsing to one knee.

Cassius sauntered behind him, raised one clawed hand,

and poised it right above my uncle's back.

My eyes widened.

"No..." I croaked. My voice was barely a breath. "What are you doing...?"

Cassius looked down at me from over Uncle Alfarr's with a straight face, voice full of smugness.

"What does it look like?" he said with a shrug. "Cleaning up your mess."

He thrust his hand forward, burying his claws straight through my uncle's back. His hand came out on the other side, twitching in satisfaction.

Uncle Alfarr tensed, then howled loud and long.

Cassius' hand remained buried there, his arm slick with blood. My uncle twitched once... then slowly sagged forward.

I stared—unable to move, unable to speak. Unable to scream. My broken arm pulsed with pain, but it felt far away now—like it belonged to someone else.

My uncle's head turned slightly.

And for a moment—just a moment—its eyes changed.

Gone was the clouded rage, the hollow, monstrous haze.

They were clear. They were my uncle's eyes.

They met mine, soft and tired, full of something I couldn't understand.

Then, his mouth moved.

"I... Isaac?"

The voice was weak and warped. But it was his.

"Why are you crying?" he asked. "Did you fall from that tree again?"

My lips trembled.

"If your aunt sees you..."

His head slumped forward, and he went still.

I stared at him—frozen.

The sound of blood dripping echoed in the silence.

Cassius pulled his arm free and shook it off, splattering blood across my face.

He glanced down at me, brushing back a speck of dust from his cloak with the back of his claw.

"...Touching," he said flatly.

I don't remember breathing.

All I remember was the feeling—

Anger.

Pure, white-hot.

Rising beneath the weight of the shock. Curling in my chest like a fire desperate to burn through the numbness.

My uncle was gone.

I hadn't done anything.

Cassius tilted his head, studying me. His lips curled into a frown, though it was anything but sincere.

"You wear such a face... grief, was it?" he murmured, his voice slow and deliberate. "Yet your anger—Drifted—it is mislaid."

He stepped closer, eyes narrowing.

"You ought not direct it toward me. No... you should blame your fool of a father. Malikai is the one who brought this to you."

He paused as if savoring his own words.

"Though I suppose... blaming him may prove difficult." A smile slithered across his face. "Seeing as he is no longer... with us."

My   eyes   widened.

His gaze lingered on mine, cold and knowing. "You know, it was only meant to be him that fateful night. But that stubborn, short-sighted mother of yours..."

He trailed off, his eyes shifting to the side briefly.

"...Even then, she still chose him."

His mouth continued moving, forming words—but I

couldn't hear them.

Not over the ringing in my head.

Not over the sound of my heart breaking.

He began walking toward me. His silhouette grew larger and larger until it blocked out the light above.

I couldn't move. Couldn't think. I was looking at him, but I didn't understand what I was seeing.

His claws gleamed in the broken light, still slick with blood.

He raised his hand and leveled it toward my head.

Right between the eyes.

I stared down the length of his arm.

"Goodbye, son of Malikai," Cassius spat.

A shattering howl ripped through the air like thunder, so fierce it shook the ring beneath us. The wood groaned, and the broken chains rattled.

Cassius froze, and his eyes slowly turned to the side.

My head slumped lazily to the side as well.

Standing at the edge of the ruined platform above—no longer secured—was a massive animal bathed in light.

A wolf, blood-orange fur bristling. Fangs bared. Eyes glowing.

Celine.

CHAPTER 38

"No..." Cassius muttered, almost choking on the word. "This is not possible."

His face twisted—not with rage, but with something I had yet to see from him.

Fear.

For the first time, he looked like a man who understood he was no longer in control.

"The blood..." he whispered. "How could I have overlooked it?"

His eyes flicked between me, still half-frozen, and the towering figure of Celine.

"All this time..." His voice lowered, as if the truth weighed too much to say aloud.

"She was a... It was her."

His head snapped back toward me. Eyes wide and frenzied.

"You!" he roared. "I must end you now!"

He threw his claws forward, intending to finish what he had started. But he didn't get far.

The sound of something tearing filled the air, and Cassius froze mid-strike.

Behind him stood the colossal Lunar form of Celine.

Fangs sunk deep as her jaws clamped around his outstretched arm, the very one he'd raised to strike me down.

I heard a loud crack as his arm disappeared into her jaws before she tossed it aside like it were nothing.

Cassius yelled in pain. Loud and unpleasant as he jumped away. He stumbled back, clutching the stump, his mouth hanging open in horror.

498

"No!" he shrieked.

With what strength he had left, he launched himself into the air to throw a kick at her.

Celine didn't flinch. Her jaws snapped sideways, catching his leg mid-air. Then with a single twist of her neck she slammed him into the ground.

Cassius hit the floor hard, the impact shaking the wood beneath me. His body went limp—arms sprawled, and his breath knocked clean from him.

Celine tossed his crumpled body through the air, and her jaws clamped down again, this time on his lower half.

I watched, speechless, as he dangled from her mouth—torso writhing, eyes wide.

His eyes met mine. A hollow clarity of someone who understood too late.

"You fool..." he rasped, blood bubbling from his lips.

"You have doomed us all."

Celine tilted her head.

Then, with a flick of her neck, she tossed him into the air—

and swallowed him whole.

I lay there on the ground, my mind trying to catch up—trying to put the fragmented pieces together.

Cassius was gone. Swallowed.

My uncle's body lay next to me, still and grey.

I heard a low rumble, and my vision snapped back to Celine.

Her fur was standing on end—bristling wildly. Her breath came out in hot huffs, steam rising from her muzzle.

As I looked at her features deeply, something stuck out to me;

Her eyes were no longer violet—they burned a deep, searing red. And though they were fixed on me, it felt like she was staring straight through me… as if I wasn't even there.

She growled as she stepped forward. Her claws dug into the wood with every step, leaving shallow gouges behind.

"Celine…" I whispered, barely hearing my voice.

She kept walking toward me, growling louder and baring her teeth.

"Celine… It's me…" I added weakly, propping myself up with my good arm. "It's me, Isaac."

She lunged at me. Her jaws opened wide, fangs flashing as the light hit them, and for a breathless moment, all I saw was red.

THWACK

A loud sound rippled through the air as something slammed into Celine's muzzle from above.

Celine's head dropped hard to the ground, her jaws forced shut mid-lunge. She crashed onto the floor in front of me, the momentum of the hit on her snout bringing her to a halt as her claws skidded on the wood.

I blinked as Sabrina jumped off of Celine's face, rushing towards me.

"Up," she hissed. "Now."

She pulled me hard, nearly yanking me to my feet.

"We do not want to be in her line of sight when she recovers," she added quickly, guiding us to a pillar. "Not like this."

I stumbled with her, the sound of my boots scraping the wood far too loud. We ducked beneath some massive roots and branches around the ring, shielding ourselves.

I looked past Sabrina's shoulder—Celine's massive body lay still, but her limbs twitched, claws flexing. A snarl was already beginning to rise in her throat.

Sabrina pressed a finger to her lips, signaling for me to stay quiet.

Celine finally rose, shakily, but still taller than ever. Her muscles tensed, and her head tilted back, as she let out another ear-splitting howl.

Sabrina and I covered our ears, but it did little to stop the shaking in my brain.

As Celine lowered her head, a group of guards burst into the arena clearing, their faces panicked.

"By the moon, what is that"

"How can she be so large?"

Celine turned, and the sound of wood splitting beneath her paws was instant as she dashed towards them.

One guard screamed, but as quickly as the sound came, he was gone. Thrown through the air with a headbutt.

The rest barely had time to react before she was upon them—slamming one into a wall, raking claws across another.

Those who could run, did.

And she followed.

Her massive frame barreled after them, deeper into the trees—toward the town.

I stayed crouched, my legs refused to move. Everything felt distant in the moment.

What was happening?

Through the noise in my head, I heard a voice. Muffled at first, then clearer.

"... Drifted."

I didn't move.

"Drifted."

A hand gripped my shoulder.

"Drifted!"

I snapped out of it, shaking my head and locking eyes with Sabrina as she stared at me.

"Can you run?" she asked.

I gave her a shaky nod in reply.

"Then come," she said. "We must follow her."

She looked down at my arm—still hanging limp at my side.

"Wait," she muttered, already moving.

She went to my side and used her claws to rip a long strip of cloth from my cloak. Then she looped it beneath my wrist, tightening it across my shoulder and chest until the weight was mostly off my arm.

"There," she said. "This should do."

I nodded again, too stunned to thank her.

"Let us move."

We started running, navigating through the ruined path that Celine had left behind. Torn trees, lifeless bodies, and broken cries littered the trail behind her.

As we moved, Sabrina glanced at me.

"How did you do it?" she asked.

My head tilted in confusion. "Do what?"

"How did you give the Princess your blood?"

I nearly tripped over my own feet.

"What? I didn't... I thought you did something."

She shook her head.

"No, Drifted. I did not."

"How did you get it in the first place?" I questioned.

"Get what?" Sabrina questioned back.

"My blood. How did you get my blood to begin with?"

Sabrina's eyes dropped slightly. "Simple. I acquired it as you slept."

My head snapped to her. "You what?! What made you think it was okay to—"

A loud crash split through the air. Choking the words in my throat.

"I do not understand why she is rampaging," Sabrina added, eyes narrowed as she focused on the tree line ahead. "Through all our training back in Sylphreach—Consort

Rowen and I never once observed this kind of behavior in her."

Another howl echoed in the distance—somehow louder this time. Purely feral.

"She... she looks different as well," I added in between breaths. "Her fur, her eyes, they're red now."

Sabrina's jaw tightened. "Something is wrong."

We kept moving faster now as the surrounding trees thinned. The town's edge was just beyond the rise.

I stumbled to a stop, nearly falling forward as my boots hit the slope of the hill.

Sabrina steadied me with a hand on my chest.

Together, we stared ahead.

The outer edge of the town lay sprawled before us—shrouded in smoke and horror. Somewhere in the distance, a building collapsed in on itself, reduced to rubble.

Lupine ran in every direction.

Guards yelled.

And above it all, I saw Celine.

Towering, blood-soaked; her eyes still glowing that furious red.

The sight was total carnage.

"We have to stop her," I whispered.

I turned my head to Sabrina. "Sabrina, we have to stop her!"

She nodded, and without another word, we made our way toward the town—dodging fleeing townsfolk and keeping low as we closed the distance.

I glanced at Sabrina as we ran. "What's the plan?"

She didn't look at me.

"I do not know if there is anything we can do," she said. "We may have to wait... until she loses consciousness."

I frowned. "It's already been too long. That should've

happened a while ago."

Sabrina shook her head.

"No. During our training in Sylphreach, Consort Rowen and I worked to extend the time she could hold her Lunar form."

She looked at me and then down at the ground. "She can hold it for around ten to fifteen minutes."

"What!" I blurted.

Ten to fifteen minutes—that was more than double the time she managed when she first transformed.

In that time, she could tear through half the town—hell, maybe even the entire thing.

The sounds of crashing and screaming in the distance didn't make that realization any easier to swallow.

The deeper we pushed forward, the worse the sight became.

What had once been relatively empty streets were now a mess of broken wood, ruptured stone, overturned carts, and still bodies. Flames covered buildings, and smoke spread through the alleys like serpents.

Celine was tearing through the heart of it all, and she showed no sign of stopping soon.

I caught a flash of her between the rumbling rooftops as she raked through them. She moved through the town without any hesitation.

A cart went flying through the air, crashing against the side of a home and throwing shrapnel everywhere.

Sabrina shoved me down just in time, and we hit the ground. I nearly landed on my bad arm, but turned my body at the last second. Still, the vibrations sent pain through my torso, forcing me to bite down a yell and turn my face against the dirt.

"Stay low," she hissed, helping me roll behind a broken

support beam.

I coughed, squinting through the smoke as we pressed against the wall of what remained of a bakery. Somewhere nearby, someone screamed. Then another voice cried out— cut short by the sound of wood collapsing and bone snapping.

I peeked around the corner and saw a guard slam against a wall with enough force to leave a smear behind. He groaned once, then went silent.

Celine was up ahead, barreling through what used to be a merchant row.

She leapt onto a rooftop, and it collapsed beneath her weight. The wood snapped, and the building sagged and groaned before the whole thing gave way in a choking cloud of dust.

"This is horrible. She's not even getting tired." I said with a wince.

"I am not sure. It seems she truly has lost herself." Sabrina replied.

I followed as Celine landed on a nearby road. People immediately ran, many of them taking their Lunar forms. But many still weren't fast enough.

An older Lupine took his Lunar form and pounced at Celine. She swatted him mid-jump, sending him sprawling through a fruit stand.

"Cel—" I started to call out from behind cover, but Sabrina clasped her hand over my mouth. "You draw her attention now and she shall rip us both to shreds."

I pulled her hand away. "We can't just sit here and wat—"

"That is precisely what we shall do," she cut in. "I am watching for signs. Signs that she is reaching her limit."

Her tone left no room for argument.

She turned her head back toward the road. And I followed

suit begrudgingly.

Celine slashed through the next building, dragging a support beam out with her teeth. Another home collapsed in a spray of flames.

I wanted to shout, grab her attention. I wanted to do something, anything.

But I stayed still. Waiting for our moment.

From the fray, I heard a sound that didn't belong in the middle of this chaos.

A voice, small, and crying.

At first, I thought I had imagined it. But then I heard it again.

"... Mama?"

I leaned forward, peering past the edge of the building we were hiding next to.

There—across the plaza—stood a small Lupine child.

Barely more than a toddler, by the look of him. His ears were drooped, and his face was covered in soot and tears. He wore a tattered brown tunic, half-hanging from one shoulder. In his arms, clutched tight to his chest, was a small wooden toy—broken in half with its legs dangling loose.

He turned in place, trembling, calling out again.

"... Mama...?"

He was standing in the middle of the rubble, all by himself.

I saw Celine's head turn, and her eyes landed on him.

"No," I breathed.

Celine crouched lower and growled. Her body tensed up and shuddered as she prepared to lunge.

My body moved before I could even think.

"Drifted!" Sabrina's voice cracked behind me.

I ran across the splintered wooden road, over the shattered planks and scorched fabric.

I reached him right as Celine pounced, scooping the boy

into my good arm and clutching him tight to my chest as I continued running.

Celine crashed down where we'd just been, her claws exploding the ground beneath her weight. The impact pushed against my back, threatening to knock me off balance. Thankfully, I caught my footing and continued in stride. The child screamed into my shoulder, gripping my cloak with tiny, shaky hands.

I darted through a side street, boots sliding across a layer of ash. Doors flew past me—some open, some hanging from broken hinges. I ducked into an alley, weaving between overturned barrels and laundry lines still smoldering.

Another howl shook the buildings, and wood splintered behind me.

Celine tore through the corner of the home I'd passed moments ago—timber exploded outward in a shower of debris. A beam hit the wall beside me, and I stumbled, nearly dropping the child as I forced us forward.

She was right behind us. I could feel the thunder of her steps and the crash of her weight as she plowed through anything in her path. Every time I thought I'd gained ground, another structure collapsed behind me.

"You're going to be okay," I whispered to the boy.

I turned hard into a narrow alley and hit a dead end.

A collapsed wagon blocked the back wall, flanked by buildings with no doors—just shuttered windows and scorched walls.

My eyes darted from side to side as I breathed heavily.

With no escape, I pulled the boy with me and crouched behind the wagon, trying to blend us into the shadows.

Celine's footsteps closed in with each crash of debris. I held my breath as her growls grumbled near the entrance of the alleyway.

A shriek farther off ripped through the sky. Celine's breathing paused briefly and listened as her steps thundered toward the noise.

I waited for a moment in the silence before letting out a deep breath, my hands trembling against the boy's shoulder.

"See? We're alright," I said to the boy with a weak smile.

But I knew we weren't completely out of danger yet.

Walking through the town now would be a death wish. Celine would hear us without me ever noticing. Our best plan of action would be to hide and wait for Sabrina, she would be able to guide us out of this.

The structure to our right was a small house. Its front was bowed from the heat of a nearby fire, but it was still standing.

I rushed to it and pushed the boy through an open window. Then I jumped through after him, sloppily as I tried to keep my broken arm from slamming into the frame.

The boy whimpered as I moved us further into the darkness. We crouched low behind a counter, tucked into the far corner of what looked like a kitchen.

I put a finger to my lips, signaling for the boy to stay quiet as we hid.

I held my breath as the wooden slats creaked above us as the wind outside roared louder.

Please tell me she didn't hear us. I thought to myself.

My prayers went unanswered as a shadow swept over the building, blocking out any light from the windows.

The roof tore open above us as Celine's massive jaws clamped down on the beams, breaking through them with ease. Her glowing eyes peered inside the ruin, breath steaming as her muzzle pushed past the torn rafters

I could feel the boy trembling in my good arm, his face buried in my shoulder. His muffled sobs had gone quiet, but I could feel the way his fingers dug into me.

Celine snarled, breath blowing dust across the room in thick gusts.

I shifted my body, turning to shield the boy completely. We didn't have anywhere left to run.

The roof groaned above me as her body leaned in further, pressing through the torn boards. Her snout hovered lower, and I could see every crack in her fangs.

As her jaws hovered just feet above us, blowing hot breath across the nape of my neck, pushing my hair back.

"Celine," I said again, pleading.

"It's me."

She opened her mouth.

I held the boy tighter; curled over him and shut my eyes.

I guess this is how it ends. I thought to myself.

But as I crouched there, waiting, there was no pain, only quiet.

I opened one eye. Then the other. Turning my head slowly.

Celine trembled as she froze above us. Her jaw still hung open, but her body swayed.

And then—

She dropped.

The ground trembled as her body collapsed, crashing through what remained of the roof.

I exhaled, only now realizing I'd been holding my breath. Slowly, I loosened my arm and looked down at the boy. He stared up at me, wide-eyed and shaking, but alive.

The air shifted, and Celine's body changed—her enormous frame shrinking, and her fur receding into skin. Her claws turned back into fingers, and her snout flattened back into the face I recognized.

She was human again.

Lying in the center of the room, breathing shallowly. Eyes closed.

Then I heard the crunch of steps through the debris.

Sabrina stepped through the wreckage, brushing dust from her shoulder as she approached.

She looked at me and held out her hand.

"Your cloak," she said quietly.

I blinked, still dazed, before unclasping it from my shoulder and handing it to her.

She took it and moved to Celine's side. Then, she draped the fabric over her unconscious body.

"She shall be cold when she wakes," she murmured, more to herself than to me.

We stood there for a moment, the air thick with dust and the scent of smoke. The sounds of chaos mostly faded, replaced by distant shouting and the crackle of dying flames.

Sabrina walked toward me and rested a hand on my shoulder.

She looked at me with a small, but tired smile on her face.

"Come, Drifted," she said softly. "Let us go home.

Epilogue

We walked through the rubble in silence. The fires died down, but the smoke still lingered.

My arm ached, but I held the boy's hand tight as we walked through the town. He was quiet now, though I could still feel his body shaking.

The sky above was grey, stained by the ashes falling like snow.

I heard the voice of a woman yell, shaking and broken.

"My boy!"

The boy flinched and then turned his head, eyes going wide. He let out a small sob and tried to tear his hand from mine, as she came into view.

The woman nearly fell as she ran toward us, her clothing frayed and muddy.

"Son!"

"Mama!" the boy cried back, stumbling into her arms.

She dropped to her knees, clutching him so tightly I thought she might crush him. Her hands moved over his face, his arms, checking every inch. She wept—loudly, shamelessly—her cries echoing through the broken street like a song of relief.

I stood still, not wanting to intrude.

Her lips parted slightly, her brows furrowing as she looked up at me. Then, she sniffed and tilted her head as though she were trying to make sense of what she was seeing.

"A human?" she whispered, disbelief thick in her voice.

She lifted her child tightly, almost protectively now, and stood. Without another word, she turned and ran.

"A thank you would have sufficed," Sabrina mumbled dryly.

My eyes drifted to Celine, slumped gently against Sabrina's back. The edges of my cloak were drawn over her, hood resting above her brow, hiding her face from the world—and maybe, hiding the world from her too.

I let out a long breath, letting all the air escape my lungs. I looked up at the clouded sky, the sun still struggling to break through.

We didn't speak much as we circled back through the wreckage, our feet retracing the path to the tree. The one Cassius had once claimed for his own.

It felt... smaller now. The grandeur stripped away in the quiet. There were no guards now. All that remained was silence, and the creak of wood as the wind passed through the tree's contorted frame.

My sword was still there as we stepped into the chamber. Laying on the floor where it had fallen during the battle. I picked it up and stared at it for a moment, catching the reflection of my face in the steel.

My eyes looked tired, and my skin was bruised. A thin line of dried blood rested near my temple. I looked exactly how I felt.

"We still have one thing left to do," Sabrina said behind me.

I didn't even need to ask was she was talking about.

We left the chamber, descending a path that curved around the tree. The air was cooler down here, but still heavy with smoke. It didn't take long to find the body—his body.

My uncle's body still lay there. Blackened veins ran down his arms, and his gray, mottled skin had patches of fungus that started to wither.

I could hardly look at him. This wasn't how everything

was supposed to play out.

Sabrina knelt beside him and offered a small prayer to the moon. Much like the one she offered to the deer in the woods.

We gathered anything around that was dry enough to catch fire. Splintered branches, old pieces of pillar.

When the fire took hold, I didn't step back.

I watched as the twisted body was swallowed in orange and gold.

The journey back to Sylphreach was long, but mostly uneventful. Almost like the word had decided, for once, we'd earned a break. The wind stayed calm. The woods stayed quiet. No fiends. No surprises.

When Sylphreach finally came into view, it didn't feel like a homecoming.

We approached the Elderwood without a word, our footsteps dragging with weariness that sat deeper than muscle. The massive tree stood out ahead, its hollowed base still casting that same serenity it always did. A crowd gathered in front, singing and cheering harmonically in a language I didn't understand.

Sabrina adjusted Celine slightly on her back before making her way toward the open roots that led inside.

I kept walking past the base, past the opening and up toward the bridge that led up to the High Perch.

"Consort Rowen will want a debriefing," Sabrina called from behind.

I didn't answer. I didn't even turn to see her reaction.

The rope bridge creaked under my weight as I crossed it. The High Perch wasn't far—only a few more steps.

When I reached my door, I didn't hesitate. I opened it, stepped inside, and let it close behind me.

The light was soft as it came through the slats in the wooden frame, and the room smelled faintly of pine and fresh flowers.

I dropped my sword by the wall and sank into bed.

END OF BOOK TWO

AUTHOR NOTE

Dear Reader,

Thank you for stepping back into the world of The Drifted Path with me. Writing Lupine has been one of the most fulfilling journeys I've ever taken. This second book in Isaac's story challenged me in new ways as I tried to dig deeper into his heart, the mysteries of Velora, and the wild world that surrounds him.

Where Drifted was about discovery, Lupine became about transformation. Watching Isaac grow and watching the scenes around him unravel was as exciting for me as I hope it was for you. There were scenes that surprised even me while writing, and moments that stayed with me long after I typed the final sentence.

I can't wait to start working on the third book! There's so much more ahead and more secrets to be discovered on Isaac's journey.

If Lupine spoke to you in any way, I'd be incredibly grateful if you left a review on Amazon, Goodreads, or wherever! It's one of the strongest ways you can support authors like me. Your words not only help others find the series, but they remind me why I started telling the story in the first place.

Thank you!

Until next time—

With gratitude,
Renton Wolfe.

ABOUT THE AUTHOR

Renton Wolfe, a passionate voice in fantasy fiction, was born in Bronx, New York, and raised in Columbus, Ohio. Balancing the demands of work and family, Renton found solace and inspiration in quiet moments, using every spare second to craft his debut novel, Drifted.
What began as a personal passion project soon grew into a full-fledged journey of storytelling, fueled by a love for immersive worlds and complex characters. His dedication to bringing this story to life is a testament to the belief that, no matter how busy life gets, there's always room to pursue your passion.

Follow and keep in touch with me and Isaac's journey on the socials below:
X/Twitter: @rentonwolfe
Tiktok: @rentonwolfe
Instagram: @rentonwolfe

www.ingramcontent.com/pod-product-compliance
Lightning Source LLC
Chambersburg PA
CBHW021836010726
47493CB00005B/1424